What Readers Are Saying About . . .

. . . *A PATH LESS TRAVELED*
(Book Two in the Miller's Creek Novels)

"Cathy Bryant weaves an amazing story. She has a maturity in her writing skill that astounds me for only having two published novels. *A Path Less Traveled* is a must read. Cathy realistically captures the struggle of the heart."
~Linnette Mullin at LinnetteMullin.com

"A beautiful book with a beautiful message, *A Path Less Traveled* is an enjoyable story! The pieces of the plot come together to form a touching picture of the release that comes with trusting God and seeking His path."
~Amber Stokes at Seasons of Humility blog

"This book was totally and completely enjoyable to read. I received the book on Friday and finished reading it on Sunday. I could hardly put it down. The storyline is very well written and grabbed my attention in the first chapter and never let me go."
~Cathy Stephens at Tales of the TCKK Family blog

"This book brings out the best ideals of faith. It is a book that can be recommended to anyone! I highly recommend this and *Texas Roads* as the best kind of reading available! These books boldly tell the truth of Christianity, a rare thing today!"
~Mark Schmidt

"A good story must have conflict, and *A Path Less Traveled* delivers and then some. I always wonder if the second book in a series will be as good as the first. In this case, it is. Cathy doesn't disappoint her readers. Her characters are genuine, engaging the reader from the start. I give *A Path Less Traveled* two thumbs up!"
~Karen Lange at Write Now blog

"Well, Cathy Bryant has done it again! See, she has this nasty little habit of writing wonderful books that get me all choked up and emotional, causing anyone around me witnessing the display to make fun of me. I guess I'll just have to forgive her and continue to read her wonderful stories."
~Kate Lindsay at The Book Buff blog

. . . *TEXAS ROADS*
(Book One in the Miller's Creek Novels)

"I LOVED this story! Cathy's writing is vibrant and fresh. It's loaded with very likeable characters and zippy dialog. This was Cathy Bryant's first novel but her writing is that of a seasoned author. She kept me turning pages from start to finish. I highly recommend this book."
~Sherry Kuhn at Love 2 Read Novels blog

"Texas Roads is a wonderful book that is like a comfy pair of pj's. I fell in love with the characters and town and wish I lived in a town like Miller's Creek. The book will make you laugh, shed a few tears, and hug those you love a little tighter."
~Vicki Newell

"Cathy Bryant's *Texas Roads* is one I want permanently on my bookshelf."
~Molly Edwards at Reviews By Molly blog

"Beautiful description, poignant characters, chuckle-worthy humor, and a heart-healing message make *Texas Roads* a not-to-be missed read."
~Julia Reffner at Dark Glass Ponderings blog

A MILLER'S CREEK NOVEL

Book Three

CATHY BRYANT

WordVessel Press

Books By Cathy Bryant

MILLER'S CREEK NOVELS
Texas Roads
A Path Less Traveled
The Way of Grace

The Way of Grace
© 2012 Cathy Bryant
Published by WordVessel Press
A Division of ASDG, Inc.
Bentonville, Arkansas

All rights reserved.
This novel is a work of fiction. Names, characters, places, and incidents are either the product of the author's imagination or are used fictitiously.
ISBN: 0-9844311-4-4
ISBN-13: 978-0-9844311-4-4

To my wonderful husband Travis.
Thank you for believing in me when I lost all confidence, encouraging me when I was ready to quit, and helping me follow my heart's desire to make Him known.
Above all, thank you for being a man of grace.

Therefore, since we have been justified through faith,
we have peace with God through our Lord Jesus Christ,
through whom we have gained access by faith into
this grace in which we now stand.
~Romans 5:1-2a

Special Thanks

To beta readers: Barbie Bray, Travis Bryant, Jimmie Croker, Maggie Culp, Carolyn England, Judy Fager, and Sherlee Grimstead. Your invaluable assistance makes what I do possible.

To my personal "Grace Fellowship," my spiritual family which literally encircles the globe: Thanks for encouraging me by demonstrating God's grace. Your friendship is a blessing, and I look forward to spending eternity with you as we forever proclaim praises to the Lamb.

To my family: Mom, you patiently read every word I write, bringing with you wisdom gained in the school of life. Josh, Jase, and Megan, like John I say: "I have no greater joy than this, to hear of my children walking in the truth." Harrisen, you brighten my eyes and quicken my step, even as my earthly tent grows more frail. Travis, I'm grateful to God for giving you to me. He knew I needed someone exactly like you to walk beside me.

To my Lord and Savior, Jesus Christ: Thank You for allowing me the privilege of being one of Your sheep, in all my human weakness and imperfection. Thank You especially for providing the way of grace.

PROLOGUE

Childhood

Graciela flinched as Papa pounded a fist on the table, his dark eyes flashing at Mama.

"We do not have money for this!"

Mama acted as if his words didn't bother her at all. "I've saved part of the egg money for weeks, Juan. It doesn't cost much for a few flowers for your only daughter. This will help her learn how to grow a garden." She kept her voice low and steady.

Papa glared at Graciela momentarily, but didn't say anything. Instead he unclenched his fists and picked up his fork to resume eating.

Her two older brothers finished their meal quickly. "Can we go outside to play, Papa?"

"*Si*. You two have worked hard today." As they scraped their plates into the slop bucket for the pig, Papa shifted his gaze back to her. "But you will do the dishes to earn the flowers your Mama is determined to give you."

"Okay, Papa." She tried to enjoy the thick tamales Mama had made, but all she tasted was unshed tears. Why did he dislike her?

The next day, Graciela hummed happily as she skipped to the backyard, her thick braid bouncing between her shoulder blades. Laughter bubbled out of her chest and molded her lips into a happy smile. She and Mama had spent the past hour choosing not only vegetable plants, but also colorful marigolds, begonias, and geraniums from B & B Hardware.

All winter long she'd longed for this moment, had poured over catalogs and picked out pictures of those she liked best, while Mama made sure the flowers would survive the brutally hot Texas summers.

A frown furrowed her young forehead as she remembered Papa's objection to the flowers. He was so hard to understand. Sometimes he was so rough and gruff, all she wanted to do was climb the wild plum tree beside their little house and stay up there forever. At other times—mostly at times when Mama coerced him into a good mood—he was fun and happy. Almost like two different people, and she never knew which one would show up.

She climbed the bottom rung of the fence, looked out across the pasture at the goats munching happily on the new spring grass, and breathed deeply. Did anything smell as lovely as spring? Next she focused her gaze on the puffy white clouds floating across the sky and the chirping sparrows that flitted from tree to tree. How wonderful it must be to soar through skies of *azul*.

"There you are, *la hija*." Mama's voice broke into her reverie. "Ready to plant your flowers?"

"*Si*." She began to prattle away in her native tongue, but one look from Mama was all it took to silence her. Graciela pressed her lips together in an effort to still her tongue. "Sorry, Mama. I forgot."

Mama sighed and shot a reassuring smile. "It's okay, but we must learn to speak the language of our new country. I must do better, too." Her mother took hold of Graciela's hand. "Come, let's get these flowers planted before your Papa gets home."

"Will Papa be upset that we're planting flowers?"

Her mother's face darkened as they made their way to the patch of ground they'd cleared of grass and weeds. "We will see, won't we?"

Mama demonstrated how to dig a hole in the soil and loosen the roots of the seedling before placing it in the ground and giving it a big drink.

Graciela stooped to sniff the newly planted marigold and made a face. "That flower stinks."

Mama laughed, a musical sound that never failed to capture Graciela's wonder and attention. "Yes, but it will keep the bugs off our tomatoes."

At the mention of the tasty summer tomatoes, her mouth watered, and she licked her lips. "Why is Papa so grumpy sometimes, Mama?"

"He has many worries. I know it must seem to you that he doesn't love you, but he does."

She tried to understand, but quickly gave up. Papa rarely gave her a second look, but always had plenty of time for her two older brothers. "I try to be nice so he will love me, but it doesn't seem to do any good."

Mama quickly folded her into her arms, undid her braid, and combed Graciela's long hair with her fingers. "Oh, sweet one, you are a good girl, and he does love you. It's just hard for him to show it." Mama held her at arm's length, her hands on both shoulders. "Don't give up on him, *la hija*. The world has a way of changing people's hearts. He'll come around one day."

Graciela picked up the hand spade and plunged it into the soft sandy soil with as much force as she could muster. Maybe Papa would come around someday, but that could be a long, long time away. And what would happen to soften his heart?

The next morning at church, Graciela nestled in the crook of Mama's arm and hunkered down in the blue cushioned pew. She couldn't help but notice how differently people treated them.

Some--like the woman who smelled of cinnamon and vanilla, the one everyone called Mama Beth--were very kind to her and Mama, always stopping to say hello and ask how they were doing. Others only looked their way with accompanying whispered words and accusing glances. She asked Mama why.

"Some people cannot see past a person's skin to see that on the inside we are all the same."

Graciela puzzled over the statement, but no matter how hard she tried, she couldn't understand. She peered down the row to a girl her age she'd seen at school. In a pretty dress with lots of ruffles and bows, and with golden ringlets encircling her head, the girl reminded Graciela of a beautiful doll. Maybe they could be friends. She sent a shy smile.

The girl didn't smile back. Instead she stuck out her tongue and jerked her head away, nose upturned.

A heavy darkness descended on Graciela's heart. Would she ever find a friend?

The service began with singing. Her heart lightened. How she loved the music. The song lilted in her heart, and as she followed Mama's finger in the hymnbook, she allowed her voice to soar like the birds she'd seen yesterday. Higher and higher she floated away from her problems and into blue skies. *Oh, how I love Jesus, because He first loved me.*

Soon the pastor stood to speak, his face aglow with joy. Graciela perched on the edge of the seat, enthralled as he spoke of a God who loved her more than she could imagine, a God who loved her as a Father. When it came time for the end of the service, she bolted down the aisle, convinced in her heart that God had personally invited her to be His child.

Later that evening, Mama peeked through the opened door to her small room. "May I come in?"

This time she remembered to use her English words. "Yes."

Mama eased to the bed beside her. "Papa and the boys have gone fishing, and I thought you might enjoy a girl's night out. Maybe supper at the Dairy Maid?"

Graciela folded her coloring book around the box of crayons and hopped from the bed. Eating at Dairy Maid without the boys and Papa meant a burger and fries all to herself with a chocolate milkshake on the side.

They arrived at the drive-up hamburger joint just as the sun set, trailing long pink fingers across the horizon. They moved from the car to the screened window where the enticing aroma of grilled burgers wafted onto the evening breeze. Mama placed their order then turned to face her, steering her toward a nearby picnic table. "I want to talk to you about this morning, *la hija*. That was a very big decision for one so young. Do you understand what it means to be saved?"

"Yes, Mama. Our teacher talked about it in Sunday school. God loves me so much He sent Jesus, His only son, to die for me. If I accept what He did and invite Him into my heart, He comes to live inside me."

Mama nodded. "That's right. But do you understand why Jesus died?"

Graciela wrinkled her eyebrows and skewed her lips to one side. Why *did* God's son have to die for her? "Not really. I know it has to do with sin, but you told me I'm a good girl."

A smile rounded Mama's lips, and she reached across the table to tweak Graciela's nose. "Yes, you are a good girl, but not all the time."

A big lady brought their burgers wrapped in white paper, and set them on the table along with white Styrofoam cups and a red plastic basket of steaming fries.

Graciela reached for the cup and sucked hard to get the thick chocolate milkshake into her mouth, where it melted and ran down her throat.

Mama rustled the white paper wrapping. "Remember when you stole a cookie from the jar and accidentally broke the lid? I asked if you did it, and you said no."

"I was afraid you'd be mad at me." She spoke around the big bite of burger she'd just taken.

"Ahh, sweet daughter, you must not let the opinions of others keep you from doing the right thing, but that is a very difficult lesson to learn." Mama leaned her head back, her eyes trained on the sky. "But you see that you are not perfect, right? That even though you are good most of the time, you are not good all the time?"

It was true. There were times she got angry with her brothers for teasing her. Times when she was so upset with Papa that she wished . . . No! She mustn't wish such things!

"I can tell by the look on your face that you know it is true. As much as we want to be perfect, we are not." Mama's voice was a soft spring breeze.

Graciela's shoulders sagged. Why couldn't she be good all the time?

Mama's fingers gently lifted her chin. "Don't be sad, *la hija*. That is why God gave us Jesus. We are born with part of us broken on the inside." Mama patted her chest with one hand. "By His grace, He will one day make us complete. Until then, we must do our best, but trust in His grace."

A sudden understanding flew to her heart. "My name." The awe and wonder she felt came out in her words.

Mama nodded, a tender look on her face. "Yes, Graciela. You are named for God's grace. I was saved right before you were born."

Warmth flooded her being, and gratitude to God for what He'd done swelled in her chest. When they pulled away from Dairy Maid a few minutes later, Graciela could not remember a time when she felt so completely happy.

They stopped at a red light, and Mama reached over to tickle her ribs.

She giggled. As she dodged Mama's wiggling fingers, she glimpsed a car headed toward them so fast it looked like a gray blur.

The light turned green and her mother pulled into the intersection.

Graciela opened her mouth in warning, but the words clumped in her throat, finally bursting forth in a scream.

1

Fifteen years later

A car horn blasted through the summer evening air, followed by tires screeching against pavement and the rancid smell of burning rubber. Grace yanked her head in Mama's direction. The noisy blast continued as a car bore down on them. Everything went pitch black as Mama's piercing scream joined her own, followed by a deadly thud.

Heart racing, Grace jerked awake, forcing herself to a sitting position. The same old nightmare. She brought both hands to her face and gulped in air to slow her pounding pulse. Why now? She'd endured the last year of law school and the bar exam without memories of that awful night plaguing her. But now that she was back in Miller's Creek to work for Tyler, Dent, and Snodgrass as a full-fledged attorney, the dream shattered her sleep for the fourth time in a week.

Grace pulled her hands away from her face—almost afraid to find them dripping with blood—then glanced at the alarm clock on her makeshift nightstand. 5:15 in the morning. She flopped back on the bed and stared at the dark nothingness above her head. There was no way she'd get back to sleep now. Might as well get an early start.

A sudden rush of excitement coursed through her veins. All her hard work had finally paid off. Now it was time to enjoy herself for a change and initiate her life plan, which included a stellar career, new house, Mr. Right, and of course, children.

She removed the band that confined her hair and gave her head a shake. Better to just focus on her career at this point, her best chance at proving her worth—to Papa, to the people of Miller's Creek, and to Mr. Right, whoever he was.

The cold floor beneath her bare feet sent shivers rippling through her body as she raced down the hallway to the tiny kitchen to make a pot of coffee for Papa. Within a few minutes the coffee machine gurgled and the fresh-brewed aroma permeated every square inch of the house. She was just about to head for a shower when Papa entered.

"You're up early." His eyes held questions.

There was no way she'd tell him about the nightmare. No need to cause him worry or pain. "Just excited about this being my first day as an attorney."

He wandered past her to pull a coffee cup from the cabinet. "It's all you've talked about for weeks." He droned the words, his voice flat.

Grace rolled her lips between her teeth. It would be nice to have a word of congratulations--anything to recognize her hard work and achievement--but wishing for it wouldn't make it happen. Instead she sent a sad smile. "I'd better get ready for work."

She hurried down the hall to the only bathroom in the house and turned on the lights and the little space heater Papa had hung from a nail protruding from the paneled walls. The power cord snaked behind the sink faucet before finding the overloaded outlet—an electrical disaster waiting to happen, but Papa's way of making do with what he had.

The pipes groaned in protest when she turned on the faucet and waited for the water to get warm. Living with Papa and his stony silence would definitely be the hardest part of her plan, but it would have to do for now. With her brothers and their families now in South Texas, it was her only option.

An hour later, she stepped once more into the kitchen, dressed and ready for work. Grace reached for the spiral notebook that served as her daily planner and checked off the tasks she'd already completed. Start laundry. Check. Make bed. Check. Bible study and prayer. Check.

Millie, the stray cat she'd taken in years ago, butted her head against Grace's leg, begging for attention. She squatted to scratch the fluffy feline behind the ears. "How's my kitty?" Grace scooped the cat into her arms and hugged her close. How would she have survived Mama's death without the perky ears always willing to listen?

The back door swung open. Dressed in his heavy brown coveralls, Papa entered, and brought with him a gust of cold air and the smell of cows. He didn't say a word, but ambled past her to the kitchen sink to wash his hands, his dirty work boots clomping against the old wooden floor, his face devoid of a smile.

She wrinkled her nose, dropped Millie to the floor, and brushed cat hair from her black skirt. Long gone were the hopes that her father would be proud of her for becoming an attorney. "Through with the chores?"

He continued to wash his hands without looking her way.

Grace forced her hurt feelings aside, her mouth suddenly dry. She should be used to his emotional distance by now. "Papa, I know you don't approve of me being an attorney, but—"

He held up one hand for silence, his back still to her, water dripping down his sleeve. "Enough, Graciela. I don't want to discuss this anymore. You made up your mind to disrespect my wishes long ago."

His displeasure hanging like dead weight around her neck, Grace blinked back tears and picked up her old book bag. It was way too early, but she might as well go to work. She'd grab a pastry at Granny's Kitchen on the way. No, on second thought, it wouldn't hurt to skip breakfast. That way she'd save money and inch toward losing those last few pounds she'd gained while studying for the bar. Without another word to Papa, she slipped out of the house, climbed in the battered old farm truck, and headed to the office.

A late autumn fog engulfed downtown Miller's Creek, and the two- and three-story hewn-stone buildings rose above the mist, silent sentinels observing the march of time. The buildings had seen over a century of use, and thanks to the grant bestowed on the town while she was in high school, had been lovingly restored to their former glory.

Though early November was a little early for Christmas decorations, Miller's Creek had them up well ahead of time for the tourists who would pour into the historic town square for shopping. Already the old-timey street lamps were festooned with lighted wreaths, while greenery draped the Victorian gazebo and lights twinkled from Christmas trees placed throughout the square.

Gravel crunched beneath the pickup tires as she pulled into the parking lot of Tyler, Dent, and Snodgrass and turned off the headlights. She let herself in the back door and flipped the switch. As the fluorescent fixture flickered on and hummed, her earlier joy dissipated. This should be a celebration—the day for which she'd toiled to bring purpose from her pain—but somehow it felt common and ordinary. No balloons or flowers. No party. No pat on the back or word of congratulations.

She shook off the self-pity and moved to her cubicle to make sure everything was in its place, then instinctively pulled a Bible from her bag and ran her hand over the well-worn cover.

Lord, You know how my heart hurts this morning. I miss Mama and I don't know what to say to Papa. Help me be all You want me to be. Lead me in Your Way. Give me an open heart and mind to receive Your truth.

As she thumbed through the whispering onion-skin pages, her Bible fell open to Romans. A verse she'd underlined some time before caught her attention. *Therefore, since we have been justified through faith, we have peace with God through our Lord Jesus Christ, through whom we have gained access by faith into this grace in which we now stand.*

Enough grace to stand in. Was it even humanly possible to be a person of grace? She slanted her lips as she pondered the question, but finally gave her head a shake. True grace was motivated by the purest love, and maybe it was just her, but she doubted she could ever love someone that much.

The thought troubled her. God commanded her to love others as she loved herself, but some people made that seem impossible. Maybe something inside her was broken and malfunctioning. Perhaps her childhood left her incapable of loving like she was supposed to.

Thump!

She jumped at the unexpected noise then sat motionless, her ears tuned to the tiniest noise. More thumps sounded from the basement.

Her pulse raced at the possibility of an intruder. In Miller's Creek at this hour of the morning? Not likely. Maybe Andy had spent the night in the basement apartment because of working late. She stood and tiptoed to the narrow stairs leading to the basement. That wasn't likely either, especially with a newborn at home.

The noise continued. "Andy?" Grace made her way down the darkened steps. If it wasn't him, at least maybe her voice would scare away a potential burglar.

She glided noiselessly across the large carpeted room. "Andy? Is that you?" Grace jiggled the door knob of the small studio apartment. Locked. Now what?

Perhaps she should call the ranch to see what Andy wanted her to do. She started back across the open space toward the staircase to place the call. But before she'd made it even halfway, the overhead lights sputtered on.

"Well, well, if it isn't Gracie Mae."

She spun around, one hand to her pounding heart, a tinny taste in her mouth. Matt?

He leaned against a wall, one stout leg crossed casually over the other, his arms overlapped. An enigmatic expression rested in his sandy brown eyes, and though his hair was damp from a recent washing, his rumpled T-shirt and jeans looked as if he'd slept in them. In the time since she'd seen him last, he'd cut his hair so short there was no evidence of the curls she'd always admired, and he'd buffed up, more muscular and lean than before.

Grace squashed the motherly instincts that rose within her at the sight of his wrinkled clothes. That's what landed her in trouble with him the first time, and she wouldn't fall for it again. A man like Matt, one with wanderlust in his blood, wasn't the one for her. "What are you doing here?"

He released a short laugh. "Shouldn't I be the one asking you that question?"

"I passed the bar and—"

"Yeah, Andy told me. Congrats." He made his way to where she stood and came to a stop a few uncomfortable feet away. "But that still doesn't explain why you're here so early."

She shrugged and turned toward the stairs. "Couldn't sleep. See you around."

Before she reached the first step, Matt blocked her way, the soft scent of shampoo clinging to his damp hair.

"Still running away from me?" Though he spoke the words softly, his tawny eyes held a challenge.

Her hands balled into fists. A million retorts built up behind her clenched lips, but she held them at bay. She wouldn't give him the satisfaction of seeing that his words affected her in the least. With great effort, she uncurled her fingers. "Nope. Just going back to my desk to get started on some work."

His posture went slack, and he sent an apologetic grin. "Sorry. Let me start over. Had breakfast yet?"

A rumble sounded from her stomach. "If that's an invitation, I accept." The reckless words were out before she had time to reconsider. What was she thinking? She'd shut this door over two years ago, a door that needed to stay shut. Nonetheless, she'd agreed to breakfast, and she'd follow through to prove she wasn't running away.

They crossed the room together, and Grace threw out a question to fill the silence. "Have you been working out?"

"Yep. Even joined the wrestling team at school. It's been good for me."

Grace followed Matt into the apartment and glanced around. In characteristic messy-Matt style, a spread-out newspaper, microwave popcorn bag, and an almost-empty glass sat on the coffee table, while a pillow and blanket hung off the couch. A duffel bag on the floor spewed its contents, bringing an odd rush of disappointment. "Just in town for one night?" Typical.

"Don't really know at this point." He offered no further explanation, but moved to the kitchenette fridge and removed the makings for an omelet. "So what's next for you?" With deft movements, he prepared the meal, the chopped onions burning her eyes. "Last I heard you were going to get your career going before looking for your soul mate. Still searching for Mr. Perfect?" His voice held a hint of bitterness.

She lowered her gaze. "Look, Matt, about our conversation two years ago. It wasn't personal. I just needed to focus on one thing at a time. My law school had to come first."

"Agreed. As I recall, I never tried to suggest otherwise."

"No, but I sensed you wanted more from me than I was prepared to give at the time."

He seemed to accept the answer. "But you have to admit, I don't exactly fit the image in your head."

Grace froze. How was she supposed to answer that? "And what image is that?"

"Smart, well-groomed, wealthy, professional, handsome."

Her eyebrows rose. He'd pretty much nailed her must-have list on the head. In fact, he'd perfectly described one of Andy's new partners, Jason Dent. The only problem was that guys like Jason didn't give girls like her a second glance.

A knowing smile touched the corners of Matt's mouth, but to his credit, he dropped the subject. "So you still haven't told me why you're here at such an early hour."

"That's because you didn't ask nicely."

His boyish chortle took her by surprise and set off unexplainable emotions. He glanced up from the cutting board. "True. How's this? Nice to see you again, Gracie. What's a nice girl like you doing in a place like this so early?"

To her chagrin, a traitorous laugh bubbled out. She cut it short and shrugged. "I woke up and couldn't go back to sleep, so I decided to come to work."

A frown wrinkled his brow. "How come you couldn't sleep?"

She hesitated, considering how best to answer his question. Might as well tell him the truth. He'd always been good at dragging it out of her anyway. "Nightmare."

The lines on his forehead grew deeper. "Same one?"

She averted her gaze and nodded.

"Have it often?"

"Not as often as I used to, but for some reason it's woken me up several times this week."

He whisked the eggs into a frothy mixture and poured it into the sizzling skillet, but didn't speak for a moment, as if thinking through her comment. "Might be the stress of starting a new job."

"But it's not really a new job. I've worked for Andy off and on since I graduated from high school. You, of all people, should know that."

A wry grin curled one corner of his mouth. "Yeah, but now you're an attorney. That worrying you any?"

She deliberated on the question. Drat! He'd done it again. How could he always discern what was bothering her?

"That's it, isn't it?"

The self-satisfied smirk on his face gave Grace the urge to whop him upside the head. "So what? That's what you're learning how to do, isn't it? Figure out what's eating people?"

"Yep." He added the omelet toppings, and folded it over effortlessly. "Now the next question. Why does it bother you so much that I figured it out?"

Grace seethed inwardly. Why indeed? Maybe because it made her feel like she needed him, and she didn't want to need him.

He moved next to her, the hot skillet out in front, and stopped, his face inches from hers, his eyelids half-closed. "Don't worry, Gracie Mae. It's okay that someone has you figured out. Trust me, it's a good thing."

"I don't think anyone has ever been able to make me as angry as you do, Matt Tyler. Ever!" Grace pelted the words through tight lips then moved toward the door.

Once more, he blocked her way, holding the simmering omelet, the tantalizing aroma teasing her nostrils. "There you go again, running away."

Rage exploded within, but no way would she dare give him the privilege of being right. She sent a close-mouthed smile she didn't feel and turned to take a seat at the small table.

Matt tossed a pot holder to the table and set the pan on it, then procured two plates and glasses from the cabinet. "Still like chocolate in your milk?"

Yes, but he didn't have to know it. "No. I've outgrown that childish habit."

He cocked one eyebrow and poured two glasses of milk, dousing his with a healthy dose of chocolate syrup.

Grace turned her head and looked the other way, fighting her chocolate craving by reminding herself how much she hated her thunder thighs.

Matt took a long slurp from his glass, then released a satisfied sigh and licked his lips. "Man, there's nothing better than ice-cold chocolate milk." He sat his glass on the table and divided the omelet before delivering a portion to each plate. "Mind if I bless the food?"

"Not at all." She bowed her head. At least one part of his life seemed headed in the right direction.

After he finished the prayer, Grace pulled a napkin from the holder and laid it in her lap, then forked into the omelet, cheese squeezing out from between the fluffy layers. A few minutes later she wiped her mouth and glanced up to see Matt staring at her with the same indecipherable look in his eyes.

"So if you woke up early, why didn't you eat breakfast at your house?" Matt took another swig of milk, his eyes never leaving her face.

"No reason, really." She shifted in her seat. At least none she wanted him to know.

"Your dad still pressuring you?"

"What do you mean?" Grace scooted her chair away from the table and stood with her plate to carry it to the sink.

Matt took hold of her arm as she whisked by. "Running away again?"

She jerked her elbow away. "No. Just cleaning up my dishes."

"I'll take care of it later. Have a seat."

Grace unwillingly acquiesced. "Papa means well. We just have different opinions of what I should do with my life."

He studied her face for a long, uncomfortable minute, like he wanted to say something, but wasn't sure he should say it. Finally, he widened his eyes and changed the subject. "So back to the attorney thing. Any thoughts on why it's bothering you?"

"Matt, you're not a therapist yet, and I'm certainly not your client. Don't feel like you have to analyze me and figure out all my issues. Nor should you feel obliged to fix me."

His eyes widened again, registering hurt. "Just trying to help."

She took in the sincerity inscribed on his face. Why did he have to be so darn likeable? Grace raised her gaze momentarily, focused on a cobweb dangling from the ceiling. And how was she supposed to talk about this with the brother of her boss? "It's not easy to explain."

"Try me."

"Okay, but you'd better not breathe a word of this to Andy."

A teasing light flickered in his eyes. "If you're not a client, then you have no client privileges."

Grace wadded her napkin and tossed it at him.

He caught it effortlessly in mid-air and laughed.

She pointed a finger at him. "I mean it, Matt. Promise."

"Okay, okay." He waved his hands, chest high, in surrender.

She inhaled a deep breath, the lingering smell of breakfast still in the air, and rubbed her arms. "You know I've wanted to be an attorney ever since Mama died."

"Yeah. Go on."

"I just didn't see it working out this way. I thought I'd be a prosecutor."

"So you feel like you're working for the wrong side of the law?"

Grace nodded. "I love Andy like a brother, and owe him so much. I wouldn't be an attorney if it weren't for him."

"But you feel obligated to work for him when your passion is to put the bad guys behind bars."

"Exactly." She gave her head a shake at the conundrum. "And I don't know what to do about it."

Matt placed his elbows on the table and rested his chin on his laced fingers. "Maybe you're looking at it all wrong, Gracie. You're focused on the situation rather than why you feel the way you do. Have you stopped to think about why you want to be a prosecutor?"

The reason flew into her brain instantly, and she straightened. "I guess for Mama, to keep someone else from going through this, and to achieve justice for others."

"To avenge her death?" The question was half-whispered, but even then sounded cold, almost un-Christian. "Don't overthink it, Gracie." Matt's tone held warning. "I see your brain spinning from here. Don't try to assign meaning and morality to your motivation. Just accept it and move on from there."

"But it does explain my nightmare." The agitation in her voice surprised her. "Don't you see? It's as if Mama's trying to remind me of that night so I'll make the right decision. Maybe I need to look for a different position, one that'll put me on the prosecution. Maybe I'm not cut out to defend guys I don't completely trust."

"Whoa, girl, you're gonna strip some gears bouncing around that fast." He stood and moved to the sink with his plate, nabbing hers as he passed. "When it comes to life, A plus B doesn't always equal C. It's just a jumping off place. Give it some time."

There it was again. Matt and his *"lo que será, sera"*-approach to life. "You would say that. You want me to work for Andy. He's your brother."

The dishes Matt carried crashed into the sink, and he made a quick trip back to the table. "That's not at all why I said what I did. Just think through things a little more carefully. I don't believe your mother's trying to communicate with you from the grave, and neither do if you think through it." He softened his demeanor. "But the dilemma you're facing is enough to make you dream about the accident."

"Think through it? That's the best advice you can give? A minute ago you were telling me not to overthink."

An exasperated sigh fell from his lips. He squatted near her chair, enclosed her hands with his own, and gazed up into her eyes. "Gracie. It's me, remember? I know you. Don't stress and worry about making the right decision. Pray about it. You belong to God. He'll put you where He wants you." His smile grew tender. "And I have no doubt that you'll be an awesome attorney, no matter which side of the courtroom you sit on."

Tears stung her eyes, and she blinked furiously to keep them at bay. How good it felt to have someone offer encouragement—to remind her God was in control—even if it were Matt. She lowered her gaze to collect herself before glancing back up at him. "Thanks."

He helped her to her feet and moved close to embrace her in a hug, the scent of his cologne toying with her frazzled emotions.

Grace sidestepped and reached for her glass. There was no way she'd let this move past a friendly level. He was more than likely here for a short time. Then he'd be off chasing his fantasies once more.

She deposited the glass in the stainless steel sink with a clunk. Besides, she had her life plan to think of—a plan that didn't include a gypsy like Matt.

2

"Tyler, Dent, and Snodgrass. Hold, please." Gracie sing-songed the words then punched another button.

Matt's mouth lifted at one corner. If it bothered her that she had to play receptionist when she'd earned the right to be an attorney, she didn't let it show. Her professional façade was stoically plastered in place.

He sipped the fragrant coffee and allowed his eyes to trail her every move. Blast it all! He hadn't been as prepared for seeing her again as he'd thought. But why? Hadn't he endured enough torture the first time? Besides, he wasn't here to find a woman. He was here to help Andy and Trish in the short term while he figured out what God wanted him to do, to hopefully find a way to pursue both his passions—music and counseling.

Matt released a short sigh, his frustration mounting. So much for putting his feelings for her behind him. She'd made it more than clear two years ago that friendship was all she was interested in. He'd accepted it and eventually moved on. Then why was he feeling so . . . so disappointed? He swigged another sip of coffee, and tried to swallow his disappointment at the same time. Perhaps some part of him had hoped that once she was out of law school she might feel differently. Obviously nothing but wishful thinking on his part.

Behind the receptionist's desk, Gracie easily handled multiple phone calls, multi-tasking through several projects like a well-oiled, organized machine. With her thick dark hair swept up into a twisted knot at the back of her head and the dark business attire, she looked almost formidable. All five-foot, four-inches of her.

"Are you planning on hanging out here all day?" Her voice held an irritable edge.

"Maybe."

She huffed a puff of air from between pursed lips and returned to her work.

Two summers ago he'd glimpsed her softer side—and her better side, in his opinion—the sweet country girl with the voice of an angel and a heart for God. He pressed his lips together. Was there any hope of getting that Gracie back? More importantly, would he ever be able to prove he wasn't the slacker and daydreamer she imagined him to be?

The phone rang again and she answered, jotting down a note while rearranging her desk to keep everything in perfect order, as though she'd marked the distance between each item with a ruler. Even notepads were placed exactly on top of each other, their sides precise and even.

He crossed his arms. Everything about her was too perfect, from her professional voice to her sensible shoes. But it was more than just role-playing. More like her thinking she could be perfect if she tried hard enough. Matt frowned. This wasn't good at all. If Gracie kept heading toward the illusory trap of perfectionism, she was destined for a fall—and not a minor one.

The back door swung open and closed with a bang. Gracie turned her head at the sound, then smoothed her hair and skirt and checked her teeth in a small mirror near her desk.

Matt swallowed a gulp of tepid coffee, his forehead tight. Who was she trying to impress?

Andy rounded the corner, and his face broke into a grin. "Bro, when did you get here?"

"Late last night." Matt hugged his brother and patted his back, careful not to spill the contents of his cup on Andy's dark suit or crisp white shirt. "Didn't wanna wake you and Trish, so I stayed at the apartment."

"You're here early, Gracie." Andy strode around her to the coffee pot.

She looked up momentarily before rifling through a stack of papers. "It's a good thing, too. The phone's been ringing off the hook. Where's Sandra?"

"Called earlier to say her youngest has the chicken pox." He hesitated, his face strained. "Can you cover for her?"

"Not a problem." She spoke the words sincerely, though the enthusiasm in her voice lowered a couple of notches.

Matt pressed his lips together, the coffee aftertaste in his mouth growing increasingly bitter. Her disease to please had grown worse. Why didn't she stand up for herself?

"Good old Gracie, as dependable as always." Andy patted her on the head like an obedient puppy. "If I didn't know better, I'd think you were after something. A raise, maybe?" He winked at Matt.

Gracie flashed Matt a "don't-you-dare-tell" look, but didn't answer.

He flinched inwardly. Him and his stupid promises. How could he help Andy see that he needed to treat Gracie more like an attorney and less like a crack-filler, yet not breathe a word about Gracie's desire to become a prosecutor? More than that, what could he do to help Gracie feel more appreciated? The seed of an idea rooted in his brain.

Andy stopped beside him. "Wanna do lunch later?"

"Sure. I'll hang around 'til then." That would give him time to work on the surprise for Gracie.

His brother checked his wristwatch. "I have a few client appointments this morning, but should be done by noon." He turned to Gracie. "Can you bring me the files for this morning's clients?" Without waiting for an answer, he stepped to his office and closed the door behind him.

Her lips tightened and her shoulders drooped. "Sure."

Matt's heart tumbled. Poor thing. Today should have been a day of celebration for her. Instead it had turned into the same boring routine. He caught her attention. "You okay?"

She nodded and went back to work.

The front door creaked open, and a spry, elderly man strode by. He nodded at Matt. "Morning, Gracie."

"Good morning, Ben."

The man tottered down the hallway and entered one of the offices.

Matt gazed after him. "Who was that?"

Gracie raised one eyebrow. "One of the new partners, Ben Snodgrass. He joined the firm about the same time as Jason."

"Jason?"

She stared at him like he'd lost his mind. "Jason Dent, the other new partner. You haven't been here in a while, have you?"

"Then why don't you fill me in?" He nodded toward the office the old man had entered. "What's he like?"

Wavy lines wriggled their way onto her forehead. "Honestly, he kind of gives me the creeps. He's always sneaking up on me, like he's part feline or something."

"And the other new guy?"

This time her face took on a certain fascination, but before she could speak, the door opened again, and a guy who looked like he'd stepped off the cover of *GQ* strode in. He wore an expensive black suit and tie which set off his dark complexion, steely blue eyes, and broad shoulders. "Good morning, Grace." His British accent was the proverbial icing on the cake.

"Good morning, Jason." Her eyes widened, and she spoke the words downright cheerfully, accompanied with a brilliant smile.

Matt's stomach lurched unexpectedly, depositing the taste of acid on his tongue. The smitten look on Gracie's face told him all he didn't wanna know.

"Any messages for me?" Andy's partner directed the words at Gracie then turned his way with a nod and closed-lip smile, obviously confident in his ability to turn women's heads wherever he went.

"Yes." Gracie reached for a stack of pink memos. "You seem to be in high demand as usual."

Jason reached for the pile of notes, his fingers casually touching Gracie's. "Thanks." He stepped toward another office as he perused them, his perfectly polished shoes tapping against the laminate floors and the scent of his tastefully expensive cologne clogging the air.

Gracie's eyes trailed after him wistfully, but then she turned to pull the files his brother requested.

"You didn't answer my question." Well, maybe she had.

She glanced up, her brow creased in a frown. "Hmm?"

"What's Jason like?"

A non-committal shrug lifted her small shoulders. "He's a great attorney."

"Married?"

"No." Her voice held hostility. "Why do you ask?"

"If I didn't know better, I'd say that you're interested in him—other than professionally."

Her dark eyes shot sparks. "First of all, I don't remember asking you. Secondly, Jason happens to be one of the best defense attorneys in this area of the state."

"I thought you were more interested in the prosecution end of things."

"That doesn't mean I can't appreciate his legal skills." Now her voice escalated in volume.

Matt gave a short laugh. "Quit deceiving yourself, Gracie Mae."

Jason exited his office, a frown connecting his dark eyebrows. "Is there a problem, Mr.—?" A protective edge colored his words.

Matt extended a hand and looked up at him. It didn't help matters that Jason outsized him by a good six inches. "I'm Matt."

Gracie cleared her throat, her cheeks still red from the argument. "Matt is Andy's younger brother."

Jason grasped his hand quickly. "Oh, I'm Jason. Sorry if I came across as rude. I thought you were harassing Grace."

"Every chance I get." He ignored the glare Gracie shot at him. "How do you like Miller's Creek?"

The handsome attorney nodded agreeably. "Love it." His eyes perused Matt's appearance. "I take it you're a college student?"

"Perpetually." Grace drawled out the word and turned back to her computer.

Matt's blood boiled. How like her to pass judgment without bothering to check the facts. He turned back to Jason. "Actually I finished my grad work this past May and started my doctoral studies online."

Gracie's mouth flew open, but she quickly snapped it shut. The phone shrilled, and she answered. A minute later, she hung up and faced Jason, her lips curved upward.

Matt's heart felt like it was ground into the floor beneath the heel of one of Dent's shiny black shoes. Gracie was clearly enamored with him, and judging by the glint in the attorney's beady eyes, he was exulting in every minute of her schoolgirl adulation.

"So what are your plans now, Matt?" Jason's cultured voice held a friendliness which had been curiously lacking until he'd learned his relation to Andy.

"Well, I'm spending some time with Andy and Trish while I check out a few career options."

Gracie turned back to the computer and typed furiously, pretending not to listen. But the smirk on her face let him know she heard every word.

"What kind of work are you looking for?" Jason continued his probe.

"Leaving my options open at this point, but I—"

Before he could mention his desire to open a counseling practice, Gracie let out a snort, then pressed her lips together and pretended to focus on the stack of papers to her left.

If the expression on her face didn't irritate him so much, it would almost be comical. Her "Dear-John-speech" two years ago had made it clear he didn't meet her high expectations. Now it was more than obvious that he still didn't qualify and probably never would, especially since her image of manly perfection had moved in right down the hall.

Jason didn't respond further. Instead he turned to Grace. "I have to leave for a meeting in Morganville in a few minutes, and don't know when I'll return. Just stack messages on my desk when you leave."

"Sure." The light in Gracie's eyes faded as Jason strolled to his office and closed the door. In a few short words, he'd effectively dismissed them both.

Unable to endure the hurt inscribed on her face, Matt stepped down to the stairwell, the smell of their shared breakfast only emphasizing his thoughts of Gracie. She just couldn't fall for someone like Jason Dent. His polished image—the Armani suit, Berluti shoes, not-a-hair-out-of-place haircut—might ooze money and sophistication, but it also screamed control freak.

Matt stopped short and ran a hand through his hair. He had to go back. How could he be so hard on Gracie for running away when he was doing the same thing?

She looked up from her work as he approached, a grumpy expression on her face. "Did you need something else?"

"I—uh, was wondering if you'd like to eat lunch with us today?"

Gracie lowered her gaze and licked her lips. "Actually I have some errands to run, but thanks for the offer."

A brush-off or the truth?

Jason exited his office with a manila folder in his hands, his dark eyebrows furrowed in a way that made him look ominous. He made eye contact with Matt. "Still here?"

Matt overpowered the malicious desire to ask him the same question. "Yeah, Andy and I are eating lunch together."

The tall dark handsome rested against the counter—obviously waiting to speak to Gracie alone—and eyed his perfectly groomed fingernails.

Matt glanced down at his raggedy jeans and wrinkled t-shirt, feeling more out of place than ever. How could he possibly compete with the likes of Jason Dent? His rapidly deflating ego pulled his head and shoulders toward the floor.

God, help me. You know how much I care for Gracie, but more than my selfish desire to win her heart, help me to want what's best for her. Even if that means Jason gets her and I don't.

Matt made his way to the stairs. The man could obviously provide her with a better life than he could ever dream about. And Gracie deserved it. She'd spent her entire existence caring for others, and it was time she had someone taking care of her for a change. Maybe it was best if he just kept his distance.

He reached the stairwell and cast one last look at Jason and Gracie, now engaged in private conversation, her face lit up like a Christmas tree. He halted, his eyes narrowed and nebulous thoughts suddenly solidified.

Why would a guy like Jason be interested in someone like Gracie?

He took in the man's too-smooth manner. Hmm, on second thought, maybe he should stick around and make sure Gracie's penchant for perfection didn't land her in a heap of trouble.

Matt toyed with the tamale. The food at Soldano's was delicious as always, as were the tempting aromas floating around his head in the bustling restaurant. Gracie's dad was good at many things, but especially excelled at mouth-watering Mexican food.

No, the problem was definitely not the food. He needed to sort through his emotions and shake this troubled feeling, and in addition, figure out what he was supposed to do with his life. Maybe Gracie's response to him—or lack thereof—was God's way of telling him to move on.

He huffed out a sigh. Why worry about it? God had it under control. And since when had he become a worrier? Easy answer.

Any time he was around Gracie Soldano. Yet another reason to avoid her like the plague.

"Sure you're okay, bro?" Andy talked around a mouthful of fajitas and guacamole.

"Eh, guess I'm not hungry."

His brother's eyebrows rose, creasing his forehead in thick wavy lines. He laid down the tortilla-wrapped fajita and wiped his mouth. "Okay, spill it. The only time you're not hungry is when something's bothering you."

Matt shook his head. "Probably nothing."

"C'mon, Matt, you know I only have a few minutes. Let it out."

He sighed. "What can you tell me about Jason Dent?"

Andy shifted in his seat, his green eyes darkening momentarily, and clenched his jaw. Holding in something he really wanted to say? "One of the best defense attorneys I've ever seen in action. His confidence level makes him almost unbeatable. Came highly recommended and at this point has done an excellent job for the firm, not to mention the town."

Won. Der. Ful. So not only was Jason an immaculate dresser, he was also Mr. Perfect in every other way. How could Gracie *not* fall for him?

"Why do you ask?"

Andy's question raised Matt's gaze. What was it about Dent that made his skin crawl? "I dunno, something about him just troubles me."

His brother let out a short laugh and forked refried beans into his mouth. "Don't worry. All us males are bothered by it. We just don't measure up when we compare ourselves to guys like him."

Matt chewed a bite of the pork tamale. Andy had hit the nail on the head. What he was feeling was nothing but the green-eyed monster. But his brother couldn't be as bothered by Mr. Perfect as he was. He had a lovely wife, two sons, and a beautiful new baby girl waiting for him at home. Meanwhile, Gracie was somewhere running errands and contemplating a perfect life with the perfect man. He tossed his fork to the plate, where it landed with a clatter, then raised fingers to scratch the stubble on his neck.

"Man, you *are* bothered. What gives?" Andy studied him.

"It's Gracie. I think she's falling for him."

"Our Gracie? You really think so?"

Matt bobbed his head.

For a long moment, Andy chewed silently, his eyes fixed on nothing in particular. Finally, he shook his head. "Ah, c'mon, Matt, you know her as well as I do. Her career aspirations are too high to be side-tracked by Jason or anyone else." Andy continued to eat, but Matt could tell his brother was considering the possibility. "Don't you think I'd have noticed if something was going on between them?"

"No. You're too wrapped up in your job and family."

Andy nodded. "True. But let's pretend your supposition is correct. Why should we care if Gracie's falling for him? He's a nice guy and could provide a great life for her . . ." His words dwindled away, and he cocked his curly head slowly to one side, revelation dawning on his face. "You're in love with her."

A comment, not a question. "I wouldn't go that far, but I care about her, and I don't wanna see her get hurt."

His brother eyed him in a way that suggested he didn't completely believe him. "Whatever. The question is, what are you gonna do about it?"

"Keep my eyes on him, and make sure he doesn't do anything to hurt her."

"That's it?"

Matt shifted in the booth and sat up straighter. "What do you mean, that's it?"

His brother shrugged. "Seems to me if you really cared about her you'd make a play for her yourself."

"Me? What do I have to offer? Besides, you're the one who always said I need to find out what I want to do with my life before I go looking for a relationship."

"Yeah, but that doesn't mean you should ignore how you feel. Maybe God brought you here, not only to figure things out, but direct your path toward Gracie. That's how it worked for me."

God, please let it be true. "Think about it, bro. The guy looks like a movie star or a model." He sighed and shook his head. "I can't compete with him."

Andy gently laid down his fork, his face and tone sincere. "You don't have to, Matt. In my opinion, Jason can't compete with you." He paused a long minute, as if struggling to find the right words. "I know it's not easy, especially with our background. Every chance at a relationship carries with it the risk of going through what we went through with Mom."

An immediate pain sprung to his throat, and Matt swallowed against it. His psych books would label it as "abandonment issues," a technical term that somehow lessened what he often felt. "I think I'll always struggle with truly opening myself up to a woman, even though I know in my head that fear doesn't come from God."

"That's how you'll know you've found the right one. You'll love her so much the fear goes away." He picked up his fork and resumed eating, the seriousness of the moment dissipating. "And don't sell yourself short. I don't know anyone as talented or as good-hearted as you. I still feel bad about taking that money."

Matt raised a hand. "Stop. I owed you for all the times you helped me out during school."

"I never expected it back. It was an invest—"

"Yeah, yeah, I know . . . an investment, not a loan." He sent his brother a grin. "And I appreciate the sentiment. But your baby brother is a grown-up now. You don't have to keep blazing a trail for me. I can do it on my own."

"Now you sound like my wife." Andy took another bite. "So you're doing okay? Financially, I mean."

"Yep. Have the royalty money for those two songs I sold saved up and spoke with a guy from Nashville this morning who's interested in a few others."

"Way to go." Andy held up a hand for a high five.

Matt slapped his brother's hand then focused on his food, adding a bit to his mouth. "I appreciate you letting me hang out here while I figure out where God wants me next."

"No problem. Glad to have you around. In fact, Trish and I were wondering if you might be interested in taking over the equine ministry while she takes care of the baby."

His radar went up. Since Andy and Trish started the ministry two years ago, the number of people they'd helped undoubtedly reached into the hundreds if not the thousands. "Sounds like it would be right up my alley, but I can't promise I'll do it on a permanent basis at this point. What all does the job entail?"

"Trish has a great band of volunteers who help the kids while they're on the horses, but you'd need to be there to supervise. We have some kids that would really benefit from counseling."

His heart did a queer flop within his chest. Counseling hurt kids would be just the sort of work he'd love to do. A way to offer others the help he'd needed as a kid. "Sounds interesting, but I need to pray about it first." Even as he spoke the words he knew this was a ministry he could be passionate about.

"The pay isn't great, but we could give you the top floor of the old Miller mansion to live in free of charge, and you could probably pick up a few clients in the area."

Big brother to the rescue once more. Matt tossed the idea around in his head. "The Miller mansion? You mean that ginormous house on the ranch you showed me last time I was down?"

"Yep. Trish's dad used to live there, but he moved to town when he married Mama Beth. Now we use the bottom floor as ranch headquarters and the equine therapy office."

Mama Beth. He hadn't thought about her until now. "How's Mama Beth doing?"

A wry grin lifted one corner of Andy's mouth. "Unstoppable as always."

Matt's lips involuntarily curved into a smile at the thought of the matriarch of Miller's Creek, her heart bigger than Texas. How many times had he been the recipient of her wisdom? A waitress hurried by with a tray of fresh food, the aroma wafting their way. His thoughts returned to the Miller mansion. "As I recall that place had a bathtub big enough to swim in."

Andy let out a laugh. "Huge. You could have a bubble bath any time you wanted." He waggled his eyebrows and winked. "Anyway, we'd love to have you stay on long-term."

Long term? A sudden flash of clarity lit his brain. There was only one way he would be in Miller's Creek long-term, and it all depended on Gracie. He couldn't bear the thought of staying around to see her build her perfect world with someone else. He attempted to clear his throat of the knot that had grown there. "We'll see where God leads."

As they finished up the last few bites of lunch in silence, a policeman swaggered to their table, his Billy stick wagging at his side. "How's it going, Andy?" He spoke the words with a friendly smile that curled his caterpillar mustache into an inverted rainbow.

"Good, Ernie. How 'bout yourself?" Andy shook his hand.

"Can't complain."

Andy held out an arm in Matt's direction. "This is my brother Matt. Ernie's the chief of police for Miller's Creek."

Ernie gave him a quick look and brief nod then turned his focus back to Andy.

Typical reaction. Small-town people always treated him that way. Sized him up with one glance then dismissed him as unimportant. He'd known when he came here people probably wouldn't accept him because he didn't act like them. Fine by him. He wasn't about to change who he was to please anybody. Matt picked up the check and excused himself from the table, headed to where Gracie's dad stood at the register. "Hey, Mr. Soldano. Good to see you again."

"Was everything satisfactory?" Juan Soldano rang up the ticket without looking his way.

"Great as usual." Matt laid down a twenty. "Saw Gracie earlier. You must be very proud of her and her accomplishments."

The man plopped the change down on the counter and glared back at him from beneath bushy black brows. "I would appreciate it if you stayed away from my daughter." Without another word, he scurried from the counter and through the stainless steel doors that led to the kitchen, his final words knifing through Matt's heart.

Apparently Mr. Soldano had the same opinion of him as Gracie and the rest of the town.

3

Everyone wanted justice unless they were the one on trial. Then they longed for mercy to rain down on them—even to the point of being willing to pay for it.

Grace ran a hand down her neck to smooth down goose bumps. Thank goodness this first week was almost over. Maybe next week Sandra would be back, and she could become an attorney at last. Outside a blast of thunder boomed, and a storm unleashed its fury on the Miller County courthouse.

Today even the warm-toned wood panels encasing the courtroom seemed cold and austere, most likely because of her close proximity to the man on trial. A shudder rippled through her body. Her first time in a courtroom since she'd passed the bar, but not at all the kind of case she would've preferred. At least it would give her a chance to see up-and-coming prosecutor Elena Delgado in action. She'd pick up some pointers and make herself known in the legal community at the same time.

She inhaled in an attempt to steady her nerves, the musty scent of the old building tickling her nose. If only it were a different case. Andy had insisted she attend the trial, though she couldn't fathom why, especially since she wasn't involved with the case, and Sandra was still on sick leave. While she appreciated the invitation, the subject matter threatened to resurrect memories she'd rather leave buried.

Jason slid into the seat beside her. "Fancy seeing you here."

She smiled and adjusted her hair. One thing she hadn't taken into consideration was Jason being here. He'd been unexpectedly attentive all week, and she'd grown to enjoy their encounters. "Andy insisted."

His lips parted in a lazy smile. "Same here."

Everything about him was exceptional, from his dark complexion to his sapphire eyes, and it didn't hurt that he'd quickly earned a reputation in Miller's Creek as an expert defense attorney and philanthropist.

Just as she gathered the gumption to initiate further conversation, a heavy wooden door swung open. Judge Clark entered, his black robe billowing behind as he made his way to the bench. Everyone rose to their feet, and the hollow thud of shoes against aged wood floors echoed like icy bars of jail cell doors slammed shut.

Though Grace stood behind the accused—who today looked more like an altar boy than a criminal—somewhere in the gallery was a grieving family for whom every fiber of her being cried out for justice. The thought dumped a bad taste in her mouth.

"Ladies and gentlemen of the jury, you're about to hear the opening statements in the case of the State of Texas against David Simmons." The judge rattled off the words routinely despite the gravity of the situation, as if his life's work had become a creek which had long since gone dry in the drought of life's pressures. "This man is innocent until proven guilty beyond a reasonable doubt. Your job is to discern the truth by the evidence and testimony presented during the course of this trial and to respond with a just verdict." He raised his gaze to the gallery, the bags beneath his eyes like those of a sad hound dog, and turned his attention to the opposite table. "Is the prosecution ready?"

A stylish woman, probably in her thirties, stood. "Yes, Your Honor." Though slight in stature, everything else about Elena Delgado was larger than life.

Grace eyed the prosecutor's designer suit and shoes and then glanced down at her own thrift store blouse and skirt. Far from perfect, but all she could afford at the moment. Hmm, maybe she should use part of her next paycheck to purchase a new outfit or two, like the flouncy skirt and fitted suit jacket Elena Delgado wore. After all, if she wanted to make a good impression in the legal community she needed to dress the part. She glanced at Jason from the corner of her eyes. His attention riveted on Elena, and his face glowed with a curious light.

"Is the defense ready?"

Andy Tyler rose to his feet in front of her, his jaw set with the determination of someone intent on seeing justice done. How could a man as kind as him represent scum like David Simmons?

"Yes, Your Honor."

"Then let's begin. We're ready for the prosecution's opening statement."

Elena's Christian Louboutin heels clacked against the floors as she made her way to the jury box. She came to a stop in front of them, somewhat like a humble schoolgirl. "Good morning. Thank you for giving time away from your loved ones to provide justice for a family who lost their only child at the hands of a negligent driver."

Grace's admiration for Elena's legal skills skyrocketed. In a few words, she'd delivered the heart of the case flawlessly, and in a way that complemented the jurors.

Elena paused in an obvious effort to control her emotions and gestured toward the screen. "This photograph of the victim, Michael Bedford, was taken a week before he was to return home for Christmas break. A time he was especially looking forward to because it had been four long months since he'd seen his family."

The screen flashed to a very different picture, and bile rose in Grace's throat. An involuntary shiver crawled down her spine. This shot revealed a darkened road and authorities hovered over a lifeless body.

A hushed gasp rose from the crowd, and a low murmur spread across the room. "This . . ." Elena's voice wavered. "This is the result of an irresponsible joy ride that ended in death."

A wave of nausea swept over Grace as unbidden memories flashed to the front of her mind. She brought a shaky hand to her lips.

The air tingled with electric anticipation as Elena moved behind the lectern, removed her designer glasses, and made eye contact with the jurors. "The evidence will prove that on the evening of December twelfth of last year, David Simmons recklessly took the life of one of his classmates, leaving a hole in this family that can never be filled."

She turned to the table where Andy sat with David Simmons. "The defense will have you believe the defendant was out enjoying an evening with friends, that he wasn't responsible. They want you to think Mr. Simmons has been falsely accused, but evidence will prove otherwise." She faced the jury once more, her voice full of conviction. "Your task is a heavy one, but I trust your common sense will win out. After hearing the facts, you'll have no other recourse but to find this monster," she gestured with an outstretched arm toward David Simmons, "guilty of vehicular homicide."

Her words seemed to gain a life of their own as they hung in the air. The defendant furtively whispered something in Andy's ear. Her boss merely patted him on the back and shot an encouraging smile before he turned his attention to the bench.

"The defense may now make an opening statement."

Grace watched in fascination. Andy's approach to the jury box was altogether different than Elena's. In typical laid-back style, with hands in pockets, he slowly raised his eyes to the screen. "I saw the looks of horror on your faces when Ms. Delgado flashed this picture. What you see is clearly the result of a terrible tragedy. We'd all agree—me included—that someone should pay. But only if Michael Bedford's death was intentional, which it wasn't." Andy spoke the words in his usual Texas drawl.

An unlikely mixture of respect and disgust rose inside Grace. Her boss had easily bridged a seemingly impossible gap. It was clear to see that the jury hung on his every word.

Grace sighed and lowered her head. She couldn't just ignore the likelihood that David Simmons was guilty. She'd seen his type before, and on more than one occasion, the stereotypical over-indulged son of wealthy parents who could afford to buy justice to cover whatever crimes their "innocent" child had committed. He'd most likely grown up with every advantage and was used to getting what he wanted. When anyone was bold enough to tell him "no," he took it anyway or made them pay.

Andy leaned his weight against the table and crossed his arms and legs, his gaze now focused on the jurors. "We'll show that Mr. Simmons was not responsible." He waved an arm toward the screen. "Ms. Delgado knows her best chance of indicting my client is to make you think he's a monster. In fact, she's already labeled him as such. In a subtle way, the prosecution has already toyed with your emotions and dislikes."

An immediate frown sprung to Grace's forehead. Some of the members of the jury turned their gaze toward Elena Delgado, as if seeing her in a new light.

Andy's voice brought their attention back to him. "I'm asking you to put all that aside and give David Simmons the benefit of a doubt until after you've seen the evidence and heard the testimonies. Prove to him that you're better and smarter than Ms. Delgado gives you credit for."

Elena visibly stiffened, her face starched crisp and hard. She lowered her head and scribbled furiously on a legal pad.

Meanwhile, Andy moved to stand behind David Simmons. "I have to admit Ms. Delgado is right on one account." He paused for effect. "You *do* have a tough job. You have to decide who's lying and who's telling the truth. The evidence we present will prove this man's innocence, which brings us to a different crime being committed here." He placed both hands on David's shoulders. "Being accused of something you didn't do."

That afternoon, Grace leaned against the polished panels of wood that lined the hallways in the courthouse and massaged both temples, hoping to relieve not only the throbbing ache in her head but also her churning stomach. Everyone deserved a fair trial, but it was sometimes a hard pill to swallow when it came to people like David Simmons.

She gazed down the crowded foyer. Attorneys, clasping their expensive leather attaches, grouped together, laughing and conversing. Her whole motive for becoming a lawyer was to ensure that guys like Simmons were put away to keep them from hurting anyone else. And now, by virtue of the fact that Andy played such an instrumental part in her education, she found herself working the wrong side of the courtroom. What she wouldn't give to be in Elena Delgado's uber-expensive high heels.

Across the hall, Andy emerged from the men's room and made his way through the crowd to where she stood. "You look beat, Gracie."

She cringed at the use of her schoolgirl name and glanced around hoping no one heard him. "I am pretty tired. Just observing this case is exhausting."

"I'll second that. Try doing it with a newborn at home. I know this is a hard one for you to watch right out of the gate, but I can explain." He latched on to her elbow and guided her toward the door, looking back over his shoulder. "Where's Jason? I wanted to talk to you two about something."

Talk with both of them? About what? "He already left. Said something about needing to get back to Miller's Creek."

Andy frowned and fell silent for a few steps. "Yeah, I hoped to get back to meet Matt for lunch. Maybe there's still time."

Grace struggled to keep distaste from her expression and her tone. "Guess he'll be here a few days before he's off chasing another rainbow."

Andy's face hardened. "Actually, he might help Trish out with the equine ministry while she's home on maternity leave. He could be here several months."

Help with the equine ministry? Matt hadn't mentioned it, nor had he let let her know he'd graduated and started on his doctorate. What else had he omitted?

She spied a small puddle of water—most likely the result of someone's drippy umbrella—and tried to dodge, but Andy crashed into her just as her foot hit the wet spot. Both feet slid out from under her, and she landed smack on her bottom.

Heat blistered her face as the room quieted and all eyes turned her way. Well, she'd made herself known to the legal community all right—just not in a good way.

At precisely that moment, Elena Delgado, as pretty and intimidating up close as she was from a distance, rounded the corner, coming face-to-face with Andy. "Trying to run me over, counselor?" She glanced down at Grace for a brief moment before she faced Andy again. Her perfectly made-up lips took on a smirk. "Guess that's one way to win a case."

"I'll stick to doing it fair and square," Andy returned lightly as he helped Grace to her feet. "Sorry about that. You okay?"

She struggled to stand, piecing together her wounded pride. Of all times to fall, it *would* have to be in front of Elena Delgado.

Musical laughter floated from the pretty attorney. "Sarcasm doesn't suit you, Mr. Tyler."

"Yet it drips so easily from you. If you'll excuse us, we were on our way out." He made an attempt to move around her, but she latched onto his arm with a well-manicured hand. "You haven't introduced your friend."

"Sorry. This is our newest attorney, Gr—"

"Grace Soldano." Grace smiled broadly and interrupted before Andy uttered the dreaded schoolgirl name. "Thrilled to meet you, Ms. Delgado. I'm a big fan of your work."

Elena looked temporarily taken aback, but returned the smile. "Nice to meet you, Grace. Are you still in law school?"

"Actually I just took the bar exam in July. And passed." *Don't sound so stupid, Grace.* Elena would know she took the bar in July, just like all Texas law school graduates. And she wouldn't be here if she hadn't passed. She somehow managed to keep her smile pasted in place and resisted the urge to check her appearance in a nearby mirror.

"Congratulations . I'd be happy to show you the ropes on this side of the legal fence some time."

"I'd love that!" Grace ignored the sour look that descended on Andy's face. "I've always dreamed of being a prosecutor."

Andy's expression changed from sour to sober. "See you in court, Elena." Without a chance for Grace to protest, he steered her toward the door and out into the overcast fall day. "What was that all about?" he groused as they strode toward the car, the air still scented with recent rain. "I'm your biggest fan, Ms. Delgado. Let me kiss the ground you walk on, Ms. Delgado." He donned a prissy look and raised his voice a few notches.

Grace couldn't help but giggle. "Was I really that bad? I was more than likely distracted by the fact that you tripped me." Oh man, she'd just made a colossal fool of herself in front of Elena.

Andy opened her car door without a smile. She scrambled inside, while he moved to the driver's side. Her boss was clearly miffed. He climbed in, started the car, and pulled out into traffic. "So you really wanna be a prosecutor?"

"I enjoy working for you."

"But?"

How did she say it without sounding ungrateful or hurting his feelings? "I've dreamed of being a prosecutor my entire life." At least ever since Mama died.

The ensuing silence was suffocating. Finally, he spoke. "Just so you know, Elena's not the saint you made her out to be. Not going into specifics, but watch your step."

Grace fingered the seat belt strap to keep it from rubbing against her neck. "You've been so good to me. I would've never made it through my undergrad work or law school if it hadn't been for you. That's why I decided to at least start my career with Tyler, Dent, and—"

"Don't feel obligated. The scholarships came with no strings attached." His words were curt and clipped.

"I appreciate that." She pressed her lips together while she gathered the courage to continue. "Honestly, I don't see how someone as nice as you can represent some of the people that come into your office."

His eyebrows ratcheted up. "Well, that's an interesting observation coming from an attorney. I'll admit some of 'em are guilty as all get out, but that doesn't mean they don't deserve fair treatment under the law."

"You think David Simmons is innocent?"

"You don't?"

She shook her head. "He puts on a good act, but I don't buy it."

"What happened to waiting until you've examined the evidence?" His green eyes bored through her momentarily.

Her muscles tightened. Was he making a commentary on her legal skills? "Granted, I haven't had a chance to study the case in depth, but I just have a feeling about this guy." A defensive edge crept into her tone.

Andy pressed the accelerator, causing the car to shoot forward. "Sorry to burst your bubble, Princess, but that ain't a feeling. It's a prejudice."

It took most of the ride back to Miller's Creek for Grace to gather the courage to break the chilled silence, but as they entered the city limits, she took a deep breath and went for it. "So what did you want to talk to me and Jason about?"

He steered the car into the parking lot of Tyler, Dent, and Snodgrass and braked to an overly quick stop. Without looking her way, he intoned, "I thought about having you two help with the Simmons trial."

Grace's heart rate rocketed upwards, partly from the opportunity to work in close proximity with Jason, mostly in excitement over her first case, not to mention the chance to hopefully impress Elena Delgado with her ability.

"But that's only if you can get past your prejudice." Andy exited the car, grabbed his briefcase from the back seat, and started for the building.

Grace slammed the car door and moved toward the pickup, rifling through her purse for the keys. "See you after lunch."

"Actually, could you come in for a minute first?"

She frowned, but made her way to where he stood near the opened door. "Sure. You need something?"

He smiled, an enigmatic grin that left her more confused than ever. "I need you downstairs for a minute."

Still puzzling over his strange request, Grace followed Andy, who now whistled a loud and cheery tune. As she reached the darkened basement, the lights came on.

"Surprise!" People from all over the community laughed and applauded.

Andy, his face lit with a big grin, pointed at her and mouthed the words "for you."

Her breath caught in her throat. A smile catapulted to her face as she gazed around the room at the people she loved more than life itself—Mama Beth and Big Bo, Trish and the Tyler kids, Steve and Dani Miller, the old geezers, and of course, Matt. Papa and Jason were even here! Grace brought shaky palms to her face.

Her boss patted her on the shoulder and waved a hand to silence the laughter and cheers. "All right, folks, settle down a second, so I can explain all this to our girl." He steered her through the crowd to a table in the back of the room, all decked out with lunch items, drinks, and a big cake. "This is to celebrate your passing of the bar and becoming a full-fledged attorney. Congratulations, Gracie. You always do Miller's Creek proud."

The people once more erupted into applause and they pushed her to the front of the serving line. Throughout lunch, people stopped by to congratulate her on her achievement.

The crew affectionately known as "the old geezers" gathered first. J.C. Watson, his clear blue-gray eyes kind and humble, patted her back. "Just wanted to say how proud of you we all are, Miss Gracie."

Right behind him was Coot, who would no doubt be a trumpet if this group ever became an orchestra. He hooked his thumbs under his suspenders, his pot belly protruding. "You make us pop our buttons," he bellowed loud enough for everyone to hear.

"No, that would be your daily slice of pecan pie at Granny's." Steve Miller, the town mayor, came up behind him and slapped him on the shoulder. The room erupted. Steve bent low to hug her neck. "Congratulations, sweet girl."

Next was Dani, the petite blonde who'd managed to capture the heart of Miller's Creek long before she was known as Mama Beth's daughter or Mrs. Steve Miller.

Mama Beth followed, and her blue eyes sparkled with unshed tears. "Goodness me, Gracie, you never cease to amaze me with how smart you are. I remember you when you were just a little girl in pigtails. Now you're all grown up." She hugged Grace.

There was no stopping tears now, and heat crept up her neck. She glanced across the table at Matt, who sent an encouraging and understanding smile.

Mama Beth moved away, sniffling and wiping her cheeks, her husband, Big Bo Miller, a gentle giant at her side.

At last the line ended with Trish and Andy, who both engulfed her in a hug at the same time. "You know we're so proud of you," exclaimed Trish. Andy nodded and beamed.

A lump landed in her throat. She'd be nothing without these people. Here they were congratulating her when she owed them so much, especially Andy. Grace swabbed at her tears as she gazed into her boss' eyes. "I can't thank you enough for everything you've done for me. Helping me through college and law school was enough, but now you've gone and done all this. Thank you."

"Helping you through school was my pleasure, Gracie, but I can't take credit for this."

She turned her head to one side.

"This was Matt's doing."

Matt? Grace whipped her head around to thank him, but his chair was empty. Instead, Jason, who sat nearby, captured her gaze with his own.

4

Matt stood on tiptoe at the back of the church after Sunday morning worship and searched the crowd for Gracie. She'd been there earlier, but must have slipped out as soon as the service was over. To make matters worse, Jason Dent had been lurking around her all morning, and now he was gone as well.

A wave of discouragement washed over him. He hadn't seen Gracie since the surprise party, tied up with finishing a requested song for a guy in Nashville. A sigh escaped. He'd hoped to ask if she wanted to join him for a cup of hot chocolate at Granny's.

People milled past, and though he was no stranger to Miller's Creek, no one spoke. Instead they chatted with each other, making him feel invisible. He looked the other way. Out of the corner of one eye, he spied Otis Thacker, the town grump, headed his direction.

Matt quickly offered a hand as the elderly man tottered up. "How are you, Otis?"

"Hmph." Otis ignored his hand and leaned closer. "I'm fine, but you're not doing too well by the looks of things." His bad breath blasted Matt in the face.

"I'm sorry?" His brow wrinkled as he shoved his fingers back into his jean pockets.

The old man waved a crooked finger in the air. "If my father was alive—he was a clothes salesman, you know—but if he was alive, he'd drag you to the store and dress you in something more appropriate for church."

Matt's mouth drooped open, but nothing came out.

"And he'd give your face a shave while he was at it." Otis tottered away, his parting words drifting behind him. "Young people these days have completely lost every lick of sense."

Mama Beth hurried up, wheezing and out of breath. "Heavens! I hope Otis wasn't too sharp-tongued. I tried to get here as soon as I saw him headed your way, but I didn't quite make it judging by the scowl on your face."

He attempted a smile, but the audacity of the other man had left a sour taste in his mouth. "Hey, Mama Beth." He leaned forward and hugged her neck. "Good to see you again. I've been hoping you'd invite me over for some of your famous cooking."

Mama Beth cackled, her face gleaming with good humor. "You know you don't have to wait for an invitation. Come any time. I'd enjoy the company. That man of mine is off with Steve on a hunting expedition right now."

"Deer hunting?"

"Yep. Maybe by this time next week I'll have some fresh venison for you."

His mouth watered at the thought. "Can't I come for a meal now *and* later?"

"Of course." Her smile faded, and she cocked her head to one side. "Something tells me it's not really my cooking you're after."

He lowered his head, released a half laugh, and dragged the toe of his right shoe across the carpet. "Good old Mama Beth, perceptive as always. Is it that obvious?"

"Probably not to anyone else. Do you have lunch plans?"

His heart lightened. A good heart-to-heart with Mama Beth was just what he needed. "None that can't be changed."

"Good, I'll see you at my house in a few minutes."

After locating Andy to let him know the change in plans, Matt crawled into the Pinto and cranked her up for the drive to Mama Beth's. Though often cantankerous, his 1976 pea-green car started on the first try. A few minutes later he perched on a stool in Mama Beth's country kitchen while she hummed and bustled about with preparations for lunch.

She raised her gaze to his while she stirred a pot on the stove. "Would you like a glass of sweet tea while you wait?"

"Sure, but let me get it. You've got your hands full." He moved to a nearby whitewashed cabinet to grab a glass and added a few ice cubes before pouring his tea.

Within a few minutes, Mama Beth placed fried chicken, mashed potatoes, homegrown green beans, and homemade bread in the middle of the oversized farm table. "Would you bless it for us, Matt?" She wiped her hands on her blue-checked apron.

"I'd be honored." He bowed his head. "Lord, bless this meal and the one who prepared it. May we be better servants for You. In Christ's name, Amen."

As they fixed their plates, Mama Beth jump-started the conversation. "So what's on your mind, Matty?"

He reached for a chicken leg. Did she mean in addition to downing a piece of her homemade fried chicken? "Not sure where to start." He chomped into the meat, the warm juices trickling down his throat.

"How about with Gracie?"

He almost choked. Leave it to Mama Beth to cut to the chase. "How'd you know I wanted to talk about Gracie?"

"You've been in love with her for a couple of years, right?"

A heat wave crept up his neck. "Well, love's a strong word—"

She sent a "you're-not-fooling-me" look.

Matt switched his gaze to the plate. "I do care about her an awful lot."

"Then what's the problem?"

"Well, now that she's finished with school and the bar exam. I hoped she and I could, well . . . " He squirmed in the ladder-back chair. This was harder than expected. "I need to know how to go about this. How to . . ." Words failed him.

Mama Beth's face lit with amusement. "I've never known you to be at a loss for words. It must be love." She patted his hand. "My best advice is to be yourself. You and Gracie are good friends. It's not too much of a leap from there."

"But what if she doesn't want a guy like me?"

White wispy eyebrows furrowed over clear blue eyes. "Good gravy, Matt. What makes you say such a foolish thing?"

Which reason should he give first? He forked potatoes in his mouth and chased it with a sip of tea. "Gracie's a planner. I'm not sure I fit the image she has in that brain of hers."

"Image has nothing to do with true love."

"I know that, but I'm not sure she does."

"Hmmm." Mama Beth gazed into space a moment then faced him. "You've got a point, but I wouldn't change who you are to fit what she thinks she wants. She's a smart girl. She'll figure it out."

Matt released a sigh of relief. Mama Beth had a knack for discerning what was really bothering someone. "Glad to hear you say that. I can't be someone I'm not." Even if it was for the purpose of winning Gracie's heart.

"Nor should you. You both belong to God. If this is His plan, it'll work out."

Mama Beth was right. He did belong to God, but what if God had other plans for both of them? Could he accept that possibility? "Well, it's a little more complicated than that."

"What do you mean?"

"Jason Dent. He's everything I'm not. Just the sort Gracie could fall for if given the encouragement." Just the sort to break her heart and make her gun-shy for the rest of her life.

Mama Beth's blue eyes clouded. "Jason's a wonderful man, Matt. Gracie could do worse."

"Are you sure?" If she had the same opinion as Andy, it proved he was way off base. He cast her a questioning glance.

Her lips drew up tight. "That man has done so much for this community. I don't doubt his integrity at all."

Matt nodded. "I'm sure you're probably right."

"I know I'm right." She lifted her chin ever so slightly. "So what are your plans over the next few weeks?"

"Well, Andy asked if I'd help out with the equine therapy ministry." And he was still no closer to reaching a decision.

She sipped her tea and looked at him over the rim of her glass. "I think that's a perfect job for you."

Matt hoisted a shoulder. "Maybe for the short term."

"Short term based on how things go with Gracie?"

The woman had a sixth sense. "Yep."

Mama Beth stood and bustled to the farmhouse sink to rinse her plate. Matt joined her. He placed his dishes in the dishwasher, and then faced her. "Thanks for all your advice and the meal. As much as I'd like to stay, I'd better git."

She reached up and hugged his neck. "I'll be praying for you, Matty. You're facing a lot of tough decisions."

They walked together, arm in arm, toward the front. As he let himself out the squeaky screen door onto the wraparound porch of her two-story charmer, Mama Beth tugged on his arm. "Come back anytime. Our door is always open."

On the drive to the ranch, Matt's thoughts centered once more on Gracie. By the time he reached Andy and Trish's house, he already felt the need for more advice. He glanced toward the garage. Andy's car was gone. Maybe Trish had time. But first he needed to call Gracie. After parking, he powered on his smartphone and touched the number to her house.

"Soldano residence." The male voice let Matt know upfront his plan for time with Gracie wouldn't come without a price.

"Hi, Mr. Soldano. This is Matt Tyler. Could I speak with Gracie, please?"

"What business do you have with my daughter?"

Before he could answer, muffled talking sounded in the background. "Papa, please hand me the phone. I don't need you to screen my calls. Hello?" A breathless Gracie answered.

"Hi, Gracie, it's Matt."

"Hey. Thanks for the surprise party. It was very thoughtful."

He lowered his head and chuckled, joy trickling over his heart. "My pleasure." He paused to catch his breath. "Would you like to go for a cup of hot chocolate sometime this afternoon?"

"Um, sure, I mean, I guess so."

His confidence deflated like an unknotted balloon. She didn't have to sound so excited about it.

"What time?"

He glanced at his watch. Already 2:30? "How about I swing by and pick you up in an hour?" That should give him plenty of time to talk to Trish and get back to town.

"I'll see you then."

Matt pocketed the phone, climbed from the Pinto, and ambled down the front porch between Austin limestone and cedar posts to rap on the massive wooden door Trish had imported from Mexico.

It swung open. "It's about time you showed up!" His sister-in-law spit out the words in a frenzied rush as she enveloped Matt in a split-second hug. "I hoped you'd be here earlier."

"Didn't Andy tell you I was having lunch with Mama Beth?" He followed her into the house.

She gave her dark ponytail a shake. "No, he stayed in town after church to do some work at the office."

"Sorry."

Trish sent a sheepish grin. "Not your fault. With a newborn in the house, some things just don't get communicated." She shut the door behind them. "Sorry if I sounded frantic. Bethany finally fell asleep a few minutes ago, but then Brady woke up. Bo just called. I need to go pick him up at a friend's house just down the road. I won't be gone long."

Gone long? She was leaving him with a four-year old and a newborn? He scratched his cheek. "Um, go on, Trish. Gotcha covered." He tried his best to sound convinced. Him? Keep kids? Not exactly in his comfort zone.

Trish snatched her purse from the hallway table, blew him a kiss, and quietly shut the door behind her on the way out.

Brady peeked up at him from the living room doorway, his ruddy cheeks and disheveled red curls proof that he'd recently awakened from a nap. Both times Matt had been to visit, Brady was already in bed sound asleep. It was good to finally see him awake. "Hey, bud, how's it going?"

Brady didn't answer.

Matt knelt to his nephew's level. "It's me, Brady. Uncle Matt."

The four-year-old frowned. "Nuh uh. Unca Matt looks diffewent."

"I just have shorter hair now."

"And hair on your face."

Matt laughed and rose from his knees. "Yep, but it's still the same old Uncle Matt underneath." He made a move toward Brady to give him a hug.

His nephew let out an ear-piercing scream and bolted for the sofa. "Leave me alone!" He added another scream for emphasis.

"It's me, buddy. I promise."

A strange sound emanated from down the hallway, and Matt stopped in his tracks. "What's that?"

"The baby. You're in twouble now. You woke up the baby and my mama's gonna be vewy mad."

"Me? I didn't wake her up. You're the one screaming like a banshee." As Matt made his way down the hallway toward the sound, chubby arms encircled one of his legs.

"Leave my sistew alone." Brady hung from him like a koala on a eucalyptus.

"I'm just gonna check on her. Let go of Uncle Matt."

"No!"

"Okay. Have it your way." He somehow managed to make it to the baby bed with extra weight clamped to his leg.

His niece, her head wrapped with a piece of shiny pink elastic, squirmed red-faced in the bed below him. How could such a gosh-awful racket come from someone so small? He patted her chest. "Shh, little one. Mama will be back in a minute. I'd be crying too if they wrapped that thing around my head." Her cries intensified until she turned a scary shade of purple.

Man, how did he get himself in this mess? Did he dare pick her up? He considered his options, and then caved. Anything to stop the noise. He cradled the baby's head in one hand and her bottom in the other just as something sharp sank into his right hamstring. "Ow!" Matt flinched and looked over his shoulder.

Brady, still clinging to his leg in a bear hug, now had his teeth sunk into tender flesh. The baby stopped crying and peered up at him through tiny eyes.

Forgetting the pain radiating down the back of his leg, Matt smiled. "Hey, sweetheart, it's Uncle Matt." A foul odor reached his nostrils. His face wrinkled. "Man! What's that smell?"

A muffled answer came from his nephew.

"Can't understand you with your mouth full, Brady."

The teeth unclamped. "She has a poopy diapew."

Matt held the pink bundle further from him. "You sure?"

"If it smells like poop, it must be poop."

He raised his eyebrows and glanced at his nephew. "Pretty wise observation from a tyke like you."

"I'm not a twike. I'm a boy." He latched to Matt's skin with his teeth again.

"Ow! Stop it, will ya?"

Bethany wriggled and screamed again, her tiny fingers curled into flailing fists.

How was he supposed to handle this? He made his way to the changing table just as the front door slammed. Good. Trish was home. "Back here!"

A second later Trish and his oldest nephew, Bo—now almost as tall as his mother—appeared in the doorway. The incredulous looks on their faces were quickly replaced with smiles and laughter.

"Here, let me take her." Trish made it across the room in a few steps, reached for Bethany and pulled her close, before making a face and quickly depositing her on the changing pad. "Brady, let go of Uncle Matt."

His nephew obeyed and moved to stand beside his brother.

Matt scowled at him. "Hope you don't have rabies."

"I don't have wabies, I have lice."

Trish burst into laughter. "No you don't."

"That was last year at preschool, Brady." Bo tousled his brother's hair then looked up at Matt with eyes that looked just like Trish's. "Wanna go for a ride, Uncle Matt?"

Though his scalp started to itch, Matt resisted the urge to scratch. Instead he bumped fists with his oldest nephew. "Love to, Bo, but I can't right now. I need to talk to your mom for a second before I meet Gracie in town."

"Gracie?" Trish eyed him with a knowing look, and then scooped the baby up to her right shoulder and cast a quick glance at Bo. "Why don't you take Brady for a ride?"

"Mo-o-om . . . " One swift look from Trish was all it took to still his objection. "Yes, ma'am." He turned to his younger brother. "Come on, Brady, let's go get your boots on."

With a hoot and a holler, Brady took off down the hallway, a reluctant Bo right behind him.

"You've done a great job with Bo, Trish. He's turned into a fine young man."

She smiled. "Thanks to Andy. I couldn't have done it without him. Bo has come such a long way." Her voice choked a bit, but she quickly regained control. "Now what did you want to talk about?"

"What's your opinion of Jason Dent?"

Her eyes widened. "I sure wasn't expecting that question. He's a great guy. Why do you ask?"

"Just curious."

Trish moved the baby to cradle position in her arms. "Andy said you might stick around to help with the equine ministry."

"Another thing I wanted to discuss. I'm torn about what to do. I only wanna say yes to the job if I'm doing it for the right reasons. Right now, I feel like I'm only here to see if . . . "

"If things work out with Gracie?"

Matt nodded uncomfortably. Gracie needed him. She just didn't know it.

Trish sent a sympathetic look. "Look at it this way. It's a chance to use your degree and help so many hurting people. And it'll give you and Gracie the opportunity to really get to know each other. But we realize that what we want might not be what God wants for you."

Bingo. She'd just hit the proverbial nail on its proverbial head. This was God's call, not his, not theirs, not Mama Beth's. "I just want to follow His plan."

A smile landed on her face. "I totally understand. When I first met your brother, I struggled with that very thing. God will reveal His plan to you in His perfect time."

"It's like I have a bunch of puzzle pieces, but I can't quite figure out how they all fit together."

"And you're wondering how Gracie fits in?"

Gracie! His pulse zoomed to cheetah speed as he glanced at his watch. There was no way he'd make it by 3:30. "Sorry, Trish, but I've gotta run. I promised Gracie I'd meet her for hot chocolate." And her pet peeve was people who were late.

Trish laughed and followed him to the front door. "Maybe she won't kill you. We'll talk later. Hope your time together helps you figure out at least part of the puzzle."

From Trish's mouth to God's ears. Matt hurried to his car with a final wave to his sister-in-law. As he pulled onto the ranch road, he prayed Gracie had chosen to wait for him.

5

Grace stationed herself at the front window to wait for Matt. With every tick of the clock, the look in Papa's eyes morphed into a triumphant "I told you so!"

The comment he made when he learned Matt was picking her up for hot chocolate replayed in her brain. "He is not the kind of man you need, Graciela. Imagine what everyone will be saying and thinking about you for hanging out with his type."

She'd argued her case for Matt with every tool she had in her attorney arsenal—accused him of judging Matt by his appearance, reminded him who'd thrown the surprise party—but now she couldn't help wondering if Papa was right.

Grace checked the time again. 3:45. Matt was staying true to form, and without knowing it, giving validity to Papa's opinion.

One way or another, once he arrived, she had to find a way to let him know she was only interested in friendship. It would be hard, but it was the right thing to do.

Just as she began to lay down her things, a yucky green car pulled into the driveway. Matt?

Rather than embarrass him with Papa's rude treatment, she opted to let herself out the front door and met him as he climbed from the pea-green car. "Where'd you get this?"

Matt squinted against the sun. "I gather from the look on your face that you don't like it?"

"The color is . . . um, rather institutional, don't you think?" Grace moved to the passenger side, and Matt followed.

"At one time, someone probably paid a lot of money for this custom color."

"I sure hope they got a good price." She eyed the beat-up car and the brown rusty hole in the back fender. Maybe no one would notice her in the car. She scrunched up her nose. Yeah, right. It wasn't the kind of car people *didn't* notice.

"All right, little Miss Perfect, may I remind you that you drive around in a beat-up white farm truck from the sixties?"

She glared at him. "That's different. Everyone in Texas drives a pickup."

"Not me." He stood with arms crossed and his chin lifted.

Grace rolled her eyes and opened the door. "No, you drive the puke-mobile."

Matt laughed and held the door while she climbed in. "Hey, I like that name!" He closed the door and moved to the driver's side.

She glanced around the shabby interior. Figured he was the kind of guy who actually enjoyed the derogatory nickname.

A few minutes later they parked close to Granny's Kitchen. Grace couldn't help but smile as she crossed Main Street to her hometown café, where light shone from the plate glass windows. She could smell the mouth-watering food from outside.

The bell above the door announced their arrival, and the usual crew looked up and waved. As Grace scooted into the booth she and Matt always occupied, a feeling of contentment washed over her. How she loved these people!

Mama Beth and Big Bo sat at a table with Steve and Dani, or "Mr. and Mrs. Mayor" as the townspeople called them. A loud burst of laughter echoed from nearby. Grace knew it was Coot without even looking. She turned her head their direction. J.C., Coot, Otis, and the rest of the old geezers congregated at a booth, most likely discussing the latest gossip.

One of the Grannies zigzagged through the tables to where they sat. "Hey, kiddos, what can I gitcha?"

"Two hot chocolates, please, and bring them in cups with lids." As she bustled away, Matt made eye contact with Grace, his sandy brown eyes apologetic. "Sorry I was late, but I can explain.

I went to see Trish, but she had to go pick up Bo. The baby was asleep and she needed me to stay with Bra—"

"No excuses necessary."

"But they're not excuses. I really did have to babysit."

Grace pointed a finger at him. "Just stop already."

He raised both hands in surrender. She could practically see words slamming into each other behind his teeth, but he kept his lips clamped in a tight smile.

The Granny arrived with two large cups of steaming hot cocoa and placed them on the table, the chocolaty aroma teasing Grace's nose.

Across the table, Matt grew unusually quiet. He stared at nothing, his eyes glazed. Uh oh. This couldn't be good. Something was brewing in that head of his.

"Earth to Matt."

He blinked and sat up straighter. "Sorry. Guess I kinda zoned out there."

She gingerly sipped the cocoa, careful not to burn her mouth. Dare she ask? "What's on your mind?"

As expected, he jumped on the invitation. "Remember how much fun we had two summers ago?"

It *had* been a great summer. One of those rare times in her life when she'd actually had fun. "Yeah, probably because we were just two crazy kids having a good time. I sometimes find myself wishing I was a kid again."

Matt laughed. "You've never been a kid, Gracie Mae. Admit it. I'll bet you acted like an adult when you were twelve."

Memories of herself at twelve moved to the front of her brain. She leaned back and crossed her arms. "Because I had to."

"Sorry, Gracie, I shouldn't have said that."

She relaxed her posture and attempted a smile. "It's okay. It's the truth, like it or not. Some of us don't get to be kids."

Matt nodded and leaned forward, his eyes glimmering with boyish excitement. "Let's be kids while I'm here."

While he was here, implying that his time in Miller's Creek was short-term as she'd suspected.

"I know we can't be kids all the time, but let's try to do something fun at least once a week."

A surprising flicker of hope lit inside her at the thought of repeating the fun they'd had two years ago. "Sounds good."

He held out his right pinky finger. "Pinky swear."

A belly laugh burst from her lips. "You weren't joking about being kids again, were you?"

Matt just sat there with a lackadaisical expression and his pinky at the ready.

She gave a quick scan of the room to see if anyone was watching them, then joined her right pinky with his, her elbow at rest on the table. "I cannot believe I'm doing this."

"Repeat after me, killjoy."

A giggle escaped. "Okay."

"I, Gracie Mae Soldano."

No way would she use that name. "I, Grace Soldano."

"Do solemnly pinky swear."

Her brows wrinkled. "Can you do a pinky swear solemnly?"

"Quit over-analyzing everything, Gracie. That's not kid stuff. Do solemnly pinky swear."

"Okay, okay, do solemnly pinky swear."

"That I will do kid stuff with my BFF, Matt Tyler, at least once a week." He finished with a wink.

She groaned. "Honestly? BFF?"

He feigned a hurt expression. "I am your BFF, aren't I?"

"Good grief! All right. I'll do kid stuff with my BFF, Matt Tyler, at least once a week."

Matt released her pinky and sat back, victory plastered on his face. He looked ready to crow.

Grace gave her head a shake. "I'm convinced you have Peter Pan syndrome."

Matt laughed. "And you harp on me for diagnosing your quirks." He slurped hot chocolate and smacked his lips, then scooted out of the booth.

"Where are you going?"

"Time for a little of that fun we just promised to have." As they passed the counter, Matt paid the tab. "Thought we could walk to the park. Is that okay?"

"Nothing like a walk on a pretty day to clear your head." She followed him out the door and waited while he retrieved something from his car. He held up a Frisbee, and a smile landed on her face. "I haven't played Frisbee in forever."

They meandered through the heart of town toward the park. Matt gave her a sideways glance. "We haven't had a chance to really talk much this week. Anything eventful happen?"

"As a matter of fact, yes. Andy might put me on my first case with Jason." Was this a good segue point into the "let's-just-be-friends" speech?

Matt's face paled momentarily, but he sent a congratulatory smile. "Way to go, Gracie Mae."

Why did he feel the need to call her that? "Have I ever mentioned how much I hate that name?"

His eyes held a teasing gleam as they crossed the street to Creekside Park, the gurgle from the creek a siren's song, beckoning them to play. "Which one? Grace or Gracie Mae?"

"Well, since you asked, both."

He looked somewhat taken aback. "I can understand the one, but what's not to love about Grace? It's a beautiful name." He motioned her to one end of an open area in the park and tossed the Frisbee.

She caught it and returned it. "And impossible to live up to. I have a hard time just wrapping my brain around the concept, much less putting it into practice."

Matt chased the disc. "Difficult maybe, but not impossible. And don't sell yourself short. I'll admit grace is pretty hard for us to comprehend. Just about the time I think I have a grasp on it, God shows me a little bit more. It's like a bottomless supply."

The same thought she'd had earlier in the week. She marveled. Yet another drop of grace.

"I used to think mercy and grace were the same, but I don't feel that way anymore. The difference between them is actually astronomical."

She cocked her head to one side. "How?"

"Grace is getting something wonderful, something you could never earn or get for yourself, something you don't deserve. Mercy is *not* getting what you truly deserve." Matt sailed the Frisbee high.

"Still sounds the same to me." Grace waited for the hovering Frisbee to drop.

"Not really. Say you're driving home and get stopped for speeding."

Grace caught the Frisbee, held it above her head like a halo, and intentionally donned an angelic look. "I don't speed."

"I know you don't, Miss Perfect, but pretend. If the cop gave you a ticket, that would be justice. You know, that concept you wear like a badge of honor."

If he meant for his words to wiggle under her skin, it had worked. She aimed the Frisbee at his head.

"But if the cop said that since this was the first time he'd caught you he wouldn't give you a ticket, that would be mercy. You didn't get what you deserved."

She sent a "no-duh" look and launched the Frisbee. "You think? I get justice and mercy. It's grace that trips me up."

He deflected the plastic disc with his hand. "Trying to take my head off?" Matt traipsed after the Frisbee. "Okay, let's say a friend pulls up behind you—a friend you've wronged, by the way—and tells the officer he knows you deserve a ticket, but to give it to him instead. The police officer tells your friend that once the ticket is paid you'll receive the best treasure ever." His voice lowered. "Then the policeman mentions that the penalty for speeding is death."

Grace let Matt's shocking words sink in. Yes, that was grace. So beyond what anyone deserved, but Christ had demonstrated it willingly, not just for her, but the entire world. She released a sigh and stepped over to where he stood. "I don't know if I could ever show that kind of grace."

"Maybe not on the same scale, but I think God uses us as tools of grace when we least expect it. And that," he paused, his eyes soft, "sets us free from the trap of perfectionism." He studied her a long minute until she got the distinct impression he wanted to say more. He glanced down at his watch. "I have some things I need to do. You ready to go?"

She puzzled over his odd comment as they trekked back to the car in silence. Was her desire to be as perfect as possible an asset or a liability?

As they drove toward the house a sudden realization pounded its way into her brain. Matt might make her furious at times, but with no one else did she share such deep and meaningful conversations.

He turned his gaze her way, one wrist steering the car. "Back to this case you're working on. Any details?"

"The charge is vehicular homicide."

Compassion softened his eyes. "Must be hard for you because of your mom."

Grace nodded. "I knew when I became a lawyer I'd face stuff like this. I guess I just didn't expect it to be my first case."

"Analyzing it to death as usual?"

She scowled at him.

"Just joking." He tilted his head to one side, his brown eyes narrowing perceptively. "Is there something else about this case that bothers you?"

How did he do that? How could he discern her struggle when she hadn't voiced one word to give him evidence? "One of these days you're gonna have to tell me how you do that."

"Do what?"

"Read me like a book."

He turned to peer out the driver's side window as they passed Andy's office. When he looked back, a mischievous grin etched his features. "It's not that hard, Gracie Mae. I've always liked books with lots of pictures."

"Ha. Very funny." Grace shot a mock glare. "Are you referencing my age or my mental capacity?"

The wicked gleam in his eyes receded. "Neither. I just know you. Something's eating you alive, and I think I know what it is." The words were spoken gently. "It's something I've really wanted to talk to you about anyway."

She inhaled sharply. "Oh, no, here it comes. You're about to launch into one of your diatribes about my shortcomings and then try to fix me, aren't you?"

"You don't have any trouble voicing your opinion of me, so chill. I'm your friend and you need to know."

It was all she could do to keep from rolling her eyes like some bored teenager, but she somehow managed to keep her gaze trained on him. "Okay, but you'd better play nice."

"It's just that your disease to please is getting worse."

A hard jolt of justification blasted through her body. "I don't happen to see anything wrong with making a good impression."

"Don't be so defensive. To me it's a serious problem, one that could potentially affect your relationship with God. Let me ask you this—how do you see God?"

Easy question. "Father."

He nodded as if her answer was just what he expected and turned on his blinker. "And what do you think of when you think of the word 'father'?"

Rules. Obedience. Sternness. The thoughts shocked her. "I've heard God described as a loving Father, and I see Him presented that way in the Bible, but sometimes I can't help but see Him as a Father who'll strike me down if I disobey."

Matt took hold of one of her hands and steered with the other. "He wants us to obey because it's best for us. But He's not like some giant eye-in-the-sky, waiting for us to mess up so He can zap us."

"Don't you think He punishes us when we mess up?"

He shook his head. "No. Christ took the punishment for us. God disciplines us so we won't make the same mistake. It may feel like punishment, but it teaches us a better way."

"And what does this have to do with my supposed people-pleasing problem?"

"Everything. You don't have to work so hard trying to please everyone, including God." He pulled into her driveway and put the car in park.

"Wait a minute." She gave her head a fierce shake. "Didn't you just tell me God wants us to obey?"

"Yeah, but you can't do it to gain His favor. Don't you see?" His voice held intensity. "If you're working to gain His favor, you're annulling His free gift of grace. There's nothing we can do to make Him love us more than He already does. Besides, if we could do it ourselves, what need would we have for God?"

"You still haven't explained how all this relates to others."

His face sobered. "Living your life to gain the approval of others is just an extension of how you live your life for God. I've been where you are. Tried keeping rules and working to please everyone, and it didn't work. All I had was worthless religion." His eyes held a moist sheen. "That's when I truly gave my life over to Christ, and He changed me. I don't care what people think of me, and I'm not driven to impress. When God looks at me, He sees Jesus living in me, and that's enough. I've put rule-keeping and people-pleasing behind me, and I don't plan on going back to it. Ever."

She sat in shocked silence. Yes, she'd tried to impress others to get them to like her. But in her attempt to please God, had she inadvertently tried to make herself acceptable by becoming religious? Surely not! Grace released a burst of pent-up air and shook her head. "That's not who I am!" She wanted to say more—felt the need to explain—but words just wouldn't come.

"Tell me you're not over-analyzing your participation in this case because you're trying to impress everyone, including the other side. You're afraid people won't like you, so you end up making decisions based on which option gives you the least collateral damage."

Her jaw flapped open and she snatched her hand away. "What a horrid thing to say."

"Gracie, I'm not trying to hurt your feelings. I'm trying to help."

She brushed aside a strand of hair that fell in front of her face. "Well, your help sure feels like hurt." What right did he have to be critical when she tried so hard—gave one hundred and twenty percent—in everything she did?

God, if what Matt says is true, You're going to have to prove it to me. I serve You because I love You. Yes, I'm afraid of messing things up—with You and others—but it's only because I want to live my life to make You proud of me.

A bitter hush descended between them. Finally Matt broke the silence. "This is so not turning out like I wanted. I keep sticking my foot in my mouth and upsetting you in the process. I really just wanted to get together to have a good time. Can we start over?"

She nodded, too afraid of crying to attempt speech.

He reclaimed her hand and turned an apologetic gaze her way. Suddenly, without warning, she found herself being drawn into his soft brown eyes. No! She pulled back, reached for her purse, and pretended to dig for something, her heart pounding in her throat. There was no way she was gonna fall for him again. He was a wonderful friend and that was it. So what if he often understood her better than she understood herself?

"Gracie." Matt's voice was low and soft. "Quit pretending to dig for something that's not there, and look at me."

She inhaled a long breath and raised her gaze, immediately wishing she hadn't. What she saw reflected in his eyes shook her to the core, a look she didn't care to identify.

"I wasn't planning on bringing this up today, but since the situation presented itself, I have to." He swallowed hard. "I kept my distance these past two years at your request so you could pursue your law career, but now I'd like us to see if there could be something more between us."

Grace suddenly felt physically ill. She lowered her head and rubbed her hands together. How could she get out of this without hurting his feelings? "Matt, I'm just not ready." She glanced up at him, resolute, but fearful of what she might see.

Though his eyes held sadness, he took her words well. "Okay. I'm prepared to wait as long as necessary."

"I can't promise you I'll ever be ready."

"Any reason why?"

Where did she start? His irresponsibility? His sponging off Andy's goodness? Papa's opinion? "I'm not convinced you're what I'm looking for." There. She'd said it.

He pondered her words for several minutes then turned his gaze back toward her, his jaw set in concrete. "Yeah, well. I guess I'll just have to find a way to convince you that I'm exactly what you need . . . regardless of what you're looking for."

What was she supposed to say after that? Here she was, trained in persuasive speech, and she had no rebuttal? Grace gathered her things, intentionally keeping her eyes down. "Guess I'll see you later." She crawled from the car and traipsed to the front door, refusing to look back as she let herself in the house. Her thoughts ran in circles as she closed the door to her room behind her. Matt was right about trying to please everyone. She'd always wanted to keep everyone happy. Well, no more.

She scribbled a quick note to Papa and laid it on the counter, then moved outside, digging for her keys. By the time she reached the pickup, a plan had formulated. Urged forward by a myriad of emotions—confusion, determination, and more than a little anger at Matt's comments—she put the truck in gear and headed out of Miller's Creek toward the mall in Morganville for a little retail therapy.

6

Grace arrived at work the next morning feeling like a new person. Attired in an electric blue suit and matching heels, with her newly-colored hair pulled back away from her face, she waltzed into the office with newfound confidence. Yes, she'd spent way too much, but the department store had extended her a line of credit, thanks to her job as an attorney.

Andy, Ben, and Jason stood in the hallway, most likely discussing the Simmons case.

"Good morning." Grace passed them with a smile.

"Gracie?" Andy's incredulous voice sounded from behind her.

She faced him. "Yes?"

"You look so . . . so . . . different."

"Thanks." Grace took in their facial expressions, eyes rounded and jaws hinged open. Her plan was working. No longer would they think of her as little Gracie, the meek and mild-mannered child they'd known all these years. They had no choice now but to take her seriously as an attorney. And if her mini-makeover had worked for them, it would also work for Elena Delgado and the rest of the legal community. It was time everyone knew that Grace Soldano, J.D. was in town.

A few minutes later she sat with all three men in the conference room. She jotted notes as Andy spoke, and waited until he finished before she asked the question at the front of her mind. "What about the Simmons trial?"

Andy lowered his head for a brief minute. "I've decided to let Jason handle it with me."

Her heart ground to a stop as her mouth hinged open. "I'll do a good job."

A sigh whooshed from her boss's mouth. "I know, but with Sandra out, I need you in other places right now."

Jason met Andy's gaze. "I think Grace would make a great addition to the team."

Her heartbeat quickened, but one glance at Andy gave her the answer.

His mouth had morphed into a thin line. "I'm certain of it, but my decision stands." He rose to his feet and made preparations to leave the room. "We're through."

Grace jumped to her feet. "Andy, could I speak with you privately?"

He pivoted. "Sure." His sea-green eyes held uncertainty. "If this is about the Simmons' case—"

"No." Yes, she was more than a little disappointed, but the move was his call, no matter how much she disliked it. "I just wanted to ask you not to call me Gracie. I think it's more professional if I go by Grace."

"Will do. Just used to you being Gracie."

"Thanks." She stepped around him, cradling her legal pad next to her chest. As she rounded the corner, she ran smack dab into Jason, who stood right outside the door, his lanky frame leaned against the wall.

"Oh!" Grace over-compensated for his unexpected presence, and started to fall.

Strong arms reached out and yanked her upward, and she found herself pulled close to Jason's chest, his expensive cologne encircling her head. "Th-thank you. I'm sorry I ran you over."

"No problem. I was waiting to speak with Andy." His British accent was a velvet glove.

Andy walked past. "Why don't we meet in my office, Jason?"

Jason gripped her arms and gazed into her eyes. "Sure." He released her with a smile and followed Andy down the hall.

Her heart pounding uncontrollably, Grace made her way back to her office, still puzzling over what had just transpired. To her surprise, Matt stood at the receptionist window.

His eyebrows puckered as she entered her office. "You okay?"

Forcing a smile she didn't feel, Grace nodded weakly. "Just fine. Why do you ask?"

The color of his eyes changed to creek mud as his face hardened. "Let's start over, and tell me the truth this time."

Immediate anger erupted in her chest, but before she could let him have it, Jason stepped from Andy's office and poked his head in the door. "Sorry, I didn't know you had company." The handsome attorney stepped closer, until he towered over her. "Would you like to have lunch with me today?"

Grace's heart skipped a beat, and she swallowed, hoping she could speak intelligibly. She opted not to sneak a peek at Matt, since she was pretty sure this would make him none too happy. While she didn't want to intentionally hurt his feelings, it wasn't like she hadn't tried to tell him yesterday just how she felt. She sent Jason a smile. "I'd love to."

Maybe now Matt would understand she meant every word.

Matt slid off the white mare's back the following Thursday morning and began to unsaddle the animal. The ride had done nothing to relieve his melancholy. As though she understood, the mare turned her head and nickered.

Unpleasant memories from last Sunday's date with Gracie filled his head. The recent turn of events was yet another rejection in a long string, the first of which left him wondering what was so wrong with him that his own mother didn't want him.

Matt groaned and raked both hands across his head, a battle raging within. He knew from past experience to keep his chin up, but his heart refused to cooperate. How could he prove to Gracie he was exactly what she needed?

God, help me through this. Help me respond to Your will without hurting myself any further.

Even as the words whispered in his heart, he sensed the truth that following God sometimes involved personal suffering and sacrifice. Hadn't the life of Christ proved that very point? While being in God's perfect will was the safest place to be, it could also be the most dangerous. Another mystery of God's kingdom.

Matt carried the saddle to the tack room and hoisted it onto the rack. Something had to give before he went bonkers. He'd hoped the ride would whisk every thought of Gracie away, but no such luck.

A heavy weight pressed against his heart, and he sucked in a deep breath, suddenly very much aware of spiritual danger. Gracie's perfectionist nature could easily lead to living life on her own terms and in her own goodness rather than letting God's grace do its perfect work. Is that why she'd exchanged her typical wardrobe for a sophisticated one and dyed her once gorgeous black hair the color of copper? How he wished he could get the old Gracie back, not this new and improved version that was anything but improved in his book.

Matt glanced at his watch. He pictured her, humming happily as she went about her tasks, dreaming about Jason and his cat-who-ate-the-canary grin. His stomach churned in response, sending acid to his throat and mouth.

Her face had been a shade lighter and her eyes a shade darker when she'd returned to her desk after her meeting with the other attorneys on Monday, yet she'd insisted she was okay. When would she learn that he knew her so well he could immediately tell when anything was wrong?

Frustration mounted like steam in a pressure cooker. He turned toward the barn wall and looked for something to punch. As he moved toward the weathered wood, his fist raised, he came to his senses. He lowered his hand and breathed deeply, putting into practice one of the techniques he'd teach the kids he'd be working with later—if he decided to stay. If nothing else, this afternoon's session should give him a feel for the work.

The horse whinnied and stamped her foot impatiently. Matt moved back to brush her down, determined to put the situation out of his mind. The best way to do that was bury himself in the mound of unfinished paper work and mail that had built up since his niece was born.

A little while later, he sat behind the massive wooden desk in the equine ministry office and sorted through the stack of papers. He'd only been at work fifteen minutes when his cellphone played a tune at his side.

"This is Matt."

"Yo, Matt. Derek. How's it going?"

A smile sprang to his face. "Hey, man! Good to hear from you. You on the road?"

"Just got back. Have a couple of weeks of break before we hit it again. That's why I called."

The hair on the back of Matt's neck snapped to attention.

"Jack's taking at least a month off to take care of some business, and I wondered if you might be interested in filling in."

Matt stared at the stacks. Push papers or play with a band? The pull of that lifestyle beckoned, but what about Andy and Trish? What about Gracie? "Interested, yeah, but not sure about able. I'm helping my brother and sister-in-law with their equine therapy ministry." He jotted a quick note on his to-do list to come up with a better name.

"Yeah, but does it have the potential to be a full-time gig?"

"Full-time? Thought you a month."

"I said at least a month." Derek cleared his throat. "Can't really go into too much detail, but Jack's starting to flake out on us. We've told him to fix it or else."

"Man, wish I could say yes right now, but I have to pray about this and talk to Andy. I can't back out of my commitments unless there's someone to cover me." In a few weeks the horse rides would stop for the holidays, but would that be to late?

"That's one reason the band wants you. You'll hang in there no matter what. Think you could call me back later today?"

"You know it."

Matt said his good-byes and pocketed the phone in a quandary. He couldn't just run off and leave Andy and Trish hanging. And there was Gracie to think about. A smirk slid onto his face. Not like it really mattered. She'd made it perfectly clear how she felt. An exasperated breath huffed out of him. How was it possible that he was already thinking about her again? Was this was God showing the way?

He set back to work on the papers, his mind half on the work in front of him and half on how to broach the subject of the band with Andy. *Lord, You know Andy and Trish need me here, but You may have someone else for this work. I need to make a decision, but I want Your will to be done.*

The weight in his chest lightened. God would take care of it. As Matt scribbled a note to talk to Andy later that day, his phone sounded again, this time with the Perry Mason theme. Andy and his impeccable timing. "Hey, bro. I was just thinking about you."

Andy chuckled. "What a nice sentiment. Warms my heart to know you think about me. Now tell me why."

Matt frantically searched for words, but none came. He should've thought through this a little more carefully before bringing it up. "I'd rather talk about it in person."

"Okay. Wanna do lunch?"

An hour later, Matt hunkered down across the table from his brother at Soldano's, a plate of chicken fajita nachos in front of him. He sniffed the steam rising off the plate, then stuffed a nacho in his mouth, pausing to savor the melted asiago cheese, grilled chicken, and freshly-made guacamole.

Matt took in the lines of fatigue around his brother's eyes. "You okay?"

"Yeah, it's just been one of those weeks. Barely had time to scarf down an apple for breakfast, and about the only time I get to see my wife is Bethany's two a.m. feeding. Don't know what we'd do without you running the ministry right now."

The words stabbed at his heart. Not a good time to leave Miller's Creek.

"What about you? You okay?" Andy gazed intently at him.

"Not really. I told Gracie I wanted to see if there could be something more between us."

"And?"

Matt suppressed a shudder. "Not good. Then on top of that you have to assign her to work on a case with her version of Mr. Perfect."

Andy's forehead wrinkled. "She's not on a case right now. That fell through." He gave no further explanation. His brother swallowed a first swig of soda pop and hiccupped. "What did you want to talk with me about? I'm guessing it's not Gracie."

"Brilliant deduction, counselor."

"Spill it."

Matt laid down his fork, wiped his mouth, and looked his brother in the eyes. Best just to tell him the truth, hard as it might be to hear. "I gotta call from a friend today, and he asked me to go on the road with him and the band."

Andy raised his eyebrows. "And what have you decided?"

"Don't know. I kind of hoped you'd be able to help me make the decision."

His brother shook his head, his lips pressed together. "Nope. It's your call."

Matt rubbed the area between his eyes. "I wanna help you and Trish, but I also know God has given me musical abilities."

"Agreed, but He's also given you the gift of helping hurt people."

And the desire to do it, but how did he decide between the two? And why did he have to choose one cherished part of himself over another?

"What about Gracie?"

His brother's question slammed into his gut. The question of the century—what about Gracie? Thoughts swamped his brain, and twisted into a big knotted mess.

"I thought you wanted to—"

"Yeah, well, what I want and what actually happens are two different things." Matt stared out the window and across the parking lot, focused on dry brown leaves clinging hopelessly to a clump of oak trees. "I can't compete with her image of perfection. It's impossible."

"Give her time. And give the situation time. She'll come around."

Hope took wing inside. "You really think so?"

"Believe it with all my heart. She needs you, and something tells me she's gonna need you even more in the immediate future." Andy lowered his head and scratched his chin. "As for me and Trish and the kids, we'd love to have you here, but I'm sure we could find someone else to at least help with the paperwork and day-to-day running of the place. It might take us longer to find a counselor, but it's not impossible."

Matt shot Andy an appreciative grin. At least now he had his blessing. "I'm gonna pray about it this afternoon and then get in touch with Derek. Want me to call you later and let you know?"

"Please." Andy, his face grim, plucked the napkin from his lap and deposited it on the half-empty plate. "Sorry to cut this short, but there's a gentleman here I need to see before he leaves. Will you excuse me a sec?"

"No prob. I'll wait outside." After paying the ticket, Matt opted to sit on the covered patio, which in better weather would be packed. From his perch, he could watch his surroundings and see when Andy exited the building.

A sleek black Maserati pulled into the parking lot, and Matt released a low whistle. Someone had laid out major bucks for that sweet ride. But who in Miller's Creek could afford it?

The car swept into a parking space and the driver's door opened.

Matt's mouth immediately went dry.

Jason Dent unfolded his lanky frame. The passenger door also opened. No, it couldn't be. Matt blinked hard to make sure he was seeing correctly. It *was* Gracie. Jason offered his elbow and smiled down into her beaming upturned face. "Are you sure you don't mind finding us a table? Sorry, but I need to make a quick call." Jason's British accent was unmistakable.

"I don't mind at all." Gracie's voice lilted like that of a songbird, and what Matt saw inscribed on her face was like a kick in the gut. She was smitten.

The tall attorney moved down the side of the building toward him, and Matt momentarily panicked, looking for a place to hide. What would he say if Jason entered the shade of the patio? Thankfully, the handsome Brit stopped just shy of the area and leaned against the wall to make his call.

"It's me." The man grew quiet, listening intently to whoever was on the other end. After a long minute, he spoke. "Play it cool. Getting upset will only cause foolish mistakes." Jason grew silent again, and brought a hand up to rub his jaw. "The new girl is no threat."

Matt's heart pounded faster. New girl? Was he referring to Gracie?

"I tell you, she's putty in my hands. No need to worry."

Sweat broke out along the nape of Matt's neck. He'd been right about the guy all along. He'd use whoever he needed to accomplish his purposes.

Jason clicked the phone shut and moved inside the restaurant.

Matt's mind raced. Should he say something to Andy? He thought back through what he'd just overheard. Nothing concrete, and Andy was already overburdened. *Lord, help me know what to do.* No verbal response came, but Matt was suddenly overcome with the most evident response of God he'd ever felt.

A combination of relief and disappointment melded inside. They all needed him—the band, Andy and Trish, but especially Gracie. His brother had seemed more than a little troubled when he'd mentioned her over lunch, like he wanted to say more, but couldn't. Did he know something—something he couldn't reveal for whatever reason?

Matt leaned forward and rested his elbows on his knees. Without a shadow of doubt, God wanted him here, at least for now, to take care of her. And no matter how appealing it was to go on the road, he'd never sacrifice God's plan for his own, especially when Gracie's welfare hung in the balance.

7

Grace flung her purse across the bedroom Friday afternoon after work. The bag landed on the bed, but scattered the contents on the tile floor, popping like firecrackers as they landed. Though part of her frustration had to do with not being allowed to help on the Simmons case, a big part of it also had to do with Matt. Andy let it slip yesterday that his brother had an invitation to go on tour with a band. But why was she so put out by the news?

She ambled to the dresser, removed the new silver hoop earrings, and deposited them in the jewelry box which once belonged to Mama. At first she'd convinced herself that she was upset because of what it would do to Andy and Trish, but if it bothered her this much, was it possible her feelings for Matt ran deeper than she realized? She removed the pins that held her hair in place, allowing the strands to fall to her shoulders, then combed them out with her fingers. This all had to be figured out, and sooner rather than later.

How she'd missed Matt! She hadn't seen him since Monday, and thanks to her stubborn pride, that hadn't ended so well. Grace raised the mini-blinds to look out over the weedy garden spot she'd started years ago with Mama. A sparse handful of marigolds still bloomed, but would die away at the first frost. Multiple questions nibbled at her brain. Had Matt decided to take the gig? Had he already left town? Was he upset with her for going to lunch with Jason?

A frown creased her forehead as her mind wandered to the past week of working around Jason. He'd been very kind and considerate and even treated her to lunch a couple of times. His legal skills were top notch, his dress and manners impeccable. Though flattered by his constant attention, there was something about him she couldn't quite put her finger on, beneath the surface, like a shadow in the muddy creek after a big rain.

Grace flopped down on the bed beside her purse. "Ow!" She stood, plucked a tube of lipstick from the bed, and tossed it in her gaping purse just as the phone rang. She hurdled her briefcase and raced down the hall, hoping it was Matt. "Hello?"

"Grace? This is Elena Delgado."

Elena? She covered the mouthpiece with one palm, her heart thumping in her ears. She swallowed hard to find her voice and moved her hand away from the phone. "Yes?"

"I was calling to see if this would be a good time for a tour of the District Attorney's office."

Her mouth went dry, but she somehow managed to plow ahead. "Sounds great."

"Wonderful. I'm actually in Miller's Creek right now. Why don't I swing by and pick you up?"

Elena come here? "Well, I—"

"I won't take no for an answer. The phone book says you live at 1351 Farm to Market Road 8204. Is that right?"

"Um, yeah, but –"

"I'll be there in a few." The line went dead.

Grace dropped the phone to the receiver and raced back to her room. After a quick over-haul, she ran to the kitchen and living area to make sure that part of the house was presentable.

Her heart sank as she scanned the room. What would Elena think? Mismatched furniture, worn and sagging, and kitchen cabinets that had long since seen better days. The bright-colored Mexican tile Mama and Papa brought with them from Mexico had been a pleasant reminder of her heritage at one time. Now it seemed to scream bad taste.

She gave her head a shake. There was nothing she could do here. Instead, she hurried to check her appearance, quickly combing her unruly hair into place. Maybe she could meet Elena outside. The doorbell rang. With her pulse racing like mad, Grace forced herself to calmly open the front door. "Hi, Elena."

Before Grace could object, the other woman pushed her way inside, glancing around the room. "Love what you've done with your hair. So this is your house?"

"It actually belongs to my father. I'm living with him while I pay off my school loans."

To her surprise, Elena smiled. "Smart idea. Are you ready to head to Morganville?"

"Sure." She followed the other attorney outside to where her beautiful red sports car was parked. Grace's eyes widened. "This is yours?"

"Yes. Isn't it a beauty?"

Classy black leather decked the interior, which still boasted that new car smell. Grace forced her mouth closed and clicked her seatbelt into place, all the while battling jealousy. Must be nice to have money to burn.

Elena turned her head to peer over her shoulder as she backed out. "If you don't mind, we'll drop by my house first. I'd like to introduce you to my family."

"Um, sure. You live nearby?"

"Between here and Morganville."

Grace checked Elena's left hand. No wedding band.

A few minutes later they barreled down the highway toward Morganville. In her designer sunglasses and chic clothing, Elena could've passed for a movie star or super model. Grace twisted sideways in the seat to face her. "Thanks for the invitation to tour the DA's office. I really appreciate it."

"My pleasure." Her smile revealed perfect white teeth, which glistened in contrast to her olive skin. "By the way, I heard there might be an opening. I immediately thought of you."

Her breath suspended in her chest. "Really?" Grace knew she must sound like an over-eager schoolgirl, but excitement pranced around like a wild horse within.

Elena laughed, a musical sound like that of tiny wind chimes. "Yes, really. Sounds like you might be interested."

Grace chewed her lower lip. Until she had given this more thought, she shouldn't say one way or the other. "Maybe."

"Didn't you mention you'd always wanted to be a prosecutor?" Elena's smile had disappeared, replaced with a colder façade—the same one that earned her the reputation of being a tough opponent in court. "What are your objections?"

"I wouldn't call them objections exactly."

"Then what would you call them?"

Grace thought through the question. "I guess misgivings would be a better way to describe it."

"Why?"

The woman's machine gun questioning was getting old. Why the inquisition. "For one thing, I owe Andy a huge debt of gratitude for all he's done for me."

"Such as?" Elena's voice took on a curious undertone.

"I probably wouldn't be here if it weren't for him. He's the one who made it possible for me to go to college."

Her arched eyebrows rose above her sunglasses. "You mean he paid for your schooling?"

"Part of it."

Elena grew quiet for the rest of the drive, obviously deep in contemplation based on the squint lines barely visible behind her dark glasses. A few minutes later they pulled off the highway and on to a tree-lined drive. Once they cleared the trees a stately home appeared.

"Beautiful." Grace breathed the word in a hushed whisper. A combination of river rock and cedar made up the exterior of the multi-gabled house, and lush evergreens flanked the large windows. This place was the home of her dreams. A monster roared to life inside her. Would she ever be able to afford a home like this?

Elena pulled to a quick stop and hopped from the car.

Grace followed. Once inside, she glanced around the home's interior. Exquisite furnishings and décor filled every room. "Did you decorate this yourself?"

"Wish I had the time. No, I paid someone."

"It's very nice."

"Thanks." Elena walked toward the back of the home, swiveling her head from side to side as she peered in room after room. "Mom?"

"I'm here." An older and rounder version of Elena appeared from a nearby doorway, her face lit with a joyous light. She held out a hand to Grace, her smile wide and generous. "This must be the young woman you were telling me about. Welcome to our home. I'm Consuela."

Now the monster clawed its way to her heart, ripping it into ribbons. As if all this grandeur weren't enough, Elena Delgado had the privilege of living with her mother. She came to her senses and took the woman's hand. "Nice to meet you, Consuela. I'm Grace."

"What a lovely name."

Elena craned her neck to look past her mother. "Where's Jessie?"

The smile on Consuela's face disappeared, aging her instantly, like she shouldered a heavy burden. "She's back here."

Grace followed the two into a darkened room. In the far corner sat a small wheelchair facing the window, and a tiny, dark head appeared above the back.

Elena moved in front of the chair, and her face softened as she knelt. "How's my girl?" No answer. She motioned for Grace to join her. "This is my daughter Jessie."

Grace wasn't prepared for what she saw as she stepped up next to Elena. The girl's body was twisted and turned in awkward positions, and her head lolled to one side. Overwhelming compassion, not just for Jessie, but for her caretakers, welled in Grace's heart. She smiled and leaned forward to caress her arm. Hello there, Miss Jessie."

The girl couldn't speak, but managed a half smile.

Elena chuckled. "She likes you already." She stood and looked at her mother. "After I show Grace the house, we're having dinner and a tour of the DA's office. I'm not sure what time I'll be back."

The older woman looked taken aback. "But we've barely s—" She stopped in mid-word, apparently silenced by something she read in Elena's eyes. "We'll see you later."

Grace stepped into the path of Elena's stare. "If you need this time with your family, I can do this some other day."

Elena waved a hand. "Nonsense. It's not like we'll be gone all night. Follow me. I want to show you something."

A few seconds later, Grace stood in the center of a gigantic room Elena called a walk-in closet. She pivoted in a slow circle to take it all in. Not only was it bigger than the bedroom she had at Papa's house, but was packed from top to bottom with clothes and shoes. The mahogany cabinetry, lit with spotlights, gave the room the appearance of an exclusive boutique.

Elena fluttered an arm around the space. "Isn't this every girl's dream closet? If you'd told me ten years ago I'd live in this kind of house, I would've laughed in your face."

Was she fishing for compliments or showing off? "The whole house is beautiful."

A broad smile flitted to Elena's face. "I hope this doesn't come across as forward and rude, but I have some clothes I no longer wear. Would you be offended if I offered them to you?"

Heat crawled to her cheeks and the tips of her ears.

"Please don't be embarrassed." Elena laid a hand on Grace's shoulder. "I remember my first days as an attorney, school loans to repay, and a woefully poor-paying position."

Swift suspicion ripped through Grace's veins, but she managed to answer in a normal voice. "I'm not offended. I could use some new clothes." To add to the pile she charged to her credit card last weekend? Where would she put them?

The other woman smiled brightly. "Great, and while we're at it, I'd love to take you under my wing. What do you say? Wanna be my protégé?"

A nervous giggle escaped before Grace could control it. Never had she felt so included, but she couldn't help but wonder about the unspoken price tag, not of dollars, but return favors. "I'm honored you would offer."

"I have some things that will make you look like you dropped a thousand bucks. Let's start with this section." She pointed toward one corner of the closet.

Grace gasped. "But they look brand new."

"Most of them are. I bought them and never wore them because I lost weight. I never got around to returning them, but I think they might be your size."

Grace pushed aside her reservations and concentrated on the task at hand. The next several minutes were spent trying on various outfits, and her stack of clothes grew larger and larger. "Thank you so much for all this." Grace pirouetted in front of a three-way mirror in Elena's bedroom, modeling a slinky pant suit perfect for New Year's Eve. "It really is too much. I'd be glad to pay you a little out of each check . . . "

"Nonsense."

Grace peered at her through narrowed eyes. How could she ask the question burning within without offending the woman? "If you don't mind me asking, why are you doing all this?"

An uneasy laugh flowed from Elena's immaculately made-up mouth. "Let's just say you remind me a lot of myself at your age. But enough of this. Let's get packed up and head to town."

Only a thin line of daylight was left on the western horizon as they left the house. Locked within the cramped confines of Elena's sports car, claustrophobia descended on Grace. She searched for topics to break the uncomfortable silence. It would be all too easy to sit and ponder questions about Elena to pass the time, but she needed to get to know this woman—for multiple reasons. "Thanks again for the clothes. I don't know how I'll ever be able to repay your kindness."

Elena leaned her head back and laughed. "I'm sure I can think of something."

Grace shifted uncomfortably. Exactly what she feared. When they finally arrived at the DA's office in downtown Morganville, she almost cheered, so ready was she to be out of the clutches of the black leather interior. Questions spun in her head like a carnival ride. How could Elena afford such a lavish lifestyle, and why was she being so generous?

Once inside, Grace relaxed somewhat, though the old building seemed to take on a life of its own after hours. Elena's now chatty conversation contrasted greatly to the uncomfortable silence she'd experienced on the drive in.

The petite attorney showed Grace around the office complex and ended in her personal office. "And here's where I work."

Tastefully decorated with a cherry desk and credenza, matching barrister bookcases filled with leather-bound law books lined the back wall. The off-white plush pile carpet whispered as they walked across it.

"Very nice." Grace spoke the words in a muted voice, no longer surprised by beautiful spaces. Her previous jealousy had waned, replaced by hopelessness.

Elena raised one brow. "I could see you working in a space like this."

Grace shook her head. "I don't know . . . "

"You'd be much more satisfied working for the DA than in defense. And there are ways to supplement your salary to get those loans paid off sooner so you could move out on your own."

Goosebumps pricked the flesh of her forearms. "Like what?"

Elena easily sidestepped the question. "I hope you don't mind, but I did some checking up on you. Graduating at the top of your law class is a major achievement. I'm glad I'm going to be your mentor."

"Thanks." Overcome by the need to escape Elena's persuasive and cloying charm, if only long enough to maintain her ability to think straight, Grace glanced around. "Is there a restroom close by?"

"Yes." She pointed out her door, across the reception area to a small door. "Right over there."

"I'll be back in a second." She crossed the reception area, bathed in the same plush carpeting, opened the door, and flipped on the light switch. Her eyes landed on the toilet paper holder.

Empty. A quick search in the drawers beneath the sink turned up nothing. She'd just have to ask Elena.

As she drew closer to Elena's office door, cracked ever so slightly, the woman's voice sounded from the other side, hushed and determined. "She's been here a few minutes. I'm telling you, we have to watch out for her. She's smarter than you give her credit for. She graduated first in her cla—"

Elena grew silent for a moment, then came back in, her voice stronger. "I don't care how naïve you think she is, I'm telling you we'll have to keep an eye on her. Yes, she's important to our plan, but this isn't going to be a cakewalk. You're gonna have to turn it up a notch in the charm department."

The air grew still and quiet again, her heartbeat pounding so loud in her ears, Grace was sure it was audible in the next county. Elena's words about graduating first in her class lodged in Grace's brain. Was Elena referring to her? If so, why did she think she think she needed to be watched out for? And who was she talking to? Grace struggled to keep her breathing shallow, tuning her ears to the faintest sound.

Finally Elena spoke again. "Yeah, well, she's also pretty attached to Andy Tyler, and that's not a good thing. You know he's on the list."

Her muscles froze, making breathing impossible. Andy on a list? What list? Her brain raced. Elena *was* talking about her and her connection to Andy.

"Listen, we'll have to talk about it later because I need to make another call." Talking ceased, and faint musical tones sounded as Elena punched buttons. "This is Elena. I can't talk long. What do you need?" Again a pause. "Just say you don't remember if the defense asks that question."

Invisible hands clawed at her throat, threatening to suffocate her. She brought a hand to her neck.

"Talk to you later. Bye." The phone banged against the receiver and a whisper of steps grew louder and closer.

Grace scrambled across the carpet to the bathroom door, pivoted, and pretended to exit, when Elena called out from her doorway. "Did you hear something?"

She gave her head a casual shake. "No. What?"

Elena's eyes narrowed to cat-like slits. "Nothing. Must have been my imagination." She stared at Grace a moment longer then headed to the exit. "Right now they're holding the job opening at my request. It won't last forever, so you need to give me your answer ASAP. Come on, I'm hungry."

The following Monday, Grace once more sat in the Miller County Courthouse, her thoughts on Matt. She'd been more than relieved when he'd showed up at church yesterday and even more pleased when he'd asked her to lunch. Afterwards, they'd walked to the creek and sat near the water to talk, and though he questioned her new hairstyle and clothing, he'd done so respectfully. Her lips curved into a smile. Just knowing that for now he planned to stay in Miller's Creek made everything better. While it was still too early to tell if things would work out between them, at least now she had the chance to find out.

Jason shifted positions to her left. Even though Andy still refused to put her on the case, he requested she attend the trial to observe Elena in action to hopefully uncover any weaknesses. The idea was laughable. Elena wasn't the type to show chinks in her armor. Nor would she make careless mistakes.

Grace moistened her lips and thought back to her dinner with Elena on Friday night. The other attorney had once more grown quiet and reticent, and more than once, she'd looked up from her plate to find Elena staring at her, almost as if she were scheming up some sort of plan.

A chair scraped against the floor and brought her attention back to the trial. On the other side of David Simmons, Andy rose to his feet, ready to cross-examine Scott Evans, a witness Elena had called to the stand. "Mr. Evans, you stated previously that you were in the car with David Simmons on the evening of December twelfth of last year. Is that correct?"

"Yes sir."

"And two other people, Gregory Johnson and Michael Bedford, were with you as well?" Andy perused the yellow legal pad he held in his hands.

"Yes."

"You mentioned that David only pretended to be Michael's friend, that behind his back, David made him the brunt of jokes."

Scott Evans nodded.

"And how was your relationship with Mr. Bedford?"

"Okay, I guess."

"So you never made derogatory comments behind his back?"

The witness fidgeted a bit before answering the question. "I guess I did sometimes."

"So it's safe to say that you and David held similar views of Michael Bedford?"

Evans rubbed his cheek. "Yeah."

Andy approached the witness stand in a non-confrontational way. "Did Michael hang out with you guys on a regular basis?"

"Not normally, but it wasn't unusual for David to invite other people to hang with us."

"And what kind of activities did all of you typically enjoy during these times?"

"Just the usual, playing basketball or football—you know, guy stuff."

On the other side of the courtroom, Elena twisted her lips then lowered her head.

Grace's spirit quickened, and a frown drew her eyebrows in tight. The witness's response bothered Elena, but why?

Andy resumed his questioning. "It's already been established that you'd all had a few drinks, but on the night in question, how much did you have to drink?"

Scott Evans practically bored a hole in the back wall of the courthouse. Finally, Evans leveled his gaze to Andy. "I don't remember."

Grace's pulse blasted off, jack-hammering in her ears, her mind zoned in on the phone call she'd inadvertently eavesdropped on only a few days ago. Elena had mentioned those very words—"I don't remember." She stole a quick glance at the prosecutor. She looked nonplussed, like she wasn't the least bit bothered by the answer. Was Elena guilty of influencing witness testimony?

Andy grew agitated and strode closer to the stand, his legal pad raised in the air. "Oh, c'mon, surely you can do better than that? Don't you know how much you had to drink? One? Two? More than that?"

Evans swallowed hard. "I don't think I had any more than anyone else if that's what you're asking."

Grace couldn't maintain her focus on the drama unfolding before her. Her head pounded, and she raised fingertips to massage the sudden ache in her temple. She had no proof for her suspicions of Elena. Anything she said would be nothing but hearsay, and she couldn't just go around accusing well-respected members of society without something to back it up.

A shudder rippled down her spine, sending bumps along the skin of her arms and legs, her mind gyrating with questions. There was more at play here than she understood.

Why had Elena introduced her to her family, given her several hundred dollars' worth of clothes, taken her out for dinner, told her about the possible job, offered to be her mentor? Was she just being nice, or was she attempting to buy her off? And who was on the other end of Elena's phone conversation? More importantly, what list was Andy on?

Everything around Grace faded away, as she rested an elbow on the rail and spun a strand of hair around one finger. Something was amiss, and it revolved around Elena. And somehow or another, she had to figure it out. Grace released a shaky breath. She had no choice.

The way grew crystal clear, like fog disintegrated by pure sunlight. Matt would be proud. For once her decision wasn't based on what others thought of her, but for the purpose of doing what she could to protect Andy, even if it meant going to work, at least in the short term, for Elena.

In one smooth fluid movement, Jason placed one arm along the back of her chair and leaned closer, his lips inches from her face as he whispered in her ear. "Interesting turn of events, wouldn't you say?"

8

It was all Matt could do to keep from screaming the word "No!" Instead he crossed his arms and leaned back against the wall to see how this scenario played itself out. At least he had to give Gracie credit for moving past trying to please everyone. Unfortunately her decision also made it more difficult for him to protect her.

Was she finally growing a backbone or was something else at play here?

She stood rooted in one place, an arm crossed around her waist and the other twitching nervously at her side, her eyes glued to the floor. "I know this is short notice, but it's something I have to do. Being a prosecutor is something I've always wanted."

Matt switched his gaze to Andy. He didn't seem the least bit surprised, but his eyes held disappointment . . . and disgust? There *was* more going on here. Something he wasn't privy to. A slow shudder ran down his neck.

Andy raked one hand through his curly hair, pivoted, then paced across the room and back. "I guess you have to do what you think is best, but don't say I didn't warn you."

Warn her? Warn her about what?

Gracie still didn't make eye contact. "I'll get my things out of my desk." She spoke the words quietly and left the room. The door closing behind her sounded so final.

Andy must have felt it too, because he resumed the pacing and looked ready to punch something. "I gotta get outta here before I blow."

Matt moved from leaning to standing. The only way he'd ever figure out what was going on was to ask Andy, but now was obviously not the time. "How 'bout lunch? My treat."

Andy stopped and brought a hand to his abdomen. "Make it some place with non-spicy food, 'cause I don't feel too well."

"That's understandable." Truth be told, his stomach felt a little punchy, too.

A few minutes later the two of them were in Andy's car headed out of town. Maybe a steak from Montana's would make them both feel better, not just for the food, but to reach some sort of peace over Gracie's decision to leave the firm. At least one good thing had come of all this. She'd no longer be in close proximity to the James Bond of Miller's Creek.

His eyes obscured behind his Ray Bans, Andy remained silent and withdrawn, making it difficult to get a read. At long last he spoke. "I still can't believe she did this. Ben thought it would happen, but I didn't think she'd go through with it."

"Ben?"

His brother awakened from his catatonic reverie. "Ben Snodgrass, the older attorney in the firm."

Matt thought back to his first day in town. What was it Gracie had said about the man? He struggled to retrieve the conversation, but nothing came.

They wheeled into the parking lot at Montana's a short while later. With several minutes remaining before the normal lunch crowd hit, the hostess immediately seated them at a table near the front on the east side, the tantalizing aroma of freshly-grilled steak in the air.

Andy took a seat facing away from the door and opened his menu. "You okay?"

"Not really. Gracie's announcement kind of knocked the wind out of me. I don't even know why, except that I won't see her as often as I'd like."

His brother raised a hand to his forehead, eyes closed, and rubbed at the furrows gathered there. "I feel the same way. I'm hurt, angry, and honestly a little worried."

"Why worried?"

Andy continued to study the menu, but gave his head a shake. "Not sure I can really say why."

Couldn't or wouldn't? Matt studied him. He wanted to push for an answer, but one glimpse at the fatigue on Andy's face kept him from following through. Maybe after lunch.

Though the delicious steak dinner didn't completely erase the unease Matt felt, it did help somewhat. By the end of lunch, Andy looked better, too.

His brother tossed the linen napkin to the table in the now-bustling restaurant. "It's amazing what a little food therapy can do for my disposition, though I must admit I feel like a glutton for putting away that huge steak so quickly."

"Same here."

An apology flickered on Andy's face. "Sorry to get so bent outta shape earlier, bro. I just hate to lose her."

A wad of emotion lodged in his throat at his brother's choice of words. Had they lost her? A sigh burst out.

"You too?" Andy's expression held understanding.

"Yeah, I just don't know how I'll have time to spend with her now that she's working in Morganville."

"Guess you'll have to do it the old-fashioned way and call to ask her out."

"Yeah." That, and find a way to do most of his business in Morganville. A mental image of himself doing paperwork at a café close to the courthouse popped to the front of his mind. Definitely something to consider.

He did a quick check of his brother's mood, before launching into the question he'd been holding in. "You mentioned something earlier about warning Gracie. Mind me asking what that was about?"

For a few seconds Andy said nothing. Instead his jaw worked like he couldn't quite decide what to say and what not to say. "Please don't repeat this to anyone, especially not to Gracie." He leaned forward and lowered his voice. "I have suspicions about the woman she'll be working with."

Matt's heart pounded faster. "What do you mean? Is she in danger?"

"I don't think so." Andy must have seen the concern on his face. "It's okay, Matt. Gracie's a big girl and can take care of herself."

"If she's in danger, I wanna know. And she deserves to know."

Andy clamped his lips in a taut line. "I can't say more than I've already said. Probably shouldn't have said anything at all, so please, stay out of it."

Matt glared at him incredulously. Stay out of it? How could his brother knowingly put her in danger?

"Oh, man!" Andy jerked his head downward to check his watch. "I just remembered an appointment I have here in town. I hate to drag you along."

Over Andy's left shoulder, Gracie and an attractive woman he'd never seen before entered and were seated on the opposite side of the restaurant. "No prob. I'll just hang here until you get through."

"You sure?"

"Yeah. It'll give me a chance to clear my head." Matt sipped his iced tea nonchalantly, eyes on Gracie, who had now headed toward the restrooms. It was best if Andy had no clue what he was up to.

"Okay. It shouldn't take more than an hour."

"Take your time. I'll be fine."

Andy strode from the table and out the door, totally oblivious to the plan formulating in Matt's head.

Grace stared at her pale reflection in the bathroom mirror at Montana's Steakhouse later that day and crunched down on an antacid tablet. Though the chalky peppermint flavor cooled her tongue, it did nothing to counteract the slow burn in her stomach, which had started the moment she'd shared the news of her imminent departure with Andy.

At first, she'd rejoiced to see Matt there, overjoyed that she'd have someone to cheer her on, but once she started speaking, his smiling eyes had turned battery-acid brown.

Her chest heavy, she brought a hand up to ease the hurt. The disappointment displayed on their faces had been almost unbearable, and she'd finished her carefully rehearsed speech with her gaze to the floor. It had been a difficult decision, but also an easy one. How could she not make an attempt to bring about justice in a situation where foul play was likely?

A headache built behind her eyes. Apparently Matt had been right about her 'disease to please,' as he'd called it. Right now it wreaked havoc in her stomach—partly because of the new job—but mostly because she'd let her friends down.

It's for a good cause, Grace. A sigh slipped between her lips. Her pep talk fell flat, and did nothing to improve her outlook. What if her plan backfired in some way? Who would she have to corroborate her side of the story? She closed her eyes. All this worry would get her nowhere. She'd just have to trust God to help her.

After one more check in the mirror, she pivoted on one heel of the stilettos Elena had given her last Friday and moved through the door to join her mentor.

The woman flashed a bright smile as Grace approached the booth. "There you are. I was beginning to think you weren't coming back."

Grace forced a laugh. "Just dealing with an upset tummy."

Elena glanced over the top her menu. "Are you all right?"

"Yes, I think the antacid is finally working." Big lie. Normally, the aroma of grilled beef would have her salivating, but today it only worsened the churning in her stomach.

They studied their menus in silence, Grace struggling with how to bring up questions in a way that sounded natural and didn't arouse Elena's suspicions.

A familiar voice intruded into her thoughts. "Well, well, if it isn't Gracie Mae."

Her gaze flew to Matt's face. What was he doing here? "Hi." Her tone held an intentional chill. She continued to peruse her menu, willing him to take the hint.

Elena's feline eyes zoned in on him. She scooted in and patted the seat beside her. "Why don't you join us? Any friend of Grace is a friend of mine."

Matt was all smiles. "Thanks. Think I will." He plopped down in the seat across and extended a hand to Elena. "Nice to meet you."

Grace came to her senses. "Forgive my lack of manners. Matt, this is Elena, and this," she gestured toward him, his sloppy attire registering in her brain, "this is Matt."

Elena smiled and returned to reading her menu.

Grace did the same, but in her peripheral vision she noticed Matt lean to one side to eye her new shoes with a frown. She shot him a glare, resisting the urge to grind the point of her shoe into his shin. "Elena, I'm having trouble deciding what to order. Any recommendations?"

"You can't go wrong with the filet mignon."

Grace scoured the menu. She could indeed go wrong at that price.

"Don't worry, Gracie Mae. Lunch is on me." His eyes half-lidded, Matt spoke the words matter-of-factly, like it was a daily ritual for him to spend lavish amounts of money on a meal. And since when did he have enough money to spend thirty dollars on a steak?

"That's very generous of you." Elena smiled her gratitude.

"No problem." He returned her boss' smile, and then faced Grace, the set of his jaw issuing a subtle challenge.

Fine. She'd enjoy every juicy, tender bite of that thirty-dollar steak, thank you very much.

A few minutes later, the waitress arrived with a basket of fresh bread, ready to take their order. Surprisingly, Matt ordered nothing but a glass of tea.

A frown wriggled onto her forehead. Was he going hungry in order to pay for their food? She toyed with the idea of ordering something less expensive, but the insolent glint in his eye urged her forward. "I'll have the filet mignon, cooked medium, with a salad and baked potato." She held up one finger like she'd had an epiphany. "Oh, and I'll probably want dessert."

A bemused smile curved the corners of his lips, and his tongue moved inside his left cheek.

"Okay." The waitress scribbled on her pad. "And to drink?"

"Coke, please."

His eyes grew small beneath his furrowed brows. "You don't drink sodas."

"I do today. Why aren't you eating?"

He shrugged. "Not hungry."

Elena also ordered the filet mignon, and then turned her attention to Matt as the waitress hurried to the kitchen. "So how do you two know each other?"

Matt faced Grace, his eyes doing a slow, but methodical study of her face, his answer thankfully vague. "My brother lives in Miller's Creek, and he introduced us. We've known each other a few years now." He snagged a piece of bread from the basket and took a bite, intentionally chomping with his mouth wide open, his gaze never leaving her face. Matt swallowed and addressed Elena. "And what do you do for a living?"

Grace licked her lips and pretended to focus on drinking her soda. Surely Matt already knew who she was, since he'd been privy to her conversation with Andy earlier that day. What was he up to?

"I work for the Miller County DA's office."

Matt maintained his poker face. "I see. Lived in the area long?"

One of the questions she wanted answered. Grace straightened. Who needed to pry with Matt here? This potential disaster had turned into a potential plus. All she needed to do was close her mouth and open her ears.

"My mother and daughter and I moved here last year."

"Daughter? Does she goes to school in Morganville?" Matt leaned back while the waitress slid plates with delicious-looking food and equally enticing smells in front of both women.

"No, she's a special needs child. A specialist comes each day to help with her physical and educational needs." A pained expression crossed Elena's face as she moved a napkin to her lap.

Matt's eyes and voice now held genuine concern. "I'm sure that must be difficult for you."

"At times." She carved off a piece of steak.

Grace followed suit, the tender steak practically melting in her mouth.

"I don't mean to pry," offered Matt, "but is your daughter's father still in the picture?"

Elena coughed uncomfortably. "No. He took off for greener pastures once he realized her condition." Her tone oozed bitterness and resentment.

Grace's heart rose to her throat, making it difficult to swallow. How difficult it must be to struggle with a child's physical ailment, bearing the weight alone, as well as dealing with her husband's abandonment. A newfound appreciation for Elena built inside her. In spite of it all, she had persevered and overcome, now providing the nicest possible life for her child.

Across from her, Matt moved his head up and down. "In my line of work, it's common to find one parent shouldering the responsibility for a handicapped child."

Elena took a sip of water then returned the glass to the circular coaster. "And where do you work, Matt?"

"A place that provides equine therapy."

Grace closed her eyes. *Please don't let him say anything about Andy.*

A small frown landed between Elena's perfectly manicured eyebrows. "The one at the Miller family ranch?"

"Yeah. I'm helping my brother and his wife with the ministry—at least for a while." He glanced at Grace, his expression sullen and dark.

Elena's eyes narrowed perceptively. "Your brother?"

"You probably know him since you're an attorney. Does the name Andy Tyler ring a bell?"

Grace's breath froze momentarily, but quickly thawed as she watched Elena's response with interest. The woman's face visibly hardened, and she stabbed at her meat with a ferocious fierceness.

Matt, on the other hand, maintained his normal unassuming expression, though he studied Elena, analyzing her every move and expression. Did he suspect something, too?

For the remainder of the meal, Elena didn't direct another word to Matt, and Grace could tell that the intentional snub wasn't lost on him.

By the time the waitress arrived with the check, the tension in the air was more in need of a knife than the steak, and Grace couldn't wait to escape to the fresh air.

Elena beat Matt to the check, but refused to even look at him as she snagged it, her lips taut.

As they stood to leave, Andy walked up, his attention focused on his brother. "There you are. I was looking for you on the other side of the restaurant." He turned his attention to Grace and Elena. "Good afternoon, ladies."

"Sorry for stealing your protégé." Elena's tone held none of the apology she verbalized. Instead a catty smirk curled her upper lip.

"Just be sure to treat her right." Andy spoke the words sincerely and glanced at Grace, a wish and warning in one brief statement. He faced his brother. "Ready?"

Matt sent Grace one last searching look, then nodded. "Sure."

Elena eyed the two as they left. "Matt doesn't seem your type. I'd steer clear of him if I were you." She flipped open a wallet full of money, pulled out a hundred dollar bill, and tossed it to the table as she scooted from the booth.

Grace fell into step behind her. The woman's last words sounded more like a threat than a warning. Elena obviously disliked the Tyler's for some reason. Enough to change her from a tragic single mom to a caustic caldron of criticism in a few minutes' time. Was it simply a rivalry? Her thoughts turned to Elena's family. It just wouldn't do to get too emotionally invested in this situation. Best to simply figure out what Elena was up to, notify the authorities, and then step aside.

The petite prosecutor glanced back at her. "Matt Tyler strikes me as the kind of guy who would sponge off anyone who gave him the time of day." She shoved open the door.

Grace stepped from the restaurant into the cool fall air. How many times had she thought the same thing? Andy paid for Matt's education and now had given him a place to live rent-free while he figured out what he wanted to do with his life. She crawled into Elena's tiny sports car and pulled the door to.

Next to her, Elena adjusted the mirror and turned the key, the engine humming as they backed out of the parking space. "Lesson number one for my new protégé. Don't hang out with defense attorneys or their family members."

Her first day on the job, and Elena was already dictating the terms of her friendships?

The woman must have read the expression on her face. "It just doesn't look good. Trust me, it's for your own protection. This way no one can accuse you of leaking information to the other side."

With the last remark swishing through the air like a double-edged saber, Elena gunned the car and shot out into traffic.

9

Grace poured another cup of coffee Thursday afternoon and doctored it with plenty of sugar and cream. She raised her gaze to the clock on the break room wall and stifled a yawn. Not even three o'clock in the afternoon and she already longed for the comfort of her bed.

The spoon clinked against the thick mug as she stirred the caramel-colored liquid. She raised the cup to her lips and drank deeply. How was it that she made it through her undergrad work and law school without giving into the lure of caffeine, but after three days on the job, now downed massive quantities in the form of coffee, tea, cokes, and even an occasional energy drink?

She closed her eyes and sipped the fragrant creamy liquid, her shoulder muscles unknotting. Her mind, immediately more functional with the caffeine, moved to the issue at hand—how to uncover whatever it was that Elena was involved in.

So far, the woman had effectively buried her with research, none of which moved her any closer to her goal—to get in, uncover, and get out—all as quickly as possible.

A stockily built woman with gray curly hair entered the room and plopped into a seat near where Grace stood. "Hey, there. Haven't seen you before. You new?"

Grace moved closer to shake her hand. "I'm Grace Soldano."

A knowing look swept across the older woman's face. "Oh, yeah, I heard about you. You're the fresh meat."

"Pardon me?"

"The fresh meat for our resident tiger lady."

Tiger lady? Was that Elena's reputation around the office? Based on her experience over the past three days it wasn't all that unbelievable.

The woman guffawed. "You already recognize it as the gospel truth, don't you?" She laughed again, a wheeze that sounded like she was about to dissolve in a coughing fit. The lady lit a cigarette, and a puff of smoke shadowed her face before she exhaled and sent the spiraling vapor hurdling toward Grace. "Yeah, you got the look all right. How long you been here? One week or two?"

"Four days."

The woman dissolved into a fit of raspy laughter that ended in a harsh cough. When she finally brought the barks under control, she took another puff. "Mercy, child. If you already look this bad, you probably won't even come close to the record."

"Record?"

"The last one. Stayed four weeks."

An uncomfortable tightness landed in Grace's chest. All she'd ever heard about Elena before taking this job was that she was one of the finest prosecuting attorneys in the county. And *now* she had to find out the truth? Grace glanced toward the door. What would Elena do if she found her in the break room chatting with someone who could potentially provide help with the questions she so desperately needed answered?

Grace took a seat. "Is she really that bad?"

"Guess that depends on your perspective. And your definition of bad." The woman tapped her cigarette against the side of the ashtray. "I'm Peg. Work in the mailroom. I've seen it over and over. You all come in here looking the same, stars and dollar signs in your eyes, your chest held high, certain that after a while under the tiger lady's tutelage you'll be the next great attorney. But after a few weeks, you can't take the punishment anymore and decide the price is too high. I've seen more than one leave with their tails tucked between their legs."

"What kind of punishment?"

Peg's chuckled. "You've obviously not been on the receiving end of her sharp tongue."

Grace shook her head.

"Interesting. You might have found favor with her."

"If she's as bad as you say, why don't they get rid of her?"

"There's the rub. She's good at what she does." Peg leaned closer, her smoker's breath almost unbearable, and lowered her voice. "Of course there's also hearsay that she has friends in high places."

Finally she was getting somewhere!

With a startling bang, the door swung open and Elena entered, a tight smile at play on her lips. "There you are, Grace." She cast a ferocious glance at Peg then faced Grace. "You look like you're hiding something."

Grace forced a laugh, feigning a bravado she didn't feel. "You probably just saw me grimace at this coffee. Whoever made it likes it dark and thick." She moved to the sink to pour the delicious drink down the drain.

Elena cleared her throat, her voice dangerously quiet. "As soon as you're finished, I need to see you."

"Okay. Be right there." She didn't turn as she rinsed the cup. Elena's heels performed a staccato march across the tiled floors. Then the door slammed. Grace placed the cup in the dishwasher, and then faced the door for a long minute, gathering her courage. As she passed the table, Peg reached out and grabbed her forearm. She looked down into the woman's rheumy eyes.

"Don't let her scare you. Stand your ground."

"I'll try." Grace resumed her walk to the door.

Behind her Peg's voice called out once more. "Oh, and one more thing."

Grace turned. "What's that?"

Peg lit up another cigarette and puffed a cloud of smoke. "You might wanna put on fire-retardant clothing before this meeting." She laughed her way into another round of emphysemic coughs.

Peg's words turned out to be prophetic. As soon as Grace entered the office, Elena, who stood with several other attorneys around the conference table, called out to her. "Over here, Grace."

She moved to where they were stationed, doing her best to keep her shoulders back and her head held high in spite of the fear searing through her veins.

Elena held up a hand to silence the man she was speaking with and focused her attention on Grace. "Would you mind explaining why you were in the break room less than two hours after lunch?" All other conversation ceased as many pairs of eyes turned her way.

"I—I didn't sleep well last night, so I went after a cup of coffee." She withered even further beneath Elena's haughty stare.

"Let me make myself perfectly clear. I stuck my neck out for you to get you this job. I won't have you tarnishing my reputation by gossiping with the girls in the break room."

"But I—"

"No excuses. You don't get paid to drink coffee. Do I make myself clear?"

Grace made the mistake of peering around at the others nearby. The men all stood with their heads lowered and their hands in their suit pockets. The women cast furtive glances at each other, glances that seemed to say, "Here we go again." Grace had the distinct impression she'd be water cooler fodder after this. Were they already placing wagers on how long she'd last, or was that strictly a game the mailroom workers played?

A flush of heat crawled up her face, and tears stung her eyes. She blinked hard to hold them at bay. "Yes."

Elena extended a stack of papers toward her. "I need you to file this brief and be back here no later than four o'clock."

Grace took the papers and stepped toward her desk to gather her purse.

"And Grace."

She stopped in her tracks and faced Elena again.

Her face held cold contempt. "You might want to avoid the break room. It makes you smell like a pool hall, and you look like you've gained a few pounds."

Snickers sounded from a group of guys standing nearby.

Grace exerted considerable effort to keep her jaw clamped shut. She managed to exit the room as gracefully as possible in spite of the storm brewing inside. All the way to the courthouse she replayed Elena's hateful words. They slashed through her over and over again, leaving her more wounded with each pass.

How dare the woman publicly embarrass her in front of her new colleagues! Who did she think she was? Angry tears hovered just below the surface, but Grace refused them an exit, stuffing them deeper and deeper.

Once at the courthouse, she sat in Papa's pickup for a few minutes trying to gain control of her emotions. The last thing she needed or wanted was the drama of yet another emotional scene. She had to make sure she was completely ready to face whatever and whoever came next.

Grace finally slowed her breathing, knowing she'd have to deal with the baggage she'd stuffed away at a later time. She rummaged in the glove box and found an old napkin. With that and the rearview mirror, she set to work to remove all traces of her reaction to Elena's verbal barrage. Then she trotted from the parking lot and up the courthouse steps, a sudden realization dawning on her. In spite of three years of very expensive law school she had no idea how to file a brief.

The heavy door squeaked as she entered the building and peered around. Was there a sign somewhere that said "File Briefs Here?"

"May I help you?" A lady behind the desk peered up at her.

Grace smiled sheepishly and approached. "I don't know quite how to say this, but I'm a new attorney and I—"

"Let me guess, first time to file a brief?" She broke into a smile.

"That obvious?"

A kind smile lit the woman's face, and immediately set Grace at ease. The lady patted her hand. "Don't worry, hon, I've been here almost thirty-seven years and I've seen it time and time again. You'd think they'd teach this in law school, but for some reason they don't. Come with me."

Though the woman was sweet and helpful, she was also incredibly slow and thorough, going through every step of the process in great detail, and more than once, in an effort to help Grace the next time around.

Almost an hour later, Grace expressed her gratitude to the lady once more and hurried down the street to the pickup. She eyed her watch as she inserted the key and buckled her seatbelt. There should be just enough time to get back before the imposed deadline. Surely Elena would be pleased she'd managed the task in the allotted time. She turned the ignition. The old pickup made its familiar grinding noise, but then began to slow.

Lord, please not now.

She pumped the gas pedal and tried again. All she heard was a bit of the same noise and then nothing but a click. Grace let her head fall forward onto the steering wheel, longing to release a scream of frustration. What was she supposed to do now? Calling Elena was out of the question. Papa would be gearing up for the dinner crowd at the restaurant. Normally, she'd call Andy, but somehow that didn't seem right under the circumstances.

Matt's face flashed in her mind. She climbed from the truck, jogged to a nearby business in her stiletto heels, and asked to borrow their phone. She punched Matt's number, praying she remembered it correctly. Her heart fluttered when he answered. "Thank goodness."

"Gracie? You all right?"

"Not really. I can't get the pickup started and I need to be back at work as soon as possible before . . . " She stopped herself in the nick of time, reminded of Elena's warning. No, it wouldn't do for her to bad mouth her boss. Not if she wanted to complete her mission and keep her job.

"Before what?"

"Never mind, it doesn't matter. Let's just say I need to be there five minutes ago. Can you come rescue me?"

Matt chuckled. "You can't have it both ways, Gracie Mae. I can't be the scum of the earth one minute and your knight in shining armor the next."

"I don't have time for this." Panic escalated her words to a near scream.

"Okay, okay. Sorry. Where are you?"

"In a parking lot down the street from the courthouse. Where are you?" She pelted out the words like they were bullets and he was the target.

"You're in luck, fair damsel. I'm headed into Morganville to run a few errands for Trish. I'll swing by there and help you out first."

True to his word, Matt arrived a few minutes later, quickly diagnosed the dead battery, and produced a set of jumper cables. In no time, the pickup cranked right up.

Grace engulfed him in a quick hug. "You've saved my life."

"Well, I wouldn't exactly go that far." Matt removed the cables and folded them.

"I would. Sorry I can't stay, but I've gotta run." Already fifteen minutes late, but hopefully Elena would understand. She wiggled her fingers at him and sped out of the parking lot.

She rounded the corner of Fourth Street, the DA's office within sight. A siren sounded behind her. Grace glanced in the rearview mirror at the red and blue flashing lights.

Her heart fell to the ground. Was this really happening?

Grace pulled over, her heartbeat hammering a hole in her head. The officer took an eternity in coming to the window. She watched him from the side view mirror as he slowly sauntered up like he had hours to squander.

"Sorry, officer. I work for the DA's office and needed to run an errand for my boss and I'm running behind and—"

"Driver's license, insurance, and registration, please." He drawled out the words, his jaws at work on a wad of spearmint gum.

Grace retrieved the requested documentation, then watched in agony as the patrolman sauntered slowly back to his car. Five minutes ticked by on the dashboard clock before he made his way back to her.

"Ma'am, I clocked you going fifteen miles over the speed limit. In addition, I'm ticketing you for not having your seatbelt buckled."

She fumbled for the seatbelt in dismay. How could she be so stupid? Grace took the ticket and tried to listen to his instructions, but with the roaring in her ears, his words melded into a mound of indecipherable gibberish.

When he finally finished his spiel and pulled around her, her tears unleashed in force. They backed up in her throat, and she sobbed all the way to the office.

Thankfully the building was empty as she made her way up the stairs to Elena's office. At least she didn't have to deal with stares or questions. Hands shaking, and feeling like a worn-out dishrag, she turned the knob of the office door, prepared to offer her resignation if necessary.

Elena, every hair perfectly in place, sat behind her desk writing on a legal pad, a pleasant expression on her face—as though she hadn't a care in the world. She didn't look up as Grace entered, but continued to write as she spoke. "It's certainly about time. In fact, it's past time. Did I not give you explicit instructions on when to be back?"

"Yes." Grace's voice quavered. She chomped down hard on her lower lip to distract her from yet more threatening tears. "My pickup wouldn't start, and then I got a ticket trying to make it back on time."

Elena laid down her pen, almost too calmly, and finally looked up, searching Grace's tear-stained face. Her upper lip curled in contempt. "Tears? Really? I credited you with so much more spine than this." She rose to her feet and moved from behind her desk. "I gave you those clothes to give you a hand up, but you're obviously not interested in looking your best. Your hair and make-up look like a schoolgirl playing dress-up."

A scene from junior high bubbled to the surface of her memory. Several girls from her class, standing around her in the gym, listing her faults—one's she'd have to overcome before they'd consider being her friend. She struggled to keep the hurtful memory locked out, but she couldn't help but notice the similarities. The only difference was she and Elena were grown women. She inhaled the biggest breath she could gather in her lungs and sent up a cry to her Maker. *Lord, help me pull it together.*

Immediate peace cascaded over her, soothing her battered spirit. She swiped at tears with her fingertips. "I'll do better. I apologize for being so emotional. I'm just tired."

"More excuses?" Elena clicked her tongue. "Go wash your face and come back."

Grace didn't hesitate. Even a restroom was a welcome escape. As she wet a paper towel and pressed it to her face, she prayed once more. *Lord, thank You for Your peace and for answered prayer. Help me understand why Elena is like this. Show me how to help her and to figure out what she's up to. But most importantly, help me respond to her in a way that's pleasing to You.*

A minute later she traipsed back to Elena's office, not feeling especially better, but more prepared to handle whatever Elena unleashed.

But she *wasn't* prepared for the immediate difference she saw in the other woman. Instead of the dragon lady, she was met with a very contrite Elena. "I'm so sorry, Grace. Please forgive me. I really shouldn't have come unglued on you like that."

Forgive her.

God had forgiven her so much, how could she not do the same? From somewhere deep inside her, Grace found a strength she didn't even know she possessed. "It's okay, Elena. I need to do a better job than I did today, and I promise I'll do better in the future."

Elena pulled her toward the stylish sofa near the window. "I want you to understand how I sometimes can be when I'm under a lot of pressure. Please don't take it personally. This will sound like an excuse, but I'm really worried about Jessie. She hasn't been responding well to a new medication she's on, and since I have to be at work here, Mama is under considerable strain. To make it worse, the Simmons case is eating up my time and energy."

Another prayer answered. She'd prayed for understanding, and He'd given it. "What can I do?"

Elena's eyes softened. "I knew you'd be willing to help."

"Anyway I can."

"Thanks, Grace. I appreciate it more than you know." Elena moved to her desk, suddenly chipper, like nothing had happened. "If you could, I'd like you to call the people on this list." She snatched a piece of paper from her desk and brought it over. "These are some high school classmates of David Simmons. Maybe they can give some insight into his character."

Grace nodded and accepted the paper. More homework. Quiet resolve stiffened her spine. Difficult? Yes. But also her best opportunity to uncover any wrongdoing on Elena's part.

The petite attorney smiled in such a kind way, it made Grace question if Elena's earlier outburst had been nothing but a huge misunderstanding. "You go on home. Oh, and leave that ticket with me. I'll see what I can do about it to make up for my blunder today."

Blunder? Is that what she called it? "You don't have to—"

"See you tomorrow."

Dismissed again.

Before she left the building, Grace stopped by the restroom once more to wash her face, then glanced over her shoulder to make sure Elena was nowhere around before she descended to the mail room in the basement.

The typical musty smell of the basement greeted her. An elderly man locked the mailroom as she arrived. A disgruntled expression descended on his face, and he cleared his throat loudly. "Just closing up shop. Need something?"

"Um, no, but I'm looking for Peg. Is she still here by any chance?" If nothing else, maybe she could meet the woman for coffee to glean more information about Elena.

"Sorry, you're a little late."

Grace smiled and nodded her thanks. "That's okay, I'll catch her tomorrow."

He shook his head. "No, I don't think you understand."

"Understand what?"

"Peg was fired earlier today. She won't be coming back."

Grace exited the building in a daze and made her way to the pickup. The street lamps buzzed awake. Why had Peg been fired? Did Elena have anything to do with it?

She thought through the bizarre incidents of the afternoon, especially the dramatic change in Elena's behavior and the way in which the woman ordered her life and then dismissed her when she was through, much like someone wadding up a candy wrapper to throw in the garbage.

Grace crawled into the relative comfort and security of the truck and turned the key. The pickup responded with a churning noise, but no motor sounds. Not again. She leaned back in the seat, trying to decide what to do.

A shadowy figure moved in front of the pickup and stopped, staring right at her. Matt! She rolled down the window as he neared.

A comforting smile crossed his face. "You got away so fast earlier today that I didn't get a chance to tell you that you probably need a new battery. So I waited for you to get off work. I thought you might just need more rescuing."

His words choked her up, and she had to wait a moment before she could speak. "Boy, is that the understatement of the year."

His smile disappeared, replaced by concern. He reached a hand inside the window and turned her chin to face him. "You've been crying."

"A little, but I'm better now."

"Wanna talk about it?"

"No, it's over, and I'm gonna be okay."

"You know when people unload on you it says a lot more about them than it does about you, so find a way not to take it personally." He pressed his lips together momentarily. "Your new boss brought this on?"

Grace contemplated telling him everything—the odd mood swing, the way the woman had of ordering her around—but thought better of it. For better or worse, the woman was her boss, and for the sake of her career, and her mission, she needed to remember her place. She faced him and shook her head. "It's just been a rough day. The Singles' Class Thursday night Bible study is tonight. Wanna come?"

He looked hesitant at first, but then nodded. "Sure, but only if I can treat you to a cup of hot chocolate afterwards." The plea in his sandy brown eyes made it impossible to refuse.

"Sounds like a plan, but we'll have to cut it short. I have some work to do." She held up the sheet of paper Elena had given her.

His smile returned. "First let's get this old truck running again, so we can get you home safely."

10

The Singles Bible study group finished with prayer and headed from the church sanctuary to a nearby home for fellowship. Matt moved closer to Gracie, who strolled in silence beside him. The weather was a good parallel to the storm raging inside him, and from the looks of it, inside her as well.

The November night was uncharacteristically muggy with gusty south winds, which more than likely meant a cold front was about to push through, bringing with it thunderstorms and cooler temps. One of those nights pressed between the changing of the seasons.

Matt lowered his head to the ground, the sound of crunching leaves beneath his feet, the smell of pumpkin pie drifting from a nearby window. During prayer requests Gracie had asked for prayer over an unspoken concern. Not too surprising. All the time he'd known her, she had the tendency to stuff her emotions and problems in a well so deep, it would take years to dig to the bottom of it.

If only she would let him in. *Lord, show me how to reach her.*

As if discerning his thoughts, she faced him momentarily. A smile appeared, but didn't erase the sorrow in her eyes.

His heart ached for her. She needed to verbalize what was bothering her. He was afraid to even consider what might happen if she continued to bury all her hurts.

They moved inside, and Gracie rested a hand on his arm. "I don't want to stay long, but do you mind waiting just a sec? I need to ask Marcy about next month's Christmas party."

Yes, he did mind waiting. Very much. He wanted every second alone with her he could manage, if for no other reason than getting her to open up. But it wouldn't be smart to share those thoughts at this point. Instead he nodded. "Sure."

While Gracie traipsed across the room, Matt leaned against the brick fireplace. His eyes landed on Jason Dent who now made his way to where Gracie and Marcy stood.

Matt pressed his lips into a line. How long had Jason been a part of the group? And hadn't he already intruded enough in the brief time he had with Gracie? The guy made a beeline to them the minute he arrived, stationing himself in a seat on the other side of her.

Marcy wiggled her fingers at the other two and moved to the back of the house. Now only Gracie and Jason remained, both completely oblivious to anyone else in the room. Gracie's face lit with a smile and her laughter sounded across the space. She nodded at something Jason said. Then another girl wandered up and joined the conversation. What was that all about?

Gracie rejoined him a few minutes later, her fingers deftly knotting the red scarf she wore around her neck. "Okay, I'm ready to go. Thanks for waiting."

"No problem. Why don't we walk to Granny's since it's warm outside?" That would keep her from running away too easily.

They stepped into the night, the few leaves still attached to tree limbs rustling in the gusts of wind. Matt struggled with how to broach his questions about Jason. The last thing he wanted was to pry or make her angry, but he needed to know.

Gracie cleared her throat. "You're like a toddler. When you're quiet, it makes me wonder what you're up to."

He released a light laugh. "Are you calling me a kid?"

"Only in the nicest sense of the word. So what's going on in that head of yours?"

"I'm not sure you wanna know."

An audible grunt of disgust sounded. "And here we go again."

He laughed as he spun around to look at her, walking backwards temporarily. "Am I really that bad?"

She smiled. "Yes, but don't hold back on my account. Besides, they say it's not healthy to hold it in, and we do only have a short while before I have to get home."

Good point. Their time together *was* limited. "In regards to holding back, I could say the same about you. But since you asked, I'll go first to break the ice."

Gracie's smile turned to laughter. "Oh, so very kind of you."

Matt pressed his lips together and fell into step beside her once more. "How long has Jason been a part of the Singles Bible study group?"

"Tonight was his first night. I invited him last week. Why do you ask?"

Matt shrugged. "I guess I want to make sure his intentions toward you are pure." He waited for her to explode over the comment, but for whatever reason she didn't.

Instead a sigh fell from her parted lips. "Thanks for your concern, but I think Jason's above-board. Though I must admit that here lately I seem to question everyone's motives."

"Including mine?"

Gracie glanced over at him. "No." She paused a second, a teasing gleam sparkling in her eyes. "But that knowledge adds its own set of concerns to my crazy thoughts."

Matt beamed. At least she didn't question his motives. Might not be much, but it was a start. "I think you must be rubbing off on me, 'cause I find myself over-thinking things, too."

"Welcome to my world. What kind of things?"

He inhaled a deep breath. "Like what your relationship is with Jason."

Her face darkened, but she maintained a steady calm. "We're just friends at this point, but so you know, he did ask me out on a date for the weekend, and I accepted."

The air he'd inhaled earlier now rushed from his chest and sagged his shoulders, his worst fear confirmed. She just couldn't fall for a guy like Jason. He gave his head a shake. No, he couldn't go there. Though the thought of her going out with Mr. Perfect devastated him, he refused to let it consume his thoughts. Not when he could enjoy this beautiful evening with Gracie.

In comfortable silence they made their way toward the Miller's Creek town square, much of the neighborhood already decked with Christmas lights. Matt raised his head to the starlit sky, the Christmas lights no competition for the star-studded heavens. "I can't look at the sky—especially this time of year—without a profound knowledge of God's existence and sovereignty."

She shivered beside him.

"Cold?" He quickly removed his zip-up hoodie and placed it on her shoulders.

Gracie smiled and snuggled deeper into the jacket. "Thanks."

A small sports car passed slowly, its motor purring, and then braked to stop a few feet ahead of them. Gracie leaned forward, her gaze honed in on the car, and gasped ever so slightly. The vehicle resumed its crawl, its lights soon disappearing around a corner.

Something prompted him to grab Gracie's hand, and she didn't pull away. Instead, she tightened her grip. "Gracie, what's wrong?"

Reflected in the streetlights, a single tear inched its way down her left cheek. Was that fear in her eyes? "I'm just feeling a little overwhelmed right now, that's all."

That wasn't all, and he knew it, but more questions would only push her further away. Matt forced himself to hold back. Maybe if he didn't push, she'd find the strength to open up.

Granny's Kitchen greeted them with delicious aromas and friendly down-home hospitality. Around the café, familiar smiling faces lifted hands to acknowledge their arrival, followed by words of welcome. How many nights during that summer two and a half years ago had they spent time here just enjoying each other's company?

Gracie made her way to their booth, and Matt followed, praying silently for wisdom and guidance during their conversation. There was so much he needed to know, but had to trust God would help her open up in His timing.

After ordering their hot chocolate from one of the elderly twins who owned the place, Matt turned to Gracie. "So other than the snafu today, how's the new job?"

"It's okay."

"Any regrets?"

She pondered the question then gave her head a vehement shake. "I'm doing the right thing. No one else may understand or accept it, but this is what I'm supposed to do for now."

Matt's eyebrows rose. Good for her. She'd made a decision based on what she thought was right, and not in some convoluted effort to please everyone else. "I'm proud of you, Gracie."

Now it was her turn to look surprised. "You are?"

"Sounds like you took this job for the right reasons."

A frown made waves above her sad brown eyes. "This was one of those decisions I knew would make some people *un*happy with me." Gracie lowered her gaze. "It may not make anyone happy, including me, but it's still something I'm supposed to do."

"Why wouldn't it make you happy? You've always wanted to be a prosecutor. This is your chance."

"Yes, but something tells me it's not going to be as enjoyable as I once thought."

"Every job has its ups and downs."

She gave a non-committal shrug. "Yeah, I guess you're right."

He slurped from the steaming cup, allowing the chocolaty liquid to roll around on his tongue while her words filtered through his brain. There was so much more she wasn't saying. Just how much grief had the Delgado lady unloaded on her? Matt placed his mug on the table and leaned forward on crossed arms. "So what's it like working for your new boss?"

Gracie didn't look up. "I'm learning a lot."

Well, that was intentionally vague. "How so?"

"She's good at what she does." Gracie looked at him, her expression immediately revealing she wouldn't budge past ambiguous comments.

But he was on to something here and he knew it. The fact that she wasn't talking was proof. "And the work?"

A wry grin splattered across her face. "Well, except for not having the faintest idea on how to file a brief, I've enjoyed it."

A chuckle bubbled out. "They didn't teach that in Law 101?"

Now she laughed, a sound that immediately lightened the heavy tug on his spirit. Good. She was moving out of her melancholy, at least for now.

"Unfortunately, no. I was thinking the same thing earlier today when I climbed the county courthouse steps. I can't believe I spent so much money on law school, and they didn't teach something so basic. The nice lady who helped me said she did it all the time for newbies like me."

"Glad to know there are still decent people in the world."

Her smile disappeared behind a mask of darkness. She didn't speak, but sipped her cocoa, once more hiding from him. Finally she spoke, but only to change the subject. "What about you? Are you enjoying the work with the equine therapy ministry?"

"It's good. At least for now."

Her eyelashes fluttered downward, effectively veiling her thoughts. "What made you decide to stay here instead of going on the road with a band?"

Did he dare tell her? "Like you, it was just one of those things I knew I had to do."

She raised narrowed eyes. "I know Trish and Andy both really need you right now."

"Yep, but they're not the only ones."

This time she held his gaze. "I'm a big girl, Matt. I can take care of myself."

"Agreed, but it never hurts to have a backup."

A lazy smile curled her lips. "So you have my back?"

His chest throbbed. "Always." *God, help her know it's true.*

A curious expression descended on her face. "Just so you know, I have yours, too."

"Never doubted it for a second. You're a good person."

She sighed again. "Sometimes I doubt that."

"Why?"

One corner of her mouth turned downward. "I just struggle with the best way to handle things."

"We all do. That doesn't mean you're bad." Was she always so hard on herself?

"I know. It's just . . . " Her words dwindled away and her face went into "I'm-thinking" mode. Finally she continued. "I have this friend who's struggling, and I don't know how to help her. One part of me wants to set her straight and the other part feels incredibly sorry for her."

Something he learned in one of his counseling classes popped into his brain. Many times when a person mentioned a friend, they were really seeking answers for themselves. Was that the case here? "Go on."

"I'm wondering if they're caught in something bigger than they can get out of. Something potentially dangerous. One minute they're kind and helpful, and the next raging mad and ready to take it out on whoever they perceive to be crossing them."

"It's okay to get angry sometimes, Gracie. It's a normal human emotion. But you also need to remember its secondary, brought on by fear, pain, or frustration."

Her eyes clouded. "But what if they take it to an extreme?"

"Maybe she's stuffed her emotions too long, and they're starting to work their way out."

Gracie's eyebrows knotted, obviously still puzzled over the situation with 'her friend.' "Just encourage her to be open."

She bobbed her head, the copper highlights in her hair catching the light. "I just hope I'm strong enough to handle it."

"You can do it, Gracie. You're stronger than you realize, and God will give you the strength to do what you need to do."

Peaceful confidence radiated from her features. "I know He's with me, and I'm trying to trust Him in all this." Her eyes glazed over as she gazed over his shoulder. "Remember when we talked about the difference between grace and mercy? How far do you think mercy should go? At what point—if any—does it become about protecting yourself?"

His pulse elevated, and he searched her eyes for clues. Did she feel the need to protect herself?

"I mean, the Bible tells us to turn the other cheek, to forgive seventy times seven, to show mercy—"

Matt laid a hand on her forearm. "Stop it right there, Gracie. I think I see where you're headed. Yeah, the Bible says all those things, but are you really showing mercy if you let someone get away with wrong behavior? Is that really what's best for that person?"

She didn't answer right away, but considered his words. "When you put it like that, I guess not, but who am I to decide what's best for someone else?"

"There are times you can't, but there are also times when it's pretty obvious."

Indecision flickered on her face.

Lord, help me get this point across. Matt racked his brain for an example. "Look at it this way. If a child at school constantly bullies others and blames it on someone else, are you extending mercy if you turn a blind eye?"

She shook her head.

"Or is true mercy shown by working with that kid until he learns a better way to live, so he won't continue in a pattern that's not only harmful to him, but to others?"

"I see your point, but what if your option appears unkind and unmerciful to the other person?"

"Aargh!" He brought both hands to his head and pretended to pull his hair out. "You type-A personality people drive me nuts!"

Grace giggled. "Turnabout's fair play. Buster. And just so you know, you easygoing types drive me crazy, too. Now quit stalling and answer my question."

"Okay. Here are a couple of more analogies. Kids need vaccinations to keep from getting serious diseases, but when their parents take them to get a shot, the kids don't see it as merciful. But it is because the alternative would be worse."

"Agreed. Now what's your other example?"

He drew in a deep breath. "I'm pretty sure you're not gonna like what I have to say."

Her eyes glinted. "What else is new? Say it anyway."

He chuckled, glad to see her more light-hearted and playful. "It's really more about self-protection than mercy, but since you're the one who brought it up." He hesitated, willing her to get the full impact of what he was about to say. "If you touch a hot stove and it burns you, it seems pretty silly to touch it again."

She rested her head on one hand, and then clamped her jaw and shook her head. "That analogy is flawed."

Matt rolled his eyes and slapped both palms on the table. She had an argument for everything. "How?"

"People aren't stoves. They're human beings. Someone God loves as much as He loves us." Her face lit with a passion he'd never seen her exhibit. "It's possible God put me in a place to be merciful to someone regardless of how they treat me."

He couldn't speak, had nothing to contradict her statement. It was possible, but what a sacrifice to make. "I can't say it's not possible, but please be careful. Whether you decide to stick it out or back away, just remember that everything comes down to motive. If you do anything with a heart of love—even if the other person thinks you're being unkind or unforgiving—you're doing the right thing."

A flash of hope flickered in her brown eyes. "I believe that."

He leaned forward and cupped her face in his hands. "I think you're one of the most grace-filled and merciful people I know, sweetheart, so don't be so hard on yourself in this situation."

Her eyes locked with his, so full of sorrow it made him want to cry. "Please keep praying for me, Matt. Showing grace is much harder than I ever dreamed possible. I think I'm just now realizing how costly it can be."

"It cost Christ everything."

She nodded as tears welled in her eyes. "Yet my selfish heart seems to only focus on how costly and painful it will be for me."

His heart pounded curiously in his chest, a heavy thud of pressure. He took her hand and prayed her words weren't somehow prophetic.

For a brief moment they sat quietly, her hand at rest in his. Matt sent a smile and caressed her fingers with his thumb.

Gracie jerked her hand away and reached for her cup.

Matt's heart cratered. Time to have this discussion. "What is it about me you can't stand?"

She set the cup down with more force than necessary. It clunked against the table, hot chocolate splashing onto the red and white checkered tablecloth. "I care about you, Matt, so please don't start with the questions. Past our friendship, I just don't think we're right for each other."

"Why?"

Her features hardened. "Do you really wanna have this discussion, 'cause I'm pretty sure you're not gonna like it."

That. Did. It. Matt opened his mouth to give her what for, but at that precise moment, Steve Miller and his old geezer buddies entered the café and made their way to a table nearby, their boisterous conversation and laughter drowning out every other sound.

Steve saw them and made his way to their booth. "Hey, guys. Saw y'all at church last Sunday, but never made it over to say hi. Y'all doing okay?"

Gracie managed a smile as she looked up at the lanky cowboy. "Fine. Didn't expect to see you here this time of night."

"Just finished up a city council meeting. Guess you've heard the news?"

Matt took a cleansing breath and pushed past his anger. "What's that?"

"Dani and I are expecting a baby." He grinned broadly.

Gracie's features took on a mixture of joy and jealousy. "How exciting! Congrats!" The shrill pitch of her voice held strain.

Matt took in her expression. She wanted a family, and not just a little. "Congratulations, Steve, and pass it along to Dani."

The glint of envy in Gracie's eyes softened somewhat. "I'll bet Mama Beth's elated."

"That's an understatement," drawled Steve.

Coot—the guy who always wore brightly colored suspenders to hold his pants up over his potbelly—hollered from the other table. "Mayor, you'd better get over here and place your order before this Granny throws us all out on the street."

Steve tipped his hat. "Guess I'd better mosey on. See y'all later."

Once he left the table, Matt glanced at Gracie, who sat with her head lowered.

He rehashed the earlier tension between them, trying desperately to see himself through her eyes. Obviously she held some preconceived notions about him, which kept a wall built between them. How could he show her he was capable of being the man she needed him to be?

Gracie wakened from her reverie and checked her wristwatch. "I'd better get going so I can get to bed at a decent hour." She scooted out of the seat, her purse in tow.

Matt followed her to the counter and paid the ticket. Soon they were back on the street, making their way back to the church. He longed to reach over and grab her hand again, but didn't dare. In her current frame of mind, she'd only lash out at him, and he wasn't sure his bruised ego could take it at the moment. "You wanna help out with the equine therapy ministry on Saturday afternoon?" At least until her date with Mr. Perfect.

"I'd love to."

"You would?"

"Don't sound so surprised. I love to be around the kids."

"Right." No mention of wanting to hang out with him.

They walked the rest of the way in silence. Just as they reached the church, Gracie sucked in an audible breath and halted, her gaze frozen on a car ahead of them, parked in the middle of the road.

Matt's eyebrows wrinkled. Wasn't that the same one they'd seen earlier?

In an unexpected move, the car peeled out, the air now reeking of burned rubber. The tires screamed and screeched as the car careened down the road.

"Who is that jerk?" Matt groused the words without even thinking and then turned back to Gracie.

What he saw reflected in her stoic face paralyzed him with fear. She knew the driver. Of that much he was certain. But that wasn't what scared him most.

What sent terror coursing throughout him was the compassion and sheer sorrow swimming in her dark eyes. With a heart like hers, she was sure to get it broken.

11

A storm had blown in during the night, and now frigid temps chilled Grace to the bone early Friday morning. She hurried from the parking lot to the courthouse, tugging on the collar of her new trench coat to ward off icy winds that ripped between buildings in downtown Morganville.

She darted across the street, a car horn blaring down the block. What was going on with Elena? Earlier that morning, she'd waited patiently at the office for her boss, eager to share the results of her research, but as time for the proceedings inched closer, it became apparent Grace was on her own.

The sports car she'd seen last night belonged to Elena, of that she was convinced. But was she intentionally following them? The woman had made her opinion of a friendship with either Matt or Andy very clear, but surely she wouldn't resort to stalking.

Her lips clamped in a resolute line. Well, whatever Elena's motivation, perhaps she'd change her mind with the information Grace had uncovered in her phone calls to high school classmates of David Simmons.

As she climbed the long expanse of concrete steps to the courthouse, her mind rolled through last night's time with Matt. They'd strolled along moonlit streets in total quiet, with a contentment she couldn't discount. Yes, Matt sometimes got on her nerves, but with no one else did she experience such a comfortable peace.

Time with him was like wearing a favorite pair of shoes. They might be a little worn and frayed around the edges, but they fit like none other. His comment about God's sovereignty had sent chill bumps down her spine, once more impacting her heart with his profound words. Her cheeks warmed as she recalled how he'd wrapped his jacket around her shoulders. Never had she felt so cherished. But how could she allow herself to have feelings for someone who didn't have a plan?

The enormous wooden door creaked as she leaned her weight against it and stepped in the wooded warmth of the stale-smelling historic building. In spite of the building's warmth, Grace shivered, her body's reaction to yet another day of the Simmons case. This time she'd be on the opposite side of the courtroom. Had it only been two short weeks since she'd wished for this? How ironic that her desire to be a prosecutor had been granted, yet now she'd give anything to be sitting behind Andy.

Grace inhaled a breath to steady her frazzled nerves before she entered the courtroom. As expected, Elena was already there. Grace gulped and made her way to the table. "Good morning."

Her boss didn't acknowledge her presence or greeting, but continued to write.

Lord, help me. How do I deal with this?
Love your neighbor as yourself.

Her mind flitted back to last night's Bible study. What was it Brother Mac said? Something about believers being most like Christ when they loved those who were difficult to love.

After she removed her coat, Grace took a seat next to Elena, opened her brief case, and pulled out the notes. The papers hissed as she slid them across the table. "I think this might help your case. It appears Mr. Simmons had a similar prior charge in high school. He served time in juvy to expunge his record."

Elena laid her pen on the legal pad and calmly picked up the notes without saying a word or making eye contact.

Grace continued. "I found a couple of people who remembered the incident. Their names and contact info are listed, and both said they'd be willing to testify if needed."

The attorney fingered the document and leaned back in her chair while she read it, her expression remarkably calm.

The back door swung open. Andy and Jason entered, shoes a-tap on the parquet floor. They moved through the swinging gate which separated them from the gallery. Jason shot her a brilliant smile, but Andy sent only a tight-lipped nod.

An unexpected knot of emotion wedged in her throat at Andy's lack of greeting. How she missed him. Missed the camaraderie they'd shared. Maybe one day he'd understand why she made this decision, but even if he didn't, she took comfort in knowing she'd done the right thing for the right reason.

The jury members arrived, and everyone stood as the bailiff and Judge Clark made their way into the courtroom. "Good morning, ladies and gentlemen." The judge peered out over the gallery as he took the bench. "At our last session, the prosecution rested. Defense, are you ready?"

Andy nodded. "Yes, Your Honor."

"Very well, you may call your first witness."

"We call the defendant, David Simmons, to the stand."

With every hair of his blonde head in place, and dressed in a conservative navy blue suit, Simmons walked to the stand.

Grace's blood ran cold as David, his blue eyes wide and innocent, raised his right hand and promised to tell the truth. The jury had most likely already formed judgments, despite their promise to wait until they'd heard the evidence. She wiped her sweaty palms against her skirt, her stomach turning cartwheels. They couldn't help but like him with his boy-next-door image.

Simmons took a seat as Andy approached. "Please state for the court your recollection of the events from the evening of December twelfth."

"Yes sir." He looked at the jury. "After I finished my volunteer work at the soup kitchen, I went back to my room to clean up and go out with friends."

"Which friends?"

"Greg Johnson, Scotty Evans, and Michael Bedford."

"Go on." Andy leaned against the table.

"We had dinner and drove around for a while, just talking and having a good time."

"Did you drive around the entire evening with your friends?"

"No. We stopped at Jerry's bar for a few drinks." Simmons possessed an innate charm that made him very likeable.

"Then what happened?"

He gave a brief shrug. "We drove around some more, you know, just cutting up and laughing."

Andy checked his notes. "According to Mr. Evans' testimony, you were the designated driver for the evening."

"I was supposed to be, but we were in Scotty's car. When we left the bar, he wouldn't give me the keys. I got in the front seat with him just in case. I knew he'd had too much to drink."

Grace glanced over at Scott Evans. If looks could kill, David Simmons would be meeting his Maker right about now.

Andy crossed his arms. "What time did you leave the bar?"

"Between ten-thirty and eleven."

"What happened next?"

David's face paled, and he lowered his gaze. "We were downtown by the old depot. Michael started feeling sick. We let him out and he went behind the building to throw up. We decided to play a trick on him, so we turned off our headlights and drove to the other side like we were leaving. Scott got carried away and started driving too fast. Out of nowhere, Michael appeared in front of us and we hit him."

Scott Evans jumped to his feet, his face livid red. "That's not true and you know it!" He made a move to climb the seat in front of him, but was immediately restricted by the bailiff and guards. As they escorted him from the room, he yelled over his shoulder. "I'll get you for this, David. I'll get you if it's the last thing I do!"

The courtroom erupted, and Judge Clark brought his gavel down on the stand with several hard raps. "Order." Silence gradually prevailed.

Grace brought a hand to her chest, her gaze on the jury. If she didn't know about his prior conviction, she'd buy every word. Judging by their faces, it looked like they'd done just that.

Judge Scott turned to a visibly upset David, his hound dog eyes soft with compassion. "It's okay, son, finish your story."

Andy stepped closer, his voice low and calm. "David, can you tell the court why you originally lied to the police about driving the car that night?"

David sniffed and nodded, swabbing tears with the back of his hands. "Scotty already had a DWI from a few months earlier. A second offense would have been bad. We'd all gotten out of the car to check on Michael. He was groaning and moving so we thought he was gonna be okay. A siren went off and I panicked. I climbed behind the wheel to protect Scotty."

"Thank you, David." Andy sent a soft smile, then strode back to the defense table. "Your Honor, I'd like to enter Scott Evan's prior DWI conviction as evidence."

The words faded into background noise in Grace's ears as she thought through the testimony. Not only was David Simmons convincing, but Scott's emotional outburst made him appear guilty. She snapped back to attention.

Andy faced the judge. "Your Honor, I request a recess for my client to gather himself."

Elena sprung to her feet. "I object. The client is still able to answer questions."

The judge didn't hesitate. "Objection overruled. We'll adjourn until two o'clock this afternoon at which time the prosecution may cross-examine the witness."

As the gallery cleared, Elena angrily stuffed papers into her briefcase, obviously unhappy with the recess.

Grace moved closer. "Is there something I can help with?"

"No, I think I know how to put my things away, but while you're here, we might as well discuss something else."

The hairs on the back of Grace's neck stiffened in anticipation, and a nasty taste developed on the back side of her tongue. This couldn't be good.

"Didn't I make it clear I wanted you to stay away from Matt and Andy Tyler and anyone else involved with the defense?"

"You did."

"Then why were you walking through downtown Miller's Creek with Matt last night?" Her voice lowered to a sibilant hiss.

"He's my friend."

"Not if you intend to work for me. We'll discuss this further in my office, and you'd better not keep me waiting." Elena turned and strode from the room, her high heels making angry snaps against the floors.

Grace slumped to a seat in the almost empty room to curb her anger. How dare Elena dictate her friendships! She breathed deep to slow her thrashing pulse. After several minutes she finally felt in control enough to leave.

In spite of her warm coat, she shuddered as she stepped into the bitter November cold, feeling world-weary. Less than a week until Thanksgiving, and maybe she could catch up on sleep and make some headway through the mental turmoil. Grace cranked up the old truck and quickly traversed the few blocks to the DA's office.

Elena was waiting for her when she arrived. "It's about time you showed up," she spouted from her office door. "As soon as you put down your things, I need to see you in here."

Though her knees trembled, Grace lifted a prayer as she traipsed to her boss's office. *Help me be who You want me to be.* A floral scent attacked Grace's nostrils as she entered.

Elena looked up. "Have a seat."

She sank into the plush chair, dreading the verbal tirade about to come her way.

An inscrutable expression resided on the woman's face. "I appreciate how quickly you did the research I requested."

Grace clamped her jaw to keep it from snapping open. This woman had a serious case of Dr. Jekyll and Mr. Hyde.

"It might be our best chance to put this creep away."

David Simmons definitely topped her creep list. What made him even creepier was his ability to appear so innocent. "That's why I've always wanted to be a prosecutor."

Elena shifted her head to one side. "Is there something from your past—" She stopped, as though unsure of what to say.

"That makes this case especially difficult?"

Her boss nodded.

"Yes, my mother was killed in a car accident where the other driver was at fault. The guy got off with little more than a slap on the hand." A thorn in her flesh that festered to this day.

"I'm so sorry." Elena's eyes moistened. She stared at her desk, but after a few seconds shook herself from the reverie. "I need to tell you something that I really don't want to mention."

Grace's eyebrows crinkled. "What?"

"I know you're upset that I told you to stay away from the Tyler's. I guess I should be more specific about why." She wet her lips. "There are rumors that Andy might be involved in illegal or unethical activity."

There was no way to stop her gaping jaw. "I don't believe it."

"I don't either, but in situations like this we can't stick our head in the sand and pretend it might not be true."

She shook her head in astonishment. "What kind of things are we talking about?"

"Some question why he wins an extraordinary number of cases involving high-profile people. Apparently the authorities are interested in how this case turns out for that very reason."

"Are you saying he's on the take?" Grace resisted the temptation to laugh.

"I know it seems ludicrous. I questioned it, too. But he does have high prominent connections. That's why you need to stay away. If the rumors are true, and they suspect you . . . "

A feather could have pushed her over. While her heart didn't believe, her brain told her anything was possible.

"I'm sorry to be the bearer of bad news."

"Is there concrete evidence?"

"I don't know. The authorities will take care of it, but it would be easy for them to suspect you, since you worked for him and have now for me. It looks more than a little suspicious."

Her head swam. How could an innocent career move hold such threat, especially in her attempt to seek justice?

"Anyway," continued Elena, "just watch your step. I have to get back to work and figure out how to call David Simmons' bluff before court reconvenes. I'll let you go."

Dismissed again. Still dazed, Grace stumbled to her desk, struggling with her thoughts. Was the information accurate or was something else at play here?

She considered her options all during lunch, and an idea took root. The spare key to Andy's office hung from a cup hook in her bathroom. It wouldn't hurt to visit his office early one morning to check his files. It wasn't like she was actually breaking in, because she had a key. And she wasn't doing it to steal anything. It was all about her attempt to reach the truth. If she found nothing it would only help her case against Elena.

A few minutes before two, Grace returned to the courtroom. As she took a seat, she gazed to where Andy stood talking to David's dad and some other man. Where had she him before?

Elena joined her at the table. "Told you so."

Grace frowned. "What?"

"About Andy and his powerful friends. The other man standing with them is John Dempsey, Attorney General for the State of Texas."

Her eyebrows shot up. That's why he looked so familiar. Were Elena's suspicions true?

At that moment, the judge entered and turned their way. "Ms. Delgado, you may now cross-examine the witness." He looked at David. "Mr. Simmons, as you take the stand, I'll remind you that you're still under oath."

The defendant strolled to the stand and sat.

Like a miniature tornado, Elena whisked toward him, a light blue legal folder in her hands. "Mr. Simmons, according to your deposition, you got off work at six-thirty on the evening of December twelfth. Is that correct?"

"It wasn't really work. I was voluntee—"

"And what time did you get home?" She cut him short while she scanned the document.

"I got back to my room at—"

"When you say room, are you referring to a dorm room?"

Good question. The jury needed to know David Simmons was wealthy and used to getting his own way, in spite of his reference to volunteer work.

"No ma'am. I share a house with Greg Johnson."

"Do you own this house?"

He shook his head. "No, my parents do."

Grace stole a quick look at Simmons' parents. His mother was reportedly a doctor and his father worked for the State Department in some sort of advisory capacity.

"Does Mr. Johnson pay for his housing?"

"Objection." Andy rose to his feet. "I fail to see how my client's roommate situation has anything to do with the case."

Elena stood her ground. "Your Honor, I'm trying to show that the defendant has the means to buy friends." She glared at Andy. "And possibly their testimonies."

Andy ignored her. "Prejudicial, Your Honor."

Judge Clark didn't answer for a moment. "Ms. Delgado, you need to watch it. Defense objection overruled. I'll allow this line of questioning to continue. At least for the moment."

"Thank you, Your Honor." Elena looked back at David Simmons. "Does your roommate pay for his room and board?"

"No." For a brief moment, David's expression changed ever so slightly, but he quickly brought it under control.

Elena studied the file. "According to the police report, you and Mr. Evans were downtown near the old train depot around eleven-thirty that evening. Is that correct?"

His eyes flashed fire for a moment. "It is."

Simmons was clearly not accustomed to being questioned. Grace considered this aspect of his personality.

The prosecutor trained her gaze on Simmons, a lioness poised for the kill. "Mr. Simmons, if what you say is true—if Scott Evans is the one who should be held responsible for the death of Michael Bedford—please explain why you'd put yourself in the position of taking responsibility for this crime."

Her tactics to wear him down were working. He fidgeted, a caged animal searching for escape. "Like I said earlier, Scotty had been drinking, and he'd had too much. We didn't know Michael was gonna die. I didn't want Scotty to get in trouble, so when the cops got there I told them I was the one driving."

Elena laughed out loud, a haughty snort followed by a derisive look. "Interesting story, but for now I'll go with it. When exactly did you realize Michael Bedford was dead?"

"I don't know."

She slammed her hand against the lectern. "You're under oath, Mr. Simmons? Didn't you intentionally run him over?"

"Objection!" Andy's eyes shot fire as he hopped to his feet. His chair slid across the floor and crashed into the railing.

"Sustained. This is the last warning you'll receive, Ms. Delgado. You're getting mighty close to contempt."

Elena pursed her lips in an apparent effort to bring her emotions under control. Her gaze rested on the research Grace had given her earlier.

Her eyes widened. Surely Elena wouldn't use it until she'd given the defense time to prepare.

The petite attorney moved to the table and picked up the research. "Mr. Simmons, would you please explain a similar incident you were involved in during high school?"

A smattering of voices tittered across the courtroom as David Simmons paled and Andy catapulted to his feet. "Your Honor, this is new evidence and information I wasn't made privy to. But since Ms. Delgado brought it up, I hereby request a mistrial based on irreparable prejudice to the defendant and his case."

Grace's heart jumped to her throat. No, this couldn't be happening. It couldn't end this way. Not until someone was held accountable for Michael Bedford's death.

Judge Clark nodded, clearly frustrated at the turn of events. "Counsel for both parties, approach the bench."

All eyes focused on the judge and the attorneys, though their words were inaudible. A few minutes later, Elena and Andy made their way back to their respective places. The judge faced the jury. "Due to substantial and irreparable prejudice to the defendant, David Simmons, I hereby declare a mistrial *sua sponte.* The rule of jeopardy will attach, so this case may not be retried. Case dismissed." He pounded the stand with his gavel for a final time and strode from the room.

Bile rose in Grace's throat. Justice had been defeated, first in Mama's case and now this one. If David Simmons was guilty, he'd just gotten away with murder.

Within a minute of dismissal Harry Bridges, the DA, approached the table, his eyes honed in on Elena. "My office on Monday morning." He pivoted on one foot and stormed out of the courtroom.

Elena paled, her mouth drawn up in a tight bow. She turned on Grace. "This is your fault. Why didn't you tell me you didn't pass on the information to the defense?" She didn't wait for an answer, but picked up her things and left.

A cold sweat broke out on Grace's scalp. Elena was the type to turn this around on her to protect her own neck. Still reeling from all that transpired, she made her way back to the office in a daze. Work proved impossible between thoughts of losing her job and fear Andy could be involved with the wrong people. Much later, her work finally complete, she glanced up from her computer to find the office empty and the sky dark.

Heart heavy, she gathered her belongings, donned her coat, and locked the office door, dreading the thing she needed to do. Each step toward the old pickup seemed to make her plan more tedious and costly.

As she approached the truck, bathed in a pool of light from a street lamp, a distinct voice sounded from nearby. A voice with a British accent. She moved to the shadow of a building and glanced toward the voice, struggling to see in the darkness.

Jason and Elena leaned against her boss's shiny red sports car, oblivious to her presence and deep in conversation.

Numerous questions let loose inside, but one stood out from the rest. Why had Elena warned her away from the attorneys of Tyler, Dent, and Snodgrass when she had no intention of following her own admonition?

12

The alarm rang way too early, and Grace silenced it quickly. The last thing she needed at two a.m. was for Papa to awaken and ask what she was up to. She slipped from between the warmth of the bed covers, and tiptoed across the icy floor in her sock feet.

A few minutes later, dressed in a black sweat suit and tennis shoes with her hair pulled back in a ponytail, she wiggled her fingers into black mittens. As quietly as possible, she made her way past Papa's bedroom and out the back door. The freezing temps momentarily stole her breath as she began her jog into Miller's Creek to Andy's office, hoping with everything inside her that she wouldn't find a thing.

While she'd rather drive the two miles' distance, the noisy pickup motor would waken Papa for sure. She pushed the thought of the warm pickup cab from her mind and concentrated on her breathing.

Puffs of white arose from Grace's mouth as she took one step after another, her thoughts once more on the Simmons trial. Questions roiled in her head, the same ones she'd wrestled with all night. Was it possible Elena had intentionally caused a mistrial? No matter how hard she tried, she couldn't wrap her brain around it, and she chalked it up to fatigue.

Within a few minutes, the homes leading to the center of Miller's Creek appeared, lawns white with frost. She arrived at Andy's office, retrieved the key from her pocket, and inserted it into the lock, then glanced around furtively, her nerves on alert.

As she turned the knob, a hedge that separated Andy's office from the house next door rustled. She froze in place, her mind racing, then slowly turned her head to peer into the darkness. Probably just a stray cat.

Making as little sound as possible, she inched her way inside. Though pitch black, she couldn't risk turning on the lights. Instead she groped her way to Andy's office, and pulled a small flashlight from her pocket.

Three hours later she closed the last file folder and leaned back in Andy's leather chair. A headache built at the bridge of her nose. Had Elena intentionally sent her on a wild goose chase, or had Andy long since suspected he was under investigation and removed anything that would convict him?

Grace sighed and picked up the last file to return it to the cabinet. She'd just put it in place and closed the drawer when the exterior door squeaked open.

Her pulse thumped hard in her chest. She flicked off the flashlight and tiptoed to the bathroom attached to Andy's office. Once in the cramped space, she pushed the light button on her watch. Only five-thirty. Who would be here this early, especially on a Saturday?

She released the button on her watch and waited for her eyes to adjust to the darkness. A shadowy figure used the light of a smartphone to slip into the room. A drawer creaked, followed by the familiar sound of a file being wedged in a drawer. Then the unknown person left the room. A minute later the exterior door clicked.

Grace remained frozen in place for several minutes, her brain spinning. She moved cautiously from her hiding place, her mouth as a dry as dust and her breath coming in shallow spurts. It wouldn't be long until dawn, but she had to see the new folder. Once more she flipped the flashlight switch and opened the drawer. An unlabeled file, inserted at an angle caught her attention. A frown plowed furrows across her forehead as she perused the contents—names and phone numbers of high-profile people, including the Governor and the Secretary of State. While the file alone wouldn't be enough to implicate Andy, with the right accusations it could certainly damage his reputation.

What now? If she left the file, anyone could find it, but taking it felt wrong, too. In addition, if she mentioned it to anyone, she would implicate herself. A weighty breath fell from her lips. The only option to protect Andy was to take the file and give it to him later with an explanation. That should be as fun as sticking her head in a lion's mouth.

Grace tucked the file close to her abdomen and zipped her jacket to hold it in place. As she moved into the parking lot, a light flashed from the wooded area behind Andy's office. She ducked behind the air conditioning unit and peered in the direction of the flash, but nothing else caught her attention.

Much relieved, she moved from the shadows to begin the long trek home. With each pounding step, more guilt rained down on her. How could she have ever doubted Andy? And who was trying to set him up?

The sky lightened to deep purple, and then a pink streak appeared along the horizon. As she neared home, the cattle lowed from the pastures and birds chirped from the oak and mesquite trees. Maybe Papa would be out feeding the cows and none the wiser concerning her overnight jog. Unfortunately, she arrived just as he returned from feeding the cows. He slammed the pickup door and sauntered toward her, questions in his eyes. "You're up early."

"Yep. Trying to lose a little weight." Her chest heaved as she tried to catch her breath.

His eyes held wariness. "On a Saturday morning? You usually sleep in."

She fell into step beside him. "Normally I would, but I have a busy day planned. I have a date with Jason Dent tonight, and I told Matt I'd help with the equine therapy group this afternoon."

Papa's face hardened as he held the back door open for her. "You know how I feel about him."

"If you got to know Matt, you might just change your mind."

"Hmphf." With his work boots clomping against the floor, he moved down the hall to his bedroom and slammed the door behind him, his way of adding an exclamation point to his objection of Matt.

After breakfast and a shower, Grace donned her jeans and boots, fatigued, but eager with anticipation. A smile fluttered to her lips at the thought of helping the kids, something she'd done since the ministry started, when her schedule allowed. And the thought of spending the day with Matt held an appeal she couldn't deny. His presence brought sanity to her crazy life.

An idea popped into her head. She glanced at the clock. If she hurried, there might be time to pull it off.

A few hours later, she shoved the vacuum cleaner back in the hall closet and hurried to her room to grab her things. Now that the weekly chores were done, she'd make a quick trip to the store to pick up what she needed.

Grace pulled up outside the Miller mansion an hour later and climbed from the old pickup, reveling in the gorgeous fall day. The ancient live oaks flanking the circular drive held out gnarled arms to embrace her.

"What're you doing here so early?" Matt, his face lit with a smile, came around the corner of the house. His brown corduroy jacket highlighted the color of his eyes.

"Just following through on the BFF pact."

He reached her in a few more steps, his head tilted to one side. "Oh, really?"

She gave a quick nod. "Feel up to a picnic? I picked up a grilled chicken at the grocery store."

His eyes widened, drawing the corners of his mouth upward. "Of course. Wish I'd thought of it myself."

"Well, there is a catch."

"Oh, there is?"

"Yep. I wanna go riding. Do you think we have time to do both before the afternoon session?"

The smile on his face broadened. "Might have to be a short ride, but it can be done."

A short while later they headed across the north pasture toward the creek on horseback. In the comfort of Matt's company, Grace released her fears over recent developments and allowed herself to enjoy their time together. He told one corny joke after another, and by the time they reached the shady grove of oaks at the creek's edge, her sides hurt from laughing.

Matt tethered the horses to a few saplings in a grassy spot, and then gathered wood for a small fire to chase the chill away. Grace unloaded the grocery sacks from the saddle bag, and before long they dined on rotisserie-roasted chicken, potato wedges, and sourdough rolls beside a crackling fire and a babbling creek.

After she gorged herself on the meal, Grace tossed chicken bones toward the creek and stretched out. "What I wouldn't give to set up camp here and stay forever."

Matt sent a questioning look. "Sounds like escapism to me." A teasing grin landed on his face, and he winked. "But I'm game if you are."

A laugh bubbled out. "I must admit I'm tempted. Especially after the week I've had." She drew her knees to her chest and held them in place with her arms, gazing off in the distance.

"That bad, huh?"

She wrinkled her nose and nodded.

For a moment he didn't speak, but finished off a chicken leg and followed it with potato wedges. He wiped his mouth on a bandana he pulled from his pocket. "Care to elaborate?"

"Let's just say there's a good chance I might lose my job."

Concern etched his features. "Why?"

She filled him in and found a nearby stick to poke the fire, sparks spiraling skyward. "Please keep this confidential."

"Of course." He paused, the area around his eyes wrinkling. "Something else bothering you?"

Him and his sixth sense. Whoever coined the term 'woman's intuition' had never met Matt Tyler. But how could she tell him about sneaking into his brother's office in the middle of the night? She shook her head. "Nothing I care to talk about."

His lips pooched bunched up, and he nodded. "Fair enough. But you know you can tell me anything, right?"

Her guilt intensified, and she lowered her head. "Maybe some other time." She stood and stepped to her horse, petting the mare's velvety nose before mounting.

Matt chuckled softly from his perch near the fire. "Guess this means you're ready to leave?"

"I'll be back in a minute." She pulled the reins to the right until the mare faced the open field, and then prodded her into a trot. No, that wasn't enough today. She needed more. "Hyeah!" With a swift kick the mare bounded over the ground in a full gallop, the wind whistling in Grace's ears. Combing out the snarls in her hair would take forever, but at the moment she didn't care. As the horse pawed the ground beneath her, she relished the moment, inexpressible joy pouring over her worries until they evaporated.

When she returned to the picnic spot a half hour later, Matt had put out the fire and packed up the meal. He stood near his horse, cinching up the saddle bag and looked up as she neared, squinting against the noonday sun. "I was about to ask if you felt better, but I can see it in your face. Looks like it wouldn't hurt you to do this a little more often." He mounted and clicked his tongue to urge the speckled bay past her. "We'd best get back so we can get the kid's ponies ready to go."

Grace gave one last longing glance at their picnic place beside the gurgling creek before she turned her horse around and trotted after him.

They saddled the last pony just as the first vehicle pulled up. Matt hurried to the van and greeted the woman who emerged from behind the wheel. Together they moved to the passenger side, and Matt helped lower a young boy in a wheelchair. "Like to pop wheelies, Garrett?"

The boy's face lit with a smile. "Yeah."

Matt pushed down on the handles, raising the front wheels. Garrett squealed as they raced up the ramp into the stable. Within five minutes, the boy sat atop his mount, wonder in his eyes as he patted the paint horse. His mom held the reins while Matt spotted, and they moved around the arena.

A lump of emotion landed in Grace's throat as she watched. Matt was perfect for this job. Just a big kid himself, his compassion and intuition resonated with child and parent in a way she hadn't foreseen.

One by one, other volunteers, parents, and children arrived, and Matt handled it all with his customary easy-going nature. He assigned Grace to a young girl named Sadie who had no physical handicap. Though she didn't seem afraid of the horse, she didn't speak or smile no matter how much Grace tried to engage her. After several minutes of no verbal response, a thought lodged in her brain. She brought the horse to a stop. "Do you like to go fast, Sadie?"

At first her eyes widened, but then she nodded slowly.

Grace smiled. "It's a lot of fun, but you'll need to hold on tight. Can you do that?"

Again the girl nodded.

"Okay, here we go." She pulled on the rein, coaxing the horse into a trot and then into a lope, her eyes constantly on Sadie to make sure she was safe.

A smile broke out on the little girl's face, and she giggled.

When Grace brought the horse back down to walk a few minutes later, Sadie was all smiles. "That w-was f-fun." A laugh fell from her smiling lips.

Matt sauntered up, his mouth open in amazement. "Sadie, you've got a smile as big as Texas on your face." He faced Grace, his eyes flickering. For a long moment he said nothing, just studied her.

Her pulse quickened and she caught her lower lip between her teeth.

"Good work, Gracie."

"Thanks." She inhaled a shaky breath and turned her gaze back to Sadie. "Ready to do that again?"

"Yes!"

By the time the afternoon ended, Grace's heart was lighter than it had been in a long time. She unsaddled the last horse and moved her out to pasture.

Matt waved at a departing car and made his way toward her, the same indecipherable light flickering in his eyes. "Just so you know, you made great headway with Sadie. She'd all but closed up on everyone, including her grandmother who looks after her."

"Glad I could help, but I think I gained far more than I gave." She fell into step as they made their way to the pickup.

"I always leave here feeling that way. It's therapeutic to help these kids, and I'm gonna miss it over the next few weeks while we take a break for the holidays."

"When you start back up, please keep me in mind."

His smile ignited a flame in his eyes. "Will do."

They reached the driver's side of the old truck. Grace looked up at him, her heart pounding curiously.

Matt stepped closer and took hold of both her hands. "Thanks again, Gracie." He peered into her eyes in a way that left her exposed and vulnerable, but also completely unafraid. "You're going to make a wonderful mother someday."

The words lit a longing inside her that she'd never voiced until now. "I hope so. It's something I've wanted even longer than wanting to be an attorney."

His sandy eyes searched hers once more, digging deeper until she felt her heart would burst. He stepped closer, then reached around her and opened the pickup door. "See you later."

Disappointment engulfed her, but she found her voice. "Okay." Grace climbed in the truck and turned the key. As she pulled away, she checked the rearview mirror. Matt stared after her, frozen in one position until he at last disappeared from view.

Grace puzzled over her feelings, to decipher what had just happened. In one minute she thought he would kiss her, but something stopped him at the last minute. Then it hit. In a few minutes she had a date with Jason. Though she'd let it slip her mind, Matt had remembered. She punched the accelerator pedal. Unless she wanted to look and smell like a wild woman on tonight's date, she needed get home to shower and remove the knots from her snarled hair.

Papa glanced up from his recliner as she entered. "Did you have a good day?"

"Very much." She hurried past. "Sorry I don't have time to talk right now, but I have to get ready for my date."

He didn't reply, which was a good thing. No response meant no objection.

After a quick shower and fixing her face and hair, she carefully removed the hot pink dress Elena had given her from its hanger and slipped it over her head, the floaty fabric dancing at her knees. Her eyes caught a glimpse of her reflection in the mirror while she buckled the dainty straps of her shoes, and she was amazed at the transformation. The day at the ranch had given her a glow that flushed her cheeks and brightened her eyes. Must be the fresh air and exercise, or was it something else?

Butterflies fluttered in her stomach as she reached for her brush and pulled it through the snarls. This evening felt different than the business lunches she'd shared with Jason, but no matter how attractive he was, she had to remember her underlying purpose—to uncover his relationship with Elena. The doorbell rang, and the butterflies danced faster.

Papa answered the door, and through the paper-thin walls of the house, she heard him speak. "You must be Mr. Dent. Graciela has mentioned you. Please come in."

Grace steadied her nerves with a slow breath, snatched the sparkly gold evening bag that matched her shoes from the bed, and stepped down the hallway with a forced smile on her face. She'd hoped to have time to do something with the file she'd confiscated earlier that day, but it would just have to wait.

As she entered the room, the conversation between Jason and her father came to an abrupt stop. Papa's mouth hung open, but Jason, dressed in a black suit, made his way to her, lifted her hand by the fingers, and planted a kiss not on the back, but in her palm, then curled her fingers around it. "You look lovely, Grace."

The butterflies moved to her heart, racing helter-skelter between the beats of her pulse. "Thank you."

Suddenly Papa was all motion. "You two will have a beautiful evening. *Buenas noches!*" With his parting words zinging in flight, Papa hurried her and Jason through the doorway and into the chilly night air.

For dinner, Jason took her to a reservations-only establishment. He steered his sleek car beneath a burgundy awning and strode to the passenger side to open her door. A young man in black slacks and burgundy jacket seated himself in the car and pulled away to park.

Once inside, Grace marveled at the surroundings. Several fireplaces divided the large area into intimate seating arrangements. The fire hissed and popped as it encased the room with a woody fragrance. Candles flickered from every table, where white linen tablecloths provided the perfect backdrop for crystal goblets and gold-rimmed china. "This is gorgeous." She longed for more eloquent words, but none came to mind.

Jason laughed softly and placed a hand against the small of her back. "My table is over here."

His table? Did he eat here that often? Who with? All these questions and more invaded her thoughts as they traversed the plush carpet, sudden fear sparking in her mind. Never had she felt so out of her league.

The handsome defense attorney proved to be the perfect gentleman all evening, and conversation flowed easily. Grace relaxed in his company and enjoyed the exquisite evening. Later, as she finished off a piece of cheesecake, she leaned back in her chair and sighed. "Thank you for a wonderful evening. I've had such a great time."

He smiled, both dimples showing. "I'm glad you enjoyed it, Graciela."

Her eyebrows rose at the use of her Spanish name.

"Hope you don't mind if I use your full name. It's lovely."

She only nodded. Normally she would have objected, but her name did sound rather beautiful with his smooth British accent.

"I must say you've never appeared quite as dazzling as you do tonight, and I'm feeling a little overwhelmed. Your beauty has cast a spell on me." His words flowed like amber honey.

Her heart pounded, and heat climbed from her neck to her cheeks. Did he really find her dazzling? She gave her head a shake to unclutter her mind. "May I ask you a question?"

His eyelids contracted, veiling his eyes beneath dark brows. "Certainly."

"Do you know Elena Delgado on a personal level?"

At first he appeared slightly taken aback, but he quickly masked it with a smile. "We've spoken of course, but the answer to your question depends on your definition of 'personal.'" He laughed softly, leaned close enough for her to feel the warmth of his breath on her face, and planted a kiss on her lips.

A sudden awareness that they weren't alone brought Grace to her senses. She pulled back, her thoughts confused.

"Well, fancy seeing you two here." Andy stood at their table, Trish clutching one arm. Neither looked particularly happy. Then they moved to one side, and Matt stepped forward. Even in the dim candlelight his eyes registered hurt.

13

Grace grabbed two fists of hair and pulled. Where was that file? It had been on her dresser this morning when she left for Sunday school, but she'd searched her room twice, and it was nowhere to be found.

Panic squeezed her heart. It had to be here somewhere. She needed the file to give to Andy, to explain what she'd done and why she'd done it. The sermon in church had been about David's sin with Bathsheba, about how people tended to justify and rationalize their wrongdoing. Convicted by her actions of the previous morning, she'd struggled through the rest of the service.

Grace rubbed a hand across her face. Maybe Papa had seen the file and moved it, but it wasn't like him to come into her room. She scurried to the kitchen, her shoes a-clop against the tile. Where was he anyway? She glanced around, hoping to spy the missing folder, but instead glimpsed a note scrawled in Papa's handwriting and held to the fridge with a magnet advertising the number of a local pizza delivery.

Graciela, I have decided to go away for a while to visit your brothers and other family over Thanksgiving. Mr. Cates is taking care of the animals, and I've left control of the restaurant to the assistant manager. Love, Papa

With shaky hands, she re-read the note. No mention of her joining him or when he'd be back. No number where he could be reached. How like him to let her know in such an impersonal way. Now what?

She laid the note on the counter and brought both palms to her face. The best use of her time was to call Andy and ask to meet him. Surely he'd understand and wouldn't think she'd gone completely bonkers. Hands still shaking, she lifted the phone to her ear. It rang several times, but no one answered. She'd just have to try again later.

Grace drifted to the couch and plopped down, her thoughts on Matt. Guilt dripped through her like a leaky faucet. She hadn't meant to hurt his feelings, and hadn't expected Jason's kiss. All of it was beyond her control. So why was she still so bothered? She traipsed back to the phone and dialed Matt's cell number.

"Hello." Even through the phone line, he sounded dismal.

"Hey, Matt, it's Gracie."

"Gracie?" His voice changed. "Is something wrong?"

"No, why?"

A huff of exasperation sounded. "Well, it could be because you never call me."

"Well, never's a pretty strong word. I called to see if you wanted to get together this afternoon for a talk."

The line silenced for a minute. "Sure, I guess so."

She grimaced. Judging by the sound of his voice, he was still hurt. "It's a pretty day." She glanced out the window at blue skies and puffy clouds. "How about the lake?"

"Great idea!" The excitement in his voice escalated. "I found an awesome trail out there not too long ago that's really pretty this time of year. Without the leaves on the trees you can see the bluffs on the opposite shoreline really well. You still remember the way to Andy and Trish's lake house?"

Just the mention of the place brought a smile to her face. "How could I forget? Some of my happiest memories took place there."

Again the line grew quiet. A more sober-sounding Matt finally spoke, a new hesitancy in his voice. "Is it okay if I just meet you there? I might decide to stay for a few days since the holidays are coming up and Andy took his family on vacation."

"Vacation?"

"Yeah, he took them to Florida for Thanksgiving."

"When will he be back?" She nibbled her fingernail.

"Sorry, he'll be gone 'til next weekend. Poor guy needs it, too. Said something about having to work over the holidays."

The guilt returned, only tripled. Even in her attempt to protect Andy by taking the prosecutor position, she hadn't thought through how the decision would affect him in the short term. She was responsible for the extra work he now shouldered when he should be relaxing and enjoying his family. "What time do you want to meet?"

"Gimme an hour."

"Okay." Grace hung up the phone and went to change clothes. She'd just finished tying her shoes when the phone jangled. Probably Matt. What had he forgotten this time?

She raced down the hallway and answered the phone. "Hey, Matt."

"This isn't Matt." Even through the phone, Grace discerned the anger in Elena's voice. "Apparently you still haven't learned."

Normally, she would have apologized immediately, but she'd had all the back and forth behavior she could take from this woman. "Matt and I are friends, and it's none of your business." Let the chips fall where they may.

"I've already told you it is if you intend to work for me."

Grace bolted her jaws shut to resist a comment about losing her job and the false allegations against Andy. Until she could talk to him personally, she'd best not play that hand.

"In fact, I'd also like to know why you went out with Jason Dent last night."

A tight frown knotted her brows. How would Elena know unless she was having her followed?

The woman lit into her, hot with anger, her razor-sharp words slicing through Grace time and time again, until when she at last finished her tirade, all that was left of her psyche was a wounded mess. "You'd better watch your step, missy. You don't know who you're messing with." Elena ended her outburst by banging the phone against the receiver.

Grace sat unmoving for several minutes, trying to piece together her emotions so she could figure out what to do next. She wandered to the window and looked out at the once pretty day. Now it had turned dark and blustery. Was Elena out there somewhere just waiting for her? Did she dare meet Matt as she'd promised?

The phone shrilled and Grace jumped, one hand to her chest to slow her racing heart. If it was Elena could she emotionally handle another scathing round of abuse? She squared her shoulders and moved to the phone. "Hello?"

No answer.

"Hello?"

Still nothing.

She hung up and backed away. Then sudden determination straightened her spine. She refused to let an emotional terrorist keep her captive in her own house. Besides, she needed Matt, needed the comfort of his arms and his words of wisdom. Without further consideration, Grace grabbed her purse and headed for the pickup, locking the back door behind her.

Intermittent tears meandered down Grace's face as she drove to the lake, her mind rehashing Elena's hurtful words. Why did she let the woman get to her like this? She angrily brushed tears from her face, but some managed to escape and slid to her lips, leaving salty residue.

Grace riveted her eyes to the road, which grew more difficult to see in the sheets of pouring rain, but she also checked her rearview mirror frequently, just to make sure she wasn't being followed. A swift wave of fear splashed over her, pulling her beneath murky torrents, and she slammed on the brakes, screeching and sliding to a halt on the wet pavement. What was she doing? Hadn't Elena made it perfectly clear that she was to stay away from Matt? And here she was running straight to him.

She buried her head in her hands. *Oh, God, help me. How can I help Elena get through this without losing my sanity?*

Forgive her.

But how? How can I forgive when she's been so hurtful without reason? The woman's words were poisoned arrows, and God expected her to forgive? The answer hammered its way into her head. Yes.

With a shaky breath, Grace resumed the drive, battling a constant threat of tears. Thankfully, the Tyler cabin soon appeared, bringing with it a rush of comfort. She pulled her coat over her head and made a run for it, water soaking her feet as she sloshed through puddles.

Matt met her at the door. "There you are. I was starting to get worried. I sure didn't expect the weather to do this."

Grace released the coat from around her head, but kept her gaze lowered to hide her swollen eyes.

He gently lifted her chin with his finger and immediately swept her into his arms. "What's wrong, sweetheart?"

Tears were unstoppable. Like the torrents of rain that bucketed from the sky, she sobbed uncontrollably.

"Hey," said Matt in a soothing tone, "it's okay." He rubbed a hand across her back. "Let it out, Gracie."

After a few minutes, her tears finally spent, she backed up and wiped away tears with her fingertips. "Sorry, Matt. I didn't mean for that to happen."

He tipped her chin with one hand and used the other to whisk away more tears. "No apologies necessary. I'm glad you felt comfortable enough to let it out." A tender smile crossed his face and lingered in his eyes. "From the looks of it, you've been holding that in for a while."

Grace laughed through misty eyes then scanned the room. A floral-designed box of tissues sat on a table near the couch. She scurried across the room to grab one before her nose dripped.

Matt followed close behind, his eyes full of concern. "You feel comfortable enough to tell me what that was all about?"

A shivering sigh fell from her lips. "There's something wrong with Elena, Matt. I know she's needy, and I want to help. I want to be God's grace to her, but . . . " Her voice cracked, and another wave of tears flooded her face.

He took hold of her hand and pulled her to the couch. "We need to talk about it, but first you need to get dried off before you catch pneumonia. Sit here while I get a towel." A few seconds later he returned, but rather than hand her the towel, he bent low and dried her hair. Then he knelt in front of her and removed her puddle-soaked shoes, wrapped the towel around each foot, and massaged gently.

She closed her eyes and leaned her head back against the couch, breathing deeply, relishing the relaxation that flowed throughout her stressed-out system. The next thing she knew, she awoke in a prone position, safely tucked beneath a thick quilt. A thin streak of light peeked from beneath the door that lead to the kitchen, and tantalizing aromas wafted in the air. Grace tuned her ears to the popping and sizzling sounds from the kitchen, as well as Matt's happy hum that soon broke into words. "Oh-oh-oh, we've got to love one another."

Grace threw back the covers and stood. How long had she slept? She peeked through the blinds, startled that night had fallen, and moved to the kitchen, intrigued by the catchy tune. Not wanting to interrupt, she quietly opened the wooden door and watched as he cooked and crooned. A smile worked its way to her face. There was more to Matt Tyler than most people gave him credit for. More than she'd recognized. "What song are you singing?"

He wheeled about, a happy glow on his face. "You're awake!"

"Sorry I fell asleep on you." Grace stepped to the stove.

His eyes softened and he swept her hair behind one ear. "You're exhausted, Gracie. I'm glad you got the rest. Hope my singing didn't disturb you."

"Not at all. What song is it? I don't recognize it."

Matt shrugged slightly. "A little something I wrote."

"Really? I'd love to hear all of it sometime."

A boyish excitement shone from his features. "Maybe after dinner?"

"Sure." Her heart did a queer flip-flop in her chest. Time with him felt so natural. "Speaking of dinner, it smells delicious." Her stomach rumbled in anticipation.

"Almost done."

"Good, I'm famished."

He cast a sideways glance while he manned the skillet. "Remind me to add that to the list of things I wanna talk to you about."

Normally, she would've taken offense to the statement, but for some reason, tonight she welcomed it. Relying on her own insight didn't appear to be working well, and any advice he could give would be appreciated.

Grace retrieved plates and glasses from the cabinets and set the table. Within a few minutes, she and Matt sat at the small table, now loaded with grilled fish, roasted potatoes, and steamed asparagus. She surveyed all the food and shook her head in disbelief. Matt had always cooked well, but when had he learned to cook like this? "You've outdone yourself."

In an unforeseen move, he took her hand and brought it to his lips, planting a soft kiss. "For you, my lady."

Her pulse quickened, and she quickly averted her eyes so he wouldn't read her traitorous thoughts. What was happening?

Matt jumped up from his chair, one finger in the air. "Forgot something. Be right back." He moved to the living room, and a few minutes later a bluesy music sounded from the stereo. He reappeared, and after blessing the food, ladled food on her plate, and then fixed his own.

She tried to make sense of the emotions twisting throughout her insides, but to no avail. "I love this music. Someone you know?"

He looked up, eyes wide. "Guess you could say that. Someone you know, too."

"Who?"

Matt leaned his head to one side. "Me." His eyes searched her face.

There was no containing her shock. He was good. Not just okay, but really, really good. She felt the need to say something, but words escaped her, so she focused her attention on the food and took a bite of the fish, moist and flaky on the inside, with a slight crunch on the outside. Grace closed her eyes, her mouth savoring the food and her ears savoring the music, as realization slammed into her. She'd misjudged him, not just now, but two summers ago, and had actually believed he was somehow beneath her. Her breath stuck in her throat. How had she been so wrong?

"You okay, Gracie?" Matt's blonde brows puckered in concern.

"Yeah, I'm just feeling a little overwhelmed." And a lot guilty.

"About?"

"Everything." She expected a rebuttal, or at least more questions, but when she glanced up, he was focused on his plate, obviously lost in deep thoughts of his own.

He glanced up. "So tell me more about your boss."

Grace stiffened. How much should she reveal? Elena's last tongue-lashing made her fearful not only for her own safety, but also for his.

"It's okay, Gracie. You're safe with me."

She felt safe, as evidenced by the impromptu nap. But safe in sharing her suspicions? Not until she had solid proof. Grace wiped her mouth with a paper towel. "Professionally, she's top-notch. I've learned a lot from watching her in action."

"But?"

She forked a bite of asparagus and considered her words. "Elena swings back and forth faster than anyone I've ever seen. One minute she's kind and friendly, the next she's chopping me into fish food. And she's so calculating."

Matt's expression clouded over. "Does she exhibit signs of possessiveness?"

The warnings to stay away from Matt, Andy, and Jason. The way she had of dictating every moment of her life, even on weekends. Grace nodded.

He frowned more, his eyebrows so wrinkled his eyes almost disappeared. After a brief silence, Matt's tone and expression abruptly changed. "I've only been around her briefly, but with job stress and being sole provider for a handicapped child, I'm sure it affects her behavior."

Everything he mentioned, she'd already considered. But Elena's behavior went way beyond the norm. "I agree she's under stress, but. . . "

"Gracie, are you sure it's worth working for her?" Matt's face held dark thunder.

Worth it? If it meant protecting Andy, then yes. "I've already told you. It's something I have to do."

He enclosed her hand in his. "Just promise you'll take care of yourself. Anytime she starts to unload, put up a shield."

Her throat knotted, making speech difficult. "Easier said than done."

"Yeah, but I know you. You'll take her words to heart, allowing them to hurt you over and over again."

He'd done it again. Read her like a book he perused on a frequent basis. She sighed. "You're right, but how do I stop thinking about it? It's like a cancer that eats away at me."

Matt forked food in his mouth. "You need a rubber band."

A giggle erupted. "What?"

His face lit with a smile. "A rubber band—you know those stretchy—"

"I know what they are, but I've never known that to be a remedy for overthinking. Did you pick that up in Psych 101?"

He laughed out loud. "It may have been 201. Put the rubber band around your wrist. When you catch your thoughts returning to her hurtful comments, snap the rubber band and think 'stop.' It's basically just reconditioning."

"It's worth a try." Especially if it kept her from ruminating on Elena's razor-sharp words.

"Let me know how it works."

"Will do." A perfect segue opportunity. "Now that we've discussed my problems, mind if I ask you a question?"

Matt skewed his lips. "Don't know. The way you phrased that makes it sound like I have a problem."

A laugh bubbled out. "Oh, so just because you counsel others with their problems means you have none of your own?"

He chuckled. "Touché, but I'm not the one who's practically perfect in every way." He wiped his mouth with a wink and a smile. "So what's my problem, counselor?"

"I know you got your feelings hurt last night, and I wanted a chance to explain. I didn't intend for Jason to kiss me."

He shook his head. "No need to explain. I can't really blame the guy. You looked gorgeous."

"Thanks." Conversation lapsed, and the rest of the meal was eaten mostly in silence, with only polite small talk. Afterwards, Matt washed the dishes while she dried and put them away. Again she marveled at how natural and unforced they were together, a cohesive rhythm and harmony between them she couldn't explain.

Once they were done, Grace hung her towel over the edge of the sink and faced Matt, who gazed at her in a way that made her heart gallop. "You promised to sing the song you wrote. And by the way, I loved the music during dinner. I had no idea you were so good."

His expression didn't change, but his intense gaze made her feel that he peered straight into her soul. "Glad you enjoyed it. Why don't you have a seat while I grab my guitar?"

Her thoughts whirled as she moved to the couch. Had she unknowingly overlooked who he was on the inside because she couldn't see past his wrinkled clothes and boyish behavior? She'd just taken a seat when he returned, his guitar in hand. Her mind flashed to the summer over two years ago when they'd relaxed around a campfire on a church outing and sung worship songs. Heavy disappointment draped her heart when he took a seat in a chair across the room rather than next to her.

He smiled. "The song I sang earlier is one I wrote last year. It's been picked up by a group out of Nashville."

"Seriously?" Her mouth swung open.

"Yeah. Pretty cool, huh?" His tone held no arrogance, only joy. He moved his capo to a fret near the tuning pegs and launched into the rollicking, bluesy song he'd sung earlier.

The lyrics spoke of the importance of people loving each other, and she couldn't keep from harmonizing the last time through the chorus. How long had it been since she'd allowed herself the simple pleasure of singing? Grace applauded when the song ended. "I love it, Matt! It's so catchy. And the lyrics are Christian, but not in a preachy way, you know?"

He beamed. "That's the best compliment ever. I don't wanna cram religion down people's throats. That only turns them off. I wanna sneak in the back door, to teach the principles Jesus taught, to help them have a relationship with Him."

Fascination captured her full attention, like she truly saw him for the first time.

"Sorry. I'm blabbering."

"No you're not." She lowered her gaze. "Matt, I owe you a big apology for misjudging you."

He said nothing, his gaze unwavering.

She swallowed against the lump in her throat. "I've let really petty and superficial things color my opinion of you and I'm so very sorry. Not only are you able to read people well and counsel them, but you're a really great guy with amazing talent."

Without a word, he rose to his feet, carried his guitar to the bedroom, and stayed.

Grace gathered her things. Had she embarrassed him? Had her admission made him decide she wasn't worth his time?

"Going somewhere?" Matt entered the room, a frown on his face.

"I probably should be getting back." She looked back at him, her coat in her hands. "Sorry if I said something to upset you."

In a heartbeat, he stood directly in front of her, his hands on her shoulders. "You didn't upset me, Gracie. You answered my prayer."

Before she could open her mouth to speak, he claimed her lips with his own.

14

For a long moment, Matt lost himself in the kiss, not quite believing he was finally kissing her, or that she was kissing him back. But fear crept in, and he pulled away. The last thing he wanted was to take advantage of her vulnerability. One glance at her was all it took to see the wisdom of his decision. She looked ready to collapse, confused and bewildered. He smoothed her hair. "That was beyond nice, but we need to talk."

She broke free from his gaze and nodded.

Matt held her hand to reassure her. Gracie was the type to over-analyze everything anyone said or did, and then she internalized it, turning even innocent comments and gestures into deadly weapons against herself. More than likely a response held over from her traumatic childhood.

He led her to the couch and sat down beside her, tilting her chin until she met his gaze. "I don't wanna scare you away, sweetheart, but I have to tell you how I feel. I'm in love with you and have been since that summer two years ago, even after you told me you only wanted to be friends and even after I thought I'd gotten over you."

Her eyes held a dark softness that threatened to pull him under. In a split second the softness turned to fear.

Hurt slashed into his heart. "Why are you afraid, Gracie? Don't you trust me?"

Gracie pulled her hand away and rested her face in both palms. She opened her mouth to speak, but no words came.

He engulfed her in a hug, rubbing a hand along her back. "It's okay, sweetie, let it out. It's safe for you to say whatever you need to say, even—" He closed his eyes against the ensuing pain. "—even if it's something you know I don't wanna hear."

They remained in the embrace a long while, Gracie clinging to his neck as if her life depended on it. Finally, she pulled away, streams of tears coursing down her cheeks.

His heart fell. This wasn't good. He forced a smile and nodded to assure her.

"My life's in such chaos right now, Matt." Her words came out choked and broken. "I want to be able to say the same things to you, but I'm so confused, and you deserve better than me telling you one thing now and something else later when things have hopefully calmed down."

The words churned in his gut, but she spoke from an honest place. "I'll accept that, Gracie, but I want you to know I'll still be here waiting. Take all the time you need."

A half sob sounded in her throat, a sound that tore at his already shredded heart.

"What's bothering you, sweetheart? Please tell me."

She said nothing, and tears continued to fall.

"Does it have to do with Elena?"

Gracie remained reticent.

"With Jason?"

Again, she didn't speak, but now chewed her bottom lip. Finally, she shook her head.

An inner alarm went off in Matt's head. She wasn't telling the truth, but who was she covering for—Jason, her boss, or both? He hadn't bought Jason's act since day one, but in many ways Gracie's relationship with her boss bothered him even more.

She fidgeted away from him, and he laid his head against the back cushion. If his suspicions were correct, the Delgado lady could have serious, even dangerous, psychological issues. But Gracie was a worrier, and he couldn't have her paralyzed by fear. That's why he'd tried so hard to act like she was worried for no reason. He started to ask another question, but changed his mind at how pale she'd grown. "You feel okay?"

She released a heavy sigh. "I'm just really tired. I think I need to go home and rest if that's okay."

"Of course it's okay. Sorry if I kept you too long. I'm just trying to find a way to help you out of the chaos and confusion you mentioned earlier."

Her lips curved into a faint smile. "Thanks, Matt, but I'll be fine. I just need time to make sense of things. Right now I'm still adjusting to the new job. I'm sure that's a big part of it." She stood and plodded to the door.

Matt followed. "You know Andy would take you back in a heartbeat, don't you?"

She nodded sadly as she donned her coat and buttoned it up. "Yes, but this is something I have to do."

He opened his mouth in rebuttal, but she silenced him with an uplifted hand.

"Before you lecture me, this job has nothing to do with vindicating my mother's death."

Matt took in the depth of sorrow in her eyes. His Gracie was on a mission—a mission that didn't include him—and knowing her tenacity, she wouldn't rest until it was completed.

He ushered her to the old beat-up truck and watched her drive away. Matt ran a hand across his mouth. Watching her leave was sheer torture, but he had to trust that God cared for her when he couldn't. Out of nowhere, a rush of joy splashed over him. At least there was hope for them now. Gracie hadn't said 'no,' just 'not now.' He rubbed his hands together to warm them, breathed in the rain-washed air entered the cabin.

Maybe he should look into the possibility of a promise ring for her Christmas gift, just to show her how serious and committed he was. As he opened the screened door, his cell phone buzzed.

"Hey, Matt. Derek here. Interested in coming on the road with us over the holidays? We're booked solid through New Year's."

Why was a patio chair sitting beneath her window?

Grace stopped in her tracks, her eyes darting around the dimly-lit backyard. The glow from the security light cast a soft glow, but also cast really deep shadows. Did she dare walk to the shed to peer behind it?

After a few seconds to think through her options, she walked casually to the chair and returned it to its position beneath the table, casting a brief glance toward the shed. Too dark to see if anyone was there. Grace fumbled with her keys as she made her way to the back door. She located the right one and inserted it in the back door knob. Something brushed against her leg, and she nearly fell off the back porch trying to get away.

"Meow." Millie sauntered toward her again and butted her head against Grace's shin.

"You scared me to death, you silly cat." She bent low and lifted Millie to her arms. While Grace scratched behind the cat's ears, her eyes flitted around the backyard. "Did you miss me, kitty?"

Grace turned the knob and quickly flipped on the light switch, relieved to find everything the way she'd left it. She dropped Millie to the floor. The phone shrilled, and she startled. *Settle down, Grace. It's only the phone.* She cradled the phone in the crook of her neck as she slipped off her coat. "Hello?"

"Well, hello. I've been trying to reach you all afternoon." Jason's cultured voice was unmistakable.

"Hi, Jason. Sorry, I wasn't here when you called. I was out with a friend."

"Anyone I know?"

Why did it matter? "Yes. Matt Tyler."

The line grew deathly quiet. "I see. Well, I was calling to see if you'd allow me to take you to dinner again tomorrow night. I'd make it later in the week, but I'm leaving on Tuesday to visit my family for the holidays."

She moistened her lips, remembering Matt's tender kiss. No, she was finally gaining some perspective on how she felt about Matt, and she wouldn't let anything or anyone—including someone as handsome as Jason Dent—mess that up. "I can't, Jason, but maybe after you return." If only to question him further about Elena, since he'd managed to evade the question the other night. That would also allow her time for a one-on-one chat with Elena.

"Surely you can squeeze me into your schedule for dinner. You have to eat some time."

He clearly wasn't accustomed to being told no. "Thanks for the offer, but I'll have to take a rain check."

"Fine." He clipped the word short. "Happy Thanksgiving." The phone went dead.

Grace hung up. She hadn't meant to upset him. Maybe she should meet with him to tell him face-to-face to let him know she wasn't interested in anything but friendship. But it would have to wait until after Thanksgiving. Right now, all she wanted to do was shower and get to bed early. She needed all the sleep she could get to confront Elena with her suspicions in the morning at work.

The house was oddly quiet without Papa there. Normally by now, he'd be leaned back in his recliner, the TV remote in one hand as he flipped between various channels. Offering a silent prayer for his safety, she sauntered down the darkened hallway toward the bathroom. The fluorescent light over the sink flickered on with its normal hum, casting long shadows around the dark-paneled room. She twisted the hot water knob and plugged the bathtub drain.

A few minutes later, she soaked in the warm sudsy water, the tension in her neck and shoulders slowly ebbing away. Her thoughts turned to Matt. How had she been so wrong about him? She brought fingertips to her lips. The kiss they'd shared had left her mind and heart spinning, but in a good way.

Grace looked toward the ceiling, and released a breath. Maybe her planned meeting with Elena tomorrow would set the record straight, and she'd feel better about allowing herself more time with him. But it wouldn't be that easy. Something told her Elena wouldn't take kindly to her questions or comments.

The phone sounded from down the hallway, but she didn't move to answer it. Surely whoever it was would call back later. But what if it was Papa? On the third ring, she stood, wrapped a towel around her and dripped down the hall.

"Hello?"

No answer.

"Is anyone there?" Probably just a wrong number. She'd just made it back to the tub when the phone rang again. Once more she traipsed down the hall, but again no one answered. Okay, this was getting a little creepy.

Grace glanced at the clock. It was already almost ten-thirty, and she hated to wake Matt over something as stupid as a prank phone call. And why call the police? What could they do about it? What if it was just Elena's strange way of keeping tabs on her?

She returned the phone to the receiver, shivering from cold in the drafty old house. By the time she made it to the bathroom, the water had already lost its warmth, so she drained the tub and put on her flannel pajamas. An idea filtered through her brain before she crawled into bed. The phone calls and the misplaced chair might have a simple explanation, but they also might not. Without Papa here, it was better to be safe than sorry.

Grace slipped on her house shoes and shuffled to the kitchen, digging in the junk drawer until she found what she wanted. She opted not to put on her coat, but left the front door open while she hurriedly did what she'd never done before in all the years she'd lived in Miller's Creek—padlocked the gate.

Restlessness plagued her sleep, her mind preoccupied with the events of the day. She'd just drifted off when the ringing phone broke the silence. Grace bounced to a sitting position, her heart pounding. The phone continued to ring, but she refused to answer. Instead she plopped back down in the bed and covered her head with the spare pillow. The ringing eventually stopped.

Early the next morning, a squeaky noise at the window near her bed awakened her. Grace forced her eyes open to peer at the clock. Only five. The sound resumed. Still half asleep, she threw off the covers and padded over to peek between the blinds. On a hasty impulse, she yanked on the cords and pulled the blinds up in one swift move. There was no one there, but what she saw sent fear coursing through her veins.

While she slept, someone had drawn a face in the condensation. The crooked mouth drooped downward, and where the eyes were drawn, water had pooled and now made a slow crawl down the face, like ice-cold tears.

Grace jumped back and released the cord, the blinds crashing to closed position. Further sleep no longer an option, she fixed a large pot of coffee and tried to gather her thoughts for the upcoming meeting with Elena. She left the house thirty minutes earlier than usual, all for the purpose of arriving early to talk to her boss. But as she hurried to the gate to unlock it, her mouth gaped open.

During the night, someone had yanked several pickets off the front fence, and the mailbox had been ripped from its post. Who would do something like this, and why? Her mind instantly flew to Elena. Would she really stoop to scare tactics?

Grace cleaned up the mess the best she could, deciding to call Ernie after work. At least he could offer her advice as to what she should do. Soon she was on her way to Morganville, and arrived in plenty of time. Her backbone and her resolve solidified as she entered and peered toward Elena's office where a shaft of light shone from the cracked door. Good, she was here. Grace deposited her things on the desk, then proceeded to Elena's office and rapped on the door.

"Come in."

She prayed as she turned the knob. *God, give me strength to say what needs to be said. Help me to speak the truth in love. Give me a discerning spirit.*

Elena perched behind her giant desk with pen in hand, once more the picture of businesswoman perfection, but she glanced up with a frown when Grace entered. "You're here early."

"Yes, I need to speak with you. Is now a good time?"

"Actually I was just on my way to Harry's office. Why don't you join me?" She made her way to the door.

So it was starting already. Grace followed her down the hallway to the attorney's office, certain Elena was about to let her have it.

Some of the anger had dissipated from Harry Bridges' face since Friday, but he still looked unhappy. He did shake both their hands before he motioned for them to sit.

Elena, very much in control, gazed directly at him. "Harry, I want to apologize for what happened on Friday, but I can assure you it was a rookie mistake."

Grace's mouth fell open, and she struggled to find words.

The petite attorney continued. "Grace did some research for me and gave it to me on Friday. I assumed she'd already shared it with the defense, or I would have never used it."

He considered her words for a prolonged silence. "So what do you think I should do, Elena? This left the district attorney's office with a huge black eye and made you look thoroughly incompetent." He shifted his gaze to Grace for a moment, then looked at Elena.

She held his gaze. "I think we should just chalk it up to a rookie mistake and move on from there." She glanced at Grace. "I'm sure Grace has learned her lesson."

Grace still couldn't find her voice.

He eventually nodded. "Okay, but the next time something like this happens, you're both in danger of losing your jobs."

Elena stood and reached a hand across the desk. "Thanks, Harry. I can assure you it won't happen again."

Before she knew what happened, Grace found herself once more in Elena's office, her thoughts spinning.

The woman gestured to one of the comfy chairs that faced her desk. "Now what was it you wanted to see me about?"

A hot spark ignited a fire inside her. Elena had the audacity to ask that question after her cutting remarks yesterday and the big lie she'd just told? Grace somehow managed to control her volume. "I'd like to talk to you about several things actually."

"Such as?" Elena maintained her innocent expression.

Grace's carefully rehearsed script flew out the window, and she struggled between letting her have it and holding back. "Well, first I want to say that you're very good at your job. It's been a privilege to work with you." Grace cringed inwardly. Her attempt to be kind was making her sound like a major wimp.

Elena smiled. "Why, thank you, Grace. I hope you know I feel the same way about you. In spite of the mix up, I'm very pleased with the research you did on the Simmons case. Which reminds me—I have a list of a few things I could use your help on." She snagged a legal pad from the left side of her ultra-organized desk, and handed it to Grace. "I need this research done before next Monday.

Grace skimmed the list. Completing the requests would eat up her entire holiday.

"I know it's a lot, but I'll be spending some much-needed time with Mama and Jessie. I knew you wouldn't mind."

"I have plans over the holidays, too." Sleep, and lots of it. She glanced down. It was now or never. "The way you speak to me is verbally abusive, and I've had all I can take."

Elena's mouth gaped uncharacteristically, but she snapped it shut, flames in her eyes. "So you're quitting on me, is that what you've come to say? It figures that you're a spineless quitter. I should've seen it coming." Scorn colored her tone.

Grace catapulted to her feet, her temples throbbing, thin cracks in her patience. "You're wrong. I didn't come to quit, I came to tell you I won't put up with your outbursts and your demands on my free time any longer. I'll continue to do my best at this job, but not at the expense of my peace of mind."

The petite attorney rose to her feet, both palms on her desk. "That's not the way it works around here. As my employee, you'll put up with whatever I choose to give you." Her voice held a chill.

Grace continued before she lost her nerve. "While I'm appreciative of not losing my job, you just told Harry Bridges a pack of lies. You gave me that research on the Simmons case last Thursday. I worked on it at home and gave you the information as soon as I got to the courthouse the next morning. You didn't tell me to give it to the defense, nor did I have time to do so. I think you threw the case on purpose."

Elena stalked slowly from behind her desk, until she stood eye-to-eye with Grace. "You have absolutely no proof."

Grace suddenly came to her senses. God hadn't called her here to start a fight. "Look, Elena, the last thing I want is to get you in trouble, but I believe with all my heart that you need professional help. I know you're under a lot of stress with your job and family, but you erupt over the smallest thing. Sometimes I wonder if you even remember all the hurtful things you say." She released a sigh as she maintained eye contact. If only she could voice her objection to the false accusations against Andy, but she couldn't, at least not without incriminating herself, something she had no doubt Elena would use against her. Better to focus on the Simmons case. "I don't know what you're involved in with the mistrial, but it's not too late to set it right."

Elena didn't speak, but relaxed her posture and glided to the window. After several long minutes, she faced Grace. "I apologize for my outburst yesterday on the phone. It was only out of concern for you that I asked you to stay away from Jason and Matt. As for your other allegations, they're completely false." Her face was a blank slate, and her voice held neither warmth nor chill. "Please work on that list for today and tomorrow. I don't expect you to do it over the holidays. Now if you'll excuse me, I have an appointment." Without further comment, Elena gathered her purse and sashayed out the door.

Grace wearily trudged to her desk and attacked the work. If nothing else, the massive amount of research Elena had given her provided a way to focus her thoughts away from her troubles, but she snapped a rubber band on her wrist for good measure.

All day she worked, only stopping to eat her brown bag sandwich and apple before gluing her eyes to the computer once more.

At the end of the day, she reached a logical stopping point, leaned back to eye the legal pad she'd filled with notes, and scanned Elena's list. She could finish the rest tonight and tomorrow. With a yawn, she stretched and eyed the clock. Already seven o'clock. As she made her way to the exit, a shaft of light glinted from the barely opened door of Elena's office. Curious, Grace crossed to the doorway and peeked. Everything was just as it had been this morning. Had she been gone all day?

An odd sensation fluttered in her stomach. Something wasn't right. She donned her coat, gathered her things, and hurried out the door. Dimly lit with red emergency lights, the hallway of the old building felt creepy at this time of day. Grace scrounged in her purse for her keys, rounded a corner, and ran squarely into someone.

She jumped back, one hand to her chest, surprised to see Jason. "You scared the wits out of me! Why are you here?"

He placed both hands on her shoulders. "Sorry to have startled you. I tried calling you at home, but when no one answered I figured you were still here. Ready for dinner?"

Obviously he hadn't accepted her 'no' from last night. Grace shook her head. "Sorry, but I can't." She held up her brief case for evidence. "I have tons of work to do before the holidays."

"Poor darling. At least let me treat you to a nice dinner."

"Maybe some other time." Grace started down the stairs.

He fell into step beside her, but didn't speak until they reached the street. She half-expected him to once more launch into why she needed to eat dinner with him. Instead, he turned toward her briefly. "I'll be seeing you." With nothing further, he strode toward the parking lot on the other side of the building.

Grace puzzled over his odd behavior all the way home. As she drove up to the house, she glanced in the direction of the fence and braked to a sudden stop. Both the fence and mailbox had been repaired, as though the scene that greeted her earlier was only be a figment of her imagination.

She steered into the driveway and stepped to the front to gaze at the fence once more, her jaw slightly unhinging as she ran a hand over the replaced pickets. Next she made her way to the mailbox and gathered the day's mail. What was going on? Who would cause the damage then return to the scene of the crime in broad daylight to repair it? After a brief search through her purse, she located the padlock, closed the gate, and snapped the lock into place. Would she be met with the same results in the morning? If so, she wouldn't hesitate to call Ernie this time.

Dazed, she made her way to the back, her jangling keys at the ready. As she glanced around the backyard, her brain and pulse hit overdrive at the same time. The patio chair once more sat in the same position beneath her bedroom window. Heart pounding, she hurried to the door and glanced down to see Millie sprawled at an odd angle on the porch.

"Hey, kitty. You ready for some dinner?"

Millie didn't move. Grace froze for a moment, her heart thumping and her breath suspended. In what seemed like slow motion she reached down to touch the cat's soft fur, but immediately yanked her hand back. She slowly turned her hand over to find her hand covered in blood.

A strangled scream erupted from somewhere deep within her, mingled with the sound of a ringing phone.

15

Her screams reached Matt's ears before he'd fully opened the car door.

Fear strangled his heart and brought a deathly stench to his nostrils. He sprang from the car and raced to the locked gate, then hurdled the fence and sprinted around the edge of the house to where Gracie stood, one hand gripping the other, as she continued to shake and scream. From inside the house, the telephone rang.

"Gracie, what's wrong?" One glance at her bloody hand compelled him to grab the keys from her grasp and unlock the door. The sooner they got that wound tended to the better. How had a cut produced so much blood in such a short amount of time? Her scream decreased to a whimper. "It's okay, Gracie. We'll get you all bandaged up." He flipped on a switch and pulled her into the house, instinctively reaching for the phone. "Hello?"

No one answered, so he returned the phone to the hook, grateful he'd given in to the impulse to check on her. What would have happened had he not been there? For the first time, he got a good look at Gracie's face. She stared blankly at the blood that dripped from her hand to the Saltillo tiles, her pupils dilated.

He steered her toward the kitchen sink, peering over her shoulder at the hand she clutched in front of her. Though completely covered with blood, there didn't appear to be an open wound anywhere. Matt turned the faucet handle, gently held her hand under the stream of water, and once more took in her ghostlike complexion, damp cheeks, and unblinking eyes. "Gracie, what happened?"

She stared at him, finally aware he was there. "Matt?"

"Yeah, sweetheart, it's me." He cleaned the rest of the blood from her hand, checking for a wound, and a frown sprang to his forehead. No cut or gash anywhere. He reached for a nearby dish towel and wrapped it around her hand. "What happened?"

Gracie started to shake, not just a little, but a lot. A low keening sound started in her throat, then worked its way out in a feverish pitch. More tears flooded her cheeks.

"Hey, you're gonna be okay." Matt placed an arm around one shoulder and held her close as he navigated to the couch. He took a crocheted afghan from the back of the sofa and wrapped her tightly before helping her sit.

Indecision ripped him in two. He needed to stay here with her, but there might be a clue to her emotional breakdown outside. After a few minutes of holding her in his arms and stroking her hair, she calmed down considerably, though she still hadn't verbalized what had happened. He wiped tears from her face. "I'm gonna check on something outside, but I'll be back in a flash, okay?"

She nodded, her normally bright eyes lackluster.

Once he assured himself she'd be fine without him, he hurried out the door into the dark night. A nearly lamppost gave just enough light to peer around the backyard and porch, but nothing seemed out of place. An old patio table and chairs sat near the garden, all awaiting warmer weather.

Matt searched the porch where he'd found Gracie. A wet spot caught his attention. He stooped and ran his fingers over the weathered wood, then raised his hand to his face. Only water, most likely a rain left over from yesterday's storm. What was going on? Something had to set her off. This wasn't her normal behavior. Disgusted he was no closer to finding answers, he entered the house. She was the only witness. In order to figure out this puzzle, she'd have to talk.

Gracie rested on the couch, her head leaned on one fist. She turned when he entered, obviously more in control.

He smiled as he sat beside her. "You wanna talk about this?"

Fine lines edged her lips. "What do you want to know?"

Matt frowned at her acidic tone. Why the quick turnaround ? "Well, for one thing where all that blood came from."

She looked at him incredulously for a moment then titled her head back and laughed—a strange, almost maniacal laugh. "You didn't find anything when you went outside, did you?"

He shook his head, befuddled. Why was she acting this way?

Her odd laughter commenced again, but was quickly silenced by a half sob.

Matt grabbed both her shoulders. "Gracie, talk to me."

She said nothing, but a stray tear wandered down her left cheek.

"C'mon, Gracie, let me in. What happened?"

For a brief moment she actually seemed to consider his words, but then shook her head. "There's obviously nothing to talk about." She snapped the words and threw the blanket into a heap on the floor. "I'll see you to the door."

"Why are you doing this?" Confusion spiraled through him as he followed her.

Gracie faced him with cold contempt. "I think you should know that you caught me at a weak moment yesterday. I'm sorry if I made you think we had any chance at a relationship."

Her steel-fisted word slammed into his gut, temporarily knocking the air from his lungs. This couldn't be happening. "Gracie, please, let's talk through this."

"I've already told you, there's nothing to talk about." She yanked open the front door. "See you around."

Before he fully realized what happened, Matt landed on Gracie's front porch with the door slammed behind him. He whirled around and beat his fist against the door. "Gracie, let me in. We need to talk." No response. He tried the handle. Cold reality trickled over him like acid. He turned, his jaw slack, and stared into nothingness for an unknown amount of time before he trudged to the car.

He drove around town for at least an hour, trying to figure out his options. There must be a way to resolve this. Maybe she'd calmed down enough to talk rationally. Matt pulled into the grocery store parking lot and pulled out his cell phone. The phone rang, over and over again. "Come on, Gracie, answer the phone." After twelve rings he gave up. When he at last turned on the road that led to the ranch, he'd reached a decision.

Gracie slammed the door behind Matt and immediately slumped to the floor, tears flowing freely, her shoulders shaking with unvoiced sobs. It had taken every ounce of her energy to pull off the drama she'd dreamed up while Matt was outside checking the backyard. Learning that during the brief time they were indoors someone had carted off Millie's body had had fueled the masquerade, as she harnessed her emotions and used them to her advantage.

Matt pounded on the door and tried the handle, sounding hurt and confused. Another wave of pain slammed into her heart and more tears from some never-ending reservoir spilled down her face. How could she survive without Millie and Matt?

She latched onto the doorknob to raise herself from the floor, tempted to swing open the door and race after him, but she couldn't risk the chance that he'd be in harm's way.

A warning—that's what Millie's death had been—a warning from Elena that she'd stop at nothing to get her way.

Grace stumbled to the sink and pulled off a nearby paper towel to blow her nose, then ran water to wash her face. After days of working at the DA's office, she had no more proof than before. Who'd believe her without any evidence—especially after the events of the past few days? She wouldn't believe it herself had she not experienced it. Or maybe she really was going crazy. Had she imagined the patio chair, the phone calls, Millie?

No. It was all real. She cupped her hands beneath the running water and drank freely. Then she sloshed the rest over her face. It dripped down her cheeks and onto her shirt.

Father God, help me.
Forgive. Seventy times seven.
The words rolled in her head like a nest of scorpions. She raised a tearful gaze to the ceiling. *I can't, God. You can't ask me to do this. She's cost me so much—peace of mind, my relationship with Andy, and now Matt. Why should I forgive?*
Because I forgave you.
The thought chafed. Yes, Christ's work on the cross had removed her sin as far as the east from the west. But she'd never intentionally hurt anyone, never murdered, tried to live according to God's Word. Surely unintentional sin wasn't as bad as someone who sinned by blatantly hurting others.

God, You'll have to give me the strength. I'm not capable. She staggered to the bedroom, her thoughts jumbled, her body weary.

The phone rang, and adrenaline surged through her. Grace ripped the phone from the wall and hurled it across the room where it landed with a crash. She had no choice but to go through with her original plan to expose Elena's evil deeds for what they were. Until her mission was completed, she wouldn't quit, no matter the cost.

At work on Tuesday Grace kept to herself—especially avoiding Elena—and did all she could to focus on her research. But her tortured thoughts turned often to Matt, and she raised prayers to heaven on his behalf, pleading for an opportunity to one day set things right between them. Late that afternoon, she leaned back in her desk chair, satisfied with all she'd accomplished. She'd complete the horrific research list.

Grace glanced toward Elena's office. The light was on, which meant she was still here. Good. There was still time to launch part of her investigation before her boss left work. Several minutes later, she pulled up outside the woman's house, her pulse thudding in her temples. This move was a risk to be sure, one she had to take, but she'd better put it in high gear before Elena arrived to complicate matters. She hurried through the beautifully-landscaped yard and rang the doorbell.

Consuela opened the door, her smile bright. "What a nice surprise! Please come in."

She entered the grand foyer, her palms sweaty as she faced Consuela.

The older woman searched her face, her smile slowly fading. She lowered her head, and then turned a knowing gaze toward Grace. "I've been expecting this day. I see questions in your eyes. Let's have a seat." With weary eyes she glanced at a pedestal clock on the fireplace, its steady tick audible in the hushed silence of the space. "We don't have long before Elena gets home, so we'd better cut to the chase. How can I help you?"

Grace sank into the overstuffed sofa and leaned forward. "I know Elena is under tremendous pressure, but . . . " How could she confront this lovely woman with her daughter's issues?

Consuela smiled sadly. "It's okay, Grace. I, of all people, am most aware of my daughter's shortcomings. I can see she's hurt you, but I can also see that you're trying to live up to your lovely name. Thank you for that."

"I want to help her, but I have to know what's going on."

The woman shook her head. "I wish I knew. This job has changed her. She wasn't always so sharp-tongued and bitter."

Sharp-tongued? That was like saying tigers had a few claws. "Have you ever witnessed Elena being cruel?"

Her eyes darkened. "Cruel? In what way?"

"More than just her sharp tongue. Things that could be considered threatening." Grace wanted to say more, but thought better of it. No need to cause the woman anymore grief.

Consuela considered the question. "I've never seen anything." She paused mid-sentence and inhaled. "But we're all capable of terrible things given the right set of circumstances."

True. Hadn't she proved the fact when she'd entered Andy's office without his knowledge or permission? She removed a business card and pen from her purse and scribbled her new cell number, then handed the card to Consuela. "Call me for any reason, but please don't share my number with anyone else."

The woman stood and pocketed the card, a kind smile in place. "I won't. I also won't tell her you were here. It could cause problems, as I'm sure you understand."

Grace hugged the kind woman. What a burden she carried. "Please know that you and your family are in my prayers."

Consuela's eyes misted over. "And you in mine."

Like a mass of interconnected gears, Grace's mind gyrated as she made her way through Miller's Creek to her house. She still had nothing concrete, but knowing that Consuela also recognized a problem somehow made her feel better.

Instead of turning into her driveway, she continued down the dusty dirt road to the Cates' place, less than a mile away. Wanda Cates, the mayor's secretary, was well-known in Miller's Creek for her sharp eyes. If anyone had seen anything out of the ordinary yesterday, it would be Wanda.

The door to the little rock house swung open on the first knock, and Wanda flung open the squeaky screen door as well. "Hello, neighbor. What in tarnation brings you down this way?"

Grace smiled at the woman's greeting. "Hi, Mrs. Wanda. I actually have a few questions to ask. Do you mind if we talk?"

"Not at all, not at all. Come in, come in." She stepped aside and waved her through the doorway.

It took a moment for Grace's eyes to adjust to the dark room. Aged oak floors, antique furniture, and over-abundant knickknacks slowly came into focus, and the room reeked of Harvey Cates' cheap cigars.

"Have a seat, have a seat." Wanda clamped a bony hand on her shoulder, motioned to the couch and then roosted in a nearby chair. "What's on your mind?"

Now *that* was a loaded question. Best to stick to the point. "I wondered if you'd seen anything unusual at my house yesterday. I think someone may have been there while I was at work."

"Now that you mention it, there was someone there when I came home for lunch. I was runnin' a bit behind because Steve had some filin' for me to do—that man always has filin' for me to do—but a white van was in your driveway. Looked like they were fixin' your fence. I was just tellin' Gladys earlier today that y'all must be havin' work done while your Papa's away."

Grace fought to keep a smirk off her face. Ahh, the good old Miller's Creek grapevine. "Well, be sure to thank Mr. Cates for taking care of the farm animals. I know Papa appreciates it."

Wanda frowned. "In all the years we've lived near y'all, I've never known your Papa to go away like this."

A point she'd considered at least a thousand times. "I know he misses my brothers and their families and wants to spend the Thanksgiving with them."

"And what about you? What are your plans? Headed south?"

Grace shook her head. "Um, no, I...I have work to do."

A stern look descended on Wanda's features. "Well, if you ask me, you shoulda never have taken that job in Morganville, especially after all Andy Tyler's gone and done for you."

The words stung, but Grace managed to keep a pleasant look on her face. "I'm very appreciative of Andy, but this is something I had to do."

Wanda sniffed. "Well, that being said, we'd be pleased and proud if you'd join our family for Thanksgivin' dinner."

"Thanks, but I already have other plans." Plans to turn over every rock until she uncovered Elena's agenda. "The person working on the fence, was it a man or a woman?"

"Goodness, child, don't you know?" She clucked the words. "I'm guessin' it was a man, but I didn't recognize him with his paint clothes and big hat. He did a mighty fine job on that fence now, didn't he? It hasn't looked that good since your Mama . . . " A look of horror fell on the woman's face.

Grace forced a smile. The awkward moments when people mouthed unthinking words were almost as difficult to deal with as her mother's death.

"Gracious me, I didn't intend to . . . I mean, I'm so sorry . . ."

"It's okay, Mrs. Wanda. I know you meant no harm."

Wanda reached over and patted her hand. "You've always been such a sweet girl, Gracie. I know your Mama would be so proud of you."

"Thanks." She attempted another smile. "Forgive me if I'm asking too many questions, but did the van have any sort of lettering on it, maybe the name of a company?"

The woman stared off into space and scratched her chin. "Not that I recall."

No lead here. With a sigh, she rose to her feet. "Thanks so much for all your help, Mrs. Wanda. Guess I'd better be going. Have a wonderful Thanksgiving." Grace stepped onto the concrete porch, Wanda close on her heels.

"You, too, Gracie. Let us know if you need anything."

With a wave, Grace hoisted herself into the old pickup and turned the ignition. It roared to life with the new battery Matt had purchased and installed. She backed onto the dusty road and headed toward the house. At least now she had proof that she wasn't going crazy. Someone had repaired the fence, and she had a witness. Though her case wasn't airtight, it was past time to let the authorities know her suspicions, especially with everyone about to be snowed under with holiday festivities. She passed the small frame house and made her way to the police station.

Ernie's older model police car still stood in the parking lot. Good. Grace parked, breathing a quick prayer for guidance. A bell rang as she entered the room, the air thick with stale coffee.

The policeman poked his bald head out of the office door.

"Hey, Ernie, you're just the guy I'm looking for."

His eyes held a peculiar soberness instead of the friendly light. "Hi, Gracie. Uh, would you have a seat for now? I'll be with you in a sec."

"Sure." A frown took up residence on her forehead. He seemed upset about something. Probably whatever case he was involved with at the moment. Grace removed her coat and took a seat in a chrome and fake leather chair as Ernie closed his office door behind him.

A few minutes later, the door re-opened, and Ernie stepped out. "You can come in now."

She gathered her things and traipsed to his office. "I promise not to take too much of your time, but I need to talk to you."

Ernie didn't respond, but moved behind his desk.

Grace rounded the corner expecting an empty office. Instead, Elena Delgado and one of the private investigators were seated in the only two chairs. The petite prosecutor looked over at her, a cold, but satisfied smirk plastered across her face.

Ernie faced her, both hands on his hips, his thick moustache wobbling back and forth. "Before you say anything else, Gracie, hear me out."

He closed his eyes and took a deep breath, as though in pain. "You have the right to remain silent. Anything you say or do can and will be held against you in a court of law." Ernie's lips continued to move, but all Gracie heard was a ferocious roar as the blood drained from her head.

16

Andy's mini-van sped by the Miller mansion early Wednesday morning, and sent leaves scattering. Matt almost choked on his coffee. What was Andy doing back from his vacation? Without stopping to grab a jacket, he headed out the door and down the path which lead to his brother's house.

Matt rounded the corner as Andy lugged a black duffel bag from the van and slammed the door. He glanced up, lines of fatigue surrounding his eyes. "Hey, bro."

"What's going on? Everyone okay?"

"Trish and the kids are fine, but you'd better come in. In fact, you might wanna sit down for this one." He slung the bag over his shoulder and moved to the garage.

Panic skittered through Matt's insides as he followed him in the kitchen door.

Andy dropped his bag to the floor, rummaged in the fridge, and produced a Dr. Pepper. "Want one?"

Matt shook his head. "You're hitting the hard stuff early, aren't you?"

His brother popped the top and took a swig. "Between phone calls, the airport, and a pretty flight, I've been up all night. I need the caffeine to keep from draggin' my wagon."

Matt straddled a bar stool at the kitchen island. "The suspense is killing me. What gives?"

"The law firm was broken into this past weekend."

"And now you tell me?"

"Just found out last night."

Why did he get the distinct impression there was more—much more—to this story? "Did they catch the guy?"

"Girl. And yeah."

"Anyone we know?"

Andy lips compressed in a grim line, his eyes sorrowful. "Gracie."

Matt's breath bottled in his chest and his mouth flew open. "She wouldn't do that. There's gotta be a mistake."

"Exactly what I told Ernie, but he says they have proof."

"What kind of proof?"

"Photos." His brother took another swig. "And she confessed."

Matt closed his eyes and brought a palm to his forehead. What had gotten into her?

Andy clamped a hand on his shoulder. "Sorry, Matt. As soon as I shower, I'm headed to the police station. Wanna come?"

"Sure."

Forty-five minutes later they parked at the Miller's Creek police station, an old rock building with bars on the windows. The elderly attorney who worked with Andy approached as they climbed from the car. Would Jason be here too?

"Mornin', Ben." Andy's tone carried fatigue. "Sorry to pull you away from your family."

"Part of the job."

Ernie met them as they entered, his hand outstretched. "Mornin', everyone. Sorry to call you on your vacation, Andy, but I thought you'd wanna know. You guys want coffee?"

"Please." The word barged from Matt's mouth without permission. He moved to the machine in the far corner and poured the black brew into a Styrofoam cup. Not that he really needed another cup, but under the circumstances he certainly wanted it. He sipped the liquid and grimaced. The stuff tasted like it had been made a few weeks ago. He retraced his steps to where the other men stood, Andy's face grim as he addressed the Ernie. "So what's the scoop?"

The balding police chief moved into his office, motioning to a few chairs. "Have a seat." He parked himself at the desk and swiveled to face them. "Yesterday Ms. Delgado and a private investigator—"

"Wait a minute. Elena Delgado? From the DA's office?" A frown darkened Andy's face and he exchanged a look with Ben.

"That's the one." Ernie's moustache crawled up and down as he spoke. "Anyway, they came to my office late yesterday afternoon with pictures of Gracie letting herself into your building at 2:30 a.m. on Saturday morning. The pictures show her leaving three hours later."

"Have you questioned her?" Andy's face held a frown.

Ernie nodded. "Yep. She's been very cooperative. Said something about looking for a file. I figured you'd know more about that. If you wanna talk to her, you can."

Matt sat up his seat. "You mean she's still here?"

Again, Ernie bobbed his head. "I gave her the chance to use the phone, but she said there wasn't anyone to call. She spent the night in the cell. All she asked for was a Bible."

A stony part of Matt's broken heart melted, and he lowered his gaze to the floor. The thought of her locked in a cell overnight affected him in a way he hadn't expected. Where was her dad? He glanced at Andy, his insides twisted in knots.

His brother shot a look of encouragement then turned to Ernie. "Can we see her now?"

The man rose to his feet and pulled a set of keys from his desk drawer. "Yep."

Matt followed the other three, his thoughts focused on one thing and one thing only—to make sure Gracie was okay.

Grace rose to her feet in the dingy gray cell at the sound of approaching footsteps and voices, her fingers tightly clutching the Bible Ernie had provided. She'd spent all last night preparing for this, praying God would help her through, praying that Andy would understand.

The men emerged from the darkened corridor, and her eyes immediately focused on Andy and Ben then shifted to Matt, his sandy brown eyes full of questions. She ducked her gaze and stepped back until she felt the small cot on the back side of her legs, her knees threatening to buckle. Why had Matt come? His presence would only make things more difficult.

The keys rattled against the steel bars as Ernie unlocked the door. Strong arms encircled her, a familiar cologne teasing her senses. She'd know Matt's scent in a pitch-black cave, the same scent and same arms that had comforted her so many times. Tears welled in her eyes and slipped unbidden down her cheeks. Hard as it was, she forced herself to stand completely aloof, not daring to give him any encouragement. He deserved better.

When he pulled away a minute later, she kept her eyes trained on the floor, and simply raised a finger to her face to catch a stray tear.

"It's okay, Gracie. Why don't we talk?" Andy's voice held kindness, and he stepped forward to pat her back.

She nodded and collapsed to the bed, finally garnering enough courage to make eye contact with Andy. "I want you to know how sorry I am, and though it sounds contrary to belief, I did it in an effort to find out the truth so I could protect you."

"Protect me?" He looked doubtful. And really, really tired.

"Long story, but it's also why I took the prosecution job."

Her former boss scratched his face, then trudged across the cell and back again. "I don't follow. How's the DA's office involved in this?"

"I don't exactly know. That's what I've been trying to figure out. I'm pretty certain Elena's up to something, but she's good at covering her tracks. I think she's influencing the outcome of cases. In fact, I think she intentionally threw the Simmons case." The thought that had plagued her all night returned. "But I have absolutely no concrete evidence."

Ben spoke from the back of the cell where he leaned against the black bars. "What makes you think she threw the case?"

"She gave me research on calling classmates of David Simmons on Thursday afternoon, which I completed late Thursday night. I gave it to her first thing Friday morning and she used it Friday afternoon. She said she thought I'd disclose the information to the defense so you'd have time to prepare. I know it makes me sound incompetent, but it's almost like she planned it to happen this way."

Matt shifted positions and crossed his arms across his chest, his eyebrows puckered. "You're not telling us everything."

His comment would've angered her at one time, but not now. Not after what she'd done. Instead she released a sigh and stared at the concrete floors. "I can't make accusations without proof."

"Yet you broke into my office." Anger edged Andy's tone.

Her eyes pleaded with him. "Elena said something about you being investigated for illegal and unethical activity."

"Me? And you believed her?"

Her chest ached and she brought a hand to her throat, hoping to make breathing easier. "I didn't want to believe it, but she made it sound plausible."

"And she'll of course admit to this conversation?" Ben's eyebrows were drawn together in a way that obscured his eyes in the dim light.

Her shoulders heaved with yet another sigh. No, Elena would never incriminate herself. Of that she was certain.

Andy stepped up. "Okay, so help me understand. You broke into my office looking for proof. What did you hope to find?"

She raked her bottom lip between her teeth. "Anything."

The attorney side of Andy took over. He paced again, his gaze glued to her face. "Did you find anything?"

"Not at first, but while I was there someone else came in and put a file in the cabinet. It was a list of pretty powerful people and their contact information. If someone made the right accusations, the file would've implicated you. I wasn't sure who planted it, but I was trying to protect you, like I said earlier."

Andy halted right in front of her, his heels snapping together like a military drill sergeant. "And where is this file now?"

Grace closed her eyes and rubbed the cramp in her neck. Why wouldn't he believe her? "I took it home with me. I was gonna talk to you about it, but you'd already left for vacation."

"It's at your house?" His voice ratcheted up several decibels, his tone thick with barely-concealed frustration. He turned away.

"It was, but now I can't find it."

Andy whirled around on one foot to glare at her. "What?"

Her breath came in spurts and she squirmed to find a more comfortable position on the lumpy bed. "Sometime between when I brought it home on Saturday and the following Sunday afternoon it went missing."

He looked ready to blow a fuse. "Wait a minute. You're telling me you broke into my office for proof that I was involved in illegal activity and couldn't find anything. Then before you left, someone came in and planted a file of false information which you took, but now can't find." He snorted in disbelief. "Sorry but I don't buy it."

The words knifed into her. *Lord, help him believe me.* "I know it sounds unbelievable, Andy, but it's the truth. I'm not explaining it well, but at least give me the benefit of a doubt."

"Benefit?" His eyes bulged, and he raised both hands. "Sounds like some cockamamie story you created to justify your actions! Just tell me the truth."

Tears formed in her eyes and sheer panic escalated the speed of her words. "I am. Please believe me. The file was there when I left for church Sunday morning. All kinds of weird stuff has been happening at my house." More things she couldn't prove. "First the chair and fence and mailbox, then the phone calls and Millie." Grace glanced around. All their expressions held skepticism. Why bother? No one believed her. Why should they? She closed her eyes to the excruciating pain in her heart.

Andy resumed pacing. Finally, he shook his head and stared her down, his jaw set in concrete. "Sorry, Gracie. I'm an attorney. Until I have proof, I have no reason to believe any of this."

The room began to spin and she gripped the bed.

Now he faced Ernie. "Let her go. I'm not pressing charges." Andy once more directed his words her way. "How'd you get in?"

"Spare key." The words seemed to come from somewhere outside herself.

"I want it back."

She nodded, as thick darkness invaded every pore of her being. *Lord, this is more than I can bear.*

My grace is sufficient.

She latched onto Andy's arm as he passed. "I'll make it up to you, I promise."

He shot a look laden with disappointment and stalked from the cell without a word, Ernie and Ben on his heels.

Pain singed inside as the darkness spiraled deeper and deeper, bringing with it the taste of death. She groaned and lowered her head to her hands.

"Gracie, what can I do?" Matt took one step and stopped.

She shook her head, too ashamed to look at him. "Nothing. There's nothing anyone can do."

He stood there a moment longer, then strode from the cell, the steel door closing behind him with a blast of finality.

Later that afternoon, Grace forced her eyelids open far enough to view her reflection in the bathroom mirror at Papa's house. Matt's departure earlier that day had brought on so many tears she could barely see to drive home. Now her eyes, red and swollen shut from the crying, made her look as though she'd been in a boxing match and lost. In her quest to uncover the truth, she *had* lost. Everything.

Surprisingly, no more tears fell. She pulled a threadbare washcloth from beneath the sink and wet it with cold water to press against her eyes. Like it or not, she had to go in to work today. Not that she had a job. More than likely Elena would send her packing. But at least she could pick up the few belongings she had on her desk. After that she'd return the spare key.

An hour later she stood outside the DA's office in downtown Morganville and stared up at the massive brick building that one time symbolized her perfect career. How had things gotten to this point? A sigh escaped. What she'd done was wrong, and her intentions really didn't matter. Best to accept the way things had turned out, learn from her mistakes, and move on if possible.

Grace inhaled to bolster her courage and entered through the revolving glass door. She'd spent countless hours trying to understand what had happened. Elena had obviously set her up, effectively clearing herself of doubt, and in the process made herself look like a hero of justice. St. Elena. If it weren't so laughable, it would almost have a nice ring to it. The woman had used the oldest legal trick in the book—discrediting the witness—and it had worked. But why? What was she trying to hide?

The thought niggled at her brain as she traipsed down the uncharacteristically quiet corridor toward the stairs. Glances cast her way were accompanied with whispers, and in hushed silence, her echoing footsteps seemed to herald approaching doom.

Once in the office, no one spoke as she cleared her desk and deposited her belongings in the tote bag she'd brought for the occasion. But as she made her way to the exit, Elena stepped from the doorway of her office, effectively blocking her path. "In spite of everything, I wish you well, Grace. Sorry things had to end this way. Be sure to give prospective employers my name, and I'll give you a glowing recommendation." Though her tone held friendly goodwill—most likely for the benefit of those nearby—her eyes revealed a contrary message.

The words hit their mark and sparked intended fear. Elena knew exactly what to say to twist the knife and make it cut deeper. Would she ever be able to work as an attorney again?

She somehow found the courage to straighten her shoulders and raise her head. The anger and bitterness she supposed would flow from her like vitriol were amazingly absent. What she felt was pity, not anger. From some calm place inside, she smiled. "Thanks, Elena. Hope you have a wonderful Thanksgiving."

As she stepped out into the unusually warm autumn day a few minutes later, an inexplicable peace blanketed her. She moved to the truck with a light step and headed to Miller's Creek.

As she drew near Andy's office, her stomach churned at the thought of facing him again. Would he ever forgive her?

Grace parked and said a quick prayer for strength, then opened the office door and approached the receptionist window. "Hi, Sandra."

Once a comrade and colleague, Sandra stared back at her, her expression completely devoid of warmth. "May I help you?"

She pulled the key from her purse and handed it over. "May I speak with Andy please?"

The receptionist snatched the key as though she feared making contact. "He's already left to fly back to Florida to be with his family." Her tone held condemnation, leaving no doubt as to how she felt about Grace at the moment.

She made ready to leave, but faced Sandra once more. "I don't expect you to understand, but not all of this is my fault."

Now her friend's face flared red. "Why can't you just take responsibility for your actions and admit when you're wrong?"

"I do, Sandra. I shouldn't have come here in the middle of the night without permission, but I had my reasons. My heart was in the right pl—"

"Whatever." Sandra stood and stormed from the receptionist's office and slammed the bathroom door behind her.

An invisible claw clutched her heart and squeezed. How far would the repercussions of her actions reach? Would anybody believe her—that in spite of doing the wrong thing—she'd done it for a noble reason? The thought plagued her all the way home.

Grace awoke the next morning, more lonely than ever. Normally Thanksgiving was a day of family, food, and fun, but not today. She padded to the kitchen, and in no time, had the house ensconced in the smell of bacon and eggs, but in the end threw most of her breakfast in the trash.

As the morning wore on, she entertained the idea of calling Matt, but changed her mind. After her efforts to put distance between them, it would only complicate matters. But the silence finally got the best of her, and right before lunch, she plugged in the phone in case Papa called. She didn't dare run up the phone bill, especially since she might have to borrow money to pay for the things she'd purchased over the past few weeks.

To her great delight, the phone emitted a dial tone as soon as she plugged it in, and only thirty minutes passed before the phone rang. For a second she hesitated, fearful of possible silence on the other end. But finally she answered.

"*Buenos dias*, Graciela."

Tears pooled in her eyes. "Papa!" Had she ever been so glad and relieved to hear his voice? "How are you?"

He laughed, the happiest sound she'd heard him make in the past fifteen years. "I've never been better, *la hija*. How are you?"

The words froze in her throat. Telling him the truth would only destroy this newfound joy. Best to wait until later. "I'm fine. I have something to tell you, but I'll wait until you're home."

"I have things to discuss with you too, but they'll wait. I mainly wanted to wish you a Happy Thanksgiving."

The phone was passed to her brothers, sister-in-laws, nieces and nephews, so that by the time she'd spoken with everyone, a half hour had elapsed. She hung up with mixed feelings. It hurt to know her family would have a great day of celebrating without her, but as least she'd had the chance to speak with them.

Grace grabbed a book and headed to the back door. Might as well read outdoors while the day was warm. The phone shrilled, and she stopped in her tracks. It wouldn't be like Papa to call again so soon, and in her current state of mind, she dared not answer. Instead she unplugged the phone and moved outside.

The weekend wore on interminably. Grace thought about looking for a job on Black Friday, but with the throng of Christmas shoppers it was unlikely anyone would have time to discuss jobs. She busied herself around the house, cleaning out her closet and the pantry.

By Sunday morning Grace was more than ready for interaction. She went through her normal routine on autopilot. Though she dreaded facing people at church, she also needed them like never before, but would they be receptive in light of what she'd done?

She arrived a few minutes early, but every attempt she made to engage others was met with uncomfortable silence. By the time the service started, her pasted-on veneer of a smile wore painfully thin, but she forced herself to carry on as best she could.

Since tears hovered just beneath the surface, she opted to sit in the congregation rather than the choir. During the welcome—what Mama Beth laughingly called 'hug and howdy' time—Grace turned to greet those behind her. To her surprise, Andy and Trish and their two boys had slipped in during the opening song.

Grace held out a hand to Little Bo, who'd grown at least two feet since her high school days when she babysat for him. Discomfort covered his face, and Trish quickly stepped in. She wore a tight smile, and her eyes held uncustomary hardness. "How are you?" Trish asked the question as she shook her hand, then without waiting for a response, turned to hug the neck of the person behind her.

Her heart fell to the floor. So this was how it was going to be.

Andy, his face still as grim as it had been last Wednesday, stepped forward and offered a hand. "Hey, Gracie."

"Hi." She managed a slight smile, in spite of her shredded heart. "Is Matt here by any chance?"

A small frown created vertical ripples between his eyebrows. "I thought you knew. He decided to go on the road with a band."

The news slammed into her with unexpected force, and she gripped the pew. He'd left without saying good-bye?

Grace turned to the front, her mind and heart reeling as she blinked back tears. Though the blow hurt worse than any other, it was for the best. Now she wouldn't have to worry about him getting caught in the crossfire while she tried to uncover the truth.

Throughout the service, an ever-growing realization invaded her thoughts. Life in Miller's Creek would never again be the same.

17

"Matt!" Derek barked out his name, effectively bringing Matt's focus back to the Sunday evening rehearsal.

"Sorry. Can we try it again?" He sent an apologetic grin.

Derek sighed. "Actually, let's take five."

The guys in the band jumped on the break, quickly exiting the basement in favor of Derek's loaded fridge upstairs. All it took was one look from his host for Matt to stay in place.

His friend pulled up a chair and straddled it backwards, elbows at rest on the back of the chair. "What's going on, bud? This isn't like you."

Matt feigned an innocent expression. "What do you mean?"

"I mean you're here, but your head's not."

His eyebrows rose. Derek had always been blunt and to the point, one of the things that drew Matt to him during their college years. "Sorry, man. I'll try to keep my head in the game."

"It's a chick, isn't it?"

A wry grin crept onto Matt's face. "That obvious, huh?"

"Seen it a hundred times before," said Derek, breaking into a smile. "Afraid she'll forget you while you're on the road?"

Though there was a smidgeon of truth to his friend's comment, that wasn't the true source of his fear. Matt shook his head. "Afraid she's in danger."

"Then why'd you agree to come on the road with us?"

Matt shrugged. "I don't think I fully realized how much danger until right before I left. Now it's all I can think about." The bags under his eyes should bear testimony to his words.

Though he'd managed to doze off a few times during the past couple of nights, his sleep had not been sound.

"Need to leave?"

"No, I won't do that to you guys. I'll get my brother to keep an eye out for her." That is when he wasn't running around like a crazy man trying to keep all the balls he juggled in the air.

Derek knocked knuckles with him. "Sounds like a plan, man. Keep me updated."

"Will do."

The rest of the rehearsal went smoother, but took more effort on Matt's part than he ever dreamed possible. Not only did his worries of Gracie constantly threaten, but fatigue from the drive to Austin coupled with two restless nights made it a struggle to keep his eyes open.

As soon as Derek released them for dinner, Matt grabbed a sandwich, bag of chips, and a Dr. Pepper, then made a beeline to his room to make a couple of calls. First up was Justin Combs, a college professor who'd also been a friend and advisor.

The phone rang only once. "Hey, Doc. Matt Tyler here. How's it going?" He put his phone on speaker setting and opened the bag of chips, nabbing one and crunching it between his teeth.

"Great. To what to do I owe the honor of this phone call?"

"Actually a friend of mine is going through a rough time, and I thought you might share a little of your professorly wisdom."

Justin laughed. "Happy to help, but I'll need a few details before I make my diagnosis."

A smile broke through on Matt's face. "Figured you might." His smile dissipated as he thought of Gracie. "This friend is a perfectionist, always striving to do better and to be better."

"Ah, real conscientious, huh? I know the type. An overachiever to boot?"

"Yeah." He took a bite of the tuna salad sandwich and followed it with a swig of Dr. Pepper. "She's always been one to control her emotions, but here lately, she's changed, done things I never thought she'd do."

"Such as?"

"Well, she broke into my brother's office for one. And her emotions have been out of control, like a yo-yo."

"Has she experienced some type of trauma?" Justin's voice held concern, and Matt could almost see his friend's accompanying frown.

"She lost her Mom when she was ten."

"Hmm, that's hard on anyone, but I meant something recent."

His mind immediately flew to Gracie's boss. "The woman she works for sounds like an adult version of the typical playground bully. And since she's new on the job, there's not a whole lot of support for her during her work hours."

Justin released a sigh. "Your friend is just the type that others prey on. A lot of people feel intimidated by over-achievers."

Matt considered his words. "I'm not sure that's the case here. I think it's more about dominance."

"And your friend lets it get to her?"

"Yep. She turns the words and actions of others against herself, so the emotional damage is multiplied. I've told her to put up a shield, and I'm sure she's trying." But was it enough?

His former professor grew quiet for a moment. "Do you know if she's experienced anything threatening? Something that might explain her unusual behavior?"

Matt thought back to the last time he'd seen her in the jail cell. "She said something about weird thing going on at her house." What was it? A chair and her cat? "But it didn't make a lot of sense." His voice came out croaky, his fear for Gracie escalating.

"You might want to keep a close eye on her, Matt. She could be in more danger than anyone realizes." He paused. "But remember that sometimes the real culprit is something or someone that no one suspects."

Panic set in before he finished hanging up the phone, ratcheting upward by the moment. Matt immediately put a call through to Gracie's house, but it was busy, just like it had been each time he'd tried to call during the past three days. He punched the 'End Call' button on his phone with more force than necessary. Andy, he needed to call Andy.

His brother picked up on the first ring. "Hey, bro."

"Thank goodness I caught you."

"You okay?" Andy's concern sounded through the phone.

"Not really. I'm really worried about Gracie."

The line grew temporarily quiet. "Well, the way I see it, she brought all this on herself."

Matt strode across the small bedroom, one hand raking through his hair. "I understand why you feel that way, Andy, but I think there's more at play than what we're aware of. I've tried to call Gracie to warn her, but the line's busy. Can you go check on her?"

"What?" Anger tinged his voice. "You're asking me to leave my family on a holiday weekend after the stunt she pulled?"

He stopped pacing, stared up at the ceiling, and sucked in a heavy breath. "Yeah."

Again the line grew silent. "You think she's in some kind of danger?"

"I don't know for sure, but I think it's possible."

"Who?"

"Maybe the Delgado lady."

Andy chuckled. "Elena's a handful all right, but I don't think she's dangerous." His tone reinforced his words.

A heavy sigh escaped. "Look, Andy, I'm not just asking. I'm begging. Please keep an eye on her while I'm gone. I'd do it myself, but these guys are depending on me. If I back out, they won't be able to keep their commitments for the holiday season."

Derek poked his head in the door and tapped his watch. "Rehearsal started five minutes ago."

Matt nodded and pointed to the phone.

Andy let out a frustrated breath. "Okay. I'll drive by her house occasionally to check on the place, and I'll see her at church."

One more question. If he could get it out. "Um, do you, I mean, could you give Gracie her old job back?"

A curt laugh sounded. "You've gotta be kidding."

"Please, Andy, for me. I'd feel better knowing that during the day she's in a safe place."

"I wish I could, but I can't. And it's not that I don't want to. There are other issues involved. Things I can't discuss at this point."

"Got it. Thanks." Matt hung up, more frustrated with his brother than ever before, and plopped down on the bed, his head in his hands. He somehow had to come to grips with the fact that, like it or not, he was apart from her for the next several weeks. The sooner he faced the facts, the better.

Lord God, help me. Keep her safe while I'm away. Give her Your supernatural wisdom and guidance, and help Andy have a change of heart. No other words came to his prayer, only a groaning from deep within, accompanied with anguished thoughts. He slid from the bed and onto his knees. Never had he felt so torn and afraid.

Grace slipped in the back door of the court room Monday morning just as proceedings began. While she couldn't keep an eye on Elena in an official capacity, she could at least keep tabs on what went on during public trials. It mattered more now than ever. The only way she'd ever regain her standing in the community was if she could prove what a snake Elena really was. As she took a seat on the back row, a thought stuck in her brain. Never would she have imagined sitting in a trial when she should be out looking for a job, but when everything she cared for hung in the balance, she'd do whatever necessary to make it right.

The morning drug on, but nothing Elena did brought on further suspicions. Grace's mind wandered to the knotted mess of questions concerning the woman, as she once more tried to make sense of it all. Only when people began to stand and leave the courtroom did Grace snap out of her reverie. She tried to wiggle into a gap to exit, but the crowd was too thick.

Elena spotted her on the way out the door, the shock on her face bringing great satisfaction. The woman stopped in the middle of the aisle, and forced those behind her to move around her to exit. "What are you doing here?"

A tremble began in Grace's feet and worked its way up, anger unleashing its fury throughout her system. Her hands balled into fists. She didn't have to explain her actions to anyone, especially not Elena. "I'm on to you, and I won't rest until I can prove it to the world."

The woman's eyes took on a haughty sneer. "As if anyone will believe you."

So she'd been right about Elena discrediting her. She didn't back down. "If you thought you could get rid of me that easily, you're sadly mistaken."

Andy and Jason walked up in time to hear the comment, and her former boss' face grew dark and foreboding. "You okay?"

She released a shaky breath and nodded.

Without another word Andy slipped past her and exited the courtroom, Elena on his heels. The door swung shut behind them. Only Jason remained, and he sent a kind smile. "Sounds like you've had a rough go of it here lately. Andy told me what happened. I'm so sorry."

His thoughtful words wrapped around her wounded spirit like a fuzzy blanket on a cold, dark night, the first comforting words she'd heard since before Matt left. Why was it that a virtual stranger was more gracious than people she'd known and loved for years? Tiny needle-like jabs watered her eyes. "Yeah, but I'll be okay, at least eventually."

"I have depositions all afternoon here in Morganville, but would you allow me the privilege of taking you to dinner tonight?"

A brief moment of indecision battled inside, as her thoughts flew to Matt. He'd left without saying good-bye. While it was true she hadn't given him any encouragement for fear of putting him in danger, he'd been mighty quick to go on the road without once mentioning it. Obviously his feelings for her weren't as deep as he'd professed at the lake house. She smiled into Jason's handsome face. "I'd love to." If nothing else, it would provide another opportunity to see if a connection existed between Jason and Elena.

His compassionate smile morphed into a full-blown boyish grin. "Wonderful. It's a black tie event. May I pick you up at five-thirty?"

Black-tie? "It sounds wonderful, Jason, but I'm not sure I have anything suitable to wear."

"I'll take care of it. See you tonight." He left the room before she could protest, his dimpled smile setting off somersaults in her heart.

Grace checked her watch. Hopefully Andy could give her a few minutes of time to try to set the record straight. She plucked the cell phone from her purse and punched in the number to the law office.

"Tyler, Dent, Snodgrass, and Rowe, this is Sandra."

Rowe? They'd already hired another attorney? The thought sent a wash of hurt. "Sandra, this is Grace. I'd like to set an appointment to see Andy this afternoon if possible."

Even through the phone, the air chilled. "He has an opening at 1:30," Sandra intoned in her best business voice.

No chitchat, no girl talk. Just straight and to-the-point. "I'll take it, please."

A few minutes before her appointment time, Grace parked the truck outside the office and made her way into the reception area, familiar smells setting off longing in her heart. How good it felt to be here. Sandra glanced up from her desk as she entered, but said nothing. Grace took a seat.

Five minutes later, Andy, now sporting rolled-up shirt sleeves and a loosened tie, stepped through the swinging door that separated the legal offices from the reception room. "Gracie, you ready?"

She followed him into his office, and took a seat.

He lowered himself to the black leather desk chair and leaned back, his elbows propped on the arm rests and his fingers steepled in front of his chest. "What can I do for you?" Though the words were kind, a certain measure of reserve colored both his tone and expression.

Grace swallowed to moisten her dry throat. "First, let me say again how sorry I am about what I did. I know you don't believe me, but I was trying to do the right thing. I just went about it in the wrong way."

He stared back, his face a cold blank slate, but didn't comment.

"I turned the key into Sandra last week."

"Yeah, I got it. Thanks."

She gathered her courage to ask the question at the front of heart and mind. Surely he'd take into consideration the years of faithful service she'd given him, as well as their friendship.

His forehead wrinkled. "Was there something else?"

"Yes. I, um, wanted to know if there was any way I could have my job back. I know I don't deserve it, but I promise—"

He held up both hands. "Stop right there, Gracie. I can't give you your job back right now."

His answer slashed through her hopes and sent tears down her cheeks. She did all she could to bring the traitorous tears in check, but they continued to flood her face as she rose to her feet. "I understand." Grace made a move for the door.

Andy was around the desk in a flash, and reached the door ahead of her. "Sorry. I didn't mean to make you cry."

Her throat clogged with more tears, making it impossible to speak. All she managed was a nod.

His ocean-green eyes took on compassion. "I'm not saying 'never,' Gracie. I'm just saying 'not now.' Please trust that I have my reasons."

The small flame of hope that flickered inside was quickly doused by ensuing thoughts of what she'd do in the meantime. Grace made it almost to the reception area before she realized she'd failed to ask how Matt was doing. She almost kept going, but decided she'd rather know something than nothing. So she pivoted and returned to his office, the door slightly ajar.

As she raised a fist to knock, Andy's voice sounded from within. "So you heard everything on the speaker phone?"

"Yep. I think you were wise not to bring her back on, at least for now." The voice belonged to Ben Snodgrass.

Grace frowned. What did Ben have against her? And why did Andy use his phone to let the man eavesdrop on what she'd assumed was a private conversation?

18

Late that afternoon Grace peered into the mirror, blown away by her reflection. Jason arranged for the dress to be delivered soon after she returned from her failed meeting with Andy. Any bad feelings she carried away from the office of Tyler, Dent, Snodgrass, and Rowe had drained away the minute she opened the package.

The red chiffon evening gown with matching shoes and bag only enhanced her recent hair and makeup overhaul, and now she felt like Cinderella ready for the ball with the handsome prince. She'd swept her hair into a classic chignon by watching a few videos online, and was delighted with the results.

She dabbed perfume below each ear and on her wrists and sighed. Jason's attention and gifts were pretty heady stuff for a girl from the wrong side of the tracks. *Lord, help me keep my wits about me.* An absolute must if she intended to coax information from Jason.

The doorbell rang a few minutes later. Dressed in a black tuxedo that accented his dark good looks, Jason offered his elbow as she locked the front door and made her way down the porch steps. "You look absolutely gorgeous. I knew red would suit you. Hope you weren't offended that I had the dress sent over."

She smiled. "Not at all. It's lovely. Thank you."

He came to an abrupt halt. "I almost forgot." He patted her hand. "Stand here a moment while I retrieve something. This will be much easier outside." Jason hurried to his car and returned with a blue velvet jewelry box. "These belonged to my mother. I thought you might want to borrow them for the evening." He snapped open the lid to reveal a diamond and ruby necklace and matching earrings.

She gasped and brought a hand to her chest. "They're beyond description, Jason. I'm honored, but I'm also terrified I might somehow lose them during the evening."

He smiled and revealed his dimples. "Never fear. They're insured."

A slight frown tightened her forehead, but she quickly forced it away lest Jason be offended. Was he only concerned about the monetary value of the necklace? Grace turned her back and held up loose tendrils of hair while he fastened the clasp, his fingers brushing against the nape of her neck.

"As lovely as the woman wearing them." He handed her the dangly earrings. "It's probably best if you take care of these."

She laughed, removed the small cubic zirconia knock-offs, and replaced them with the earrings Jason offered, surprised at their weight.

Jason smiled his approval and offered his elbow once more. "Shall we?" After he seated her in his luxurious sports car, he moved around to the other side and eased into the seat.

Grace faced him. "You have my curiosity up. Where are we going?"

"There's a political fundraiser at the Morganville Expo Center for the Attorney General while he's in town. I feel very fortunate to have snagged such a lovely dinner date and companion. Hope you enjoy this evening as much as I know I will."

Grace leaned her head back against the black leather seat as they sped out of town. Enjoy? After the happenings of the past two weeks, this felt like utter decadence.

Within a half hour, Grace descended a flight of stairs leading into a large carpeted foyer lit by enormous chandeliers. The relaxing sound of stringed instruments played softly in the background and the aroma of fresh seafood drifted to her nose. She clutched Jason's arm and her red handbag more tightly and prayed she wouldn't lose her footing in the stiletto heels and tumble headfirst to the floor below. Below them, people turned heads their way. "Why is everyone staring at us?"

Jason leaned in close, his lips near her ear. "They're all wondering who the stunning woman is accompanying me. Relax and smile. They just want to know who you are."

Of course. She *was* with Jason Dent, probably the most eligible bachelor within five hundred miles. It made sense that they'd want to know who was with him. "Did I mention how grateful I am for the pleasure of spending this evening with you?" She spoke the words through a pasted-on smile.

He laughed and smiled into her eyes, resting his hand on hers. "Trust me, the pleasure is all mine."

Before the dinner and concert portion of the evening started, Grace lost count of all the important people she met—state senators and congressman as well as a couple of U. S. senators. What amazed her most was how at ease she felt. Maybe it was the clothes and make-up, or perhaps it was having a man like Jason as her escort, but she somehow managed to carry on intelligent conversation without fear or trepidation.

She blinked. Now, here she was, sitting next to the man of her dreams while he lavished his attention on her. All through the evening he'd been a perfect gentleman, had anticipated her every need, and been quick to provide. An irresistible urge to pinch herself flashed through her consciousness. Was she dreaming? If so, she never wanted to awaken.

A troubling thought crossed her mind, and brought a frown with it. In spite of the wonderful evening, she had to hold back, wary of succumbing to Jason's charm and persuasion. While part of her wanted to relax and enjoy the enchantment, a deeper part pulled on invisible reins.

They dined on lobster, asparagus spears, and potatoes au gratin followed by a creamy tiramisu for dessert. The orchestral performance by a string ensemble from Dallas only added to the magical aura. Before she knew it, the evening came to a close. Grace stood with the rest of the audience to applaud the orchestra, and then squinted against the glare as the house lights were brought up.

Jason placed his hand in the small of her back. "So did you enjoy tonight?"

Happy laughter fell from her mouth. "How could I not? Thank you for a lovely evening." She gathered her evening bag from the table, where a centerpiece of fragrant roses spilled their perfume into the air. As they turned to leave a familiar voice sounded.

"Gracie?" Andy stood nearby, Trish on one arm. Questions glistened in his eyes. Next to them were Ben Snodgrass and a woman she'd never met. Andy's gaze focused on her. "You look quite different, Gracie. I almost didn't recognize you." His eyes now traveled to her date for the evening. "Hey, Jason. Thought I might see you here."

Palpable tension hung in the air. Even Jason seemed slightly uncomfortable in the awkward moment, though he quickly masked his discomfort with a good-natured grin, and patted Grace's hand. "I couldn't pass up the opportunity of spending the evening with this lovely young woman, now could I?"

Grace made the mistake of glancing at Andy. There was no mistaking his displeasure. Defensiveness roared inside. Why should it matter to him that she was out with Jason? Did he really view her as the enemy?

As if things weren't already tense enough, Elena swept into their midst, her gold lame dress rustling. "Well, well, if it isn't Andy Tyler and his cohorts. My, Grace, but you do clean up well. That outfit must've set you back a pretty penny."

"I—uh, that is—"

Jason stepped in to save her. "She's been turning heads all evening."

Disgust etched on her features, Elena moved her focus to Grace, making no attempt to disguise the hostility in her eyes. Then just as quickly, she moved onto the woman standing beside Ben, her voice now exuding friendliness. "I've met Mr. Snodgrass and Mrs. Tyler, but I don't think I've had the pleasure of meeting you. I'm Elena Delgado." She extended a hand.

"Deborah Rowe, the new attorney with Andy's firm."

Grace trembled with pent-up emotion, the realization of all that could have been hers hitting her squarely in the face. How unfair that in her attempt to protect those she loved, she'd lost out on so much.

Jason must have noticed her sudden distress, for he tucked her hand more securely in the crook of his elbow and covered it with his own, at the same time moving closer to her side as if to provide a place for her to lean. "Well, it's been lovely chatting with you all, but we'd best be getting on."

A few minutes later, after Jason made sure she was seated comfortably in the passenger seat of his sports car, he climbed in the driver's side and easily maneuvered their way through traffic. Soon they sped down the two-lane highway that led to Miller's Creek.

"So glad you enjoyed the evening." Jason's velvet voice was particularly sonorous, as she gazed out the window at the moon and stars, the fields bathed in beautiful light.

She leaned her head back against the seat and turned his way with a smile. "I feel like I should pinch myself to see if I'm dreaming."

He gave a slow lazy laugh. "You're not dreaming, but after seeing how beautiful you look tonight, I wonder if I am."

Grace didn't know how to respond.

"Please accept my apologies if I was too forward."

She placed a hand on his arm. "Not at all. I'm just not used to looking or feeling like this. I don't quite know how to act."

He smiled at her through the dim light of the car's interior. "You've definitely shown a different side of yourself tonight, and I must confess I'm intrigued. You handled yourself so professionally. Do you realize how many influential people you hobnobbed with tonight?

She laughed. "I know. It's been unbelievable. I wish it would never end."

He grew silent a moment. "I feel the same. I just wish we could erase the confrontation that occurred before we left. You were understandably upset."

A heavy sigh rushed from her mouth before she could contain it. "Thanks for coming to my rescue." She paused, unsure if she could trust him with her thoughts and feelings. "Life's so unfair sometimes."

"Yes, it often is." His comment was so cut and dried and formal—so British. "Unfortunately, we have no control over what happens to us. We only can control our response to it."

"What a wise thing to say." She hadn't expected him to have such depth.

He glanced toward her, his face illuminated by the moon and lights from the dashboard. "You've had a difficult week, haven't you?"

"Yes, it's been a real winner."

"Pardon me if I'm being too forward, but do you feel like you were set up by Elena Delgado?"

Something about the question unnerved her, and an invisible wall rose around her heart. She thought through the question. Yes, Elena had masterfully manipulated her into doing something she wouldn't ordinarily do, and had done so for the purpose of discrediting her. In addition she'd covered her wrongdoing by laying the fault entirely on her shoulders. "I can't place all the blame on her. I was the one who broke into Andy's office. She didn't force me."

"It shows great character on your part for taking responsibility for your actions."

His words were salve to her bruised spirit. "I wish others could see it that way, but they seem determined to condemn and punish me." She shifted in her seat so she could see him better. "Aren't you concerned their perceptions of me will cause them to view you in a negative light? Aren't you even a tiny bit afraid to be seen with me?"

He lifted one shoulder casually. "How others perceive me is of little importance. If they do perceive me negatively, they'll come around in time. But I do care what you think of me."

An unexpected chill skittered down her spine and she shivered. "Why?"

Jason pulled into the driveway, put the car in park, and faced her, his face an enigmatic mask in the moonlight, his eyes completely hooded by his brows. He took hold of one of her hands.

Grace swallowed against the panic moving from her stomach to her throat. "I mean, you could have your pick of anyone. If I were to see you for the first time in a group of people, I'd never have the nerve to approach you." She rattled out the words in rapid-chatter mode to cover the electric silence. "So why does what I think matter?"

He brought his other hand to a ringlet that had escaped her chignon and fingered it for a moment before cupping her face with his palm. "You have no idea how exquisite you are, do you?"

A shaky breath shuddered out of her as she reached for the door handle. She couldn't let this happen, not when she cared so much for Matt. "Thank you again, Jason. I'd better get inside. I had a lovely ti—"

Jason silenced her babble with a kiss that stole her breath.

Only minutes later, when she once more stood in the safety of the little house, the door locked behind her and currently holding up her weight, did she realize that in the midst of the most fairy-tale-like night she'd ever experienced, she'd completely forgotten to quiz him about her suspicion of a possible connection to Elena.

Her thoughts flew to the brief moment they'd seen the fiery prosecutor. Jason had seemed uninterested and nonplussed by her shiny dress and scornful comments.

Grace gave her head a shake and headed to the back to get ready for bed. No need to worry. It was obvious Jason had no relationship at all with Elena.

Matt attempted a smile for his friends as they left the concert on the first Friday in December, but just couldn't make it happen. The only thing on his mind was making with contact Gracie, but it was too late in the evening.

"Wasn't that just the coolest concert ever?" Derek's eyes flashed with an energy and excitement Matt envied. "I mean, the way the crowd responded, and we got an invite for next year!" The guy was obviously stoked.

Other band members added their comments, but Matt had no words. This was so not what he expected. Was it just because he was so worried about Gracie, or was there more? He tried to wrap his head around the question, but finally gave up, his brain too exhausted to form a coherent thought.

Derek moved into place beside him. "You did an awesome job tonight, Matt. I gotta say I was a little concerned about bringing you on after our first few rehearsals, but you really stepped up to the plate. Glad to have you on board."

"Thanks."

"We're headed to a place on the other side of town. Might be able to drum up a future gig. Wanna come?"

Matt eyed his watch. At midnight? "No, thanks, man. I'm exhausted."

His friend nodded agreeably. "Totally understand. We're scheduled to leave in the morning at ten to get to our next venue. Get some rest, and I'll see you on the van." After a friendly slap on the shoulder, Derek hurried to join the rest of the guys as they crossed the street and headed the other direction.

Matt made his way through the semi-empty streets to the downtown Dallas apartment to crash, his mind still on Gracie. If it weren't already so late, he'd call Andy to check on her, but it would have to wait until morning. He'd tried her phone again earlier in the day, but still only heard the same old busy signal. Was she okay? She'd been so down when he'd seen her last—over a week ago now--and it hurt to think of her on her own, without a job, and totally stressed over the whole situation.

In a few short minutes, he reached the old brick building. The sign above the door read Dallas View Lofts, but the cramped apartment provided by their host bore no resemblance to a loft, and the only view was the ramshackle building next door. At least it was better than sleeping on the van.

He used the spare key Derek had given him to let himself in and checked behind as he entered to make sure he was alone and safe. After he locked the door, Matt snatched his overnight bag from the pile of luggage and headed to the bathroom.

In spite of low pressure and sparse hot water, the shower did wonders at washing away his worries. Afterwards, Matt located a quiet corner where he wouldn't be disturbed when the guys came in and unrolled his sleeping bag. Though it was stifling-hot close to the furnace, he opted to sleep inside the bag just in case any critters tried to get cozy during the night.

Sleep came quicker than expected, but Matt was awakened two hours later when the guys finally made it in, loud and boisterous. There was no going back to sleep, and as the long night wore on he found himself once more praying for Gracie.

When the first cracks of light filtered through the mini-blinds, Matt crept quietly to the kitchen to make a pot of brew to get rid of his nappy morning breath. He searched the dingy and worn cabinets, but found nothing—no filters, no coffee, not even a coffee maker. He gazed around the space and rubbed his grainy eyes. It figured.

Careful not to trip over the sleeping bodies of his snoring friends, he tiptoed to the bathroom, dressed, and eased his way out the door to find some breakfast—and at least a potful of coffee. His nose soon located a mom-and-pop joint right down the street, and he inhaled a full breakfast of scrambled eggs, bacon, hash browns, and biscuits with gravy, then downed another cup of coffee before he called Andy.

"Yeah, bro. What time is it?" His brother's words were a drowsy whisper.

Matt cringed. "Sorry, man. Thought you'd already be up."

"Not a problem. You okay?"

"Guess so." He opted not to paint a picture of life on the road. "Just wanted to see if you've seen Gracie."

"Saw her Monday night. She's doing just fine."

Matt's brows rose. "How so?"

"Let's just say you wouldn't have recognized her in the evening gown and jewels."

His brows crinkled so much they hurt. "Huh?"

Andy let out an exasperated sigh, and Matt could almost picture him a hand through his bed hair. "Don't mean to bring you down, Matt, but Gracie was with Jason Dent at a high-priced political fundraiser in Morganville dressed in a very expensive dress and even more expensive jewelry, rubbing elbows with some very important people."

His chest deflated and his shoulders slumped forward. Well, it certainly hadn't taken her long to get over her jail trauma. And he'd been worrying and losing sleep for nothing! No wonder her phone was always busy. He imagined her chatting happily on the phone with Jason, and then inhaled a deep breath, forcing himself to cool down. "I'm glad she's okay."

"Well, you've sure changed your tune. What happened to keeping her away from Jason?"

"Did she seem happy?"

Andy's brief silence came through loud and clear. "Yeah, come to think of it, she did."

The words stabbed his heart, and he closed his eyes against the pain. "In the long run I just want her to be happy and safe. If Jason is as good as everyone in Miller's Creek seems to think, she'll be fine."

The other end grew quiet once more. Finally, his brother spoke. "Sounds like you've given up on her."

"Not at all." Matt blinked against the pinpricks in his eyes. He could never give up on her, no more than he could ever stop loving her. "But I am giving up on the two of us ever being together."

19

"Coming!" Grace sped down the narrow hallway to the front door and yanked it open.

With one hand in his pocket, Jason clutched a bouquet of fragrant lavender roses. Dressed in an off-white cable sweater, blue jeans, and black leather jacket, he looked like an ad for the latest men's fragrance. Had she ever seen him dressed so casually? Or looking so good?

His handsome face broke into an even smile, revealing his perfect white teeth. "There you are. I've been trying to call you all day, but your line was busy." He leaned forward to kiss her cheek and handed her the bouquet at the same time. "Beautiful flowers for a beautiful lady."

Her heart pitter-pattered. "They're gorgeous. Come in." She stepped aside to let him enter. So many things were going right in her life. If only she could find a job to pay the bills beginning to pile up. And Christmas was just around the corner.

He gave the room a cursory glance and moved to the sagging sofa beside the scrawny Christmas tree she'd put up yesterday.

"Have a seat while I put these in water." As she hurried to the kitchen sink she sent up a quick prayer. *Lord, help him not to think less of me because of where I live.* Another reason to find a job—to live in a nicer place. She took a vase from beneath the counter, filled it with water, and placed the long stems inside, fluffing out the leaves. "These are so pretty, but you shouldn't have gone to the expense."

"Nonsense." Jason shoved a crocheted cushion behind his back. "Have you been on the phone all day?"

She joined him in the living room and sat in Papa's ratty recliner. "Not at all. It was ringing off the wall the other night, so I unplugged it and forgot to plug it back in."

A brief frown crossed his face, but he quickly whisked it away with one of his killer grins. "Well, that makes it kind of hard for people to reach you."

"Sorry. It was just an oversight on my part." She hurried to the phone and plugged it in. If the anonymous calls returned, she could always unplug it again.

"Good, I feel better knowing I can reach you. How's your father?" He glanced down the hallway.

"Fine. I expect him back sometime this week. He's visiting my brothers and other family members."

He crossed one leg over the other, the couch groaning its complaint. "I came to see if you'd like to go to dinner with me tonight."

"Sounds wonderful." The week had dragged by, painfully slow, with no one to talk to except prospective employers, all of which said "No" when she'd asked for a job. The bad economy made the job hunt incredibly difficult, especially in a small town where there weren't many to begin with.

"I'll wait here while you change. You might want to dress warmly. It's a little nippy out there."

"Okay." Grace hurried to her room and locked the door behind her, frantically searching the closet for an outfit to complement what Jason wore. She finally decided on the designer jeans and black boots Elena had given her, coupled with a creamy white turtleneck and fitted lambskin jacket she'd purchased with her first credit card. The one she'd default on if she didn't find a job. And soon. She zipped the boots, then sprayed a mist of perfume and stepped into it before she sped back to the living room.

Jason flipped through a family photo album she'd put together for the purpose of remembering Mama. He glanced up as she entered. "You look nice." He hoisted the album an inch higher. "Hope you don't mind. I'm perusing your photographs."

Not really asking permission, just stating a fact. Grace didn't answer. She *did* mind, but why? "I'm ready when you are."

His gaze once more honed in on the book. "You look very much like your mother. At least, I assume this is your mother?"

"Yes." For some odd reason, her eyes filled with tears.

Jason cocked his head to one side, a frown at play on his forehead. "Did I say something wrong?"

"No." The word came out in a croak. "Mama was killed in an automobile accident when I was a child."

He dropped the book to the coffee table and strode to her. Then he placed a hand on each of her shoulders and peered deep into her eyes. "I am so sorry, Grace. I didn't know."

She nodded, still battling tears. "It's okay."

He engulfed her in his arms, her face pressed to his chest, as he rocked back and forth. He didn't speak, but only held her close, his scent and embrace comforting.

The tears could no longer be controlled, but in fear she'd mess up his cream-colored sweater with her eye makeup, she pulled away, wiping the area beneath her eyes with her fingertips. "Sorry. I didn't mean to get so emotional."

He placed one hand on her face and used his thumb to caress her dampened cheek. "Don't apologize. I can't imagine how hard that must have been for you and your brothers and sisters."

"No sisters. Just brothers." She traipsed to the tissue box near Papa's recliner, and wiped her nose.

"That must have made it doubly hard on you, being the only girl in a houseful of men."

She nodded. Time to change the subject before she gave in to the sobs of self-pity hammering on her heart.

In two steps he stood beside her. "You look so forlorn, love. Please accept my apologies again for bringing this on."

Grace stepped back and gave her head a shake. "It's not your fault. It's just been a rough couple of weeks, and I'm feeling a little sorry for myself. Can we just go?"

"Of course." He took her hand in his and escorted her out the front door, pausing only long enough for her to lock up.

Soon they zipped down the road toward the far side of the lake, Jason leaning on the curves like a fearless racecar driver. "Hope you feel up to something a little different. I have a very special evening planned for you."

She swiveled to peer out the window at the blur of trees and pressed her lips together. He'd made plans just assuming she'd agree to the date? On one hand, it was nice to have everything arranged, but it was also disconcerting, like overkill.

Half an hour later, they pulled into the circular driveway of a very large estate. A steel-spiked gate towered over them with dark rock columns on either side. Jason braked quickly, lowered his window, and punched buttons on a keypad.

Uneasiness trickled through her. "This looks interesting."

He released a short laugh as he raised the window and drove through the open gate. "You haven't seen anything yet." Jason cast a sideways glance. "Don't look so frightened, goose. I'm not going to eat you."

Grace attempted a laugh, but it came out sounding high-pitched and nervous.

As they made the curve in the driveway, a dark house loomed from behind tall evergreens. Jason parked in front of the massive double doors and came around to the passenger side to help her from the car. The wind blew eerily through the tops of the trees. "Welcome to my house."

"It's lovely." She inhaled deeply to quiet her out-of-control nerves. Why hadn't she thought to let someone know her whereabouts?

"I still sense fear." He chuckled and led her away from the front door, around the right side of the house on a rock pathway.

When they finally cleared the dark stone, the view that unfolded before them stole Grace's breath. "I don't think I've ever seen anything so breathtaking." The words were hushed.

An expansive and tastefully-landscaped patio overlooked the lake, every tree and shrub lit with miniature Christmas lights which twinkled off the water, and mimicked the sky. A flagstone terrace stepped in tiers to the lakeshore, a table decked with a white tablecloth and candles in the midst of it all. A white-coated server stood near a hewn-stone fireplace, a crackling fire within, and a guitarist strummed soft, relaxing music. Blanketing it all was the fishy stench of the lake.

Jason laughed, obviously pleased by her awed reaction. He took her hand in his, escorted her across the terrace, and seated her at the table like a perfect gentleman.

Grace viewed her surroundings once more. Another fairy tale. "I don't mean to sound rude, but why are you doing this?"

"Isn't it obvious? I like you, Grace. I want to spend time with you, to see if there's a future for us." Ice clinked in their glasses as he filled them with water from a nearby pitcher. "I must confess, it bothers me that you question my motives."

She placed a hand on his arm. "Don't be upset. I've never been treated so royally, and I just wanted to understand why."

His eyes bore through her like a laser beam in search, and her discomfort grew. She fidgeted, struggling to maintain eye contact. A slow, one-sided smile curved the corner of his mouth. "So you enjoy the princess treatment. I'll keep that in mind."

Grace longed to explain how she'd served as little more than a housekeeper for her family her entire life, never feeling fully loved or accepted by anyone. Who wouldn't have their head turned by fineries and attention with that kind of background? Instead she simply nodded and focused on the meal set before them by the man in the white coat.

Shrimp cocktail, pan-seared fish, twice-baked potatoes, and lightly steamed vegetables were set before her, but she reached for a steaming hot roll, so light it dissolved like sugar in her mouth. The conversation grew more amiable during dinner, and Grace relaxed into her surroundings.

After dinner, Jason moved his napkin to the plate and took a sip from his glass. "Mind if I ask you something, princess?"

"No, what?"

"Why did you break into the office?"

She swallowed the bite she was chewing and laid down her fork. "I heard a rumor and wanted to see if it was true." Grace turned her head to listen to the peaceful sound of the lake lapping at the shore. "I should've handled the situation differently. I did the wrong thing for the right reason."

He didn't answer.

"It sounds like an excuse, or like I'm trying to shirk the blame, but I'm not. I've kicked myself ever since. I just hate how everyone's reacting, almost as if they hate me. The crack in her heart deepened.

"I believe you."

A weight disappeared from her shoulders. "Thank you. That means more than I can express."

Jason leaned in closer, his breath warm on her face, and rested an arm along the back of her chair. He briefly lowered his gaze to her lips, and then stared into her eyes. "I think you and I share a common connection."

Grace battled to disengage herself from the penetrating intensity of his gaze, but something about his eyes hypnotized her. Her heart pounded in her chest and her breath came in short spurts. "How so?"

His entrancing gaze still had her pinned down, like a butterfly on a piece of cardboard. "Well, as I see it, we're both attorneys with a stronger-than-normal desire for justice."

Her eyes widened at the accuracy of his words. At least it was true for her. "Sometimes I think it's easier for people to disregard wrongdoing than it is to do what they can to stop it."

"And that bothers you."

"Yes."

He took another drink from his glass, never breaking eye contact. "Is that why you went to work for the DA's office?"

How had he figured that out? And how much should she reveal? Her brain zoomed in high-speed pursuit of answers, though it sounded like he already knew the truth. "Yes."

"So you had suspicions and you attempted to achieve justice by proving them true."

Grace nodded, willing her spastic breaths to an even pace.

"And did you find anything?"

"Nothing that can be proved. At least not yet."

At last he broke eye contact, his gaze moving past her for several minutes. When he once more focused his attention on her, a calm and cool demeanor had settled over him like a familiar cloak. "I'm guessing Ms. Delgado set you up for the purpose of silencing you."

"That's what I think, but I could be wrong."

"Always trust your instincts." Jason fingered the stem of the glass. "It will serve you well in life and as an attorney."

"If I ever get to be an attorney."

He placed his hand atop hers. "It will happen. I'll see to it."

Grace searched his face, only his chiseled jaw hinting at staunch determination. "It would mean so much to me if you could put in a good word for me with Andy."

"That," he said, leaning back in his chair, "could be problematic. Right now, he sees you as the enemy. Your best bet would be to find a job in another place and work your way up from there. I have a friend in Bellview County who could probably use your services. Would you like me to check with him? I think he would be understanding when it comes to your situation."

She thought through the offer. Never had she imagined working anywhere other than Miller's Creek, but a job was a job, and her financial situation grew more desperate by the day. "That would be wonderful."

His head tilted ever so slightly and he smiled. "My pleasure. It's near enough that we could still see each other on weekends."

"I'd like that very much." Now how to turn the conversation back to Elena? "What do you know about Elena Delgado?"

Jason's cool mask morphed momentarily to a startled one, but he quickly lowered his head. "I've a confession to make, one I hope you understand. You asked earlier about Elena, and I dodged the question." He raised his gaze to hers. "I apologize for not being truthful. I guess I feared she'd already poisoned you against me." He swallowed. "Elena and I were once married."

Now it was Grace's turn to be surprised—so surprised she had no idea what to say.

Jason spoke again. "Please don't share that information. It could cause unnecessary problems as I'm sure you understand. Jessie is my daughter. I moved to the area to be closer to her and hopefully convince Elena to let me see her, even though she has full custody."

"Why did the judge grant her full custody?"

He inhaled a deep breath that noticeably raised his broad shoulders. "I suspect foul play, but like you, I have no way to prove it. Another point of connection—Elena has duped us both."

Her emotions twisted inside, and his sorrow became her own. How sad to be unable to see his child because of Elena's ability to manipulate situations to her advantage. "I'm so sorry. This makes what she did to me seem small in comparison."

His Adam's apple bobbed beneath his sweater. "In response to your original question, all I can say is that in my dealings with her, she's proved to be rather eccentric, hyper-sensitive, and unstable. It drives me crazy that she's the one raising our daughter." He rose to his feet and heaved a frustrated sigh, staring off into the distance. "After Jessie was born she changed and then punished me . Our marriage disintegrated in spite of everything I did to keep it going."

Overwhelming compassion cracked open her heart removing the walls between them. In less than a beat of her heart, Grace wrapped her arms around him. *Lord, help him through his grief. Show me how I can help.* "Do you want to talk about it more?"

"Not at the moment." His voice sounded hoarse.

"I understand." Grace's cell phone buzzed within her purse. She reached to silence it, but noticed the number. Consuela. Was she in danger? "Sorry, but I need to take this call."

He nodded his consent, his eyes distant and dark.

She stood and moved a few feet away, intentionally keeping her voice low. "Consuela? Are you okay?"

"*Si.* I am so glad to have caught you." Relief sounded even through woman's Hispanic accent. "I need to speak with you. Tomorrow if possible."

Jason strolled closer, both hands in his pockets, his gaze focused on the lights of a nearby boat.

Grace feigned a cheery tone since he was within earshot. "Of course, will ten work for you?"

"Yes, that will be good. I must go now."

"Bye." Grace clicked the phone off and hurried to where Jason stood staring out over the placed lake.

He turned at her approach and smiled slightly. "Anything important?"

"Just meeting a friend tomorrow."

Jason clasped her hand in his own and headed back to the table.

She dropped the phone in her purse. "May I use your rest room?"

"Certainly. James will show you the way." Jason snapped his fingers and the white-coated gentleman stepped quickly.

"Yes, sir?"

"Show Miss Soldano to the rest room."

"Yes, sir." He headed toward the house.

Grace sent Jason an encouraging smile and followed James. When she left the restroom a few minutes later, she gazed around the lavish interior of the house, her jaw agape. The great room faced the lake and soared at least three stories high, lit by the largest chandelier she'd ever seen. How could he afford this?

Just as she was about to explore the area a little more carefully, a voice sounded behind her. "Mr. Dent is waiting outside, Miss Soldano."

She brought a hand up as she twirled to face the butler. "Oh, you scared me!"

His face revealed nothing. Instead he merely pointed the way with one hand.

Grace obeyed and rejoined Jason on the terrace. She trailed a hand along the nubby fabric of his sweater. "Feeling better?"

He latched onto her fingers and brought them to his lips. "Seeing you always makes me feel better."

How was it that he always knew the perfect thing to say? She searched his face. No trace of his previous sorrow remained.

"Sorry about earlier. I didn't mean to get sentimental." His words held no emotion and were spoken matter-of-factly.

The flesh along her neck tingled, as though a multi-legged insect crawled along the surface. Something about the emotionless comment disturbed her. She quickly dismissed the feeling. Everyone handled grief in different ways, or perhaps the calm reserve the British were known for had come into play.

He stood. "I should get you home before it gets any later. Don't forget your cell phone." Jason pointed to the table.

A frown crept onto her face as she picked up the phone and dropped it into her bag. "I could've sworn I put that in my purse earlier."

He laughed and moved closer. "I do the same sort of thing all the time. Yet another example of how much we're alike." He planted the softest of kisses on her lips.

Part of her heart melted as she returned the kiss. What was happening? And what about her feelings for Matt? Confused thoughts clouded her brain. He'd left without even saying goodbye, and Jason, in so many ways, was what she'd always wanted in a man. Besides, he obviously needed her more. Matt would always be, well, Matt—happy-go-lucky and carefree as the wind.

Jason pulled away. "I definitely need to take you home." He tucked her hand in his and led her to the front of the house.

Soon they were headed back to Miller's Creek, with not a word passing between them. Strong emotions swirled inside, but the more Grace struggled to bring them into sharper focus, the more twisted and irrevocably knotted they became. They finally arrived at her house, which now seemed downright dowdy compared to Jason's lakeside mansion, and the evening ended with a polite kiss to her forehead.

Her sleep that night was restless and agitated, her dreams shrouded with intermittent images of both Jason and Matt. She slept late the next morning, but finally forced herself from the warm covers to fix a pot of coffee.

Grace released a sigh as the machine gurgled. She'd hoped her thoughts would be more cooperative this morning. If only she could see Matt. He had a way of grounding her like no one else. But wouldn't that only make things more complicated?

She poured the aromatic liquid into her cup, doctored it with extra sugar, and sipped it as she padded to the bathroom to get ready for her meeting with Consuela.

At exactly ten o'clock, she parked in front of Elena's perfect house and made her way up the perfect flagstone walkway to the perfect front door, all the while battling resentment that her former boss had cost her the chance at the same perfection. Maybe Jason would make it possible again.

Consuela answered on the first ring, her eyes glancing around furtively. "Come in." She didn't stop at the living room, but bustled to the back of the house and out to a stone patio overlooking a large pool. Wisps of steam rose from the water into the frigid air. The woman kept walking and didn't stop until they reached a noisy waterfall that flowed into the pool. She motioned to two metal patio chairs and fastened her gaze on Grace as they sat. "I don't have long. Jessie is sleeping and I never know when Elena will choose to come home."

"Are you in danger?"

The older woman's eyes held fear. "I believe Elena is involved in something dangerous. That is why I moved us out here. The house may have ears."

Her breath caught in her chest for a long moment. So her suspicions had been correct. "Any idea what she's involved in?"

Consuela shook her head. "I only know that a man arrived in a chauffeured car last night. After he left, I went to check on her, and she was crying." The woman twisted her hands in her lap.

"What did the man look like?"

"Older. Wealthy. Powerful."

Great, she could have described any number of people. "What can I do to help?"

She reached into the pocket of her apron and withdrew a jagged slip of yellow paper. "I found this in Elena's trash can. She usually shreds everything, but missed this. Can you check it for me? I'd do it myself, but I'm afraid the house . . . " Her words died away as she glanced toward the house, the terror in her eyes more pronounced.

Grace took the paper and nodded. A phone number. "I'll see what I can do." She latched on to Consuela's arm to catch her full attention. "Promise me you'll call if there's any trouble."

The woman nodded and stood, obviously agitated and nervous. "You need to go now."

"Quick question. What do you know about Jason Dent?"

Confusion bathed the other woman's face in a frown. "I do not know him. Now, go!"

She wasted no time in doing exactly what Consuela said.

20

Matt pulled the cell phone from his pocket, praying Sandra hadn't already left for the day. One phrase Justin used in their recent phone conversation kept nibbling at his brain—'the people you least suspect.'

He hurriedly tapped the numbers on the screen of his smartphone and brought it to his ear. How many people had he asked about Jason Dent, and they'd all said nothing but good things. And in spite of the nagging suspicion in his gut, he'd let their opinion sway his own.

As the phone rang on the other end, Matt glanced over his left shoulder. The guys in the band were still setting up the equipment for a Monday night company Christmas party and concert.

"Tyler, Dent, Snodgrass, and Rowe, this is Sandra, how may I help you?" She ran the words together in one sentence, obviously in a hurry to end the day and get home to her family.

"Hey, Sandra. Matt Tyler here."

"Hey. If you're calling to talk to Andy, he's not here at the moment. May I help you?"

Perfect. "As a matter of fact, you can. I need Jason Dent's birth date. Can you get it for me?" He held his breath, fearful she'd ask why.

"Sure. Hang on."

He released a relieved breath. Canned music streamed through the phone line for a few minutes, but Sandra returned in record time. "May 6, 1978."

"Thanks, Sandra. You're a doll."

Matt powered down his phone and checked the band's progress. They were still setting up and more than likely miffed at him for not helping. It couldn't be helped, and he had no time to explain that this was far more important.

He hurried out the door opposite the stage and into the alley where the investigator he'd hired waited near a smelly dumpster. The retired cop had come highly recommended for his investigation skills. He handed the slip of paper with Jason's info to the man. "This is the guy I need you to research. Goes by Jason Dent, and his birthday is May 6, 1978. He's currently an attorney in Miller's Creek."

"Got it." The wiry man folded the slip of paper and stuffed it in his wallet.

"Please let me know any information as soon as you get it, okay?" Matt made eye contact with the guy to make sure he got the point. "Someone's life might depend on it."

A wisp of smoke spiraled from Matt's mouth into the cold December day as he watched the man turn the corner and disappear from view. *Lord, help him find answers as soon as possible.* Anxiety once more gnawed on his brain, and no matter how hard he tried to quell his runaway thoughts, he couldn't. Last night he'd awakened in the wee hours of the morning, overwhelmed with fear for Gracie. And even though Andy thought she was fine, he could no longer ignore his troubled feelings. He checked his watch and strode to the door. Time to get inside and do his part.

The evening whizzed by. As they finished up the last set, the private investigator entered and took a seat near the stage. Once the final song ended, Matt hurried to where he sat munching on peanuts and pulled out a chair. "Find out anything?"

"Yeah, but I don't think you're gonna like it. The man supposedly born on the date you gave me doesn't exist. There are plenty of Jason Dent's out there, but none born on that day or living in the Miller's Creek area."

Matt frowned. "You're positive?"

"Yep." He crunched a few more nuts.

"So whoever this guy is, he's someone besides Jason Dent. But why would he do that?" All sorts of unsavory possibilities ran through his mind.

The investigator shrugged. "Don't automatically assume the guy's a criminal or wanted. Sometimes it's for legitimate reasons."

"Such as?"

"Maybe an unfortunate accident that would be associated with him for life if he kept the same name. Or perhaps he's operating undercover for his real job."

"You mean a spy?"

The guy's brows disappeared under his shaggy hair. "Or someone like me."

Matt considered the statement. It could be true, but the possibility still existed that he wasn't a good guy at all. He reached in his back pocket, removed his wallet, and handed the guy the agreed upon amount. "Thanks for your time."

"Sure thing." The man pocketed the money and exited through the side door.

Matt's mind whirled. Now what? Andy deserved to know that his law partner wasn't really named Jason Dent. More importantly, Gracie needed to know. But how could he tell her if she wouldn't answer her phone? He rubbed a hand across his mouth and eyed the clock. Too late to call tonight anyway. It would just have to wait until first thing in the morning.

With a weary sigh, he trudged up the steps to the stage to help tear down and load the equipment. He removed his guitar from its stand and ambled to the case which sat beneath a speaker tower that Derek disassembled. Matt snapped the last latch on his case as Derek's voice cried out. "Matt, watch it!"

He looked up as a speaker sped toward him. Then everything went black.

Grace peered around the unfamiliar landscape. Where was she? A pristine country church, its steeple scraping bullet-gray skies, lay beside plowed fields. Distant trees, leaves missing, took on a haunting persona in the dense fog as they stretched out brown claws.

Her legs attempted to shift position, but felt leaden and heavy. She sensed that she needed to figure this out. Needed to understand so she could make the right decision. The white tent above her head rippled and popped in a brief burst of cold wind, then sagged, dead-still.

A congregation of people she knew and loved sat in perfectly-placed rows of metal folding chairs atop fake turf. The unfamiliar place reminded her of a graveside service where heavy rains had left a muddy mess.

A frown creased her forehead. The people didn't talk or smile or even move. Like cardboard cutouts they sat, apathetic and uncaring, unable to help. A center aisle stretched down the narrow, makeshift church, and men in dark suits gathered at the back, ready to proceed down the corridor of plastic grass. Grace was suddenly aware of someone behind her. She turned.

Dressed in an exquisitely-tailored black suit, Jason ducked beneath the tent top, his face cold and expressionless. In one hand he carried a Bible. With his lips molded in a grim line, he nodded to the men in back, and they advanced, their faces long and somber.

When they reached the front they spread out in a straight line and revealed two suited men who accompanied Matt. In his normal attire of jeans, t-shirt, and flip-flops, his hands were bound and his ankles shackled.

At the sight of his ropes and chains her throat grew dry and gravelly, and she jerked her gaze to his face. His eyes held an incredible sorrow, like she'd somehow let him down. Or had he let her down? She lowered her head and for the first time noticed the forest-green trench coat she wore. Her hands, stuffed in the pockets, shifted until she gripped something cool and hard.

A gun.

Grace trembled as her hand conformed to the pistol, her index finger against the trigger.

Jason nodded to the men once more, and like menacing shadows, they advanced toward Matt. Heart racing, she attempted to pull the gun from her pocket. He had to be stopped. But her hand froze in place. She couldn't do it. Couldn't force herself to repay evil with evil, no matter the cost.

Far-away voices sounded, but none of the cardboard people moved their lips. A rapping sound broke through the foggy mist. With a moan, she stirred and sat up in bed, the dream more vivid than reality. What time was it?

The bedroom door cracked ever so slightly. "Sorry to wake you, *la hija*, but I wanted to let you know I was home."

Grace scrambled from the bed. "Papa! I'm so glad to see you. I missed you." She engulfed him in a hug, which he surprisingly returned.

"I missed you, too. There is someone I want you to meet." He smiled at her then motioned down the hallway for someone to join him.

Every nerve in her being instantly snapped to attention as footsteps pattered outside her door. What was going on? Was she still dreaming?

A round Hispanic woman with a beautiful smile stepped into view, and Papa put an arm around her shoulder. "Graciela, meet my new wife, Maria."

Her jaw unhinged as his words landed a blow. In a daze, she somehow managed to move forward and shake the woman's hand, but couldn't find her voice.

A reprimand moved into Papa's eyes, and he opened his mouth to give words to the stern look, but the woman placed a hand on his arm. "It's late, Juan. I am sure Graciela is tired. Why don't we talk about this in the morning over breakfast, hmm?"

Her father smiled at the woman still tucked protectively beneath his arm and nodded. "*Si.*" He turned his gaze back to Grace. "Goodnight, *la hija*." Without another word, he pulled the door closed, leaving her standing there with her mouth agape.

Grace fell back on the bed. First the dream and now this. Her brain flip-flopped between the two, neither making much sense. Why had Jason appeared as the bad guy in her dream, when he'd done nothing but show her kindness after kindness? Earlier that day he'd called to let her know that he not only had a job lined up for her in Bellview, but a place to live as well.

She brought both palms to her face and rubbed her sleepy eyes. The dream had nothing to do with Jason and everything to do with her worries of starting a new life in a new location. And now that Papa had a wife, moving away was for the best. She would just be in the way here.

Grace gauged her feelings about Papa having a wife. Never had she imagined he would remarry. Though it hurt that Mama had been replaced in his affections, another part of her rejoiced to see him happy again. A soft curve settled on her lips. Nothing could bring Mama back, so it was good that Papa had found someone who could make him happy.

A shiver moved up her spine, and for the first time since Papa's news, she took note of her bare feet on the cold floor. Grace rushed to the dresser, located a pair of wooly socks, and slipped them on. Next she removed her thick winter robe from the hook on the back of the door and wrapped it around her. There would be no going back to sleep now. Papa was married!

A sudden rush of energy hummed in her chest. Yes, it was late, and yes, she was wide awake, but it was all good. She'd use the time to pack her clothes and get ready for the move.

An hour later, spent from her late-night packing spree, she positioned the last suitcase in the corner and yawned. After she returned her robe to its hook, she crawled into bed and clicked off the lamp. Her head had barely hit the pillow when her cell phone buzzed. Sleepily, she eyed the alarm clock's bright red numbers. Who could be calling after midnight?

She squinted at the light as she turned on the lamp and reached for the phone. The display read 'unknown.'

"Hello?"

No answer.

Grace dropped the phone to the bed as if it were hot. She'd purchased the cell phone to escape the anonymous calls, but obviously whoever wanted to scare her now had her number. Her brain whizzed through the possibilities. Finally she decided that Elena must have found the card she'd given Consuela. Without hesitation, she turned off the phone and crawled back into bed.

The next morning Grace entered the kitchen, dressed and ready for the day, curious about the new woman in her father's life, but also dreading the news she had to deliver. She'd promised Jason she would be in Bellview in time to work that afternoon.

Papa and Maria stood at the stove, both busy with preparations for breakfast. The mouth-watering smell of *chorizo* wafted from a sizzling skillet.

"Good morning."

The other two turned at her greeting. Papa laid down his spatula and made his way to her, engulfing her in an embrace. What had come over the man who a few short weeks ago had refused to even make eye contact with her? As he pulled away, Grace once more marveled at the miraculous change.

"Good morning, *la hija*. You slept well, *si?*"

She chose not to answer. Instead, she smiled shyly at the woman whisking the eggs.

"*Buenos dias,* Graciela. I hope you were able to get back to sleep after we woke you." She placed the bowl on the counter, and wiped her hands on her apron. "You look very pretty."

As Papa and Maria turned back to the food, a sudden rush of comfort flowed through her. In spite of the recent chain of disasters, God's grace was still at work. How happy Papa seemed, and all due to this woman she barely knew.

A few minutes later, they sat down to dine on breakfast burritos wrapped in fresh homemade tortillas. At first the conversation seemed forced and awkward, and an uncomfortable silence developed.

Papa cleared his throat and laid down his burrito. "Graciela, I want you to know that although I love Maria very much, it doesn't mean I love your Mama any less." He paused, his frown bearing testimony to deep thought and careful attention to his words. "I didn't do this on a whim. Maria and I've known each other for many years. We grew up next door to one another and were childhood sweethearts before she went away to school. I know it must seem to you that I've gone *loco*, but when we saw each other, it was like we were young again. Like it was meant to be. I hope you understand."

Grace nodded, glad he'd shared the story. It somehow helped to know that he hadn't just gone to Mexico for the purpose of finding a woman. "Thank you for explaining, Papa. I can tell you and Maria are very happy, and I'm elated for you both."

"I hope we haven't made you late for work." Papa said, joy still inscribed on his face.

The perfect opportunity to share her news had fallen into her lap, but it still wouldn't be easy. "Actually I need to talk with you about that. I've taken a job in Bellview that starts today. I need to leave pretty soon to allow myself time to unpack. If it's okay, I'd like to use the old pickup until I can afford to buy a car."

A heavy cloud descended on Papa's face as she spoke, and he looked ready to explode.

Maria noticed the approaching storm and laid a hand over his. "A new job. How exciting. Isn't it wonderful, Juan?" She sent Grace an understanding smile.

"You are no longer working in Morganville?" Papa's face and voice held familiar gruffness.

She shook her head. "It didn't work out, Papa. I don't really have time to explain it now, but I promise to write you a letter once I get settled into my new place."

"So you have a place to live?"

"Yes, and I'll be fine. Please don't worry. This is for the best, and I'll be back in a few weeks for Christmas."

He still looked doubtful.

"Graciela is right." Maria patted his hand. "She's a grown woman now with her own life to lead. This is a good thing."

Papa gazed into his new wife's eyes for a long minute before he finally nodded. "Yes, it is good." He turned his gaze to Grace with a sad smile. "Go, with my blessing, *la hija,* but I would like that letter sooner rather than later."

After sending them both an appreciative smile, Grace rose to her feet and carried her plate to the sink. Papa moved up beside her, wrapped an arm around her shoulder, and drew her in close. "I hope you know how much I love you, Graciela." Unshed tears glistened in his eyes.

Grace planted a kiss on his weathered cheek. "And I love you, Papa."

A half hour later, she backed onto the dirt road and waved at Papa and Maria one last time. The old house seemed somehow brighter with the fresh start of the couple standing nearby, the future ripe with possibility. And now, with the mistakes from the past behind her, God in His great mercy had given her the opportunity for a do-over as well. More than anything, she needed to get it right this time around.

21

A bell jangled above her head as Grace entered the small bakery in downtown Bellview early Wednesday morning. Filled to capacity, the room quieted temporarily as eyes turned her way.

Heat flooded her cheeks. Though the place was quaint and rustic, she longed for the familiar faces at Granny's Kitchen. But this was her new home now, and the only way to get to know these people was to join them. It was time to put the past behind her. She released a slow breath. The aroma of fresh-baked cinnamon rolls floated around her head and drew her closer to the counter.

"Can I help you, miss?" The middle-aged woman, her red apron dotted with flour, drummed her fingers against the counter, obviously running a tad shy in the patience department.

Grace grimaced at the prices. "I'll have a cinnamon roll and water, please." She counted out the money while the lady wrapped the pastry and rang it up on an antique cash register.

Her hands full, she turned to find a place to sit, only to realize that every table was taken. Close to walking out and traipsing back to her apartment, an elderly man near the door sent a smile and motioned her over to the table he shared with his wife.

He stood as she approached. "We'd love to have you join us." He offered his hand as she set her plate and glass on the table. "I'm Jake, and this is my wife Julia."

"So nice to meet you both." Grace smiled and pulled out a ladder-back chair which instantly reminded her of Mama Beth.

"Are you new in town?" Julia, her salt-and-pepper hair clipped close to her head, smiled broadly.

"Yes. My third day here. I'm working for Mr. Thomas and leasing the small apartment above his office."

The couple exchanged a knowing look in the noisy café.

Grace forked a piece of gooey roll in her mouth, savoring the cinnamon and cream cheese frosting. A cold glass of milk would make this even better. She sipped her water. "So have you two lived here long?"

"Going on seven years." Jake's white bushy eyebrows arched slightly. "I'm the pastor at Grace Fellowship down the road."

She brightened. "Is that the cute little country church I passed on the outskirts of town?"

"That's the one. We'd be tickled pink to have you join us Sunday."

A smile blossomed in her heart and moved to her face. Only here a few days, and already she had a place to go to church. Though the thought brought joy, it also brought a bit of apprehension. Bellview was smaller than Miller's Creek. What if no one welcomed her? "I'll be there."

Though conversation was a bit uncomfortable, Grace forced herself to make small talk. Both Jake and Julia had a way of making her feel like a long-time friend, and by the time she finished her breakfast, she felt less lonely.

Before leaving for work, she jotted the times for Bible study and worship on her napkin, and then hurried out the door and down the street.

In less than a minute, she entered the office of the Thomas Law Firm, a dusty old building sorely in need of a good dusting and several gallons of paint. A sneeze erupted. It always took a good half hour for her nose to grow desensitized to the reek of stale cigars.

Mr. Thomas stepped from his office as she put her purse away, a stogie clamped between his teeth. "You finish that research I gave you yesterday?"

"Yes sir." She handed him the file folder from her desk.

He perused it with an occasional snort. Something about him reminded her of pictures she'd seen of Winston Churchill, though Mr. Thomas was much less noble-looking.

The phone shrilled from her desk. "Thomas Law Firm. May I help you?"

The same rough voice she'd heard yesterday on at least two occasions sounded again. "Let me talk to Thomas."

She decided against asking for a name, since yesterday's attempts had proved futile. "Just a moment please."

Grace held the phone toward Mr. Thomas. "It's for you. The same gentleman who called twice yesterday."

His eyes flickered with some indefinable emotion as he uttered a curse and moved into his office.

Thankfully, he left a few minutes later, with a comment that he'd be out the rest of the day. She finished the work he'd given her by mid-afternoon and spent the remainder of her time cleaning up around the office. When the day ended, the front windows were clean enough to see out, but her clothes now needed washing, a task she'd have to do by hand.

A few minutes after five, she headed upstairs to her apartment to change clothes and then walked a couple of blocks to purchase a few groceries with the small amount of money she had left. Hopefully Mr. Thomas would pay her on Friday so she'd have enough money for next week's food. As she made her way back, a small mew sounded from behind her. She turned to see a scrawny yellow kitten following. He looked up at her and mewed again, a strangled plea for help.

Her memory flew to Millie. To take on a new pet somehow felt like high treason. Besides, she barely had enough funds to feed herself. "Shoo, cat." She lunged toward it and waved her hand.

The cat sat back on his haunches and continued to mew piteously.

Frustration pushed the air from her lungs. "Oh, all right."

A few minutes later she shared a can of tuna with the cat, which only stopped eating long enough to scratch.

A sudden wave of loneliness passed over her. Right now it felt like her only friend in the world was a flea-bitten, scrawny yellow cat.

A pounding throb pierced his skull. Matt groaned and forced his eyelids apart. Afraid to turn his head for fear of intense pain, he kept it immobilized and moved his gaze around the unfamiliar space. Was he in a hospital?

"Hey, bro, glad to see you're awake." Andy stepped into his line of vision, his eyes concerned, his voice comforting. "How you feel?"

"Like someone tried to beat my brains out with a crowbar." The whispered words made his throat feel like he'd gargled with acid. "What happened?"

"You mean you don't remember the fight you had with a tower speaker?"

Matt tried to shake his head, and immediately winced at waves of pain. "I'm guessing the speaker won?"

"Good assumption. Let me call the nurse." His brother punched a red button on the bed.

"I'm in a hospital?" Where at and for how long?

"Yep. That's what happens when you pick a fight with a speaker bigger than you."

"And the band? Did they go on to the next concert?"

A wry expression crept across Andy's features. "And a few after that."

Matt's eyes opened wide, and he struggled to sit up, in spite of searing pain and wooziness. "What day is it?"

Andy gently pinned his shoulders to the bed. "Whoa there, bucko, take it easy. You've had a nice three-day nap."

Gracie! Thoughts of her exploded in his mind. "I've gotta get to Gracie."

"I already told you. She's fine."

Too weak and tired to overcome his brother, Matt stopped struggling and laid back against the bed. "What about your work?"

"Everything's on hold until you're better."

The door swung open, and a tall dude dressed in a white coat entered with an electronic tablet, a young woman in scrubs behind him. "Our guy's awake, I see." He laid down the computer, retrieved a pen light from the breast pocket of his coat, and leaned in to check Matt's eyes, the scent of his cinnamon gum wafting in the air. "I'm Dr. Stevens. I'd ask how you're feeling, but I'm pretty sure I know. Major headache, right?"

"If that's all you learned in med school, I sure hope you got a tuition break."

The dark-haired man laughed. "Glad to see that knot on your head didn't take away your sense of humor. Thirsty?"

Matt nodded, slowly this time. "Like I swallowed the Sahara."

"Melissa, let's get our new friend some water."

Her brown hair pulled back in a bouncing pony tail, the nurse whisked to the counter, poured water into a plastic cup, and brought it to Matt. "Hold on. I'm gonna raise the bed so you can drink without taking a bath." She reached below the side of the bed, and the top whirred to a slight incline.

He guzzled the lukewarm liquid. Never had warm water tasted so good.

She pulled the cup away. "You might wanna slow down a bit. Take small sips."

"Don't wanna lose it as soon as you drink it, do you?" The doctor used a stylus to punch the tablet screen and then raised his gaze to Matt. "I don't know how much your brother told you, but you came here by ambulance late Monday night with a concussion and a huge gash. No fractures, but you were unconscious and had quite a bit of swelling." He pocketed the stylus. "Sometimes swelling can cause seizures, so we kept you in a medically-induced coma to let the swelling go down."

"What day is it?"

"Thursday."

His throat constricted. What if something terrible had already happened to Gracie? He once more struggled to sit up, the pain in his head like a white-hot icepick plunging through his ear.

The doctor and nurse immediately held him down, with the former getting most irate. "This ain't gonna work, Mr. Tyler. If I have to tie you to the bed, I will. We need to observe you for the next few days. Your motor skills, memory, and verbal skills all seem to be intact, but we need to run a battery of tests to make sure."

Tears welled in Matt's eyes and slid down his cheeks as he relaxed the weight of his head on the pillow. Normally he'd have whisked the tears away, especially in front of other people, but at the moment nothing mattered except getting to Gracie. *Lord Jesus, watch over her and protect her.*

Dr. Stevens tucked the electronic pad under one arm and turned his gaze to Andy. "Depression's pretty common after this type of brain trauma. Keep an eye on him and let us know if it gets worse. If necessary, I'll prescribe medication to help him sleep."

Sleep? He'd been asleep for three days, and they wanted him to sleep some more?

"He might also experience confusion, so what he says might not make sense." Now the doctor faced Matt. "You can have sips of water in small quantities, and I'll have the nurse bring you some broth. Only liquids for a while to make sure you can keep food on your stomach. I'll be back later this afternoon to check on you, okay?" He strode from the room, his tennis shoes squeaking against the tile floor.

Andy refilled the cup and brought it to Matt's lips. "Here's some more water."

"I can do it." The words erupted in a growl, but he didn't care. "Can you at least help me sit up so I don't drown myself?"

His brother's eyebrows scuttled up his forehead. "Sure, but you'd better lose the 'tude."

Matt pressed his lips together. Andy was only trying to help. "Sorry. I'm just worried about Gracie."

"Worrying won't help you get better any faster, Matt. I'm sure she's fine. She's got a pretty good head on her shoulders. Well, except for the breaking and entering episode." Andy raised the head of the bed. "What has you so bothered anyway?"

Matt sipped the water while he relayed the information the private detective had given him. "Anyway, whoever you have working for you isn't really named Jason Dent."

Andy stood with hands akimbo, his mouth at work like he wanted to say something, but wasn't sure he should.

"What is it? Tell me." Matt didn't care if he sounded demanding and curt. He had to know.

His brother raked both hands through his curly hair. "Okay, but promise me you won't do anything stupid."

"Okay. I promise I won't do anything stupid."

"I've known for some time that Jason wasn't who he claimed to be, but I haven't been able to say anything. I've been working with the FBI while they keep tabs on him."

Matt's jaw went slack. "FBI?" His mind raced, immediately honing in on the conversation he'd had with his professor buddy. "Do they think Jason's dangerous?"

"Nah. They think he works with some political powerhouse for the purpose of affecting the outcome of various cases. That's about all I know."

"Do they suspect Gracie, too?"

"I think they were afraid she'd get involved."

Matt brought a hand up to gently massage his forehead. While she wouldn't intentionally get involved, her insatiable desire for justice could be a problem. He closed his eyes and groaned. "I've gotta make sure she's okay."

Andy moved to the window and opened the curtains just enough to let in natural light, his jaw cemented. "Not gonna happen, so don't even go there. We'll go only when the doc says it's safe, and not a minute before. Got it?"

Matt nodded weakly, too tired to protest.

The day crawled by, with his tormented thoughts never far from Gracie. When he wasn't making conversation with Andy, he pretended to watch TV, but used the time to pray that God would protect her. As the day passed, a frenzied restlessness surged within, accompanied by a burning desire to hear her voice.

The following morning, a nurse delivered a real breakfast, but Matt could only eat a few bites at a time. Too much made him nauseous. By Saturday, the solid food had renewed his strength, so when Dr. Stevens stopped by for a visit—this time with an elderly nurse who hummed incessantly—Matt was ready to impress him with his improvement.

"Hey, Doc." The doctor reached out a hand. Matt leaned forward, ignoring the pain in his head, and squeezed a little harder than necessary to prove his strength. "I've kept solid food down yesterday and today and walked to the bathroom on my own. Think I'm good to go?"

"Not yet." He leaned against the wall at the foot of the bed. "Just because you're doing better doesn't mean you're ready. Yesterday's CT scan still showed a little swelling, and to caution you, trying to do too much won't get you out of here any faster. If anything, it could hold you back. Try to do too much too fast, I'll keep you here two more weeks if necessary. Understand?"

Beneath the covers, Matt's hands curled into tight balls, and his clenched jaw pulsed erratically. He released a slow breath to keep his anger in check and simply nodded, unable to verbally agree.

The doc checked the chart. "I'll prescribe more sleeping meds for you tonight, and we'll wheel you down for another CT scan in the next hour or so. If that looks good, I'll have a physical therapist stop by to take you through your paces. Prepare to be worn out. If you do well today, and have no setbacks, I might let you go home tomorrow, emphasis on the word 'might.'"

Red hot heat rocketed from Matt's feet to his head. Didn't *anyone* realize how badly he needed to get to Gracie? As soon as Dr. Stevens left the room, Matt looked at Andy, struggling to keep frustration from his tone. "Can you bring me my phone?"

"Sure." His brother shuffled through the duffel bag in the bottom of the closet. "Calling Gracie?"

"Yep." If he could get through.

"Okay, I'm gonna step out to the waiting area and call Trish. Need anything before I go?"

"No thanks." Matt waited for Andy to exit the room, and then punched the power button. Nothing. Dead as a doornail. His head fell back against the pillow and he stared at the acoustical ceiling tiles. Now what? He could either wait until Andy came back from calling Trish, which could take a half hour or better, or he could get the charger himself.

He contemplated the doctor's words of warning, but in the end decided he was up to the challenge. Matt sat up slowly and waited till the lightheadedness to pass, then carefully swung his legs over the side of the bed and pushed himself to a standing position.

He gripped the bed rail, and with small shuffling steps, made his way to the closet and peered down at his duffel bag. Why did it seem a million miles away? He stared at it for at least a couple of minutes, trying to determine if he had the stamina to stoop over without passing out.

The door swung open without warning, and the same nurse, with the same annoying hum, entered with a dinner tray. Her eyes took on schoolteacher sternness. "What in the world are you doing?" She laid the tray on the table and rushed to him. "Dr. Stevens will not be happy about this." With both hands on his arms, she turned him around and steered him back to bed.

He had to find a way outta this mess, and quick. Matt glanced at her name tag. "You're not gonna tell on me, are you, Margie?"

"Hmmm." A hint of a smile played on her lips. "I suppose that depends on why you were out of bed after you'd already been given very specific instructions."

Matt leaned back against the pillows she'd plumped. "There's a girl I need to call—"

The woman's face softened and her lips lost their vertical lines. "Say no more."

Leave it to a woman to fall for the sappy stuff. "But if I don't say more, how am I gonna get my cell phone charger?"

She laughed and headed to the closet. "You're a regular riot, aren't you? I'm guessing the charger is in your bag?"

"Yes ma'am."

Within a minute, Margie had the phone plugged in and within reach. She sent a smile and wave as she hummed her way out of the room.

At last. Matt made the call, happy to hear the phone ringing on the other end, instead of the monotonous busy signal.

Juan Soldano answered.

"Hi, Mr. Soldano. This is Matt Tyler." He tensed, expecting opposition.

But no lecture came. Instead the man practically bubbled over. "How are you, Mr. Matt?"

"Been better, but I'm gonna live. Is Gracie available by any chance?" Just one sound of her voice. That's all he needed to determine if she was okay.

"No. She is working in Bellview now."

Matt's heart landed at his feet, and he lowered his head to one hand. How he needed to hear her voice.

Mr. Soldano continued. "Jason Dent found her a job there."

At the mention of Jason's name, his pulse careened into overdrive and his spine straightened. Why would Jason find her a job? And in Bellview of all places? "Is there a way I can reach her? I really need to speak with her."

The older man hesitated. "She does have a cell phone, but made me promise not to give out the number."

Why would she keep the number a secret unless she didn't want him to call? "Mr. Soldano, I don't know how to say this, so I'm just gonna come out and say it. I care about your daughter, and I'm very concerned about her right now. If you hear from her, please tell her I called." The phone went quiet for a brief moment. Had he revealed too much?

The man lightly cleared his throat. "I am very touched by your words. The next time I speak to her, I will tell her you called."

His chest raised and lowered. "Thank you so much, sir."

"*De nada.*"

Long after the phone call ended, Matt puzzled over the change in Juan Soldano. What could've happened to cause such a drastic difference?

In a short amount of time, his thoughts returned to Gracie. Hearing her voice wouldn't happen now, and he had no idea how to reach her. All he could do was pray, do everything he could to get better, and then make his way to Bellview to find Gracie.

22

Early Friday morning before work, Grace leaned back against the small sofa and closed her eyes, her heart heavy. *Lord, open my eyes to see Your goodness all around me. Help me get past this loneliness and to be patient with the process of living in a new town. Show me how to put the past behind me and move forward.*

In spite of her desire to get on with her life, her thoughts turned to Matt and how much she missed him. She'd almost phoned several times, but changed her mind at the last minute, fearful of interrupting a rehearsal or waking him too early after a late-night concert. Maybe he'd be back in Miller's Creek over Christmas, but would he have anything to do with her after the way she'd treated him?

She took a sip of coffee and then sat her cup on the box she used as a coffee table, reflecting over the first week in Bellview. Mr. Thomas had proved to be short-tempered. If something she said or did didn't suit him, he hollered about it until tears threatened. Thankfully, her new boss was out of the office more than he was in.

The still-unnamed cat jumped to the box and sent her cup crashing to the floor. Coffee splashed onto her skirt and quickly soaked floral-design scarf Grace used as a tablecloth. The pesky animal then leapt to the floor and licked up the rest as though the heinous act was intentional.

Grace hurriedly snatched up the scarf and ran to the sink to rinse it before it stained. The scarf was one of only a few items she had that once belonged to Mama. After draping the wet scarf over the countertop to dry, she stepped to the bedroom to change.

Her cell phone rang. That would be Jason. At least he'd been faithful in calling to check on her, though she hadn't yet garnered the courage to ask why Consuela didn't know him. It seemed too personal a question to ask for some reason. She answered the phone and infused her tone with a cheerfulness she didn't feel. "Good morning."

"How's my girl? Is Thomas treating you well?"

How was she supposed to answer that question without sounding like a total ingrate?

Jason interrupted her thoughts. "Can't talk long this morning—busy day ahead—but I did want to let you know I won't be calling tonight or tomorrow."

The news fell on her ears like an aftershock to an earthquake kind of week. Great. Now she had an extra twenty minutes of twiddling her thumbs over the weekend. "How come?" Grace hated the neediness in her voice.

"I can't really say, but I promise to make it up to you. Trust me?"

Good question. Did she? She shelved the thought and turned back to the conversation. "Of course, but I'll miss talking to you."

Jason's soft laughter filtered through the phone. "Have a great day, love."

"You too." The deep aching loneliness returned. Was it because the weekend stretched ahead of her like a lonely gaping hole and no way to fill it?

Snap out of it, Grace. A determined deep breath bolstered her flagging spirit. She rushed to change clothes so she could get to work on time. It wouldn't be wise to anger her cigar-chewing boss on payday.

The day flew quicker than she expected. Mr. Thomas was out most of the day—only at the office long enough to give her a stack of work and a lower-than-expected check. During the lunch hour, she allowed herself the luxury of daydreaming about how she'd spend her first weekend in Bellview, refusing to sit around and mope.

As soon as the clock hit five, she was out the door, eager to be free of the confines of the smelly office. She traded her skirt for a favorite pair of blue jeans. Her first stop would be the thrift store on the opposite corner to pick up a few things for the apartment. And tomorrow she'd visit the public library.

After feeding the cat, Grace moved to the stairs that exited the building in the back. She'd just clomped down the rickety steps when a fancy black car pulled into the overgrown alleyway. Her heart bounded to her throat. Jason?

The car screeched to a stop and the door swung open. It *was* him. She hurried over as he unfolded his tall frame from the sports car. "Jason!"

Though his face held a frown its familiarity instantly boosted her spirits. He returned her embrace. "Where were you going?"

"I thought I'd explore the town. What are you doing here?"

He planted a kiss on the tip of her nose. "Here to make sure you stay out of trouble. It appears I arrived at just the right time."

Now Grace frowned. Why did she get the distinct impression that he hadn't intended the comment as a joke?

Jason treated Grace to a nice dinner Friday evening, driving several miles to a well-known steakhouse. They pulled into a gravel parking lot full of vehicles. Though the unassuming building and middle-of-nowhere location gave no clue to the quality of food within, the heavenly smells brought a rumble to her stomach as soon as she exited the car. A private plane landed on the restaurant's airstrip as they entered, yet another tribute to the delicious menu.

Determined to enjoy this brief respite from her lonely life, Grace scarfed down her chicken-fried steak and creamed potatoes in short order, most likely the after-effects of a week of rationing her meager supply of food. In sharp-contrast to her jolly mood, Jason stared into the distance throughout their time together, lacking the warmth he'd exhibited on previous occasions. Instead he alternated between bored and demanding, like being here with her was the last thing he wanted. At other moments, he clung to her and refused to let her out of his sight.

On the way back to the apartment, Grace gnawed the lining of her cheek. Had she said or done something wrong? Several times during the course of the evening, she'd tried to bring him around, but to no avail. Why was he acting so strange? The confusion that plagued her steps during the last few weeks in Miller's Creek returned, a heavy fog which enveloped her brain and heart.

Jason jerked to a quick stop in front of her building. "I'll pick you up in the morning for breakfast." He made no attempt to kiss her or to come around to open the door, nor did he wait until she safely reached the top step of the worn stairs before he sped off into the night.

After breakfast at a local pancake house Saturday morning, they drove to Abilene for a day of Christmas shopping. Though it was pleasant to stroll through the mall decorated in fragrant Christmas greenery and to sing along with familiar carols, she had no money to spend on gifts and was too embarrassed to tell him why she made no purchases. Finally they both agreed to end the day early. Mid-afternoon Jason deposited her at the exterior staircase with a quick peck on the cheek. "I have to get back to Miller's Creek, but I'll try to call tomorrow."

The tail lights of his car disappeared around the curve in the road, and an overwhelming sense of relief came over her. She rolled her head in a circle to relieve the tension that had built in her neck and shoulders from trying to please him. Was it wrong to be glad she had at least one day left in her weekend to enjoy?

Sunday morning she woke with a smile. She'd looked forward to this day since Wednesday morning when she met Jake and Julia. The name of the church had first captured her attention on the drive into town—Grace Fellowship. If there were any two things she needed most, these most certainly fit the bill—grace and fellowship.

After a tepid shower, she fixed a bowl of cereal and spread the Miller's Creek newspaper that had arrived in the mail late yesterday afternoon out on the counter. In the upper center on the front page, a picture of Elena loomed below a headline that simply read: "Delgado Investigated." She gasped and dropped her spoon to the table.

Grace scanned the article, her mouth still open wide. Just as she'd expected, Scott Evans had been arrested for the murder of Michael Bedford. No mention was made of David Simmons, the original suspect. The thought that Simmons had managed to frame his friend for the crime nauseated her.

She focused in on Elena's picture, obviously taken shortly after the news had broken. Instead of the confident and classy woman she'd once admired, the person who stared back at her exhibited no hint of pride or vanity. Her once perfect hair and makeup no longer existed, replaced by a disheveled appearance, which mirrored the pain inscribed on her face.

Grace moved to the couch, unable to peel her eyes away from the picture. Something inside her broke and gave way, and tears flooded her face, depositing their salty tang on her tongue. Gone was her previous resentment and vindictive desire, replaced by a love and compassion she didn't know was humanly possible. Yes, her suspicions had at last been justified, but her heart ached to think of how this would affect not only Elena, but also Consuela, Jessie, and even Jason. She offered up a heartfelt prayer for the situation and the people involved, then headed back to the bedroom to get ready for worship.

An hour later, both excited and a little nervous, she entered the back of the country church, and gave her eyes time to adjust to the low light. The building smelled of the same orange oil Papa used on the wooden tables at the restaurant, and the small nave led into a sanctuary lined with wooden pews. The worn benches and stained-glass windows hinted at the age of the building, but the place was obviously tended with care.

Jake shuffled toward her from the front of the church, Julia close behind. They both greeted her with hugs.

"So glad you could make it, Gracie." Jake spoke her schoolgirl name as though he'd used it her entire life. Surprisingly enough, she took it as a compliment, though it set off a longing in her heart to see Matt and to hear his voice.

She moved a hand to her abdomen to still the restless butterflies and returned their smiles. "Thank you. Good to be here."

"Come on in and have a seat. The rest of the congregation should be here shortly. We're not a big group, but what we lack in quantity, we make up for in quality." He finished the comment with a wink.

The morning went by in a blur—a brief meeting together for song and prayer before dismissing to different rooms behind the main building for small group Bible study. Afterward they all returned to the peaceful sanctuary for more music and a sermon.

Jake spoke the sermon with such fervor and authenticity Gracie could only attribute it to moving of the Holy Spirit. His face glowed as he relayed the familiar story of Jonah, and left her more enthralled and in love with God and His grace. To the prophet, the Ninevites seemed barbaric, but to Sovereign God and His holy heart of grace, they were a people greatly-loved.

The congregation rose to their feet and began to sing *Amazing Grace*. She focused her thoughts and prayers on the message God placed in her heart.

"Amazing grace! How sweet the sound . . . "

She drank in the sweetness, though she suspected her finite mind could never fully comprehend or plumb its depths.

". . . that saved a wretch like me!"

Gracie closed her eyes, lifting her palms to the heavens in praise. Matt was right. There was nothing good enough in her to merit such a gift.

"Twas grace that taught my heart to fear, and grace my fears relieved..."

Through difficulty her heart had feared and turned to God, making even Mama's tragic death an act of grace. That same grace had turned her fears to faith.

"... How precious did that grace appear the hour I first believed!"

The scarlet thread of grace wove its way through history, from the blood on the doors of the Hebrew people on that first Passover, to the blood shed by the perfect Lamb of God.

"Through many dangers, toils and snares..."

She brought one hand to her chest and thumped to the beat, swaying with the music. God's grace surrounded them all, even the people who'd tried to destroy her.

"... I have already come..."

Circumstances which once seemed impossible brimmed with His grace, a grace which prodded her to gaze on her sinfulness and respond to His invitation to change and become more like Christ.

"'Tis grace hath brought me safe thus far, and grace will lead me home.

Her eyes fluttered open, her gaze at rest on the rough-hewn cross on the back wall of the baptistry.

"When we've been there ten thousand years, bright shining as the sun, We've no less days to sing God's praise than when we first begun."

Inside her heart ached with the fullness of what Jesus had done for her. A tear slipped from her cheek to the worn wood of the ancient pew in front of her. Her sins had been washed away by wave upon wave of grace. God didn't dispense grace in drops, but in torrents. Grace was a never-ending ocean, and Christ's rough-timber cross the bridge that spanned the distance between sinful man and Holy God.

When the song ended, Jake dismissed the service in prayer, and afterwards many members of the congregation shook her hand or even hugged her neck and told her they hoped she'd come back again. Julia hurried by, calling out over her shoulder as she passed. "Please don't leave yet. We'd like to have you over to our house for lunch. I have just a few things I need to pick up from my classroom first."

The parsonage sat directly behind the church, and a brief walk landed them in its cozy comfort. As they entered the front door, the fragrance of pot roast wafted to Gracie's nose. Mama. The smell reminded her of Mama, a sweet memory she'd almost forgotten.

She gazed around the tiny space as Julia bustled to the kitchen cabinets to set the table. Worn and sagging furniture lined the living room, covered with crocheted love . . . just like the home she'd shared with Papa and her brothers in Miller's Creek. Tears filled her eyes and slipped unbidden down her cheeks.

"Are you okay?" Loving concern radiated spilled from Julia's face and voice. Jake moved in closer as well, the same tenderness shining from his eyes.

Gracie managed a nod.

The elderly man sent an understanding smile. "Why don't we ask the blessing and eat. Then we'll take it from there."

After a delightful and delicious lunch of roast, potatoes, carrots, and homemade rolls they moved to the living room. The conversation turned to Gracie's life, and she released the entire story—Mama's death, her tenuous relationship with Papa, the problems she'd had with Elena, her confused feelings for Matt and Jason, even the terrible mistake of breaking into Andy's office. An hour later, she rested her head against the cushy couch, a weight lifted from her chest and shoulders.

Neither Jake nor Julia treated her like the sinner she was, but continued to extend the same kindness and grace they'd shown from the beginning. Jake patted her hand, his eyes kind and wise. "I know it doesn't feel like it, but you're actually in a good place when you recognize your sinfulness."

A smile touched her face. "After my experience today, I think I actually get that. It's only when I recognize the depth of my depravity that I also recognize my need for a Savior and can fully accept His gift of grace. But the hardest part is coming to grips with my sinfulness. I belonged to Him and still went the wrong way."

The old man gave his head a shake, his eyes bright beneath his white bushy eyebrows. "Where sin abounds, grace abounds even more, Gracie. God doesn't change. His grace is—and always has been—enough. Not just for your sin, but for the sin of the entire world throughout history."

Guilt continued to prick her insides. "Then why can't I forgive myself?"

Jake nodded, one corner of his mouth lifted in a half smile. "That's the tough part, isn't it? Part of the reason lies with the enemy of our souls. Satan wants to keep us in a position of guilt. He'll keep reminding you—and use others to remind you—but one day you'll reach the point where your understanding of God's love and grace is greater than the guilt the accuser lays on your shoulders. The only way to get to that place is to remind yourself that Christ has already paid the price."

Her throat so engorged with tears she could barely speak, Grace peered into Jake's kind eyes. "I'm like Jonah. I let my anger, vindictiveness, and my selfishness become an excuse to not do what God wanted me to do—to forgive, to extend mercy, and to seek reconciliation."

"That's always been His plan." The gracious old man released a soft sigh and stood to refill his coffee cup. "We're all like Jonah to a certain extent. To forgive really is divine. It doesn't come so easy to us humans, even when we've been the recipients of it on a far greater level than we'll ever realize." He took a sip, shuffled back her way, and eased his frail frame onto the worn-out chair, the scent of his coffee preceding him. "But the real question you should be asking is what are you going to do now?"

What indeed? The question consumed her thoughts. *Lord, help me know and do what You want.* Her cell phone vibrated and buzzed from within her purse. When she reached to silence it, the number caught her attention. Consuela.

With apologies to her hosts, Gracie stepped outside under an ancient live oak to take the call.

Consuela's tearful voice pleaded with her. "Oh, Grace, we need you. Elena is not doing well. Can you please come quickly?"

What are you going to do now? Jake's question resounded once more in her head, and she brought a trembling hand to her lips. While part of her longed to linger in the shade of the vine God provided as a temporary respite, deep down she knew she couldn't stay. Her place was in Miller's Creek. Of all people, Elena Delgado needed her help.

She whispered her one-word answer into the phone. God had lavishly bestowed His grace and forgiveness on her. How could she do less?

Gracie turned and moved back inside, Jake and Julia's gazes locking with hers as she entered. "Looks like I'm headed back to Miller's Creek."

23

Dr. Stevens stared at him. Hard. "I mean it, Matt. You need to take it easy for at least a couple of weeks."

"I'll make sure he stays away from all types of amplification." Andy grinned as he spoke the words early Sunday afternoon.

An unstoppable laugh gurgled in Matt's throat. It wasn't just his brother's joke that brought it on, but joy in knowing at last he could see Gracie and make sure she was safe. He rose from the hospital bed and stretched a hand toward his new friend. "Thanks for everything, Doc."

The white-coated man clasped his hand with both of his own. "My pleasure, Matt. If you ever get knocked in the head again, you know where to find me." He waved as he left the room.

Matt hoisted the duffle bag to his shoulder and glanced at his brother. "Ready?"

"You better believe it." Andy held up his car keys as proof and jangled them, already headed toward the door. "Ready to see my wife and kids."

They strode down the hallway, and they reached the elevator, it opened and they stepped inside. As the doors slid closed, the events of the past week marched through Matt's thoughts. "I really appreciate all you've done for me, bro. Don't know how I would've made it through this without you."

"No prob, but I'm pretty sure you'd have busted outta this joint a couple of days ago had I not been here."

The elevator opened into a parking garage, with the Z parked a few steps away. "I'm pretty sure you're right." Matt deposited his duffle bag in the back and climbed in.

After starting the car, Andy adjusted the rearview mirror and backed out. "I've been meaning to ask how your call to Gracie went the other night."

"It didn't." Matt's voice flat lined. "I got hold of her dad, but he said Jason found her a job in Bellview. Think we could swing through there on our way to Miller's Creek?" The incredulity that covered Andy's features might have been funny under different circumstances. "Please, Andy. I know you're ready to see Trish and the kids, but I have to make sure she's okay."

Andy gave his head an exasperated shake and pulled into the far right lane for the upcoming turn that would take them through Bellview. "I wouldn't do this for just anybody, you know."

Later that day, after yet another failed attempt at finding her, Matt climbed back into the car at Bellview Burger & Fries Drive-In and slammed the door behind him. He ran a hand across his mouth. No one he'd spoken to had even heard of Grace Soldano. Had she disappeared? Had Jason rigged the job to get her out of Miller's Creek and then done away with her?

His fear escalated. A burning sensation moved from his stomach to his throat and dumped a sour taste in his mouth.

To his right, the driver's side door opened, and Andy folded himself into the seat, his eyes full of compassion. "Sorry, Matt. I know you're disappointed."

He couldn't speak. Couldn't find words to express what he was feeling.

Andy peered out the front window, searching the clouds. "Looks like quite a storm we have rolling in. We'd better hightail it back to Miller's Creek before it hits. Forecast is calling for ice and lots of it."

As they left the dusty streets of the town behind, Matt stared out the window at the gathering clouds. *God, You know how much she means to me. Please let me find her.* They passed a quaint and picturesque country church, just the kind of place that would appeal to Gracie. "Stop!"

Andy braked hard and steered to the shoulder. "What?"

"Turn around. We have to go back."

His brother sighed. "Matt, we looked all over Bellview already and with this front pushing though—"

"Go back to that little church we just passed."

"Why?"

Matt made eye contact with Andy, praying he'd understand. "I know this sounds crazy, but her name is on that church. I have to look there."

Andy sent a 'you-gotta-be-out-of-your-mind' glare, but pulled a U and headed back to the church.

As they pulled into the grass-covered parking lot, an elderly couple walked hand in hand toward them from a small house behind the church. Matt opened the car door and stood behind it, the wind beginning to blow strong from the north, whipping through the brown leaves still clinging to the trees.

"Can we help you, son?" The old man's white hair practically glowed from a shaft of afternoon light on the western horizon.

For some reason, the word 'son' sent peace spiraling in and around him. Matt nodded and stepped to where they stood. "I think you can. Do you, by any chance, know Gracie Soldano?"

At the mention of her name, the man and woman shared a smile before the man spoke again. "We know her. Had lunch with her just a while ago."

Relief washed over him, and he offered up a silent prayer of thanks.

"You must be Matt." The woman's voice held natural friendliness mixed with more than a little curiosity.

He glanced back at Andy—who stood behind his car door with his mouth hinged open—then turned his attention back to the couple. "That's me. Is Gracie here?"

The man shook his head. "She's gone back to Miller's Creek. Got a phone call from a friend needing her help."

Matt half-walked, half-ran back to the car, his heart a-dance in his chest, and called back over his shoulder. "Thank you, both. I can't thank you enough."

"God bless!" The man shouted out the words as Matt reached the car.

"You, too!" He gave a final wave, then ducked into the vehicle and snapped his seat belt into place. "Miller's Creek, please, and step on it."

Andy looked somewhat dazed as he backed out and pulled the Z onto the two-laned road, quickly picking up speed. "I'm not believing what just happened. Think that guy was an angel or something?"

Matt shrugged, a grin spreading across his face. "He was to me."

An hour later they pulled up outside the Miller mansion, its giant two-story columns standing at attention like they'd guarded the place for him while he was gone. Never would he have imagined missing this place so much. Matt jumped from the car with his bag in tow, then leaned in through the open window. "Thanks again, bro. Go on to that family of yours, and give Trish and the kids a big hug from me."

"Don't have to tell me twice." His brother smiled and put the car in gear. "Are you sure you're up to finding Gracie on your own?"

"You know it." Matt slapped the top of the car as Andy pulled away. He looked up at the ever-darkening skies as fine pellets of ice began to fall, then took the front steps two at a time and dropped his bag to the marble floors in the foyer. Time to make a run into Miller's Creek to find Gracie.

As he made his way to town, he put in a quick call to her house. Mr. Soldano answered again, and it soon became apparent the man was surprised by the news that Gracie was back in town. "She is not here, Mr. Matt, and she hasn't called."

With a promise to call if he found her, Matt said good-bye. Where could she be? The old man at the church had said something about her helping a friend. But which friend? Jason?

Creekside Park spread out in front of him as he left downtown Miller's Creek. A thin coat of ice already blanketed the telephone wires. He pulled into the park's gravel lot to think through his options. One by one, street lamps flickered on around him. He'd just about decided to make his way home before the full brunt of the storm hit when three blocks ahead, on the main highway, a familiar white pickup drove by, headed toward Morganville.

Matt punched the accelerator—hoping Ernie was nowhere around—and maintained a safe distance behind Gracie. When she turned off onto a private drive a few minutes later, he pulled onto the grass at the side of the road. Now what?

He didn't have to think long. The misery of the past few weeks proved he cared about her too much to let her put herself in danger. If nothing else, he'd make sure she was safe. Then if she made it clear she didn't want him around, he'd leave.

As he traversed the tree-lined drive, Gracie appeared in front of him, silhouetted against an expensive-looking rock house. She held a hand up to shield her eyes from the glare of his headlights.

His heart thudded in his chest. He parked quickly and stepped from the car, holding back, afraid of making a fool of himself again.

"Matt!" Her face aglow with a giant smile, Gracie raced toward him and wrapped him in a big hug. "I'm so glad to see you!"

He stood there a moment, unsure of what to do next. His resolve quickly melting as he glanced down at her, he put his arms around her, and enjoyed her nearness and the scent of her soft perfume, at least for a brief moment.

Gracie pulled back part of the way and studied his face. She gasped at the dressing on the side of his head, her face awash in compassion, and brought tentative fingers to the bandage. "Are you okay?"

Matt battled against losing yet another part of his heart to her. "Better now that I've seen you. Whose house is this?"

She pulled from his arms, turned her gaze away, and pulled her coat hood around her face to protect it from the freezing rain. "Elena's."

"What? Are you crazy?" Had she learned nothing?

The all-too-familiar stubbornness revealed itself in her eyes and the tilt of her chin. "Her mother called. She needs me."

"Why? So she can chew you up and spit you out again?" Matt reached for her fingers, ice-cold in the freezing weather. "She hurt you over and over and then threw you under the bus to protect herself. Haven't you had enough?" The look on her face proved the theory he'd just spouted was true.

Surprisingly, Gracie didn't pull her hand away. Instead she looked him square in the face, her eyes lit with conviction. "I'm doing this because it's the way of grace. It loves and forgives even when there's no reason to do so." She blinked rapidly, on the verge of tears. "At one time I couldn't fathom how I was supposed to show grace, but now I know. I can't go back to how I used to be no matter how much my earthly side would like to."

He had no answer. Nothing to refute her heartfelt words. Clearly the recent ordeal had strengthened her faith.

She stepped closer and raised a palm to his face, her eyes soft and pleading in the light of the nearby lamp. A wisp of smoke drifted from her mouth in the frigid air. "Remember all our talks about grace?"

He nodded. How could he forget?

"I think part of grace is doing for someone what they can't do for themselves."

A frown pulled his eyebrows together. "Even when they're your enemy?"

A tender smile lit her face from the inside. "Especially then. Isn't that what we were to God when he demonstrated His grace to us at the cross?"

Matt lowered his gaze, drawing a circle in the dirt with the toe of his shoe. She had a point, but just how far was she willing to go to demonstrate grace to someone who probably only throw it back in her face?

He looked up to see Gracie peering into the darkness and followed the direction of her gaze. Jason's jet-black car sat almost obscured from view behind a giant oak. What was he doing here?

She tugged her hand away and stuffed it in her coat pocket, her gaze not meeting his.

"Do what you want, Gracie, but I'm coming with you. I can't stand idly by while Elena or Jason or anyone else stomps all over you." If that comment didn't let her know how much he cared, nothing would.

"Jason? Why bring him into the conversation?" Her dark eyes smoldered.

Matt puzzled over the question. She'd seen Jason's car and knew he was here, but for some reason wanted to keep the information from him. How could he get the point across that the man she fancied wasn't what she believed? If he brought up that his name wasn't Jason Dent, he'd also reveal that he'd had the guy investigated. Better to play it safe, at least to begin with. "I know you don't want to hear this, Gracie, but I believe with everything in me that Jason has a serious problem."

"What are you talking about?"

He pressed his lips together and searched for words that wouldn't incite her Latin temperment. "There are several pathological disorders that—"

Gracie laughed. "Oh boy, here we go again." Her full-lipped smile faded as she peered into his eyes, almost as if she were seriously considering the possibility.

Please, God. He wanted to say more, but didn't dare. Instead he had to trust that the Lord would take care of it. "Just please be careful around him. Are you . . . ?" He swallowed against the fear that crawled up his windpipe. "Are you still seeing him?"

She looked away for a long, silent moment. Finally she faced him, her eyes lit with determination. "Yes. We're pretty serious. I think he might propose."

His heart crumbled, and he sucked in a gulp of the ice cold air until it burned in his lungs. So this was how it felt to be totally broken. He felt the need to say something to end the awkward silence, but what? Finally he simply nodded, unable to make eye contact for fear of breaking down. "Well, I guess I'd better be going."

"Yes, that would probably be for the best." Her voice hitched in a strangled sort of way.

Without another glance in her direction, he turned and walked away, his feet crunching the frozen grass. He reached his car, not quite sure how he got there, then crawled in and drove away. Only as he neared the trees that lined the driveway did he find the strength to look in the rearview mirror.

Gracie was nowhere to be seen.

Her feet heavy as lead, Gracie trudged through icy semi-darkness to Elena's blood-red door, but waited in the shadows to allow the ache in her heart to recede before she faced Jason and Elena. She'd lied to Matt again, but she had no choice. As soon as she'd seen Jason's car in the shadow of the oak tree and allowed Matt's comment about pathological disorders to register, she knew what she had to do.

She momentarily zoned out, her mind on Jason's odd behavior the last time they'd been together, her brain immediately accessing information from college psych class. His possessiveness and on-off behavior—how could she have missed it? The answer came in a split second. Because she'd turned him into a living, breathing illusion of what she wanted him to be—an idol built not with her hands, but with her thoughts.

She brought her palms to her mouth and released a heavy breath, both a sigh and a way to warm her frozen fingers. As much as it had hurt to get rid of Matt, it had to be done, especially with his head bandaged from whatever had happened to him. Neither Elena nor Jason held a high opinion of Matt, and he would only be prey for them in what could possibly be a volatile situation.

After gathering her courage, she rang the doorbell on the beautiful rock house, a sudden insight washing over her. No longer did the earthly trappings of this life enthrall her like they once had. It was almost as if a veil had lifted from her heart and her eyes. Now she could see what was truly important. A fancy house, a great career with great pay, nice clothes, and a nice car could never replace peace of mind, something both Jason and Elena obviously lacked.

The door opened, and Consuela appeared, her face lined with anxiety. "You couldn't have come at a better time. Hurry, there's no time to waste." She latched on to Gracie's hand and pulled her through the house toward Elena's suite of rooms. "She just went into her office."

In a blur of movement, one of the wooden double doors swung open, and Gracie found herself once more in the presence of her enemy.

Hair disheveled and unkempt, and her face stained with tears, the woman she once feared now seemed shriveled and small as she raised her gaze to Gracie's face. An almost maniacal laugh sounded from her throat. She brought the shot glass she held in one hand down to the desktop with a bang. The amber-colored contents sloshed over the side and sent the unmistakable odor of hard liquor throughout the room. "You! Of all people to see me like this it would be you." The crazed cackle continued for a minute more, then turned to sobs. "It's all a stack of cards." She broke into fresh tears and lowered her head to the intricately-carved desk.

A compassion she didn't expect erupted in Gracie's chest, and she moved quickly to Elena's side and knelt. "It's okay. I want to help anyway I can. What can I do?"

Her former boss sobbed even harder.

Gracie eyed the woman and struggled to make sense of the situation. Yes, she was in serious trouble, but nothing that should cause this type of reaction. Her thoughts flitted to the night she found Millie dead. In retrospect, her own response had been over-the-top, but only because of her heightened fear.

Alarms rang in her head, and sent a slow shiver down her spine. Was Elena experiencing something similar, or was her behavior based on one-too-many drinks? As Gracie considered the possibilities, Jason's dark face filtered through her consciousness. The torn-up fence, the mailbox ripped from its post. All this time, she'd suspected Elena, but it had never quite added up. How could someone as small as she—someone so polished that she always looked like she'd just stepped out of the salon—be responsible for such destruction? Now Jason's car was parked outside, almost invisible in the shadows. Grace glanced around the room. Where was he?

Elena lifted her head, her eyes red and swollen. "Why would you want to help me after what I've done to you?"

Why indeed? The woman had destroyed her life and left her dreams in a pile of ashes. "I don't know how to answer that question. I just know that we all go through rough patches, some of our own making and most beyond our control. I want to help. Believe it or not, I care about you."

The other woman searched her face as though not quite sure how to believe her.

Gracie rose to her feet to remove her coat, but stayed close. "I read in the paper that you're under investigation. Is that why you're so upset?"

Elena nodded and stared off into space, her eyes unblinking.

Should she ask if there were another reason for the tears? Gracie took in Elena's fragile emotional state and decided against bringing up Jason directly. Maybe a backdoor approach was best. "Did you take a bribe to affect the outcome of the Simmons case?"

Again she nodded.

Gracie tossed her coat to a nearby chair. "Why?"

"He would've killed me. He also threatened to have our daughter institutionalized if I didn't cooperate."

The words chilled Gracie to the bone. Was he capable of such behavior? The answer flashed to her brain in neon red. "Jason?"

"Yes. He's more powerful than anyone realizes. His grandfather is the head of the drug cartel in Columbia, and is responsible for buying off political positions in the state government to get drugs smuggled into the country."

"Columbia? How did he get the British accent?"

"His father was a British diplomat. His mother is Columbian."

Gracie searched the woman's face, but found no evidence to suggest she was lying. The story Jason had told her at his house by the lake had only been partially true, while Elena's story explained so many things, like how she and Jason could afford to live so luxuriously. But there were still unanswered questions. "I asked your mother for information about Jason, but she told me she didn't know him."

"His real name is Alessandro Delgado."

Her brain revved to high speed. If what Elena said was true—and she had no reason to disbelieve it—then Jason was more dangerous than she could've ever imagined. And he was somewhere nearby. Of that she was certain. She knelt beside Elena, intentionally keeping her voice low. "Where's Jessie?"

"Asleep in her room. Why?"

"And how quickly can we get her and your mother and get out of here?"

Elena paled. "He's here, isn't he?" Her whispered words blasted the scent of alcohol.

Gracie nodded. "His car was hidden behind the big oak tree next to your house when I got here." If Matt hadn't shown up, she wouldn't have even seen it. How she wished she hadn't been so quick to send him away.

A closet door opened and shut behind them, snapping them both to a standing position. Jason, his face an impenetrable mask, approached slowly, and something glinted from his gloved hands.

A gun.

24

Matt steered onto the side of the road and killed the engine, his heart in turmoil. He groaned and leaned his head against the steering wheel. Something just didn't add up. He'd seen with his own two eyes how glad Gracie had been to see him, had glimpsed the loving concern in her eyes when she'd brought her fingertips to the bandage on the side of his head. Then, in less than a heartbeat, she'd told him she and Jason were in a serious relationship and it would be best for him to leave.

Frozen rain spattered against the windshield and stuck there. He forced the torturous thoughts and pictures of his last encounter with Gracie through his brain. There had to be a way to unravel all of this. One minute he'd actually hoped he was getting through to her about Jason, and then . . .

He sat up in the seat, his back ramrod straight. His car. She'd seen Jason's car and immediately sent him packing. Matt's mind travelled to the night he'd found her screaming on the doorstep. One minute she'd been practically catatonic, but after he'd checked outside, he returned to a totally different Gracie. She'd sent him packing that night, too.

Matt pounded a palm against the steering wheel, partly in excitement that she knew the truth about Jason, but mostly in fear she was in danger. She'd intentionally lied both times, all for the purpose of protecting him.

Gracie loved him.

His chest tightened and the hairs on the back of his neck stood on end in spite of the new revelation. She was in danger, and now it was time for him to protect her. He reached for his cell phone. Ernie needed to know about the situation brewing at Elena's house. He clicked the button to turn on his phone, but the phone diddly-dinked and the screen went dark. No time to waste. He'd drive to the police station and tell Ernie what was going on, then hurry back out to Elena's house. But what if he got there too late?

Matt tossed the phone to the passenger seat and cranked the ignition, his mind on one thing and one thing only—to get back to Gracie as soon as possible. The starter whirred for a moment, but died down to a click. No. This couldn't be happening. He tried the key again. This time just a click.

He yanked a flashlight from the glove box and opened the car door just as a gust of wind sent bits of ice biting into his face. His body shivered in response, so he zipped his coat and pulled the collar up over his ears. In a few seconds time, he had the hood raised and located the problem. The posts on the battery were corroded. He wiggled the cables back and forth to dislodge the powdery-white deposits then tried the car again.

This time the Pinto started right up. He quickly lowered the hood and climbed back in, trying to decide what to do. *Lord, keep her safe, and give me wisdom.*

Matt turned the defroster to high and flipped on the windshield wipers. Though the lights of Miller's Creek beckoned ahead, he'd already used up too much time. He put the car in gear, pulled the steering wheel hard to the left, and turned around. Hopefully he'd be able to use Elena's phone to call the police—if he needed to.

In horror, Gracie watched Jason moved to the large double doors, flick the locking mechanism into place, and gaze around the room with unnerving calm. "Beautiful space, Elena. You always did have an eye for beauty."

He focused his attention on Gracie. "You're too good for her, Graciela. While I applaud your good heart, don't waste your time trying to help her." Without blinking or any change in his demeanor, he took a step closer to where the two women stood.

Beside her, Elena shivered violently. *Lord, help me.* Though her heart pounded furiously in her chest, Gracie quietly drew a breath, pulling from a power deep within. No matter what, she had to protect Elena. The woman's eternal destiny depended on it. "Jason, you don't want to do this." How could her voice sound so calm, when her heart threatened to leap from her chest? She moved slowly in his direction until she stood a few feet away and gazed up into his always-hooded eyes, the same eyes that had drawn her in like a moth to a flame on more than one occasion.

Sobs once more erupted from Elena. "Alex, please." Her trembling voice pleaded in the midst of her tears.

"Alex? Your name is Alex?" Maybe questions would provide a diversion while she figured out a way to get the gun from him.

He brought his steady gaze back to her. "Alessandro, but don't let it worry you, love. I'll explain everything. After I do what I have to do, we'll go away where we'll be safe. You don't have to be afraid. You belong to me, and I have the means to keep you safe."

A shudder coursed through her body like an electrical shock. She tried her best to not appear afraid, but if he hadn't already seen her shiver, surely he sensed the fear in her heart.

Gracie faced Elena. "Why didn't you tell me the two of you were once married?" She intentionally raised her voice and infused her tone with anger on the off chance Consuela would hear.

"Once?" Elena shot a poisoned glance at Jason, and a laugh loaded with contempt sounded from her throat. She raised the shot glass to her lips and downed the remaining liquid. "We're still married. I wanted a divorce but he wouldn't give it to me without dragging my name and reputation through the mud and putting our daughter away in a home."

The words rang true. "Is that the truth?" She directed her question at Jason this time, and tried to sound hurt. "All this time, you were married to her?"

He glanced quickly between the two women. "I told you I can explain. You'll just have to take my word for it."

"Don't believe him, Grace. He talks a good game, but if you go with him, you'll never escape."

Jason smiled coolly. "Oh, but you escaped, Elena. Remember?" He waved his left hand around the room. "And you sure weren't living as well as this when I found you."

Gracie's brain vacillated between the opposing stories that unfolded in their conversation, and tried to think of a way out of the situation. Time. She had to buy time. "I'm sorry. I don't follow."

"Elena and I had a great life as part of a law firm in San Antonio until she decided to run away." He laughed in derision. "She should've known my people have eyes everywhere. I found her in a hovel in southern New Mexico, reduced to digging in dumpsters to feed herself and our daughter."

"I would've eaten worse than that to stay away from you!" Elena's eyes flashed vitriol, and she moved toward the fireplace.

Gracie stepped between the two again, careful to keep her body in the line of fire. "And how did you both end up in Miller's Creek?"

"Just another part of his grandfather's evil plan." Her tears apparently spent, Elena now seemed bent on revealing everything. Why? To warn her? To protect her? "The Simmons case brought us here. The cartel protects their own, and as advisor to the Attorney General of Texas, David's father plays an important part in the scheme. As long as he plays their game, he'll always be protected. I was brought in to throw the trial."

"Watch it, Elena." Jason's tone and features held portent. "Your attempt to warn Graciela away might just backfire. Say too much, and I'll be forced to kill you both." Jason raised the pistol.

Elena began to weep and tremble once more. "What about our daughter? Don't you care what happens to her? Or are you as heartless as I think you are?" She returned to the desk and slumped in the chair.

Fear built in Gracie's chest with each careless word Elena uttered. Was she intentionally trying to bait him? And why? With bravado she didn't feel and couldn't explain, Gracie hurried to Jason's side and wrapped her arms around him. The best thing to do was play along until Consuela had a chance to call the police. Maybe she could at least delay the worst-case scenario. "Jason, please let's leave. We can go away right now. You don't need to do this."

He stared at her calmly as if he had all the time in the world, his gaze penetrating through her.

Could he sense her underlying motivation?

"I have to do this, Grace. If I don't, they'll come after me. Besides, she deserves it after what she's done to both of us. When I think of how she made you the scapegoat . . . " His voice broke off, and he slowly and methodically lowered his gaze and the gun directly at Elena, who sobbed louder now and covered her face with trembling hands.

Gracie moved in front of the gun. He wouldn't shoot her, at least not at this point. "Jason, I care too much about you to let you do this. Please let me have the gun."

"Move out of the way."

A commotion sounded in the hallway, and the doorknob jiggled. Someone pounded on the door. "Open up!"

Matt! Raw terror ripped through her veins. If Jason could kill his wife in cold blood without blinking an eye, he wouldn't stop there. "Jason, please. We can leave through the window. There's still time."

Matt pounded on the door again and then grunted as the weight of his body slammed against the door. "Gracie! Get out of there!" His voice held sheer panic.

In an unexpected move, Jason hurled her to one side. She landed against a chair, and her forehead clipped the chair's wooden arm. Gracie sat up quickly, the room spinning from the force of the blow. The metallic taste of blood landed on her tongue. She pulled herself to a standing position, still clutching the chair for support.

Jason once more raised the gun slowly at Elena, a look of pure satisfaction curling his lips. "Good-bye, Elena."

"No!" Gracie flung herself toward the gun just as it went off. Pain seared through her lower abdomen, followed by the softest, most beautiful light she'd ever felt or seen.

25

The door gave way against Matt's shoulder just as a gunshot pierced the air and Gracie slumped to the floor in a heap. His heart stopped. *Lord, please keep her alive.* A sudden rush of adrenaline coursed through his veins and a smoky smell developed in his nostrils. Matt tackled Jason at the knees, toppling him to the floor as the gun dropped. He kicked at the gun and sent it spiraling across the room and wrestled the tall attorney into position beneath him. Dent outsized him by at least several inches, a fact which made Matt immediately grateful for the training he'd had on the college wrestling team.

Before he realized it, Jason wiggled free from his grasp and slammed a fist into the side of his head. Matt reeled from the blow, but forced himself to ignore it and focus on his goal of stopping Jason before he did any more damage.

The man stood and made a move toward the gun, but Matt grabbed his ankle and pulled him to the floor. He yanked the guy's arms behind his back and placed a knee along his spine right between his shoulder blades. That should hold him.

Matt barely had time to glance Gracie's way before Ernie and others came thundering into the room. "Come get this guy so I can help Gracie."

The policemen moved quickly to cuff the man, while Matt crawled to Gracie, cradled her head in one hand, and gently stroked the hair around her face.

Her coal-dark eyes opened slowly and a sweet smile curved her lips. "You came back. I sent you away. I didn't want you to get hurt." Her eyes were glazed over and drowsy-like, as if it were all she could do to keep them open.

Unstoppable tears poured down Matt's cheeks. "Yeah, I finally figured that out, sweetheart. Wasn't the first time you pulled this stunt, huh?" Like the night he'd found her screaming on the back porch. Were there others?

She moved her head from side to side. "Is—is Elena okay?" Her words came out in a faint whisper.

Overwhelming emotion rendered him temporarily speechless. Here she lay, gushing lifeblood, and all she cared about was that Elena—the woman who had cost her everything—was okay. He glanced to where the woman slumped in a chair behind the desk, her face pallid and drawn, her eyes wide and empty. He swallowed against the sudden tightness in his chest. *Why Gracie, God? Why?* "Yeah, she's fine. How about you? You handling the pain okay?"

She shook her head slightly, her speech slurred. "No pain." Her heavy eyes began to close.

Good. At least she wasn't in pain. Matt patted her cheek to keep her focused. "Stay with me, sweetie. No sleeping yet, okay?"

Voices sounded from the hallway, and then two paramedics raced into the room, lugging a stretcher. They placed it close to Gracie and checked her over. "Gunshot to the abdomen, no exit wound," said one as he moved the earpieces of a stethoscope to his ears and listened to her heartbeat. The other one inserted the IV. "We don't have much time. Wish we could call for a helicopter, but not in this ice storm." He glanced up at Matt, his expression sober. "Keep her awake. Talk to her. Whatever. Her life could depend on it."

Matt's pulse roared in his ears, and tears formed in his eyes at the thought of losing her. He quickly blinked them away. "Gracie?"

"Hmm?" Her eyelids parted slowly.

"Remember all our talks about grace?"

"Mmm-hmm."

"Well, I think you pulled it off."

The tiniest of frowns wrinkled the area between her brows. "What?"

"You lived up to your name."

She didn't answer, but blinked slowly, her gaze still trained on him, question marks in her big brown eyes.

"Don't you see? What you just did for Elena. That's what Jesus did. He took what we deserved, took our punishment, took the bullet intended for us."

Gracie winced and closed her eyes, but then opened them again. "One big difference."

He cupped her precious face with one palm. "What's that, sweetheart?"

Now her gaze didn't waver as she stared past him toward the ceiling. "I deserve death just as much as everyone else in this room. Jesus didn't." Her eyes closed again.

A siren sounded outside. One of the paramedics spoke to Gracie in a loud voice. "Okay, Miss, we're going to move you to a stretcher and let you go for a ride."

She didn't respond.

In swift and seamless motion, the first responders tied Gracie to the stretcher in a matter of moments, covered her with a blanket, and then carted her stilled form outside into the wintry night air, still thick with ice.

Matt followed, his heart in his throat. "Which hospital?" He yelled the words to make himself heard over the sound of the chopper.

"Morganville to start out with, but once she's stabilized they'll probably send her on to Dallas." An unspoken 'if' suspended in the air between them, and the solemn expression in the paramedic's eyes shook Matt to the core. This was worse than anyone was saying.

The ambulance pulled away, siren blaring, lights flashing. Matt raced to his car, slipping and sliding in the ice, fear stomping through his thoughts, and the cold air incinerating his lungs. His little green Pinto roared to life. He slung the car in reverse and tore down the road toward the highway that led to

Morganville, one tormenting question ricocheting like a Ping-Pong ball off the walls of his mind.

What if he didn't make it in time to tell her how very much he loved her?

Gracie cracked open her eyes to a steady beep somewhere near her right ear. The room was almost completely dark except for a small light above where she lay. She tried to shift positions to get a more comprehensive view of her surroundings, but couldn't. The place looked and smelled like a hospital.

What had happened? She closed her eyes, trying to remember. Yes, the gun Jason pointed at Elena went off, and she'd jumped in its path. The possibility that the other woman could be killed before making things right with God had been unthinkable to her. But at what cost?

She swallowed several times to get rid of the dry desert taste in her mouth, and then twisted her neck to the left to see a large window covered in heavy draperies, with cracks of light rimming the edges in blue. Must still be night. She craned her neck even further at the sound of heavy breathing. Two chairs in reclined position both bore blanketed bodies. Even in the dim light she could make out Papa. But who was the other one?

The second person startled awake and sat up. Gracie tried to make out features in the darkness, but without success. Maria, maybe? That would make sense. Then the person stood and sauntered from the chair toward the bed. Only one person she knew had that loose-limbed, free-spirited gait.

A sudden comfort wrapped around her soul. She could get through anything now. *Thank You, Lord.* Hopefully she could soon give voice to her feelings for him.

His face, covered with several days' growth, leaned closer, his eyes red-rimmed with fatigue. "You're awake." He spoke the words with a sense of awe and wonder.

"As are you."

He chuckled softly. "Yeah, but I've been awake. You haven't." His voice broke and his chin trembled. He fell to his knees, his head lowered to the bed, his thick shoulders shaking with sobs. "Thank You, God, for bringing her back to us."

Her heart went out to him, but it also leapt for joy. He truly loved her. Of that there was no doubt. She laid a hand, which seemed extraordinarily heavy, on his head, his hair length finally to the point where she could discern curls. "It's okay, Matt. I'm not going anywhere."

The words seemed to hurt rather than help, because now his shoulders shook violently. Only after several minutes and obvious concentrated effort was he able to raise his gaze to hers, his lashes wet and clumped. He looked embarrassed. "Sorry. I didn't mean to do that."

"Please don't apologize." She struggled to find the next words to say. Part of her wanted to find out the details of the past few days, but a bigger part of her wanted to confess her love. Unsure of how to best tell him her feelings, she opted for the first choice. "The details of everything that happened are a little fuzzy. Can you fill me in?"

His sandy brown eyes closed slowly, as though even the thought of reliving that time was painful.

"Never mind, Matt. We can talk about it later."

He lowered his gaze and shook his head, swallowing hard. "No, it's okay. It's just—" His voice cracked again. "Sorry." He pressed his trembling lips together for several seconds before he was able to look at her. "Jason meant to kill Elena. You stepped in front of the bullet."

"Well, that much I remember."

A tired smile touched his lips. "Oh, so the sarcastic Gracie is also awake?"

"To know me is to love me."

Now his face grew solemn. He probed her eyes for a moment, like he wanted to say something, but couldn't bring himself to form the words. "Anyway, Ernie came and carted

Jason and Elena away. Based on what I've read in the papers, Elena has agreed to cooperate with the authorities and testify against him."

"And Jason?"

His face hardened. "He'll most likely be out of commission for a very long time."

Sorrow flooded her heart and made its way to her face.

Matt's expression fell, the tired lines around his eyes deepening. "You still love him?"

"It's not like that, Matt, and it really never has been." She glanced behind his head to the brightening light beginning to stream around the edges of the curtain. "I care about him and wish things could have turned out differently."

Disappointment joined the fatigue on his face. "Still wishing for Mr. Perfect, huh?"

"No." Gracie gave her head a vehement shake to re-emphasize the word. "If I've learned anything from this experience it's that the old saying is true. All that glitters isn't gold." She paused to catch a breath and stave off her dry throat and the bad taste on her tongue. "In fact, if it glitters at all, that's a pretty good sign I need to run fast and furious in the opposite direction."

The smile returned to Matt's face, only bigger.

Her heart thumped furiously. She needed to let him know how much she loved him, but surely he'd find her words insincere after the many times she'd made him think she didn't care for him at all.

Just as she gathered the courage to express her love, the door swung open. A woman in a white coat entered, a man in scrubs right behind. "Good. You're awake." The kind-eyed woman poked the button on a container of sanitizer on the wall, rubbed her hands together, and then leaned forward to shake Gracie's hand, the smell of rubbing alcohol heavy in the air. "I'm Dr. Jackson. You gave us quite a scare. We didn't think you were going to make it there for a while." The woman straddled a nearby stool.

Gracie glanced at Matt, who had closed his eyes, like the memory was more than he could bear. What she wouldn't give to erase his sorrow. Getting well was the first step, but then would her words of love be enough?

Papa joined them, his eyes still bleary with sleep.

She sent him a smile and turned her gaze back to Dr. Jackson. "Well, I'm tougher than I look."

"Glad to hear it, because you've still got some hurdles to overcome." Her words were hushed, but sincere, giving them greater weight.

A slow shudder raised goose-bumps on the flesh of her forearms. "Sorry, but I'm not following. Other than being weak and thirsty, I feel just fine."

Matt now hung his head between his shoulders, and without raising his eyes, he reached over and took her hand in his, caressing her fingertips. Papa also stood with his head down, but one hand rose to wipe away tears.

A heavy sigh escaped from the woman beside her. "The bullet lodged near your spine, Gracie. It caused pretty extensive damage." Dr. Jackson paused and swallowed, her kind eyes full of compassion. "There's a pretty good chance you'll be paralyzed for the rest of your life."

The news seeped into her spirit in clumps. At first she wanted to laugh and shake her head, to tell the doctor there must be some mistake. Instead she decided to prove them all wrong. She threw off the covers and tried to move her legs and toes. Nothing.

The room began to spin and grew distorted, like she viewed them all through a long, dark tunnel. "Any other great news you care to share?" She knew the bitter acid words she spoke sounded harsh, but at the moment she didn't care.

Dr. Jackson nodded. "The bullet destroyed your uterus."

A feral sob that seemed to come from a place outside her pierced the dark silence. Her act of grace had been more costly than she'd ever imagined possible.

She made the mistake of glancing at Matt. Though his form was blurred by her tears, his head still hung low, like he couldn't bring himself to even look at her. Why would he want to?

Who would want a future with a crippled woman who could no longer bear children?

26

Matt stood in the waiting area at Baylor Medical hospital in Dallas, a sleepy island in the midst of a sea of noise and hubbub, trying to summon strength to help Gracie through the challenges of another day. The hours had stretched into days and the days into weeks. Christmas and New Year's had come and gone, and now the doldrums of February had set in. The weather seemed to mirror how he felt—completely iced over. And to make matters worse, today was Valentine's, a day for couples to celebrate their love.

Another piece of his heart crumbled to ashes and fell to his feet, but he couldn't give in to despair. Not when Gracie needed him.

A few nurses smiled as he wandered past their station to the coffee machine to pour another large cup. The smell drifted to his nose, bringing a small measure of comfort. Where had the past few months gone? Sometimes he found himself wondering which day of the week it was. At other times, he could think of nothing he'd like to do more than just run away from it all. A shuddering sigh escaped. He couldn't. He loved her too much.

Gracie's depression was a giant wall yet to be scaled. Most of the time she merely toyed with her food, and though confined to bed with absolutely no exercise, weight continued to drop from her petite frame. She hadn't shed one tear since that fateful day when Dr. Jackson had given her the news.

Matt plopped into a blue chair in the waiting room, not quite ready to face her, and sipped his coffee. Gracie's surgery had been eight grueling hours of praying like he'd never prayed before. At least the surgeons now held some hope of her walking again, but it grew increasingly obvious that if it happened, it would be later rather than sooner.

The news that she might walk again seemed to help Gracie, but not near as much as they'd hoped. It was as if she'd closed herself away in a dungeon of her own making, only allowing brief glimpses of the person she once was.

Matt rubbed his forehead as yesterday's painful ordeal joined his thoughts. She'd started rehab with great exuberance, but it hadn't gone well. If anything, the day left her more defeated than ever, with depression once again rearing its ugly head.

Was there no end in sight? He stood, chunked his cup in the trash can, and ambled to the window. Below him, people scurried like ants into surrounding buildings to escape the bitter cold, and he couldn't help but wish he were one of them.

The worst part of this time was Gracie's constant rejection. She completely dismissed him anytime he tried to hold her hand or converse with her. No matter what he said or did, each incident drove the wedge between them even deeper, and he had no idea how to make it stop.

The night of the accident he'd regained some confidence that she cared about him. The way she'd reacted when he pulled into Elena's driveway had renewed his hope, but that hope had long since departed.

Lord, I don't know how much more of this I can take. Please send answers and help. Show me how to reach her. Inner groans that words couldn't express continued in his spirit for several minutes.

Finally he shoved his hands deeper in the pockets of the old jacket he remembered to bring back from a recent trip to Miller's Creek. His hand hit something hard. He fished it out of his picket, angst turning the coffee in his stomach to acid. The promise ring he'd bought to give Gracie for Christmas.

A sudden desire to chunk it across the room skittered through him, but he stilled it with a deep breath.

Give it to her.

The quiet voice in his head brought a frown to Matt's face. That had to be the stupidest idea he'd ever heard. Give a ring to her when she usually refused even eye contact?

Give it to her.

The voice was still soft and low, but pressing.

Lord, I don't know how to do this. She bites my head off if I look at her the wrong way. How can I risk it?

The answer came immediately. If this one simple act made a difference in her outlook and progress then it would be more than worth it in the end. If she got upset with him, he'd just have to deal with it until she got past it.

Was he ready for this? He opened the black velvet box and examined the simple gold band with tiny diamonds creating a heart. With this ring, he'd promise his love and commitment to her, with the intention of one day asking her to be his wife. Yes, the fact that he was still at her side proved his readiness. Was *she* ready?

His shoulders raised and lowered as he heaved a sigh. There was only one way to find out, but first he had a few details to take care of.

A few hours later, his heart reinforced with newfound resolve, he strode down the antiseptic-smelling hallway to her room, knocked on the door, and entered. Encircled with flowers, stuffed animals, balloons, and other gifts from the people of Miller's Creek, the room bore testimony to the love others had for her. Many folks had made a special trip to see her, but even then, she kept a wall up, like she couldn't quite bring herself to completely trust anyone's friendship.

Gracie didn't face him when he entered. Instead she kept her head turned toward the plate glass window, her eyes unseeing.

"How's my girl?"

"Fine."

Her emotionless response didn't shock him in the least. Most of her answers nowadays were mono-syllabic. But impatience flared inside him, a sleeping monster easily awakened. *God, give me the words to say, and help me not to say anything I shouldn't.* With quiet determination, he moved between her gaze and the window. "I need you to come with me."

She said nothing.

Matt pulled the wheelchair from the corner, unfolded it, and moved it closer to the bed.

Her face darkened in a scowl. "What are you doing?"

"I already told you. I need you to come with me."

"Well, that's kind of hard to do when my legs don't work, isn't it?"

Her sharp words stabbed holes in his fragile patience. He calmed himself with another deep breath and stepped closer to the bed, raising it to an upright position. He punched the red button to call one of the nurses he'd just spoken to.

Bridget appeared a moment later and sent Matt a conspiratorial wink as she bustled into the room. She threw back the sheet and blanket covering Gracie's legs. "Are you ready for an adventure?"

"That depends." Her voice held an acidic undertone.

Bridget ignored the comment and motioned Matt to Gracie's other side with her head. In a moment's time, Gracie rested in the wheelchair. Matt stooped to slip her fuzzy red house shoes on her feet and dismissed the daggers she shot at him.

She didn't say a word as he wheeled her down the hall to the elevator and down two levels to the room the nurses had helped him procure at the last minute. But as he maneuvered the chair through the door, she gasped.

Miniature twinkle lights sparkled from the faux trees he'd confiscated from several places. In their midst sat a small table for two, wrapped in a white tablecloth and more lights. Two tall tapers flickered from the table and soft music played from a nearby boom box. The smell of grilled steak permeated the space.

Gracie's jaw hung open, her eyes reflecting the lights. "I don't know what to say."

Pure pleasure trickled through him. Just the reaction he'd hoped for. "And this is just the beginning, sweetheart. I figured you could use a break from hospital food, so I arranged for a catered meal. Later we'll watch a movie." He pointed to the other end of the semi-darkened room to a big-screened TV. In front of it lounged two recliners with small tables on either side to hold their drinks and popcorn. "Just another one of those BFF things."

Her eyes softened momentarily, but then went stone cold. "Thanks, but you don't have to entertain the crippled lady."

Flames of fury flashed, and his jaw cinched into a hard knot. *Lord, help me to remember all she's been through, but show me how to not let her get away with self-pity and rudeness.* Matt squatted in front of her so she wouldn't look past him.

"What are you doing?"

"I'm about ready to pound some sense into that pretty little head of yours."

Her eyes widened.

At least he'd gotten her attention. Matt rose to his feet and rolled her to the table. He lowered himself to the chair next to her and snapped open a napkin to place in his lap. "I can't begin to imagine what it's like to go through what you're experiencing right now, but I can tell you what it's been like for me and the other people from Miller's Creek." He stared her down. "We hurt, too, Gracie. Maybe not in the same way, but we still hurt. It hurts to see you so distant and aloof. It hurts us that none of our efforts to help seem to affect you in the least."

Her facial features tightened, but she still didn't speak.

"I have something I'd like to give you. Regardless of your response, I want you to know I'm gonna stick to you like glue until you make it through this. But you get to decide what happens after that."

Her dark eyes, so big in her pale face, held questions. "I don't understand."

"You will." Matt reached in his pocket and removed the box of candy hearts he'd bought at a ridiculous price in the hospital gift store. All but one heart had been removed, and he'd cushioned it in white tissue paper so the message showed through the cellophane window. It simply read, 'Be mine.' He dropped it to the table and slid it across to sit directly in front of her. "Read it, and then open the box."

She stared at it for a moment, then moved her gaze to his, still silent. After what seemed like an eternity, she picked up the box and gingerly opened it, the ring rolling into her cupped palm.

"It's a promise ring, Gracie."

Her face twisted and contorted, then heavy sobs racked her body. Matt scooted his chair closer and took her in his arms to stroke her long dark hair, praying her tears would be the catharsis she so desperately needed. The sound of her sobs and the soft scent of her soap sent an ache through his chest. "It's okay, Gracie. Let it out."

The tears she'd held back for the duration of time she'd been in the hospital now flowed with no end in sight. For a good half hour, Matt held her. Finally, and much to his regret, she pulled away.

With a sniff, she wiped her face for the millionth time and peered at him through puffy eyes. "It's lovely, but I can't accept it."

The softly-spoken words gouged into tender flesh. "Why?"

"You think I want to be promised to someone just because they feel sorry for me?"

Fatigue forced his impatience to a quick angry boil. He leaned back in the folding chair and struggled to control the edge to his words. "Is that what you think? You really believe I've put up with you and your foul moods for the past two months because I pity you?"

"You can't deny that you feel sorry for me."

"You're right. I can't. But I can say with all honesty that I didn't give you the ring because of pity. I bought it after that Friday night at the lake house."

Her mouth fell open. "You did?"

"Yeah. I planned to give it to you for Christmas, but there were other things more pressing at the time. Since then, you've done nothing but push me away. And honestly, I've had about all I can take." His voice raised in volume with each word.

Tears pooled in her sorrow-filled eyes. "But why would you want to marry me?" Her gaze dropped to her lifeless legs. "I have nothing to offer. I can't walk, and I can't—" She buried her head in her hands, the tears flowing freely once more.

Matt's heart broke for her, and he pulled her wheelchair to face him and took her in his arms. "Oh sweetheart, don't you understand? I fell in love with you, not your ability to walk or have children. I love you."

She pulled back and searched his face, her long eyelashes clumped with tears. "But that night when Dr. Jackson told me I couldn't walk or have kids, you kept your head down and wouldn't look at me."

He brought a finger to her face to catch a stray tear that wandered down her left cheek. "Because I was praying for you. I knew how much you want to be a mother and how especially hard that news would be for you to take." Matt reached for the ring. He brought her left hand to his lips, and then placed the ring on the finger that would one day hold a wedding band. Holding her hand in his, he brought it to rest on his heart. "I promise to love you always, Gracie. I promise to cherish you and help you in every way I possibly can. I promise to be with you through good and bad, thick and thin. And I promise to faithfully commit myself to you with the intention of one day making you my wife. Will you accept this ring as a token of my promise?"

Her eyes held a softness they'd not held in so very long, and did he dare hope they also held love?

His pulse pounded against his chest as she shook her head. "Only if you let me say a few things first."

He sighed in exasperation. Would a day ever come when she didn't try his patience? "Only a few?"

Gracie punched his arm. "What exactly do you mean by that?"

"Well, you're an attorney, and they make their living by really long arguments."

She balled up her right fist and punched him twice more.

"Ow! Cut it out." He gripped his arm with the other hand, happy to see this playful side of her again.

With a lovely, heart-stopping smile on her lips, Gracie nodded. "Only if you're ready to listen."

"Okay, but do try to give me the condensed version if you don't mind."

She laughed, and Matt relished the sound. When was the last time he'd heard that soft girlish giggle?

Gracie's intense gaze pierced to the depths of his soul. "I've loved you for a lot longer than I've been able to let on, Matt. I so desperately wanted to tell you, but wasn't in a place where I could be completely ready to show how I felt. There was so much going on in my life, and I was so very confused. Under those circumstances it wouldn't have been fair to you to lead you on when I couldn't totally commit."

He released the question that burned within him. "And where does Jason Dent fit in all this?"

"I turned to him when you left to go on the road without even saying good-bye. Part of me felt betrayed, like you didn't really care for me as much as you said you did."

Matt stopped her. "Wait a second. As I recall, you were the one who pushed me away."

Her head tilted to one side, and a thick strand of hair touched her elbow. "That's true. But I did it because I was being stalked. I was afraid of putting you in danger."

"Stalked?"

"Or terrorized. Whichever way you want to put it."

The small frown that started earlier now pulled his brows so tight they ached. "Jason?"

"At the time I thought it was Elena, but I'm almost certain now that he did it. He called me on the phone at all times of the day and night, but wouldn't answer. Then one of the patio chairs was moved beneath my window. And," she hesitated, swallowing hard, her eyes taking on a dark distance, "and then Millie was killed." She whispered the words.

He thought back to that night he'd found her screaming, her hands covered with blood. He'd been so engrossed in taking care of her he hadn't noticed a dead cat. When he went to investigate, he'd only found a puddle of water. In the short time they'd been inside, Jason must've removed the body and cleaned up the blood. He opened his eyes wide and shook his head, his mind still reeling. "I'm so sorry, Gracie. Sorry I didn't catch on to what was happening. You were acting so strangely that evening, and then you kicked me out of your house."

"To protect you." She squeezed his hand. "I also wanted to tell you how I felt that night at Elena's, but I saw Jason's car and decided it wasn't safe." She stopped, a frown creasing her forehead. "What made you come back that night?"

"I saw his car, too. I was afraid for you, but I also felt like you loved me and had pushed me away. It finally dawned on me that you knew you were in danger and wanted to protect me."

Her eyes once more took on a distant glaze. "I was so blind. You were the only one who saw who Jason really was. I'm sorry for not listening to you. So terribly sorry."

Matt caressed her cheek and smiled. "It's okay. He put on a good show, and you were looking for Mr. Perfect."

Gracie closed her eyes, a slight smile on her lips. "I'm just grateful God spared me from my personal pursuit of that so-called perfection." She turned her focus back to him. "And so incredibly happy His plan won out over mine." She leaned forward and planted a tender kiss on his lips, her soft scent swirling around his head.

A knock sounded on the door.

"Come in." The lilting joy in her voice—missing for so long—returned.

Dr. Jackson entered, a knowing look in her eyes. "The nurses told me I just might find you two here. While I'm sorry to interrupt your Valentine luncheon, it sure is good to see my favorite patient looking so happy."

Gracie tilted back her head and laughed. "Favorite? I'll bet you say that to all your patients."

A broad smile spread across the doctor's face, and she glanced at Gracie's hand. "Is that a new ring I see?"

Her face glowed as she held up the ring for Dr. Jackson to examine, and Matt marveled at the difference. *Thank You, Jesus.*

"There's no medicine in the world like love." Dr. Jackson leaned her weight against the table. "So, are we ready for round two of rehab after lunch?"

Apprehension flooded Gracie's face as she turned her gaze to Matt. He cupped her chin with his right hand and gazed deeply into the dark eyes he loved so much. "I love you, Gracie, and I'll be with you every step of the way."

A peaceful smile came to rest on her face.

Matt squeezed Gracie's hand and looked up at the doctor. "We're ready."

27

The fellowship hall of Miller's Creek Community Church bustled with activity. Voices melded with the noise of chairs and tables being moved into position to create a cacophony of sound. Matt stepped aside to let a white-aproned waiter from Soldano's Restaurant pass, the silver warming pan he carried wafting the aroma of chicken fajitas throughout the space and causing his mouth to water.

Gracie's dad had spared no expense on the food for his only daughter's homecoming, and Matt felt obliged to help out however he could, even though it meant letting Dani, Trish, and Mama Beth pick Gracie up from the hospital instead of him.

He'd struggled with the decision, but when he'd talked to Gracie on the phone, she said she understood his need to stay in Miller's Creek to work. Of course, he couldn't tell her why. The whole shindig was meant to be a surprise. He pressed his lips together and released air through his nose. Hopefully Gracie was up for a surprise that involved most of the residents of Miller's Creek.

Juan moved up beside him, his red chef's apron showing signs of a full morning of cooking. "*Hola,* Matt." He held out a hand.

Matt shook his hand, wondering about the change that had come over him. Had it really only been a few months ago that he'd asked him to stay away from Gracie? "Hey, Mr. Soldano."

"How are you?" The man smiled revealing a gold-capped tooth.

"Good. Just a little nervous this might be too much for Gracie."

"*Si*, I have wondered the same thing myself. This started off as just a few family friends, and before I knew it, everyone in town had invited themselves. *Ay yi yi.*" He spoke the words in his thick Hispanic accent and gave his head a shake. "But I know Graciela will do her best to handle it well."

"No doubt about it. She always seems to rise to the occasion." Matt winced at the unfortunate choice of words. In spite of several weeks of rehab, Gracie still couldn't walk. And it wasn't from a lack of trying. Everyday she'd given it her all, refusing to give in to despair and hopelessness. And every night she'd cried when her efforts failed to produce the results for which she'd so desperately hoped and prayed.

Mr. Soldano cleared his throat, drawing Matt's gaze. His eyes held a pleading look that very much reminded him of Gracie. "Do you have a few minutes to talk?"

"Yes, sir."

Matt followed him outside to the church pavilion, peaceful and quiet in comparison to the bustling fellowship hall. Gracie's dad chose a picnic table on the far end, where they were less likely to be disturbed. An April breeze danced among nearby cedar bushes, the fresh fragrance floating through the air.

"I wanted to thank you privately for all you did to save my daughter's life. And you've stayed by her side over the past months." Tears formed in the man's eyes.

"No thanks necessary. When you love someone, you do what you have to do."

Juan nodded. "That's how I know you are the right man for her. It was the same with my new wife, Maria, and also with Graciela's mother."

A flicker of hope ignited in Matt's chest. "So if I were to ask Gracie to marry me, we'd have your blessing?"

"A thousand times, yes." He momentarily lowered his gaze to his hands which rested on the table. "I know at one time I was not very kind to you. I underestimated you and didn't think you were good enough for my daughter. I was wrong. Please accept my apology."

Matt sent up silent thanks to God. Only He could have brought about this change in His timing. "Of course. Glad to know that your opinion of me has changed."

The older man reached over and patted him on the back. "I'd be honored to have you as my son. Now we'd better get back to work, eh?"

"Yep." He stood and followed the older man back inside, his nervousness returning. Somehow he had to find a way to make this whole experience easier for Gracie.

Unbridled panic coursed through Gracie as Dani and Trish made certain her wheelchair was secured with safety straps, and Mama Beth scooted closer to the window to begin building her nest for the trip back to Miller's Creek. These were some of the very people who shunned her before she left for Bellview. And now, on this beautiful April morning, she had at least a two hour's drive with them in a confined space. Would they once more make her feel condemned and worthless?

She used her arms to pull herself to a more upright position. Just a couple of hours and then she'd be home. The first thing she'd do was call Matt and invite him over, even if she were still a tad bit disappointed that he hadn't come to pick her up.

Dani's blond head bobbed up to her right, a happy light in her clear blue eyes. "There. That should keep you from sliding around in this big old van. I'll try not to weave in and out of this horrible Dallas traffic." With her baby bump just starting to protrude, the mayor's wife eased out of the van's side door and made her way to the driver's seat.

Now Trish stood, but unlike Dani, stooped to keep from hitting her head on the van ceiling. She flashed her brilliant smile which always seemed especially bright in contrast to her dark skin. "Ready to roll, Gracie?"

"That depends on your definition of roll."

Trish laughed. "Spoken like a true lawyer. Maybe we should make you sign a disclaimer first." She winked and backed out of the van, slamming the door shut behind her before she crawled into the front passenger seat and buckled her seat belt.

"Okay, ladies, here we go," Dani's cheery voice called out.

As they pulled away from the hospital parking lot, Mama Beth reached over and patted her leg. "We're so glad to finally have you back, Gracie. We've all missed you."

She nodded, unsure how to respond. "Thanks. I've missed y'all, too." Though they might not believe it, she meant every word. The time in Bellview and the hospital had honed her appreciation of them, in spite of how they'd treated her. But would she ever truly fit in? *Lord, please tear down these walls. Help me do what I need to do to not just feel comfortable around them, but connected to them.*

Gracie peered out the window as the skyscrapers of downtown Dallas came into view. A scripture she'd read earlier that morning popped into her head—something about being humble and considering others as better than herself. Yes, that should help remove at least part of the walls. "Thanks to all of you for coming after me. I really thought Papa or Matt would do it, but I know they have things to do, especially with all the time they've both spent at the hospital with me."

"Our pleasure, Gracie." Trish turned her head and flashed another vivid smile.

Dani made eye contact via the rearview mirror. "Your Papa and Matt both wanted to be here." Her expression oozed sympathy.

Hurt raked long claws throughout her insides. She didn't want anyone's pity! Is that why they were here?

Mama Beth leaned over and gave her a sideways hug. "I, for one, am glad they couldn't come, so we get the chance to spend time with you. I think we all need a nice long chat."

Uh-oh, here it comes. Gracie held up both hands before this went any further. "Look, I know how you all feel about what I did. All I can say is how very sorry I am. It was wrong and I shouldn't have done it."

The van grew uncomfortably quiet for several minutes, the only sound the noise of passing cars and eighteen-wheelers. Hmm, maybe she'd spoken too soon.

Trish finally broke the awkward silence as they drove past Six Flags theme park in Arlington. "You're not the only one who needs to apologize. I should 've handled things a lot differently. I judged you without knowing the full story." She turned around in the seat, her tawny brown eyes full of tears. "Please forgive me, Gracie. I know now that you were only trying to help Andy, and I'm very grateful."

"That goes for me, too." Mama Beth, her voice cracking with emotion, snatched her purse from the floorboard, rifled through its contents for a tissue, and dabbed at her nose and eyes.

"Me, three." Dani's face held sincerity. "I know how it feels to be an outsider in Miller's Creek, so I should've known better. I treated you shamefully, and I'm so sorry."

Tears flowed unbidden down Gracie's cheeks, and her throat closed, making it impossible to speak.

Mama Beth glanced over and noticed the tears, then began to cluck around like a mother hen, going through her earlier routine to procure a tissue for Gracie.

"Thanks," she at last managed to squeak out with a sniffle. "Your friendship means more than I can say, and it feels good to have everything out in the open." But would the rest of Miller's Creek follow suit?

Mama Beth reached across and patted Gracie's left hand. "Just so you know, we were all very hurt and confused by what happened." The older woman paused, her pale blue eyes questioning. "I know it's none of my business, but what happened to make you act in such a way?"

At last! Someone finally asked the right question. All the words of defense and vindication and justice she'd harbored inside over the past few months rushed to the tip of Gracie's tongue. But she clamped her lips together as the Lord's still small voice sounded in her head.

Love God and love people, my child. That's all you need to fulfill My commands.

She lowered her head until the angry feelings abated. How she'd longed for this moment! But all that really mattered was doing what God's Spirit led her to do. Gracie gave her head a slight shake and raised her gaze to Mama Beth's kind face. "It no longer matters. I won't say one more word to defend my actions or to damage another person's reputation. End of subject. If that makes me look guilty, then so be it."

The older woman's face glowed with wisdom gained only from a rough life and a close walk with God. A sad smile appeared at the corners of her mouth. "I've never met a young woman as wise as you, Gracie. I'm as proud of you as if you were my own daughter."

Her heart once more in her throat, Gracie lowered her head. "Thanks. I know you all care for Andy very much, and I'm sure to you it must have seemed like I'd betrayed him."

Mama Beth nodded. "And I'm sorry we hurt you in return. It was a knee-jerk reaction to the pain we were feeling. The entire situation was one of the most difficult things I remember ever going through."

Regret plunged its razor-sharp blade deep into her soul. Mama Beth had endured so much. The whole town knew how Big Bo Miller had been the love of her life and had married someone else. So for her to say it was one of the hardest things she'd ever faced was almost more than Gracie could bear. She lowered her gaze to her lap, her right hand fiddling with the balled-up tissue. "I believe Satan's had a field day with all of us."

Dani pounded a palm against the steering wheel, effectively bringing all eyes her way. "Steve and I were just talking about this over breakfast. Isn't it just like the enemy to cause discord and strife among God's people?" Her cornflower eyes flashed with a warrior's light.

In a moment's time, the atmosphere inside the van changed, as though they were returning from a day of shopping. Now they all talked at once, more like old times, four good friends sharing their experiences with one another. When they pulled up outside the church two hours later, Gracie almost wished the drive could last a while longer, though she had to admit to being a little curious about why they'd stopped at the church.

Trish was the first one out. She stepped to the sliding door near where Gracie's wheelchair was parked and yanked on the door handle, while Dani moved into the Fellowship Hall entrance of the church.

Gracie glanced at Mama Beth. "Something going on that I need to know about?"

She tilted her head to one side with a coy smile. "Guess you'll just have to wait and find out."

Trish untied the straps, humming all the while.

A wave of panic swept over her and sent her pulse rate into rocket range. *God, please don't let this be a surprise party. I'm not ready for everyone to see me like this. I'm not ready for the pity and sympathetic looks and awkward silences when people don't know what to say.* She chomped down on her lower lip.

Trish patted her arm, an understanding look in her eyes. "It's gonna be okay, Gracie. These people love you. Give them a chance."

She pushed a rogue strand of hair aside while she pulled at the floral cotton skirt she'd worn for the ride home. Yes, she needed to give them a chance. Needed to forgive and forget. Needed the fresh start this day might provide. But could she do it properly without time to get herself prepared?

The chair lift vibrated as Trish lowered her to the sidewalk, and the church door hinged open with a bang. Matt strode out, breaking into a lope as soon as he saw her, a broad grin spread across his face. He bent down and embraced her in a bear hug, then looked up at the other two women. "I'll take it from here, ladies."

Relief poured over her like a refreshing waterfall on a stifling hot day. How blessed she was that Matt was able—had strangely always been able—to read her like a book. Without a word between them, he somehow knew she was apprehensive. When the other two moved out of earshot range, he gave her a soft kiss and knelt in front of the wheelchair to look her in the eye. "It's so good to have you home, Gracie Mae."

"It's good to be home." She glanced toward the church. "If it weren't for you, I'm not sure I could do this."

"So you're doing okay?"

She inhaled a deep breath, the scent of nearby honeysuckle helping to calm her spirit. "I'm a little nervous about how everyone will treat me. I don't think I can stand it if they feel sorry for me."

Kindness seeped from his sand-colored eyes. "I'll do what I can to keep that from happening, okay?"

"Thank you, Matt. I love you."

His face took on a soft glow, a look that revealed how he still marveled at their relationship. This was a man who would never take it for granted. "And I love you." He kissed the tip of her nose, and then smiled into her eyes. "You ready to do this?"

She nodded, Matt's presence giving her the boost of confidence she so desperately needed. "Let's roll."

He laughed at her pun, and then rose to his feet to push her up the sidewalk and through the doorway. As they entered the room erupted in cheers and applause.

Overwhelming joy and grateful humility flooded her being as she scanned the crowd. There were people everywhere, the faces of those she loved dearest and best, people who loved her in return.

Andy, his golden curls slicked back, knelt beside her and raised his voice so she could hear him over the crowd noise. "As soon as you're ready to come back to work, let me know. It appears I'm in need of a new partner."

Her eyes popped open wide. Never in a million years would she have believed he'd give her the job again. "But—"

He raised his eyebrows, his sea-green eyes staring her down. "I won't take no for an answer." He leaned closer. "I know now that you had my best interest at heart when you broke in. I should've believed it then. And I was also trying to protect you from Jason. Matt's probably already told you that Ben Snodgrass and Debra Rowe were undercover agents. They thought it would be for the best if I kept you away from Jason as much as possible."

Gracie took note of the honesty in his eyes. His explanation made sense, and even if it hadn't, she owed this man much more than she'd ever be able to repay. She hugged his neck. "Thanks, Andy. I'll do what I can to be there on Monday."

"No need to rush, but we want you when you're ready."

The applause and cheering died down, so Andy stood and faced the crowd. "I can tell y'all are ready to see our guest of honor, but why don't we let her get some lunch first? As soon as we've all eaten and Gracie's ready, we'll make a line so you can all come by and say your piece."

Heads bobbed in agreement, and a voice bellowed from the back corner. "Just make sure she leaves some food for the rest of us."

A grin burst onto Grace's face as the crowd erupted in laughter. Leave it to Coot to make that sort of comment. As Matt wheeled her through the line, peace blanketed her soul. Miller's Creek was where she belonged, not just for now, but for always. These people and this place were in her blood, and nothing could ever change that.

A half hour later she leaned back in her wheelchair and glanced across the table at Papa. How happy he looked, with Maria sitting next to him and seeing to his every need.

"The food was delicious, Papa. I've missed your cooking."

"You only say that because you've been eating hospital food." His high-pitched giggle sounded across the room, and others sitting nearby laughed along with him.

Steve Miller, who sat down the table from Gracie, his cowboy hat at rest on the table near his plate, stood and gave a shrill whistle to get everyone's attention. "Y'all know this is a special day for Miller's Creek as we welcome back a hometown hero." He took the plaque Dani handed him. "We have this little memento to give Gracie from the whole town. It says: 'In honor of Gracie Soldano, one of Miller's Creek's finest.'" He looked her way, his grin as wide as Texas. "Miss Gracie, as mayor of Miller's Creek, it's my honor and privilege to announce that from now on April 18th is Grace Soldano Day in Miller's Creek. We love and appreciate you, and we're glad you're back home."

People rose to their feet, the applause thunderous.

Tears sprang to her eyes once more.

Matt rubbed her back with his palm, and leaned over to whisper in her ear. "You're doing great. Hang in there."

"Would you help me stand?"

He frowned. "You sure?"

She gave an emphatic nod and used her fingertips to swipe away tears. "I need to do this for them."

Matt leaned over and whispered something to Andy, who moved to her other side. Together they helped Grace to her feet. The applause grew even louder, and then died down. The sound of metal chairs scraping the floor echoed across the room as people took their seats.

She moistened her lips and gazed around the fellowship hall at the people who meant so much to her. Today said much more about them than it did about her. "I'm so very grateful for this wonderful reception. While I don't deserve it in the least, I appreciate it more than I can express." Her voice wavered and she paused to harness her emotions. "Thank you for so many things—for praying for me while I was in the hospital, for loving me even when I mess up, and for your gracious friendship. I can't think of any place on earth I'd rather be than at home in Miller's Creek."

The people applauded once more. Andy and Matt helped Gracie sit before they wheeled her near the door at her request. Matt stayed close by her side the entire time, giving her much-needed assurance through winks, smiles, and an occasional shoulder squeeze.

As Gracie expressed her thanks individually, she couldn't help but remember back to the previous Thanksgiving when she could find nothing to be grateful for. In complete contrast, her heart now sent up a prayer of thanksgiving to the One who made all things possible, including her ability to give thanks.

28

Through the rearview mirror from her position in the backseat, Gracie took in the firm set to Matt's jaw and the anger flashing in his eyes. Okay, this wasn't quite the response she'd hoped for. Only a week had passed since her arrival back in Miller's Creek, but this was something she had to do—even if he didn't understand or agree.

"I can't believe you actually wanna go through with this." Matt pulled the borrowed van into the apartment parking lot and threw the gearshift into park. "Haven't you suffered enough without asking for more?" He didn't even bother to make eye contact, but instead slammed the door behind him and moved to the sliding door on the passenger side. Without a word, he stooped to undo the safety straps that held her wheelchair in place, his anger evident in his fast, forceful movements.

"I'm sorry this upsets you, Matt, but I have to do it."

His shoulders sagged as he released a heavy breath. He righted himself from the stooped position and looked her in the eye. "I'm sorry, Gracie. I don't mean to be a jerk about this, but I don't see what can possibly be gained from this meeting with Elena. Once I touch a hot stove, I know not to touch it again."

"You've used that analogy already. In case you don't remember, it didn't work then either." She tried to soften the blow of her words with a smile.

He planted both hands on his hips, raised his gaze to the sky and rotated in a circle, his exasperation unmistakable.

A sudden thought dissolved Gracie into a fit of the giggles.

Matt stopped and glared at her. "You think this is funny?"

No matter how hard she tried, she couldn't stop laughing, and had to speak around the uncontrollable chortles. "You look like you're doing the Hokey Pokey."

At first he simply shook his head in frustration, but then a mischievous glint hovered in his sandy eyes. Without warning, he began to sing at the top of his lungs. "You do the Hokey Pokey and you turn yourself around. That's what it's all about." Matt included the accompanying motions, drawing horrified stares from bystanders.

Now Gracie was mortified, but still couldn't quit laughing. "Stop it. You're killing me." She held her hands over her aching ab muscles and leaned her head against the back of the wheelchair.

Matt stepped closer, his expression and voice taunting. "Only if you give me a kiss."

She tilted her head and gave him a sideways glance. "Do you promise to behave?"

He released a mock sigh. "I guess." He leaned in and gave her a kiss that stole her breath.

A minute later, she pulled away and smoothed imaginary wrinkles on her skirt. "I'm not sure that's behaving."

Matt winked and stooped to finish untying the straps. Then he lowered the chair to the sidewalk and pushed her toward the downstairs apartment where Elena now lived with Consuela and Jessie.

The woman met them at the door and moved aside as Matt pushed Gracie inside. Decorated simply, the room held an unstated elegance, and a soft floral scent hung in the air. She turned to face them, her hands twisting. "I was surprised to get your call." Her gaze flitted in various directions, but never to either of them. "Mama has taken Jessie to the park, but wanted me to tell you hello."

"Please tell her hi back." Gracie smiled and studied Elena, amazed at the drastic difference in the woman she'd once idolized. Gone was the confidence she'd worn as easily as her designer suits. Now her features held an unexpected humility.

Elena motioned toward the living room. "Why don't we move in here? May I get either of you something to drink?"

"No thanks. We won't stay long. I just wanted to clear the air." Again she smiled, but Elena wouldn't look her way.

Matt rolled the wheelchair next to a small sofa and took a seat beside her.

Elena lowered herself to a Queen Anne chair across the room, wiping her palms against her jeans. "Please let me begin by saying how terribly sorry I am for what happened." Her eyes locked with Gracie's, sorrow in their depths.

"It's okay, Elena. I don't bear you any ill will at all, and I want you to know that."

A frown lingered over the woman's tormented eyes. "If I were you, I would hate me." She lowered her head to her hands and began to weep. "I'm so sorry, Grace. So terribly, terribly sorry for the way I treated you. For the way I used you. For the way things turned out."

Gracie quickly wheeled her chair across the span that separated them and placed a hand on Elena's shoulder. "Please don't cry. Though I don't completely understand why, I know God has His reasons for what happened. He can bring good out of even tragedy. I've come to a place where I've accepted things as they are."

Elena lifted her head, tears still coursing down her cheeks. She searched Gracie's face. "Then you are truly blessed. If only I'd accepted things as they were instead of trying to make things happen the way I thought they should be." She suddenly appeared very weary and ancient. "I knew Alex had issues, but when he promised to leave me alone and give me enough money to take care of Mama and Jessie in style, I chose to get involved."

Sorrow for Elena nipped at Gracie's heart. "I know you can't give any details of the case, but what happens after the trial's over?"

"We become fugitives again. We'll be given new identities in the witness protection program."

"Will you be able to practice law?"

She gave her head a sad shake. "No."

What a shame. She was so good at it. "What will you do?"

"Probably teach, but please don't share the information with anyone."

Elena would make a great college professor. "I won't, and I wish you and your family all the best."

A puzzled expression crossed Elena's features. "I'd give anything to have your peace and joy."

Gratitude erupted inside and she gazed toward the ceiling with a smile. The opportunity she'd prayed for. She faced Elena. "It's available to you. Want me to tell you how?"

"Please."

A short while later, the three of them bowed their heads together as Elena accepted Jesus as her Lord and Savior.

The next afternoon Matt stood behind Gracie as they both stared up at the razor wire spiraling atop the fence encircling the maximum security prison in Huntsville. Heavy clouds tufted the April sky, menacingly low and anvil gray. The light mist conferred a dusty smell to the earth.

Why had he agreed to this? "I don't know if I can let you go through with this, Gracie. I admit I was wrong about Elena, but this is different." He moved from behind her, his hands laced atop his head. "Please don't do this. Some people will never change." He didn't care that his voice held a whining plea. He'd get down on both knees if it would change her mind.

"I don't have a choice, Matt, I feel like God—"

He put both palms chest high and closed his eyes. "I know you think God wants you to do this. And if that's the way you feel, I won't stand in your way. I just don't want you to get your hopes up."

"Point taken. Now are you going to push me in there, or do I have to go by myself?"

He lowered his head with a shake and trudged to his position behind her. He'd done all he could to prepare her, now he'd have to settle for protecting her. "If I didn't love you so much, I sure wouldn't be here."

She leaned her head back and grinned up at him coyly. "Thanks for loving me."

"I guess you're welcome." He finished the comment with a teasing wink.

A half hour later they peered at Dent and his uniformed escort through a bullet-proof window, Jason's face completely void of emotion. "Well, I certainly didn't expect to see the two of you." He leveled an icy glare at Gracie. "You especially."

Matt's anger boiled, but he shoved it down with a breath. He had to maintain control for Gracie's sake.

Her face fell. "I never meant to hurt you, Jason. Please forgive me if I did." She hesitated a second. "I want you to know that I don't hold anything against you."

"Nor should you. I wouldn't have shot you if you hadn't jumped in front of the gun." His voice held contempt.

Gracie shivered, but quickly brought it under control. "Are you being treated well?"

His arrogant shrug revealed his cold heart. "Well enough I suppose, though it's certainly not as nice as the life I could have given you."

"Jason, even in this place, there's a better way to live." The words spewed from her mouth as though she feared not being able to get them out. "I don't know what you endured in your life to make you so angry—to make you hate so much—but I can tell you about—"

"I don't want to hear about your God!" He thundered the words, his face black with rage as he pounded a fist against the table. "You people are all alike. You think you can solve all the world's problems with love, peace, and joy."

The guard cleared his throat in warning. Matt gripped Gracie's shoulder to encourage her, hesitant to be too demonstrative and risk drawing more of Jason's wrath down on her head.

She glanced over at him, tears pooled in her eyes. "I think it's time to go." She faced Jason once more. "I'll be praying for you."

"Don't bother," he sneered, his voice colder than the iciest place on earth.

Chills ran down Matt's spine. He couldn't get Gracie out of here fast enough. He moved behind her and wheeled her away from the icy confines of concrete walls.

She cried all the way out to the van and for several minutes on the drive back to home. Finally, her tears spent, she wiped her eyes on a tissue he'd passed back to her. "I'm not sorry we went. At least I had the opportunity to tell him I forgave him and to ask him to forgive me."

Matt pulled to a stop at the red traffic light and glanced back at her. "You've done nothing for him to forgive."

Gracie turned her head to stare out the passenger side window. "No one's perfect, Matt. I've learned that even if someone perceives that we've hurt them, even if we never intended to, it's worth an apology."

His eyebrows rose as he thought through her comment. Quite a turnaround for someone who once tried so hard to be perfect. How had he managed to snag such a treasure? And would she say "yes" when he finally gathered the courage to ask for her hand in marriage? He peered at her once more through the mirror. "You're never gonna let me win an argument, are you?'

A mind-blowing smile blossomed on her face. "Not if I can help it."

29

Gracie parked her wheelchair beneath an old oak next to Miller's Creek Community Church and gazed toward the field of bluebonnets that streamed down to the babbling creek. The scent of the bluebonnets combined with honeysuckle and fried chicken as people jammed the area for the church's annual spring picnic. Laughter and happy voices rang out all around her, bringing a smile to her face. What happy memories she had of times past at this very same event.

Sudden longing gripped her. What she wouldn't give to go back in time to the relative innocence of her childhood. She shook off the heavy feeling and glanced to where Matt played catch with his nephew, Brady.

"Hold your glove like this, buddy." Matt demonstrated and his nephew imitated the motion. "Perfect." He softly tossed the ball so it landed in the boy's mitt.

"I caught the ball!" Brady jumped up and down, his red curls glinting in the sunlight.

Matt laughed and watched his nephew race to Andy with the news. What a wonderful father he'd make. She'd give anything to be able to give him children of his own.

The familiar heartache returned, but she practiced pushing it gently aside and turned once more to the One who lifted her head. *Thank you, God, for giving me such a godly man. Help me walk again so I can be a better partner for him.* Maybe then he'd ask her to marry him. As far as she was concerned, walking was a prerequisite for marriage, and for being engaged, for that matter.

Gracie marveled at the change that had taken place in her heart. She had the Lord to thank for it. For one thing her desire to be a prosecutor had waned, replaced with a compelling desire to defend. If the events of the past several months had taught her anything, it was that everyone needed a defender. The world was full of accusers, headed by the chief accuser, the enemy of her soul. But Christ was the ultimate advocate for those who belonged to Him.

A frown crossed her face. Somewhere along the way she'd confused God's justice with human judgment. How had she gotten so far off track? Judgment belonged to God, and God alone. And human judgment only resulted in return judgment. God's justice and grace were interwoven—opposite sides of the same coin. He couldn't be separated from His justice any more than He could be separated from His grace.

A scene from her childhood flashed to mind. In her typical spontaneous way, Mama had pulled her out into a gentle spring shower. Together they'd danced in the rain until they were sopping wet. Gracie made no attempt to wipe away the tears that sprang to her eyes. Yes, that was grace. Not just a speckled dot here and there, but something you splashed around in, floodwaters from an endless source. There was no place it couldn't reach. No heart it couldn't change. No life it couldn't redeem. Every breath—every heartbeat—was immersed in His grace.

Unexpectedly, she laughed out loud from sheer joy. The latest splashes of God's marvelous grace concerned her relationship with Matt. God hadn't given her Mr. Perfect, but the man that was perfect for her. The magnitude of His gift washed over her.

Movement in her peripheral vision captured her attention. Matt sauntered up, hands on hips, just a few feet away to talk to Steve Miller and his old geezer buddies. A gust of wind whistled and tossed his sandy curls in several directions. With his flip-flops, rumpled t-shirt, and disheveled hair he could easily be mistaken for a beach bum. He was a free spirit and always would be.

The thought brought a smile to her lips. She brought her gaze to the ground beneath her, tufts of spring grass now blowing in the gentle spring breeze, when just a few short weeks ago the area had seemed dead and devoid of life. Maybe there was hope for her lifeless legs as well. She'd recently felt a strange tingling in her legs, but told no one, too afraid it wasn't real. Had almost felt like she could walk on her own at therapy a few times, but feared she couldn't handle the disappointment if she failed.

"A penny for your thoughts." Matt's soft voice sounded beside her.

She whipped her head around and brought a hand to her chest.

"Sorry, sweetheart. Didn't mean to startle you." He took one tentative step forward then stopped, as though unsure whether to proceed, indecision etched on his face.

"My thoughts aren't worth much."

In less than a heartbeat, Matt knelt in front of her, his hands gripping her bare arms. "Oh, Gracie Mae, don't you see what a lie that is?"

He was right. Another one of the devil's lies. Would she ever learn to ignore them? She lowered her head. "I'm trying to do better." His soft chuckle brought her eyes to his. "What's so funny?"

"That was just such a typical Gracie Mae thing to say. Always trying to do better, to be better." His eyes lit with the kindness she never tired of.

She tilted her head to one side. "What are you doing here anyway? I thought you had things to do at the ranch."

"I did, but I felt the need to clear my head this afternoon. A wise person once said that there was nothing like a walk on a beautiful day to clear your head." He placed a finger beneath her chin and tipped her head back to gaze into her eyes. "And you know what I think?"

"What?"

"I think God led me here to find you. In fact, I was just talking to Him about you." He stood, tucked his hands in his pockets, and sauntered to the oak to lean against it, the look in his eyes indecipherable.

"You were?" Grace turned her gaze to her entwined hands at rest on her non-working legs. Already she dreaded the turn this conversation was taking. "And what were you saying?"

"Oh, lots of things."

She scowled at his evasion tactics. "Like what?"

He laughed his familiar boyish laugh, his eyes taunting. "What's wrong, Gracie Mae? Am I getting you riled up?"

Gracie crossed her arms and glared. "Why do you always do that?"

"Do what?"

"Intentionally goad me until I'm ready to slap you."

His laughter echoed off the red bricks of the church wall. He stepped toward her again, his lips curved upward. "'Cause you're so pretty when you're furious."

Her palm itched to smack him, but one look at the tender smile on his face was all it took to make her irritation slip away. "Whatever. You'd better watch it, mister."

A faraway look entered his eyes and he sobered as he sauntered closer. "Actually I have something to ask you."

Her pulse pounded in her temple as she fingered the promise ring. No. Not yet. She wasn't ready. Not until she could walk—no, make that run—into his arms. He deserved at least that much. Not someone confined to a wheelchair. Her hands twisted in her lap as she pleaded with her eyes.

Matt took another step, his eyes revealing his determination. He went down on both knees, held her trembling hands, and planted a kiss on each one. "Gracie—"

"Don't do this yet, Matt. Please."

He lowered his head a moment then looked up at her once more. "Remember when I didn't want you to go see Elena and Jason?"

Yes, but this was different. She nodded hesitantly.

"And you told me it was something you had to do."

Her eyes closed slowly then reopened as she nodded again. "Yes, but—"

He placed a finger on her lips. "Shh, sweetheart. Hear me out." Matt moved his hand back to hers. "I love you more than life itself and I want you to be my wife." He reached into his pants pocket and pulled out the ring, holding it up for her to see. "Will you marry me, Gracie?"

Her pulse hammered in her head, as she eyed the ring, her upper lip tucked between her teeth. *Lord, help me through this. I don't want to hurt him.* She pinched her lips together and lowered her head in total torment. A half cry tore from her chest, and she peered up at him, tears tracing a path down her cheeks. "I can't, Matt. Not until I can walk. You deserve at least that much."

Matt's lips pooched out, and he nodded. "I understand." He pivoted and pocketed the ring, then headed toward his puke-green Pinto.

Her heart cratered. No. She couldn't lose him like this. Her eyes blurred by tears, she gazed up into the gnarled arms of the oak tree. "God, help me. I don't want to lose him." She choked out the words. "Show me what to do."

Walk.

I've tried, Lord. I can't walk.

Try again.

Gracie lowered her gaze to Matt's still-retreating back, his shoulders slumped. It was worth a try. "Matt!" She screamed his name.

The picnic crowd quieted, as though holding their collective breath, and gathered to watch the scene playing itself out in their midst.

With her arms, Gracie lifted each foot from its perch and sat them on the ground, then bent low to lift the flaps. Next she used her arms to pull herself to the edge of the seat.

A murmur rose in the crowd behind her as she stood. Andy and Papa stepped out of the crowd, but she waved them back. "Stay away from me."

Papa's eyes pleaded with hers. "Let me help you, *la hija.*"

"No, Papa. I have to do this."

Andy shook his head, his expression grave. "Don't you understand yet? Matt doesn't want perfection. He wants you. You don't have to try so hard, for him or for any of us. We love you just like you are."

"You're the one who doesn't understand. The perfection I once strived for was for me. But it's different this time. I don't wanna walk so I can be perfect. I wanna walk for Matt." Gracie glanced at her tingling legs that at least for the moment supported her weight. Would they work or would she fall on her face in front of all of Miller's Creek? "Matt, wait!"

He kept walking.

Pure agony exploded inside, worse than any pain she'd ever experienced, as if her heart were being excised from her chest. "Please, Matt!"

He stopped, frozen in position, his head down. His shoulders rose and lowered as he turned back to face her. When he saw her standing, Matt lifted one hand and started toward her. "No, Gracie, don't try it without help. You might hurt yourself."

She gave her head a shake, tears dripping off her cheeks to the ground. "Stop right there, Matt Tyler. Don't you dare come any closer." She willed her legs to work. *Please, Lord.*

What do you want Me to do for you?

She looked into the bright blue sky. "I want to walk."

Then walk.

Her forehead knotted as she gritted her teeth to pull her right foot forward. A tiny sliding step, but a step all the same. Gracie released a gut-wrenching cry as she forced the left leg to do the same.

Voices began to sound behind her.

"You can do it, Miss Gracie." J.C.'s soft words made it to her ears. She could almost see his kind eyes urging her forward.

"Yes, *la hija,* you can."

"C'mon, Gracie girl." Andy added his words of encouragement.

She glanced over at her boss, his face beaming. Behind him, Mama Beth swabbed at tears. One step, and then another, as the crowd began cheering her on.

"Atta girl, Gracie!" Coot bellowed above the crowd.

Gracie focused her gaze on Matt. His cheeks wet with tears, he stepped toward her, his eyes tender and soft. Her feet started to give way, but in a heartbeat, he raced forward and caught her up in his arms, swinging around in a circle so that her legs flew out behind her. "You did it, Gracie, you did it." His joyous sobs and laughter sounded in her ears.

When at last he stopped spinning in circles, she took a moment to gather her bearings and smiled at him flirtatiously. "I'll take that ring now."

He laughed through the tears. "Oh, you will, huh? Well, what if I've changed my mind?"

She held up her hand with the promise ring and wiggled her fourth finger. "Guess I'll have to take you to court. When it comes to love, verbal agreements are binding, you know."

"In that case, I guess I'd better finish the job." With one arm clasped tightly around her waist to keep her from falling, Matt fished around in the pocket of his wrinkled shorts, and then with all of Miller's Creek as witnesses, he placed the ring on her finger and sealed it with a kiss.

About the Author

A Texas-born gal, Cathy's desire and call is to write heart-stirring stories about God's life-changing grace. Her first novel, Texas Roads, was a 2009 American Christian Fiction Writers' Genesis finalist. Her second novel, A Path Less Traveled, was published in 2010. The Way of Grace (book three in the series) was launched in the fall of 2012, and she hopes to write several more stories about the fine folks of Miller's Creek.

Cathy also writes devotional articles and posts on writing and life and general at her blog WordVessel. She's written devotions for The Upper Room magazine, and for two collaborative books, Spirit & Heart: A 30-Day Devotional Journey and Faith & Finance: In God We Trust. She's the wife of a music minister, the mother of two grown sons, the mother-in-love of the daughter of her prayers, and the Nana of Harrisen. She currently lives in the Ozarks with her husband of thirty years, where she writes, tends the chickens and garden, and spends time with the world's cutest grandson.

Visit her website at www.CatBryant.com.

Dear friends,

As a lifelong perfectionist, I finally came to recognize the spiritual danger of trying to improve myself. In this way, Gracie's struggle is my own. Our world tells us to pull ourselves up by our bootstraps, go for our dreams, and be all we can be. Shelves around the world are lined with self-improvement books. Advertisements boast picture-perfect images we feel compelled to emulate. External appearance is ranked on the same level or higher than internal character.

This philosophy has no place in the spiritual realm. Instead, God's Word tells us to clothe ourselves with Christ, grow up in Him, and allow Him to transform us from the inside out. The only way that is accomplished is by dying to ourselves. Any effort to make ourselves "better" in our own strength cheapens Christ's sacrifice and God's grace.

In the story I also wanted to address the concepts of grace, mercy, and justice. For the longest time I couldn't wrap my brain around how God could be a God of both justice and grace. Through studying His Word, I found that justice and grace aren't the polar opposites I expected, but are woven together as one glorious attribute of our heavenly Father. Even the most difficult of circumstances bears testimony to His justice and His grace. To think otherwise is to deny His Sovereignty.

My prayer for all of us is that God will open our eyes to see the lavish grace He bestows with each breath we take, open our minds to grasp His love and goodness, and unlock our hearts and arms to share it with others.

Immersed in grace,
Cathy

Book Club Discussion Questions

1. How does Gracie's trouble with perfectionism reveal itself in the story? Why do you think people struggle with wanting to be perfect? Is perfectionism dangerous to our spiritual health? Why or why not?
2. What are the pitfalls of making plans without taking God into consideration?
3. Define justice, mercy, and grace. Is mercy and grace the same thing? Can you think of a place in the story where God's grace and justice come into play at the same time? Why do we need an accurate understanding of God's grace?
4. Why does Grace goes back to thinking of herself as Gracie by the end of the novel?
5. Name some of the ways Gracie attempts to improve her image? What does she do to impress others? What are the results of her self-improvement and attempts to impress?
6. Both Matt and Gracie learn that what they want is not always best, and that God's plans for them are much better. Can you think of a time you received something you really wanted only to be disappointed?
7. In the first part of the story, Elena is believed to be the "bad guy," but in reality is controlled by someone else. How is this same scenario played out time and time again in history?
8. The chapter near the end where Gracie visits both Elena and Jason shows two typical reactions to God's love, forgiveness, and grace. What are they? Can you think of a moment in the crucifixion account where these same reactions are displayed?
9. Evil is personified in this story. What are some ways Satan tries to trip us up. Is Satan always recognizable? Why or why not?
10. How does Gracie's suffering bring about good in her life? How does she get past physically- and emotionally-crippling circumstances?

Also Available

One secret kept, another uncovered . . .

Dani Davis just wants a place to call home. With quaint country charm, quirky residents, and loads of business potential, Miller's Creek seems like the perfect place to start over . . . except for the cowboy who gives her a ride into town. Then malicious rumors and a devastating secret propel her down a road she never expected to travel.

Grief paints a celebration in shades of gray . . .

Trish James is tired of being rescued. When a spooked horse claims her husband's life, she's determined to blaze a path for herself and her traumatized son without outside help. But will that mean leaving the place etched on her heart?

NEXT MILLER'S CREEK NOVEL
Pilgrimage of Promise

CPSIA information can be obtained at www.ICGtesting.com
Printed in the USA
LVOW06s1609161015

458582LV00001B/196/P